MERCILESS

Books by Robin Parrish

Dominion Trilogy

Relentless

Fearless

Merciless

Offworld

MERCILESS

THE DOMINION TRILOGY: BOOK 3

ROBIN PARRISH

BETHANY HOUSE PUBLISHERS

Minneapolis, Minnesota

Cover design by Brand Navigation

Published by Bethany House Publishers
11400 Hampshire Avenue South
Bloomington, Minnesota 55438

Bethany House Publishers is a division of
Baker Publishing Group, Grand Rapids, Michigan.

Printed in the United States of America

ISBN 978-0-7642-0645-0 (Trade Paper)

The Library of Congress has cataloged the hardcover edition as follows:

Parrish, Robin.
Merciless / Robin Parrish.
p. cm. — (The dominion trilogy ; 3)
ISBN 978-0-7642-0179-0 (hardcover : alk. paper) 1. Heroes—Fiction.
2. Armageddon—Fiction. 3. Supernatural—Fiction. I. Title.

PS616.A7684M47 2008
813'.6—dc22

2008014234

For Karen

I loved you before I knew you.
And I love you more every day.

PREVIOUSLY . . .

GRANT BORROWS and his friends have superpowers. Each of them is the recipient of one of the mysterious Rings of Dominion, mystical relics of a time before time. Their benefactors? A secret society known as the Secretum of Six, an organization with nefarious goals, shrouded in shadow.

Grant moves things with his mind. His unrequited love, Alex, manipulates emotions. Deadly swordsman Payton moves at inhuman speeds. Along with a dozen or so other superpowered Ringwearers, they choose to live lives in service to mankind, helping the helpless and trying to make the world a better place.

But the Secretum has plans of its own, plans that reach back to a prophecy made seven thousand years ago and are now on the brink of fulfillment. Using technology and resources the rest of the world hasn't yet developed, they've unleashed a brutal series of disasters and plagues upon mankind, destabilizing the global economy and reducing the populace to lives of fear.

It's the penultimate act in a series of manipulations and machinations casting Grant Borrows as the central figure in a grand plot that has brought him to the vast underground city the Secretum calls home. There, deep beneath the earth, a man named Devlin has given Grant the answers he's sought for so long: Every event in Grant's life was manipulated and preordained, luring him here to the deepest part of the Secretum, to a sacred chamber called the Hollow.

There, poised on the rim of a pit, Devlin murders Grant's sister and shoves Grant into a gaping hole in the Hollow. As Grant's friends fall into various forms of mortal peril, Grant falls into forever . . .

And every clock on earth stops.

1

Beneath the Taurus Mountains, Turkey

Hand over hand, Oblivion climbed.

The total absence of light surrounding him did nothing to slow his progress, his fingernails digging like talons into the black rock below the Hollow, ensuring a steady hold.

This was a mechanical process for him, nothing more than a necessary step of his birth. He did not tire, he did not feel fatigue or shortness of breath. There was moisture of some kind upon his face, but it was not sweat. He did not sweat. A drop reached his tongue and tasted of iron and salt.

Blood. It was the blood of the sacrifice. Of course.

Hand over hand, he climbed. Ever upward.

Oblivion knew everything that had brought him to this moment. He knew who he was and how he had come into being. He knew his purpose, knew the steadiness of his actions with detached confidence. He knew who awaited him above and what *their* purpose was. He knew a great deal more than he suspected they knew about what he had been brought forth to do. He knew what had happened to the world with his passage into mortal existence, and what was happening even now, to every surface he touched.

He knew the name of this container he existed within. Knew what this Grant Borrows had done since becoming the

Bringer . . . and now Oblivion. His great destiny, fulfilled at last.

Hand over hand.

The rock grew thicker now, but still Oblivion's fingers dug deep. The blood of the sacrifice flowed down from the rim of the Hollow, which he was drawing nearer to. It was the very blood that had allowed this process to commence. He felt no remorse for the loss of Grant's sister; he never felt remorse. He was not capable of such things.

It was all part of the process after all. Everything, from the notorious day this mortal container named Grant Borrows had first realized he was no longer the man he had once been—it was all part of the process. Every step he had taken, every path he had walked, every choice he had made. It was preordained—all of it—from a time before time began. It was the ultimate fail-safe, the final insurance. And now, after millennia of planning and preparation, it was happening.

A few initial semblances of light streamed flickering down, touching his gray skin for the first time, and he looked up to meet it with blazing red eyes. He noted the red mark on the back of his left hand, a fresh scar from Grant's encounter with a severed hand only days ago.

A chorus of voices reached his ears over the shaking of the earth. They were singing—no, chanting—in unison.

One voice rose above the others as Oblivion neared the top of the rim. One voice roaring with terrible conviction . . .

Hand over hand, Oblivion climbed, until he was born into a brave new world.

"WE HAVE FOLLOWED THE ANCIENT COMMANDS!!" Devlin bellowed, standing five feet from the rim of the Hollow. His heart hammered as he thought he saw a trace of movement in the darkness at his feet.

"Pario Atrum Universitas! . . ." the Secretum continued to chant behind him.

Devlin glanced down momentarily at the pallid, lifeless body of Julie Saunders, the Bringer's sibling, lying on the ground at the mouth of the Hollow.

Had it worked? Did her blood activate it, as intended?

Of course it had. This was the appointed day, the appointed hour, the appointed place. There was no question. Everything was unfolding precisely as the Secretum had known it would, for thousands of years.

"WE HAVE DRAINED THE BLOOD OF THE INNOCENT!" he thundered in ritualistic tones, a renewed conviction thundering through his voice so completely that his hand quaked. "SO THAT A WAY MIGHT BE MADE!!"

"Pario Atrum Universitas! . . . Pario Atrum Universitas! . . ."

"THE BRINGER HAS PASSED THROUGH THE VEIL! THE PROPHECIES ARE FULFILLED! LET OBLIVION COME FORTH!!"

"Pario Atrum Universitas! . . ." the Secretum chanted.

"PARIO ATRUM UNIVERSITAS: *BRING FORTH THE DARKWORLD!!*" roared Devlin.

With the suddenness of a candle being snuffed, the great Hollow instantly plunged into foreboding silence as the chanting and Devlin's shouting stopped. At the same moment, the monumental shaking of the ground beneath and above them came to an abrupt halt. His skin tingled with anticipation at the eerie stillness as he watched and waited.

And right on cue, the slate-colored hand of Oblivion appeared, climbing up from the gaping pit, followed by his body, and soon he was standing before them all. Calmly, with an indifferent, almost alien-like quality, he examined them without curiosity as he stood in their presence.

"The prophecy," Devlin declared in a reverent whisper, "is made flesh. Thousands of years we have waited and prepared for the fulfillment of this promise. Countless generations of our people have made endless sacrifices, but it was not in vain. Oh no, our faith has borne fruit—"

He broke off the speech he'd prepared years ago as Oblivion turned without warning and moved slowly toward the vast room's exit.

Momentarily thrown, Devlin stood frozen in place. Whatever he had been expecting of Oblivion's grand entrance, this wasn't quite it.

Another senior member of the Secretum of Six—a woman named Angela, who had been standing very near to Devlin, and whom Devlin had never particularly cared for—rushed forward, confusion tormenting her features. "Great one! Oblivion! Are you not here to begin your great work?" She reached out and touched the brown leather jacket he wore, pressed it until she felt the hard flesh beneath the folds of fabric . . .

She collapsed. Devlin and a few of the others rushed forward, bending over her. She'd gone cold instantly. Her eyes were rolled up, her jaw slackened.

She was dead. Oblivion's touch killed her.

If Oblivion noticed her, he made no consideration of it. He turned mechanically to face Devlin. His eyes blazed, and his gaze was wilting. "The DarkWorld is begun," he spoke for the first time, and Devlin fought the urge to place his hands over his ears at the sound. "It was set in motion the moment I entered this flesh. This place, this Hollow, is an unworthy relic of a different age."

Devlin's mind raced. *Unworthy?* What did that mean? *Unworthy of what?*

There was something odd about Oblivion's physiology when he spoke, and it took Devlin ample consideration to put his finger on it: Oblivion's chest was not rising or falling. Where a normal person's chest rises before they are about to speak, to take in breath, Oblivion merely opened his mouth and the sound issued forth.

“The DarkWorld cannot be appreciated from below,” Oblivion explained with unnerving calm.

Once again, he began to walk, and Devlin and the others followed close.

2

The earth shook from its foundations, and many were those who feared it might shake itself apart.

Then, as suddenly as it'd started, the shaking stopped.

Alex struggled to get her bearings, looking around through the bright haze in her eyes. Ethan's bulky silhouette still stood before her, and a dozen or so inhabitants of this underground city were also within her field of vision. All of them, everyone—including herself—still cowered, disoriented and frightened. They'd expected the cavern to come crumbling down. She was surprised it was still in one piece.

The city had been a din of pandemonium, thanks to her team's efforts, but now everyone and everything had just stopped. Everything had drawn to a complete pause, with people looking around in confusion, when Alex realized she felt different.

In fact, the whole world felt different.

Very different.

She had no idea what was happening, but she knew something fundamental about existence had just changed. She couldn't explain why or how she knew. It was an internal instinct, as pure as knowing how to breathe without ever having to choose to.

It was a terrifying feeling that left her sick to her stomach, as if something too big for her had just taken place, and she felt infinitesimal next to it, like standing in the path of an F5 tornado and being too terrified to move. In the handful of times in her life when she had stared down her own mortal coil and very nearly shaken it off, in those moments when her life was about to end and her past flashed before her eyes, when she expected to feel calm but instead felt so panic-stricken she couldn't catch her breath . . . this moment felt exactly the same.

She still couldn't see well because of the glowing of the Rings of Dominion throughout the cavernous city. She wore one of the rings on her right middle finger and it glowed brighter than she'd ever seen before—even brighter than that incident months back that Grant called The Forging. Then suddenly they'd flashed out, like a candle that had been violently blown by a gust of wind. But the concussive effects lingered on her retinas, and she put out an arm, bracing herself on a nearby wall as she waited for the blinding to clear.

Shapes around her soon began to come into focus, and in another moment she saw Ethan's face. He still stood only inches from her, dressed in his black jumpsuit and balaclava that had been peeled back over the top of his head. He held a pistol at his side, pointed down at the ground. His bleary eyes met hers, and there was no masking the fact that he too was utterly horrified by whatever was happening.

"I'm too late! It's already begun!" he whispered so no one else could hear. *"HE'S COMING!!"*

As Ethan spoke, Alex noticed a strange tingle that seemed to be spreading across her entire body, from her hair down to her toenails. It was the oddest sensation she'd ever experienced, like a mixture of a mild electrical current and a cold trickle of water. She didn't like it at all.

Ethan turned away from her and looked out at the city, where the glow from the Rings had flashed out, shrouding the cavern in foreboding shadows once more. "I'm sorry," Ethan was saying, and Alex had no idea what he was talking about. "I got here too late. Maybe we could have prevented it if . . ."

Alex's mind swam with strange new sensations, her limbs suddenly heavy and slow. And it wasn't just her. Everyone and everything was moving the same way. It was like trying to swim through syrup. Her senses also seemed to have sharpened considerably. She could see the tiniest grains of dirt in the ground beneath her feet with perfect clarity; she could hear the trickling of water running into pipes that lined the small lake on the other side of the city, as if she were standing right next to the sound.

All around her a new sound grew and built, rising throughout the city. Panic and alarm and terror rang from voices everywhere. She wasn't the only one noticing these weird new sensations, and soon a cacophony rose—a terrible combination of fear and excitement.

"I don't understand!" Alex shouted over the increasing commotion, her own voice painfully loud in her ears. "What's going on? What's happening?"

Ethan's face fell ashen as he looked up and scanned around, taking in their surroundings and the people who lived here. It was the first time she could recall ever seeing him afraid. Alex could tell from Ethan's expression that he felt what was happening to them every bit as much as she did.

"We'd better find Grant!" she shouted.

"He's gone," Ethan replied, his expression grave and sorrowful. It was the same expression the doctors wore whenever they passed on news to her mother before Alex's Shift.

With only the slightest hesitation, he turned and began to run.

"What are you doing?" she shouted.

He flung a glance back her way but never stopped running. "I'm sorry, it's too late now!" he cried, but then stopped and faced her. "There's nothing I can do! For *all* our sakes, I have to get out of here—"

“What’s going on?” she demanded. He obviously knew more than he was saying, and there wasn’t time to keep secrets. “What’s happening?”

“I’ll come back for you. For all of you. I’ll save you if I can. I promise. I’m sorry . . .”

With eyes filled with deepest regret, he turned from her one last time and vanished into the darkness.

3

London, England

Lisa knew her heart was going to stop beating.

Daniel had killed himself and all she could feel was a desire to be with him.

Squeak, squeak.

His feet dangled and swayed. Dangled and swayed.

Lisa's mind kicked into overdrive. He couldn't have done this to himself; he couldn't have committed suicide. There was no way for him to string himself up there; he had nothing to climb on. She looked about her cell, thoughts grasping for something, anything—

There!

In Daniel's adjacent cell, she spotted his walking cane, leaning against the corner between their cells. He'd nearly worn the thing out in Jerusalem; the MI-5 agents were good enough to allow him to keep it for moving about inside his cell. It was made of a lightweight aluminum, so it would do him little good as a weapon, they'd reasoned. But Lisa thought it *might* just be strong enough to . . .

She strained her arms inside, reaching, *reaching* . . . It was too far, just outside of her grasp.

"GUARD! HELP ME! SOMEBODY, PLEASE!!"

Lisa untied one tennis shoe, shoved it between the bars separating her cell from Daniel's, and flung it one-handed against the corner space where the cane stood.

Please . . . !

The shoe knocked the bottom of the cane, toppling it with a clang against the metal bars, the handle somehow falling inside her grasp.

She pulled the cane through the bars, stood, and extended it again. The end of it touched Daniel's noose, but she couldn't quite manipulate it . . .

Lisa pulled the cane back in, flipped it around so she held the bottom, and stuck it back through the bars. Carefully, she hooked the rubber grip handle down through the coiled fabric around Daniel's throat and tugged on it with all her might.

With a surge of strength that had to be pure adrenaline, she broke the light fixture above Daniel free from its attachment to the ceiling, and Daniel and the entire apparatus crashed to the ground. The racket was so loud that if the guards hadn't heard her screams, they would surely have heard this. Anyone passing by on the *street outside* was likely to have heard this.

But she didn't wait for them. She was just able to curl her fingertips around Daniel's lower pant leg, and she strained, sweating, until she'd pulled enough on it to bring him closer.

It was an awkward maneuver, but she finally managed to reach through the bars and untangle the noose until she could slip it off of his now-purple neck. Kneeling on the floor next to the bars, she flipped him over on his back and began pumping his chest up and down with both hands. The bars were too narrow to allow her head to squeeze through so she could breathe air into his lungs, so she kept pumping away. It was all she could do.

Please, please, please . . .

Daniel coughed, his eyes opening wide.

Lisa scooped him up as best she could and sobbed openly, wrapping her arms around him through the bars, as he continued to gag and gasp for air. His back was to her, so she couldn't see his face, but she didn't care.

He was alive. She clung to him as tightly as she could.

After several minutes, he pulled himself free of her grasp, and she noted with relief the purplish pallor retreating from his cheeks.

"What . . . what happened?" he choked, using one hand to massage the raw ring around his neck.

"I don't know!" Lisa cried. "There was an earthquake and I woke up and found you hanging by your neck!"

With tremendous effort, Daniel visibly swallowed, and the motion caused him great pain. He shook his head, eyes still huge.

"So, um . . ." Lisa sniffled. "I mean . . . you really didn't—?"

Daniel was shocked. "*Of course not!* I fell asleep and the next thing I know I'm strung up by the neck!"

"Then someone tried to kill you . . ." Lisa said.

" . . . again," Daniel finished, and then he passed out.

Lisa clutched him tightly in her arms, swaying back and forth, powerless. Waiting for whoever had failed to return and finish them for good.

4

Payton stared at his glowing Ring, allowing the blinding light to pierce his eyes and refusing to close them. His oxygen was running out, and he was determined not to deny himself any sensation that remained before death seized him.

Lost in the shattering brightness, he felt suddenly aware of how ready he was to die. Nearly anxious. It was only strange that it was now so near. This was the first time he'd truly felt in mortal danger in years, and so it was the first time he'd considered the very real possibility of dying. Again.

Knowing all he'd done, all of the darkness in his life and the death dealt at his own hands, knowing the heartache he'd suffered and the love gained and lost . . . Considering it all, Payton welcomed death.

And cursed it, in equal measure.

He'd managed to find a tiny pocket of air to curl up in, between the collapsing rocks during the cave-in. His ultra-fast bursts of speed had helped him move from spot to spot as the boulders fell, until he was able to find a hole to wedge himself between, where he would be protected from the rest of the earthquake. But the earth had packed itself in too tightly around and above him, on every side. He was unharmed save for a few scrapes, but the rocks were too big to move, so now there was nothing left but to wait.

But then the Ring continued to glow brighter and brighter than it ever had before. It had temporarily blinded his eyes long before it began to fade, long before he first felt the strange sensation that there was something wrong with . . . everything. His skin, the air he breathed, the way his body moved—it all felt drastically different, as if the very nature of existence had changed.

He knew this feeling. He'd felt it once before. In another cave, far from here, nearly ten years ago . . .

And it was growing warmer. So very hot there, buried alive. Again.

He was still unable to see much when the vibrations began.

Payton craned his neck around as if trying to see the source of the movement, but realized how fruitless that was. Everything was rock and dirt. But soon he didn't need to see, as the vibrations turned to blunt movement and he felt the rocks all around him rise up into the air.

His vision cleared and he staggered to his feet. He looked up to see every one of the boulders and stalactites and rubble that had crashed to the floor now hovering in the air only a few feet above him, all across the large cave where he'd slain several dozen Secretum soldiers. And he still couldn't shake this feeling that reminded him of what it was like to be in that cave in France, on that awful day . . . on the day—

The day he died.

If anything in this world was capable of instilling fear into Payton, it was this sensation, because he recognized it for what it was. It wasn't death that he feared; it was the memories that still haunted him from that defining event, the event that had changed his life forever. He had no regrets about the path his life had taken in the wake of his death and resuscitation, after Morgan's betrayal and abandonment of him. But some minuscule part of him mourned the loss of the man who had died that day. He had been so different before . . . So different. It had been such a different time. A different life.

Slowly, Payton turned to face the doorway where Grant had disappeared—when was that, *hours* ago now? Only, the doorway wasn't empty; Grant stood there once more, but now he was being tailed by an entourage that included Devlin, Payton's old mentor.

What is this?

What does Grant think he's—?

Payton froze.

He was a good fifty feet away from this unlikely group, but he knew as soon as Grant stepped inside the large cavernous room that whoever or whatever he was looking at . . . this was not Grant Borrows.

Or was it?

It looked like Grant. Up to a point, at least. But the eyes and the skin were wrong, and his expression . . . it was so devoid of emotion, so mechanical and lifeless . . .

Instinctively, his hand fell upon the hilt of his sheathed sword.

The *thing* that may or may not have been Grant noticed Payton's reflex immediately. He thrust out his right hand in Payton's direction, and Payton braced himself, but nothing happened.

"Grant," he said, stepping forward, "what are you—?"

Payton's body suddenly went rigid and his hand left his sword to rest easily at his side. His other arm did the same. Grant turned very intentionally away from him, ignoring him completely, and he began walking toward the opposite exit on the other side of the room that led back to the city above. The Secretum members followed behind.

Payton was alarmed to discover that his body was no longer obeying his directives. He wanted to draw his sword, to scream at Grant to snap out of whatever thrall he was held in. He wanted to send Devlin, who smiled subtly at him as he passed by, to a well-deserved grave.

But nothing happened. He merely stood there like a windup toy that had run out of juice. His mouth wouldn't open, his muscles wouldn't move, his eyes wouldn't even blink.

Sweat ran off of him in sheets from the cave's newfound heat. And something was wrong with the ground; it was changing colors, growing darker . . .

His left foot rose slightly into the air and his weight shifted forward. His right foot did the same, and he realized that his body was walking outside of his control. He couldn't even look down at the ground to see it pass beneath him, or around at the walls of the cavern, or up at the still-floating massive rocks and debris dangling above their heads. He could only stare straight ahead, like a robot locked into position, as his body carried him forward.

He fell into place behind Grant and the members of the Secretum of Six, his old masters. A few of them turned to cast furtive gazes at him but quickly resumed their loyal following of Grant, who led them from the room.

Grant and the others entered one of the elevators that would lead up to the underground city above, and Payton watched them through rigid eyes as he obediently boarded the same elevator, unable to stop himself, unable to lash out at each and every one of them as he so badly wanted to.

The last thing he heard as the elevator began to rise was a booming roar as the floating boulders and rocks that had held him trapped crashed once more to the ground. And yet he was more a prisoner than ever.

5

London

The white hot light of Trevor's Ring began to fade as he tore down the dark streets of old London. The light went out entirely, and then there was a sensation that felt like a *click* in his soul.

He felt sick with the sudden, inexplicable knowledge that everything about human life had just changed. He could feel it in his skin, bones, and blood, in his heart and mind.

Time was gone.

He was still in motion, the cool night air still caressed his skin, and his heart was still beating in his chest. Time had not *frozen*; it had simply been taken out of the equation.

"Oh no," Trevor whispered. "No, no, no . . ."

He drew his hands up before his face and flexed them, balling them into fists and opening them again. It felt different, thick and unnatural, as if the air were heavy. But it didn't weigh him down; if anything, he felt lighter and more graceful. His movements were almost smoother, like a powerful fish cutting through open water.

"They did it," he whispered to no one. "It's over. It's done. This is the end."

No! No! No!

He had a fleeting, sickened desire to run, to escape, to find a place to hide where he might be safe, indefinitely.

But no such place exists, he knew. *Not anymore.*

They really did it.

What would happen now? Nothing in history could prepare the human race for what was taking place right now. How *could* the world respond to the altogether absence of history moving forward?

He looked around helplessly, his eyes falling on a couple on a date, a pair of elderly women, a businessman out for a late-night stroll. Each of them looked puzzled, examining their hands, their bodies, the air around them, the night sky . . . None of them had a clue what was happening, but they felt it. They felt the sudden change, the sense of *otherness* that had overtaken the world, and they were showing increasing signs of worry, of panic and fear.

Poor fools, Trevor thought. *Oblivious. Their way of life is at an end, and they have no idea.*

His mind went back to words he'd heard spoken years ago by a member of the Secretum: *"No act of man can prevent the torment that day will herald."*

A brick settled into the pit of his stomach as he walked without direction.

This is it. The day of torment has come.

And with no more measurements of time . . . this day would last forever.

Ethan ran as fast as he could.

With all of the upheaval Alex and her people had caused in the underground city, it had been surprisingly easy infiltrating the place. His black jumpsuit had made it even easier to not be spotted; the place wasn't exactly bursting with light. Not until all of the Rings had begun to glow, anyway.

But if getting in had been a piece of cake, getting out was proving far more difficult. The hubbub had come to an end, and the city's population was standing around in a daze, some of them still regaining their eyesight, others looking about with unmistakable glee, knowing all too well what was happening. And what was about to happen.

As the only fast-moving thing in the entire city, he was more conspicuous now than ever. But he had no choice; there could be no slowing down or stopping. It was too late for that. He could only pray that he would be fast enough to escape, before Oblivion emerged.

Poor Grant . . . his thoughts wandered momentarily. *I'm sorry, my friend. You deserved a better fate than this.*

He drew within eye line of the outskirts of the town, around the edge where the outer walls of the cavern met the perimeter of the city. A child some thirty feet ahead screamed and pointed in his direction, and the kid's father, who was nearby, suddenly rushed toward Ethan with an unholy roar.

Thinking fast, Ethan slowed and pulled out a Glock from the holster on his left side. He trained it on the running man with ease, his years of FBI training and experience coming to his aid. When the man didn't stop, Ethan lowered the gun and shot at the ground near the man's feet. The running man stopped and pulled back, and Ethan pointed the pistol at him once more. He had no idea if these people spoke English, and talking out loud would only draw more attention to him, so he simply shook his head sternly.

He heard more screams—the result of his discharging his weapon—and saw more people running toward him from his peripheral vision.

Ethan didn't have time for this. Oblivion was coming! And now he was outnumbered. . . .

A circle of five men and women formed around him, angry looks on each face. Ethan kept his gun up but spun in place, shifting his aim to each person in turn.

"Fool!" one woman scolded him. "You can't shoot us all!"

The men and women each took a step closer, tightening the circle around him. Ethan turned his gun to the woman who'd spoken. "You sure about that?" When he spoke the words, they came out low and menacing.

"Let him go," called the man on the sidelines—the one Ethan had shot at a moment ago. "He cannot outrun the Dark-World. No one can."

Ethan took advantage of these strange words and broke into a sprint, throwing both arms out as he charged through two members, stiff-arming them out of his way. Ahead he could see the carved entryway that led to the long set of stairs that would eventually bring him to the landing high above, and to his way out: the underground tunnels the Secretum called its "Conveyor" system.

Oblivion would be upon them all long before he could reach the top. It was a suicide run.

It was his one chance.

6

"Fletcher?" Alex called into her earpiece. "Nora? Anyone?" If they were out there in the city somewhere, they were as dumbstruck as she was by whatever was happening.

First the earthquake and then the Rings glowing like the sun. And now this. Silence. Silence and an unnerving sensation like none she had ever experienced. Like nothing she ever *should* have experienced. Still, she knew this feeling; she had no trouble putting a description to the sensation, even though her brain logically knew that it was impossible.

She knew what she was feeling, even if it was utterly ridiculous.

She had stepped outside of time. But not just her. Everything and everyone.

Everything was now.

Then Ethan had run off. Probably back to wherever he'd come from, before he'd mysteriously turned up in this city.

The group had lost track of him in London, assuming that he had been captured. So what was he up to now, showing up here out of the blue, carrying secrets and going on about Grant being dangerous?

Alex imagined that most of the people in this city were probably still processing the feeling of time not passing, accounting for how eerily quiet it had become. Her eyes shifted upward, tracing the concave walls of the massive cavern that enclosed the city, the enormous stalactite running down its center and touching the floor right in the city's centermost point.

Like her hearing, her eyesight was sharper too. Everything was different. So different. Reality itself had been heightened, or at least her sense of it.

Alex whipped around as she heard gunshots half a mile away, back in the direction of the way she and the others had entered the city.

"Who's shooting?!" she cried into her earpiece, not really expecting a reply from any of her team.

She wiped sweat from her brow, for the first time noticing how much warmer it had grown inside the city. It had been cool and comfortable in the cave when they'd first arrived; why was the temperature climbing now?

What on earth was going on here?

She cocked her head down to wipe the moisture away from her cheek with her left arm. That was when she saw it.

The ground beneath her feet was spontaneously . . . changing. Without sound, without warning, it was turning black, and the blackness was spreading. The cavern's brown dirt, rocks, and clay were being altered into something that looked more like volcanic rock. The overpowering smell of sulfur met her nostrils and she covered her mouth, trying not to breathe it in.

Alex looked up, down, in all directions. There. Near the tip of the giant stalactite, where it touched the ground at the city's core—the blackened earth seemed to be originating from there. As if someone had upturned a giant bottle of black ink there in the center of the city and slowly the ink was spreading outward in all directions, staining and ruining every piece of earth in its path. The primitive, lotus-topped buildings were unchanged, and the people standing atop the blackened earth didn't appear affected either. But the strange effect spread out relentlessly, as if consuming the soil.

Alex watched as the phenomenon passed beneath her bare feet, and she could feel the ground become harder and more jagged-edged as it passed under her and continued to spill throughout the entire city. It showed no signs of stopping.

She had just placed a finger on her earpiece to call out to the team again, thinking that maybe it was time for them to retreat and regroup, when she heard gasps from a pair of the city's residents a few dozen feet behind her. She followed their gazes to the central core of the city, where an elevator had just arrived, and a large group of people exited into the city. They were being led by a lone, familiar figure.

Alex's heart leapt.

"Grant . . ." she whispered.

It didn't matter that a group of well-dressed, refined-looking strangers were following him, or that a blank and battered Payton pulled up the rear. She had eyes only for the man in the lead, and she ran toward him faster than she'd ever run toward anything in her life.

She was drowning, she couldn't catch her breath, the world was changing too much too fast and nothing made sense, but Grant was here now. And the one thing she knew for certain in this life was that that meant everything would be okay.

She just needed to touch him, to feel the electricity that passed between them every time their skin met, as it had only a few hours ago when they'd arrived in this godforsaken place . . .

Wait.

She didn't stop running, but she could see it. Something was off.

Grant's eyes were afire.

Where his eyeballs should have been, small fires burned and licked his eyebrows. They burned a deep red, a richer shade of the same hue she had seen a few times before. It went all the way back to that night in Grant's apartment at the

Wagner Building when Hannah died, when Alex had seen the first hint of it as Grant's anger nearly consumed him . . .

As she drew nearer, she noticed something else: his skin had changed. His face and his hands, and wherever else his skin peeked out beneath his clothes and that signature brown leather jacket that he rarely took off . . . His skin wasn't the pinkish color of healthy flesh anymore. It was a sickening gray, as if it were comprised of rotted bone or wet cement.

Alex finally slowed her pace, coming to a stop.

Grant was the color, the very embodiment, of death.

7

Alex was too stunned by the sight of him to form a coherent thought. Around her, a handful of small wildfires had inexplicably broken out upon the ground—fueled by nothing in particular—flaring like torches five or ten feet above the earth.

She was twenty feet away when a cry escaped from her lips before she could stop it. It was a desperate noise filled with pain and disbelief, and she didn't realize she was the one making it until after it was done. She didn't know herself capable of such a bloodcurdling sound, and it terrified her.

"GRAAAAAANT!!"

She swallowed the remainder of her revulsion at Grant's changed appearance, and rushed toward him. "Grant? What is this? What's happening!?"

Grant—*was* this Grant?—ignored her, until she was close enough to touch. She was about to grab his hand in her own when he pivoted to her, and those flames that had once been eyes fixed upon her, burning a little hotter.

Alex's feet left the ground as a crushing pressure closed in around her throat. Tears of pain poured from her eyes almost at once, and she clawed at the invisible hand forcing her to strain for a single breath. She wanted to scream, but her voice might as well have been back on the surface high above.

When Grant opened his mouth, it was not Grant's voice that came out. It was an otherworldly screech, low and gravelly yet somehow high-pitched and painful to the ears, like fingernails across a chalkboard. A sound like nothing she'd ever heard.

"Know your place, Ringwearer," Grant said without a trace of emotion, "and keep it."

An almost imperceptible flick of his head, and Alex was thrown through the air like so many rags. She flew more than thirty feet aside, out of Grant's path, landing hard on her stomach, gasping at the air now rushing down her throat. It was a good five seconds before she realized she was lying atop one of the wildfires that were burning the ground. No more than two feet in diameter, it nonetheless burned hot and bright, and a searing pain bit at the flesh covering her stomach. Her right arm had landed beneath her chest and the arm felt as if it were on fire as well.

The pain overwhelming her, she kicked off with one leg and began to roll, praying with all her might that the fire burning her skin would go out and leave her to die in peaceful agony.

She turned over a full six times before she was spent and could roll no more, landing harshly on her back. Moaning from the pain, she wanted nothing but a sensation of cold to wrap her body in a frozen embrace. Tears streamed freely down either side of her face, dampening her temples and then her hair as one thought consumed her mind.

Whatever that is . . . it's not Grant.

It can't be.

She clutched at the bloody skin over her abdomen with her good arm. There had once been a white tank top covering her stomach where the burn was, but now that part of the shirt was gone, stray fibers mingling into the blood of her injuries. Some of her skin burned white hot while other parts had lost all sensation.

Alex felt light-headed. She knew what this was—she was going into shock. She was about to fall asleep.

The world was going to Hell and Grant had been replaced by she-didn't-even-know-what and her skin was burning her alive and yes, how she welcomed the blissful darkness creeping in around her vision. It was the warm embrace of a beloved family member, welcoming her to an eternal rest . . .

Moments later, she came to. Only she was no longer prostrate upon the charred earth.

She was upright, and in motion.

Sleepwalking, that's what she was doing. It had to be. She'd passed out and somehow her body was so traumatized from her injuries that her body was doing what came naturally. Her bare feet knew how to pound against the earth, even if it was dark and black and smelled musty and acrid.

But . . .

Alex willed herself to stop walking, yet she stayed in motion. And her ambling legs were only one part of the problem. Her head wouldn't swivel or tilt, her arms refused to do anything but sway slightly in time with her walking, and she couldn't even wiggle her eyes in their sockets. They remained stubbornly fixed, wide open, pointed straight ahead.

If human beings could be maneuvered by remote control, this was surely what it felt like. Just as these words came to mind, the pain in her abdomen returned full force, and the relentless motion of her body merely aggravated the intensity of the burning sensation on her torso and right arm. But it was useless; she couldn't stop it, couldn't even clutch at her midsection to soothe the pain. She was on autopilot, controlled by some outside force—

Grant.

The Forging.

She just knew. The power that had given Grant the ability to sense the presence of other Ringwearers, and even issue them silent directives, was being twisted into some form of total control over every part of her body.

Between agonizing steps and breaths, she caught sight of the other Ringwearers here in the city—Hector, Nora, Mrs. Edeson, Cornelius, Fletcher, and several others—walking ahead of her, or to the side, or perhaps behind where she couldn't see. She tried to open her mouth, to say something to them, but they continued the same brisk walking pace that she was forced to endure. They were moving toward the exit of the underground city chamber, and though she could only catch the tiniest glimpses of the front of the line so far ahead of her, she was certain it was Grant who was there, setting the pace.

There were others ahead of her in the line, others she didn't recognize. They were well-dressed and looked as though they weren't used to doing this much walking, at this kind of pace, though each of them was bright-eyed and excited. These were the ruling members of the Secretum, she reasoned. There was no one else they could be.

The rest of the group was made up of her fellow Ringwearers, all walking along like lifeless zombies. Just like her.

Alex felt blood trickling down her legs and soaking her jeans. The pain over her stomach felt as if a hot poker were being pressed into her flesh—she would bear permanent scars from an injury this severe, if not worse. And she could feel the blackness creeping in around her senses again, threatening to render her unconscious. The pain she felt was beyond imagination, and even though she had no idea what was happening or why, she knew without a doubt that she would never be allowed to stop and seek desperately needed medical attention.

So she merely walked, allowing the burning to wash over her and through her and hopefully render her unconscious again. She tried to divorce herself of the feeling of marching forward in this obscene procession, moving toward the same entryway that all of them had used just a few hours ago to enter this city from the hidden entrance in the side of the mountain so high above.

One of the last things Alex noted before passing out was the grunting exertions of someone marching right behind her. If she wasn't very much mistaken, it sounded like Payton, moving with a limp, robotic cadence.

She wondered if they were marching to their deaths. Was that where Grant was leading them?

Where else was there to go, in such a state?

Or maybe they were dead already. That's what it felt like.

Maybe she'd died and gone to Hell.

INTERREGNUM

JULIE!

NO!!

Everything around him was black. There was no up or down, no walls or floors or ceiling, no boundaries of any kind. The darkest black he'd ever seen pressed in upon him from all around.

The soul of Grant Borrows was swimming through the ether of existence.

He looked down. He still had his body, but it was different. For one thing, he was naked. To his great astonishment, seeing himself this way didn't feel shameful or out of place. It felt natural. Normal.

His body also seemed to have a faint glow, or a . . . shimmer.

Yes, that's what it looked like. He was shimmering.

Full circle. How poetic.

If this was death, he found it unappealing so far.

Was he dead? Is that what this was? Or was it another Secretum ploy?

The last thing he remembered was watching Devlin shoot his sister right before shoving him into a gaping chasm deep beneath the earth. After that, he fell.

He fell, until . . .

Well, until he arrived here. Wherever *here* was.

Oh, Julie . . .

His sister was dead, shot in cold blood by Devlin, Keeper of the Secretum of Six. For no other reason than to throw Grant off-balance, no doubt, to make pushing him into that screaming hole all the easier. The entire walk through the Secretum's underground city had been another carefully planned manipulation, right from the start. They abducted Julie to lure him there, and then used her to get him to the innermost heart of their facility, a place Devlin reverentially called "the Hollow."

Julie was the one thing in all the world that he could count on, the one thing in his life that always made sense, always resembled "normal."

But he had failed her, and she was dead.

So, was he dead too?

Grant opened his mouth. "Hello?"

There was no echo, no resonance to the sound whatsoever. He had no sense of the size of the space he was in, nor its depth nor density. His voice was flat and dull, as if the words dissipated into nothing. Perhaps he had heard it, then through the vibrations, felt in his own body.

"Julie?" he called out, raising his voice. It was no use; he could hear himself no differently than before.

He looked around into the aching darkness, knowing he should feel panicked and distressed right now, yet feeling none of these things.

Grant decided to try to reason his way out of his situation.

He had watched Julie die, only seconds ago. The flash of the gun, the surprise in her eyes, the crumpling of her body. He saw that. He knew his sister was dead.

Then, Devlin had shoved him into quite possibly the deepest hole inside the deepest cavern beneath the surface of the earth. How long had he fallen? Thirty seconds? A minute? Five minutes? Longer?

He couldn't say. One moment he was falling, flailing madly into the blackness, and the next moment the rushing of the air passing his ears and the scrapes of his fingers against the sides of the chasm—they all vanished. Perfectly still in the black, he was no longer falling but sort of standing or floating in the middle of absolutely nothing. There were no sounds, no smells, there was nothing touching his skin, and his clothes were gone.

And he was all alone.

"No, you're not."

He spun in place, fast. The whisper had come from behind, but it was in motion, as if made by a passerby on a bicycle. He looked about but saw nothing.

"Who's there?" he tried to call out, but his voice was still muted, as before.

Grant gazed around, taking in the empty darkness that surrounded him, wondering where he was, what was happening, and whose voice was speaking to him. Naked and solitary in the dark, he felt vulnerable, but not in danger.

"The time has come," the voice said, and this time the sound seemed to come from everywhere at once. It sent rippling waves of power through Grant's entire form.

"Time for what?" Grant asked.

"Time for *us*," the voice replied. "You and I have a great deal to talk about."

8

Half an hour passed (or maybe it was a hundred years?—it was impossible to tell anymore) and Lisa clung once more to Daniel from behind, through the bars of their cells, as he rested with his back against them. Neither he nor his former lab assistant had spoken in a very long while.

Daniel was consumed with thoughts of an awfully big world out there that they were alone in now—with no help from their superpowered friends—and the knowledge that a secret organization had tried twice to kill him in the last forty-eight hours. Once by impersonating members of the British police, and next by dangling him by the neck from a light fixture. He ignored the strange new sensations that gripped them, as if their movements were happening underwater. It hardly mattered just now.

There was no chance of rest or idle conversation. There was only that desperate clinging to each other.

What an odd road it had been, bringing the two of them here. Daniel was a bookish, late thirty-something lab junkie, hopelessly consumed with his science. Lisa was his erstwhile young assistant, his very own gal Friday. He'd once tried to deny it, tried even to convince himself that he found her plucky charms annoying, but he knew in his heart of hearts that she was his soul's counterpart. They were a perfect team, and a more devoted friend he would never find. She would gladly follow him to the ends of the earth.

And that was where they seemed to be now.

Despite the terrible racket they'd caused freeing Daniel, no guards or policemen had ever shown up. And now they knew why—they could hear it.

Their cells bordered the city streets outside, and beyond those walls they heard the sounds of anarchy. It was like the riot in Los Angeles all over again: screaming, looting, sirens, gunfire.

"Your watch," Lisa mumbled.

"What?" Daniel whispered, his voice still dry and raspy after the hanging.

"Your watch stopped," she replied, slightly loosening the arms that were clasped around his chest.

He glanced down, only vaguely interested. "Huh."

"Batteries?" Lisa asked.

Daniel slowly raised his head. "I don't think the watch is the problem."

Lisa understood. "Yeah, I feel it too. That knot in your stomach? It's like . . ." she grasped for the words.

"Like there's nothing but *now,*" he whispered, finishing the thought for her. "No past or future. It's as if our existence is summed up entirely in today, this hour, this moment. And the moment never passes."

Lisa swallowed, listening to the riotous sounds outside again. "How's that possible? And what's going on out there? What's happening to us?"

Daniel knew Lisa meant more than the two of them alone in their cells. "I don't have any answers," he sighed. "Not anymore. We're venturing way outside the realm of science here, or even para-science. Everything I know tells me that what we're experiencing is categorically impossible. Time is a constant; it's one of the few unchanging laws of the universe. Even when it's curved due to the effects of gravity, it still *exists* and its effects are bound by the laws of science. It's predictable, it's bankable. It's the fourth dimension, and it's how we measure any and all change. If time has somehow been removed from the equation, then I wonder what other scientific laws have been broken . . ."

"All bets are off," Lisa offered.

He wiggled free from her grasp to turn around and face her, a quizzical expression on his face, as if he was trying to remember something.

"That's what you told me," she explained, "back when everything first began. Remember that day when Grant first breached the Threshold? You said that all bets were off."

Daniel regarded her for a moment. "You think *Grant* is responsible for what's happening?"

There was no hesitation in her reply. "I think you were closer to the truth than you knew."

"If we could just get out of here, maybe we could . . ." Daniel sighed and leaned back again, allowing her to hold him.

Part of Daniel couldn't believe he was allowing himself such an open display of affection. That wasn't like him; he was stuffy and professional, though not without his own charms, but he never betrayed his true feelings so freely. But things had changed now, hadn't they?

After their conversation the previous night, after his admissions of guilt and her—well, what *had* she admitted, exactly? That she'd secretly funded his research for years? That she had ulterior motives for doing so—motives that if he couldn't grasp on his own, she didn't know if she could express?

Another unmeasured expanse of time passed between them in silence. Never once did Lisa let go, holding on to him fiercely. The way a drowning man holds a plank of wood. But he was the one sinking. He was the one who'd brought so much pain into her life. Pains he himself had suffered and then vicariously inflicted upon her . . .

The brutal street-corner beating that had nearly claimed his life, leaving permanent damage and impairing his ability to walk . . . Taking the life of a hateful, vindictive man that the law could never touch, and then having to live with the overbearing guilt the murder caused . . . The Secretum attempting to take his life just hours ago, by hanging . . .

So much had happened to him—to *them*—and he'd given her so many reasons to walk away. He'd never tried to intentionally push her away, but he couldn't have planned a better way of accomplishing it.

And yet she was still here, holding him as if there were nowhere else she'd rather be.

Daniel had told her once the story of his youth, when he was often getting hurt but would always manage to bounce back. And even now, he had bounced back again. He'd even come to terms with his mistakes and made an admission of guilt. With this clearing of his conscience, his long-missing confidence seemed to be returning by the moment.

Daniel wondered if he was an evil man. He was a murderer; there was no doubt about that, even if the man he'd killed had definitely deserved it. But still he felt the death, as though he had *willed* death upon that vile man without the use of a gun. He'd enjoyed it, but it hollowed him out. He knew even as he was doing it that the ends didn't justify the means, but at the time, he didn't care.

He cared now. He'd explained all of this to Lisa last night, and he longed for someone to condemn him, to confirm that he was the evil man he knew in his heart he was. But instead, she'd said three words that he was not prepared for.

I forgive you.

What an absurd thing for her to say. He hadn't shot *her* in the head. Why should her forgiveness make any difference?

But even as he thought of these things, his eyes moistened again. It was such a remarkable thing, those three little words. They had unmade him.

Lisa sniffled quietly to herself from behind him, and he suddenly wondered if her thoughts were lingering on the same things that his were.

"I love you," she whispered. He hadn't moved in quite a while, enjoying the feeling of her arms wrapped around him, so she probably assumed he was asleep.

Daniel's heart lurched, and several moments passed as Daniel debated whether or not to reply, or acknowledge that he'd heard her.

Finally he could take it no more. He stirred, slowly loosening himself from her grip and turning to face her. Shame was etched across his features, along with no small amount of alarm.

Lisa reeled backward on her hands and feet. Her eyes looked ready to pop, and her mouth fell open.

Daniel shook his head miserably, struggling to find words, any words at all. "I'm . . . But . . . I'm a murderer. And a coward," he said, his raspy voice barely audible. "I don't deserve you. How could you possibly . . . ? Why . . . ?"

Tears fell unrestrained from Daniel's eyes as Lisa suddenly relaxed and smiled as if relieved and thrilled and utterly calm all at once. She nudged herself up against the bars again and took his hands. "Because the choice is mine to make," she replied. "And I've made it."

9

Ethan Cooke wiped sweat away from his face, glanced up, and read a stamped beam above his seat, printed with the words *Conveyor Pod #168*. Already the black opalescent Pod—big enough to carry twenty or more, though he was alone on this trip—rocketed through the Secretum's underground electromagnetic tunnel system at a bullet's pace.

The Pod was circular in shape, but flattened like a straw on its side that's been pressed down. There was nothing terribly eye-catching about the vehicle other than its sleek, futuristic design—a stark contrast to what he'd seen of the subterranean city where the Secretum lived, with its ancient architecture and caveman feel. Comfortable seats were stationed in simple rows; he sat near the vehicle's front, a single knee bobbing up and down anxiously. There was no pilot or cockpit; the Pod was entirely automated. All he had to do was enter and select his Entry Node destination from a screen at the front of the passenger area that listed all possible destinations, and he was off.

Only one destination had come to mind, and he'd chosen it almost without thinking. The computer's readout display periodically flashed on-screen with the time and distance remaining until he reached his destination. The time remained frozen, but the second readout said *2,811 km*— 2,811 kilometers to go.

In their arrogance, the Secretum had never bothered installing security measures within the Conveyor system. They believed that no one from the surface would ever be able to find it—or if they did, it would not deter the Secretum's plans—so why bother securing it?

Ethan's escape from the Secretum's city had been narrow; Oblivion emerged from below just as Ethan was starting up the stairs that led to the alcove high above. He tried not to think about what would have happened to him if he'd been discovered by Oblivion. Just like he tried not to think about what was happening to his Ringwearing friends right now.

Oblivion . . . he thought, the name new in his mind. He'd first heard it less than two days ago when he was abducted and drafted into a covert agency, which operated unimpeded by local or even national jurisdictions. The world had become unpredictable, unencumbered by rules. They seemed a better hope in such a world than the CIA or his former employer, the FBI.

Oblivion has come. It's really happening. Everything I was told . . . It's all true, and it's all happening.

Right now.

His new superiors hadn't given him a contingency plan, in case he couldn't get to Substation Omega Prime and stop what was destined to happen in time. They placed so much responsibility on his shoulders so fast . . . It was almost as if they knew he would fail. Knew there was no way to stop what was destined to happen.

Then why send me at all?

I am *the lowest guy on the totem pole. Guess that makes me expendable.*

Still, something felt wrong about it. Ethan was an unknown quantity to them. Wasn't he?

Had they known he would be too late? That Oblivion would emerge shortly after he arrived?

But that would mean they meant for me to see him, to witness it in person . . . But why?

An old feeling returned. Ethan's thoughts went back to his last few days with the FBI, when he'd received cryptic messages that put him on the path to finding Grant Borrows and his friends. That path had led him to resign from the FBI, only to find himself picked up by this mysterious group he knew very little about.

Was it all part of the same path? Was he still being guided along by his anonymous benefactor?

If so . . . to what end?

He looked up again.

A new idea occurred to him. At first, he brushed it aside impulsively. But then his sense of responsibility kicked in.

A cellular phone call was out of the question—he was traveling at supersonic speeds underground. Not to mention the fact that the earth's satellites had entered deteriorating orbits and would eventually burn up in the atmosphere.

Ethan glanced around. Beside each seat in the Pod was what looked like a high-tech communications terminal, complete with a twelve-inch LED screen. He touched the screen and it blinked to life, presenting him with several options. After a bit of toying with the device, he decided it was a secure communications system, apparently used by members of the Secretum. It took more work to find out how it operated: some kind of advanced, underground communications telemetry based on sonar technology, of all things.

With a little fast thinking, Ethan was able to trick the system into hacking its sonar-based signal into a telephone landline on the surface.

After a familiar dial tone emerged from the device's speakers, Ethan punched in a phone number that provided privileged access to the Hoover Building in Washington, D.C.

He sighed, dreading this conversation almost as much as he'd dreaded encountering Oblivion.

2,440 kilometers.

"Code in, please," answered a male voice on the other end.

Ethan rolled his eyes. He no longer had any valid codes. "This is former special agent Ethan Cooke. I need to speak to Director Stevens immediately. Tell her . . . tell her I have intelligence on what's happening to the world's measurements of time."

A noteworthy pause later, the man replied, "One moment, sir."

Ethan watched the clock count down to 2,203 kilometers before Stevens's curt voice spoke into his ear.

"This better be good, Mr. Cooke," she said, putting extra emphasis on the *mister*. "You've just pulled me out of a briefing with the Joint Chiefs, so skip the pleasantries and tell me what you know. If it's good enough, I might *not* have you hunted down as a deserter with a 'kill on sight' order."

Ethan ignored her threats. This conversation was necessary to keep the U.S.—or anyone else—from making a terrible mistake.

"Whatever your scientists are telling you about time having stopped moving forward—however outrageous it sounds, I can verify that it's one hundred percent true."

"And how do you know—?"

"Later," he said, cutting her off. "The source of the phenomenon is a person. A single, superhuman individual capable of inconceivable power. An individual currently located in the nation of Turkey."

"And do you know who this individual is? Consider your reply very carefully, Mr. Stevens. You may not be under my command anymore, but you did take an oath to uphold the sanctity and sovereignty of this nation. I would advise you to keep—"

"Listen to me very carefully, Director," Ethan said with urgency, as static intruded upon her words. When it cleared, he continued. "I am calling you to urge you *not* to advise the president to take military action against this individual—no matter what happens next. Hear me clearly on this, because I can't possibly overstate it: There is no power in the arsenal of mankind capable of harming this man. Any action taken against him is tantamount to condemning the entire planet to destruction. No matter how many men or weapons you throw at him, it will never be enough. *Do not engage this target.* Do you understand me?"

A pause. "I want to know who this 'target' you seem to know so much about is," Stevens replied. "*If* he even exists, which I'm not entirely inclined to take your word about."

"I don't know anything about him," Ethan lied. He knew quite a lot about Oblivion, but he wasn't going to tell her that. He didn't know *everything,* though.

He looked up at the readout again. 1,972 kilometers to his destination.

"You're not a good liar, Mr. Cooke," Stevens replied at last. "I believe you that this mystery man exists, if for no other reason than you're so intent on keeping his identity from me. Which leads me to conclude that your friend Guardian is connected to all of this."

"Trust me," Ethan retorted, "this has *nothing* to do with Guardian."

Stevens *hmph*ed in his ear. "I'll see about confirming your . . . *intel* . . . And I'll take your counsel under advisement. But I promise you, Cooke, if I find out that Guardian is connected in any way to this, I will personally deliver his head *and* yours to the president on the shiniest platter in Washington."

Click.

10

No . . .

Payton emerged from the secret entrance to the underground city behind Grant, the Secretum, and the Loci. The path led out into the open night sky of the Taurus Mountains.

They were very high up, so high that he didn't have to attempt to move his neck to be able to see the clouds rolling violently, churning and boiling. Fire seared the clouds, licking at its edges. It was a colossal sight, the entire sky offering its angry protest at what the world was becoming. It left Payton feeling tiny, like a single grain of dirt, in comparison.

A hot wind blew across the steep mountain slope, and Payton, still in thrall to Grant's commands, was also able to see that the phenomenon turning the earth black as ash had followed them from below. Even now it was creeping outward from the spot where they stood. The storm above seemed to grow to the same proportions as the dark earth below it spreading outward; the storm was keeping perfect pace with the changes to the ground.

No, that wasn't quite right. It was creeping outward from the place where Grant stood. He was the epicenter of this—whatever *this* was. Wherever he moved, the earth seemed to die and turn black, like the inside of a volcano, and the black death radiated outward from his position, consuming every piece of dirt or sand or stone in its path. Even the sparse trees and plant life here in the Taurus Mountains turned to ash and became dehydrated, dying fast once the blackness touched them.

Payton took all of this in, in the merest fraction of a moment, and it changed everything for him. His thoughts, his desires, his attitude—it all shifted now. Because while he had no frame of reference for the phenomenon happening to the ground beneath his feet, he knew exactly what was happening in the skies overhead. He'd witnessed it before. As had most of the other Ringwearers.

It was the firestorm. The very same firestorm that had blistered the skies over Los Angeles several months ago, the day Grant had squared off against his grandfather.

It was happening again. Whatever had happened to Grant, whatever the Secretum had done to him, or he'd become—*this* was exactly what Grant's grandfather was trying to achieve back in L.A. Where Maximilian Borrows had failed, Devlin had succeeded. But Grant wouldn't be stopping the storm this time, reining it in with his emotions. It would be allowed to roam free, unabated, consuming the skies above the entire world.

He caught sight of Devlin, hovering at Grant's right hand with reverence and self-importance, as if it were a place reserved just for him.

The old git's loving every minute of this, Payton thought of his former mentor.

Payton silently vowed to choke the old man to death with his bare hands the second Grant released his hold over the Ringwearers.

But that was assuming Grant *would* release the Ringwearers from his thrall. At the moment, Payton had every reason to believe that his existence from this point on would continue just as it currently was. An automaton, slave to Grant's will. Forever trapped inside his own mind, with no means of escape. Very likely he would die this way, and he cursed every single person he could think of—including himself—at this most bitter of thoughts. He was a warrior. Anything less than a death earned by a superior opponent was an unworthy means of passing into whatever awaited beyond.

But why were he and the others being made to suffer this way? There had to be a purpose to all of this, but he had no idea what it might be.

Grant began to walk. The Secretum fell in behind him at once, whispering among themselves and casting nervous glances at the Loci marching lifelessly behind them.

All of this was Devlin's doing. And Grant's. How could Grant have allowed this to happen? He was a smart man; perhaps a little idealistic, but Payton knew him to be decent and noble, and not entirely unclever. Now they were marching as one, in a very long line, and who knew where their walking would come to an end.

Was this all Grant's fault? Whatever had happened to change him this way . . . had Grant had the chance to turn away from this fate, and refused to do so? Or was he powerless against destiny's plans, powerless from the very moment of his birth?

Payton thought to himself that he would probably never know. He couldn't save *or* destroy Grant. He was incapable of doing anything except walking, which his body was doing once again, following Grant.

Payton had no answers, and no hope. But he had his anger, and that was something he knew how to use. He would be the one to stop Grant. Somehow, he would find a way to get free from Grant's hold. He would stop this *thing* wearing Grant's body from changing the entire world into whatever he was changing it into. He would kill Devlin and the rest of the Secretum and put a final end to their scheming and plotting.

And he would save his friend Grant Borrows from this fate, by bringing a swift and painless end to the man's life. Once and for all.

A first hint of rain touched his cheeks. At last, some good news. The suffocating heat that seemed to emanate from Grant would finally meet its match and be forced to cool a little. Those clouds up above, spitting fire and keeping the skies in unending darkness, were good for something after all.

Unable to move or flinch at the cool caress of the water, he didn't notice its appearance until the liquid began soaking into the clothes of the people around him. The smell was powerful and sickening. Payton recognized it at once. Some of the Secretum members were frightened by what was raining upon them, while others like Devlin turned their heads skyward and outstretched their arms, rejoicing and reveling in the moment.

Grant continued to lead their march up ahead, oblivious to the sky pouring out thick red fluid on them all, soaking their hair and clothes down to the skin.

Somewhere far away in the distance, a terror-filled scream could be heard.

It was raining blood.

INTERREGNUM

"WHO ARE YOU?" GRANT called out into the darkness.

"I've been close to you since the day you were born," said the voice. He didn't quite recognize it, but there *was* something familiar about it.

"I don't understand," Grant said.

"Wiser words have never passed beyond your lips," replied the voice. "For this is the reason you are here: to understand. To see the truth for what it really is."

"Where am I?" Grant asked. "I need to get out of here! My friends, they're in danger—"

"No way out," the voice replied, unconcerned with Grant's pleas. "You are far outside of mortal existence. It would be easier for you, in the long run, to disconnect yourself now from such concerns."

"What is this place? What's happening to me?"

The voice laughed. "Did you think the bottom of that hole led to some sort of bright, shining place full of puppies and rainbows and laughing children? Far from it, Grant. *Far from it.*"

Grant nearly snapped. He was terrified now, shivering even though there was no sensation of temperature here.

"I believe you are familiar with an object humankind calls 'the Dominion Stone'?" the voice asked.

"Yes. It predicted . . . well, it predicted *me*."

"Indeed. But it predicted a great deal more. You never read all of it, did you?"

"It was stolen before I had the chance. Then I broke it—"

"No, no. It was broken already, long ago, and then reassembled by your friend Morgan. You merely disassembled the pieces that day you shoved it off of its easel in your grandfather's presence. The Stone is made of a substance harder than diamond. You couldn't have broken it, even with the powers you possessed."

"Then how *was* it broken?"

"What if I told you *I* broke it?"

"Then that would tell me that you're powerful, but I already knew that: You're talking to me when I'm *dead*. Now, either tell me what you want with me, or let me out of here," Grant said.

"There is no 'out,' Grant," replied the disembodied voice. "I've already told you this. You're dead. Your mortal life is over. Regarding what I want . . . I want you to see the truth."

"What truth?"

"You have known great power, Grant Borrows. Power beyond that of any mortal man who ever lived and breathed. But now the entire universe has paused, holding its collective breath, watching as the fate of mankind is decided. The world that you know has arrived at a destination that was first charted more than seven thousand of your years ago. And all the power that you once knew has been stripped from you. You cannot stop what is happening, so best to put it out of your mind and focus on what's in front of you."

"There *isn't* anything in front of me," Grant replied, confused. He continued turning around and thought he caught a glimpse of a moving figure out of the corner of his eye, but it was gone before he could focus on it.

"Are you sure about that?"

The voice was closer this time. Grant turned, trying to find his sole companion in this empty place. He disliked this newcomer already. "Stop playing games and show yourself!" he demanded.

From his immediate right, a figure strode into view as if walking on ground, even though there was no ground there. He stood before Grant, and Grant took him in fully, not believing his eyes.

"Finally, you've asserted yourself," the other figure replied. "It's about time."

A man stood before him, relaxed and observant but also naked. He matched Grant's stance with a mirror's precision.

He was Grant.

"What would you like to talk about?" the mirror Grant spoke, while Grant looked on with widened eyes.

"Am I really dead?"

Mirror Grant almost smiled. "You keep asking this, but the answer has not changed. *Yes.* You are most decidedly no longer among the living."

"But I can't be dead . . . I'm not finished! I have to stop the Secretum—"

Grant's rising feelings of desperation had just reached a new peak when the other man held up a hand to cut him off, a curious expression on his face.

"Why is it, Grant Borrows, that you assume death is the end?"

11

London

Ethan trudged up the outdoor steps. There had been nowhere left to go.

His thoughts were so far away, it was a wonder he was able to ascend the steps at all. He'd been to this place only one time before. It was the attic space formerly occupied by the "Upholders of the Crown." He couldn't remember how he'd gotten here. His feet had just sort of guided themselves in this direction.

In one master stroke, the Secretum had turned the world's greatest hero into its gravest threat.

The people he'd passed on his way here, confused as they were over the stoppage of time, had no idea what was about to happen to this planet. They were already living in fear, thanks to the machinations of the Secretum: destabilization of the global economy, unleashing countless natural disasters onto the populace, boundaries and governments left in total upheaval. But all of that . . . it was nothing but the warm-up.

Oblivion would bring pain, suffering, and death in unprecedented quantities. For what purpose, Ethan didn't know. But he knew it was going to be an unmatched event in human history.

Before coming here, he'd tried returning to his new superiors, but one of the quirks of their organization was that it constantly moved from place to place, never staying put for very long. It was one of their methods for keeping the Secretum (and the rest of the world) from knowing that they existed. So of course, Ethan hadn't found them waiting patiently and helpfully at the last place he'd encountered them.

He had no other way to reach them than a personal meeting; his arrangements with them had been rather vague, but he'd gathered that his relationship would be more of the "don't call us, we'll call you" variety. And so far . . . they hadn't.

Next he'd tried locating some of his contacts in Scotland Yard, but the renowned agency was closed and inaccessible, like most everything else in the big city. All local government installations had closed up shop, fearing it was no longer safe because of the riots in the streets. The whole town had gone crazy in the wake of the "strange weather and geological phenomena" being broadcast all over the news. Not to mention the fact that time had stopped and everyone could feel it—even if no one fully understood it or could put it into words.

Left without options, he'd headed here, hoping that maybe one or two of the Loci might still be there, left behind by Alex's group when they found the Conveyor under the London Library. Ethan wondered if he might get back to the attic and find the entire building burned to the ground. Thankfully, it was still standing, dark and silent.

Grant had blown the outside door off its hinges that one time—which was only days ago but felt like months—and it hadn't been fixed yet. But the last time he'd seen it, it was at least propped in the doorway. Now it was lying aside on the kitchen floor, just inside the doorway. Dim lights were on in the large sitting area with the exposed cathedral rafters he remembered from his last time here. And he could hear the sound of voices—voices that carried the distant, tinny sound of coming from a television speaker.

Ethan instinctively drew his pistol and dropped into the lithe, ready-to-spring stance he always adopted when entering an unsecured location. He withdrew a knife with an eight-inch serrated blade from somewhere on his belt, and held it in the same hand with which he steadied the gun, deciding it was best to be prepared for anything.

He stepped lightly, the rubber soles of his black combat boots making no noise on the kitchen's linoleum floor. Creeping through the small room, he slid to one side of the door that led to the sitting room, and leaned around cautiously to get a closer look inside.

A single lamp was lit at the far corner of the room; it was the only illumination in the room, aside from the flashing television screen, which was facing away from him. Various bags and belongings of Grant Borrows and his friends were situated where he last remembered them, only now most of them were open and their contents scattered about all over the floor.

Blasted looters, he thought, frowning. *Riots bring them out of their holes, every time.*

He made out no activity inside. If anyone was still here, they must've been hiding. The room was sparse, only a sofa and some armchairs for furniture, the television set, lamps, and a few end tables. A hallway to his left led to some kind of sleeping area; he'd head there after checking this room. Gun still readied, Ethan checked under the tables. All were clear. The sofa came last, and as he approached it, he heard the slimmest whimper. Springing around it, he found a young boy crouched on all fours. Without thinking, he yanked the kid to his feet by the hair, and stuck the edge of his knife against the kid's throat.

"Who are you?" Ethan barked in his best drill-sergeant rage.

The teenager was so frightened he looked sick. He put both of his hands up in surrender, one hand holding a television remote.

It didn't escape Ethan's notice that the boy was wearing one of the Rings of Dominion on his right middle finger.

"I-I'm sorry, I was just looking—" the kid stammered.

"I said, *who are you*?" Ethan shouted even louder. He turned loose of the boy's hair and shoved him against a nearby wall. He withdrew the knife and stepped back, but trained his pistol on the boy, holding the gun even with both hands.

The kid swallowed. "Trevor," he replied shakily. "I'm Trevor. I'm a friend of Grant Borrows."

Ethan considered this, then lowered his weapon and returned it to its holster, relaxing. "You probably don't want to go around announcing that to strangers, son," he replied. "Being associated with Grant Borrows has just become a very dangerous thing."

To his surprise, the teenager nodded, nervously. Even though Ethan had relaxed, the boy hadn't yet calmed down. "I know. I was hoping to find some of his people here . . . b-but they're all gone."

"Not all of them," Ethan grunted.

Trevor nodded again. "Yes, I saw you with him! *Before,* that is." When Ethan registered a suspicious expression at this, Trevor quickly spoke up again, changing the subject. "Do you know what's happening? To the world?" He gestured with the remote control to the images flashing on the television set beside them.

"Some of it," Ethan replied, turning to face the screen, where it seemed that every channel was showing news coverage. Trevor was channel surfing, but he stopped suddenly on one that bore big letters at the bottom of the screen: *Unexplained Time Phenomenon*.

Both man and boy stood still, listening to the newscaster.

" . . . that despite earlier reports, British authorities are now entertaining the notion that—as odd as it sounds—the problem may lie with the passage of time itself, and not in a more conventional predicament rooted in electrical or mechanical issues. We can confirm that the phenomenon *is* global, but we're being told that the world's scientific minds can think of nothing that might cause such a radical shift in one of nature's most fundamental laws—"

Trevor abruptly changed the channel. It landed on CNN International, which was showing a blurry videotape captured by an amateur photographer on vacation in Ankara, Turkey, according to a headline at the bottom of the screen. The footage showed the spreading fire clouds, slowly cloaking the city in darkness.

It's already reached Ankara. And this tape is probably several hours old . . . Ethan mused in wonder. *Man, it's moving fast.*

"—CNN's continuing coverage of the mysterious weather pattern plaguing the Middle East. From what we can tell, this meteorological disturbance was not formed by any standard weather patterns in the region. We can also exclusively reveal that the strange weather is being accompanied by a disastrous geological disaster of equally unknown origin. The phenomenon is leaving behind nothing but black rocks, ash and soot. Wildfires have sprung up throughout this growing area, and ground temperatures are escalating rapidly. Local authorities have no explanation for how any of this is occurring, and have declared a state of emergency throughout the entire nation—a declaration that is expected to soon be echoed throughout all of the Middle East.

"CNN has also received reports that crops and plants in the ruined ground appear to wither and die in less than an hour's time. And every kind of ground surface—be it sandy beaches, rocky deserts, or even paved roads—turns into this bizarre black ash you can see here on the video. The amateur photographer who sent in this video told CNN that he almost didn't notice the change to the ground, because the skies are so violent and tumultuous that bystanders are preoccupied with the awe-inspiring display above their heads, not realizing what's happening below their feet. Even more disturbing are the rumors we are receiving that the strange weather pattern is currently causing a downpour of a sticky red substance that some eyewitnesses claim is *blood,* if you can believe it . . ."

The sounds of rioting outside the building seemed to reassert themselves, becoming louder. Ethan looked down at the television, viewing the strange footage of the dark boiling skies over Turkey and the black ground beneath them. Somewhere in that mess, his friends were completely helpless, at Oblivion's mercy, desperately waiting for someone to save them.

Trevor was turning the television volume down. "They really did it, didn't they?"

Ethan's head snapped around to look into the boy's eyes; Trevor was transfixed by what he saw on the screen. But Ethan was taken aback by Trevor's revealing remark. This was no ordinary Ringwearer. He knew of the Secretum and their plans.

"Yes, they did," Ethan replied.

Hardening his expression, Trevor turned to Ethan and asked, "Then how do we stop it?"

Ethan shook his head. "I don't know. But I can think of someone who might be able to help us find out. Tell me something . . . Two of Grant's friends never left London with the rest. Do you have any idea where we might find them?"

12

As near as Alex could tell between blackouts, Grant was leading them on a roughly eastern course. She could tell because every so often, among the blackened, charred ash mountains they traversed, the nation's southern shoreline would come into view. And it was always to her right.

The blood that had rained on them and soaked her clothes had caused quite a commotion near the head of the group where the Secretum council members were, but the blood was the least of her worries. First of all, there was the ocean. As the darkened ground spread to the point where it touched the massive, nearby body of water known as the Mediterranean Sea, a violent chemical reaction took place. As the blackness made contact with the water, the sounds of the reaction could be heard for miles around, growing ever louder as the darkness spread, until it was almost impossible to hear anything else.

The ocean boiled. And then it evaporated. Already the parts of the ocean nearest to the shoreline had vanished into hot white clouds of evaporation that saturated the air and them with a sickening humidity. The mists spread to where their ragged army trudged ever onward, and it was enough to wash the blood from their faces and hands, but not from their clothes.

Alex's second problem was her blacking out. It was an incredibly odd sensation, to wake up and find her body in motion, her eyes already open. It startled her every time, not that she was able to show any such reaction outwardly. She'd never known that she could sleep with her eyes open before, but the pain cascading through her abdomen and arm, and the sheer overwhelming exhaustion, sent her helplessly into unconsciousness again and again. Hours passed this way, possibly days. There was no way to know how long it had been, not anymore.

Whenever she caught glimpses of her fellow Loci, it occurred to her that she might be the luckiest one among them, in this madness. At least she was able to occasionally lose awareness of what was happening. The rest of them, it seemed, were fully awake but equally unable to stop themselves from marching forward. She hoped and prayed that the tiredness from walking would overtake them each at some point and give them a brief respite.

The final problem plaguing her came as a simple, awful truth: Whoever or whatever was leading them on this forced march of death, it was most decidedly *not* Grant Borrows.

So she wondered who it was. And she wondered if Grant was dead, gone, lost to the world. And to her.

It occurred to Alex somewhere along the way that Julie was not marching with them. Before all of this insanity had happened, had Grant been unsuccessful in rescuing her? Or was Julie . . . ?

The heaviness came over her again, and before she could ponder it much longer, she blacked out.

The next time she awoke, the group was marching along a lonely highway through rolling desert hills. In the twilight, she could see far ahead to the front of the line. The silver-haired man who seemed to be the most prominent member of the Secretum—was this Devlin, the new Keeper she'd heard about?—was marching next to this other Grant, speaking to him. She couldn't hear what Devlin was saying, but he was gesturing animatedly, if respectfully.

She felt hungry. Time's stopping seemed to have had no impact on her physical needs. Was it breakfast time? Dinner? Back in L.A., the remaining Loci might be sitting down to a group meal right about now. Did they know what was happening to their friends here in this awful place?

The darkness cast by the fiery clouds above deepened. She felt like she'd been marching for days without a single break. She felt the sting of blisters on her bare feet and the sharper anguish of blisters already burst. Sometimes it was a relief to be able to focus on this pain rather than the still-burning sensation that was at times excruciating just above her stomach.

The group rounded a bend, and in a small valley to their left she caught sight of what looked like some kind of Turkish military installation. High gates covered in barbed wire surrounded a square half mile or so of land in the middle of the desert. Inside the base were a variety of smallish, nondescript buildings, most no more than a single story high. Vehicles were busy massing in one corner of the installation, and there were at least two hundred soldiers marching in that same direction. It looked to Alex like they could be massing for deployment; perhaps the Turkish government knew something about what was happening and was preparing to retaliate against this being occupying Grant's body?

How surprised would they be when he showed up right on their doorstep?

And for that matter, how would the world react to the presence of this unprecedented power? Was he really a threat to them? If he was causing what was happening to the sky and the ground and to the laws of time . . .

The world would wage war against him. Of course they would. And in that scenario, it suddenly occurred to her that she would be a soldier herself, forced to fight in Grant's army.

The thought made Alex wish she were dead.

She wondered if she threw up right now, would Grant know it and let her expel it from her body? Or would she be forced to hold it in her closed mouth for a very long time? Not wanting to find out the answer, she fought back her nausea.

The group slowed to a stop in front of the military base, and Alex thought that finally, mercifully, this thing-that-was-not-Grant might let them rest. Not to mention get some food and water. She would have collapsed long ago from dehydration and lack of nutrients in her system, if it were any longer possible for her to collapse.

Her suspicions were confirmed when Grant walked by himself the hundred feet or so down to the entrance of the installation. The massive wire gates ripped themselves free from their foundations and sailed far out into the dark sky.

An alarm sounded almost at once, and the marching troops didn't have to wait for orders—they ran as one to block the entrance and Grant's path. They were all carrying rifles that were trained on Grant, and they shouted in a language Alex didn't understand. But the tone in their voices made their intentions perfectly clear.

Grant walked forward and they opened fire. Bullets seemed to bounce off of his newly hardened gray skin, which was very much like granite.

She found herself kneeling on the ground and then lying on her stomach, completely prostrate. Everyone around her was doing the same thing, and the Secretum members quickly joined them. Her head was turned to one side, and it was just enough to allow her a glimpse of Grant as a powerful wave of energy exploded from where he stood, rippling outward. The soldiers opposing him were annihilated, the flesh searing from their bones as if they'd been superheated, and then their bones exploding like powder.

It was the most horrible thing Alex had ever seen, but she couldn't close her eyes or turn away from it. Wave after wave of energy emanated from Grant, and she felt the powerful surge rush over her body, but not harm her. If Alex could have moved or spoken, she would have gasped or probably screamed.

It was so effortless, so casual and carefree, how this creature in Grant's body had taken the lives of these soldiers. Grant showed no emotion at the act, as if he were doing nothing more harmful than throwing out the garbage. Alex had seen Grant use this particular power only twice before, and even then he only used it with great provocation, or when no other options were before him. This new Grant, with his gray skin and fire for eyes, issued forth the awesome energy blast without second thought, and her questions about his character were set. He had just slaughtered hundreds of men without mercy, without remorse, and without hesitation.

It was over, it occurred to Alex. Everything they'd worked for as a team, all of their hopes of making the world a better place. It was all for nothing.

Whatever had been done to Grant deep beneath the Secretum's underground city, it had turned him . . . evil. It sounded silly and clichéd in her head, but there was simply no other word for it.

It's not fair, she thought in futility. It was heartbreaking to watch. Here was a good man, a noble person who stood up for what was right and helped those in need. How could the Secretum twist that man into the ultimate evil?

The thought made her angry.

How dare they!

NO!! You have to fight it, Grant! she wished desperately at him, tears spilling from her immobilized eyes. *I know you're still in there somewhere, you have to be! Remember what your sister said—never give up, never give in! Fight it with everything you have!*

Don't let them do this to you!

Why was this happening? What had the Secretum done to Grant? And where was he taking them?

13

Detective Matthew Drexel lay delirious and terrified on the sidewalk in front of Daniel Cossick's lab in Los Angeles. Daniel was a masked thug standing over him, two similar masked men on either side of him, holding a baseball bat and displaying a general distaste for Drexel's groveling on the ground below.

Daniel and his two friends—whose names and even faces he couldn't place at the moment, though that didn't seem odd in the slightest—kicked, punched, and beat the daylights out of Drexel's smallish, crumpled form on the ground. Daniel took no small amount of pleasure at the sight, and continued beating Drexel until he was all but dead.

As Daniel hefted the bat high above his head for one last brutal blow, Drexel moaned and rolled over in agony onto his back. Only now he wasn't Drexel anymore, but Lisa.

Her bruised and bloodied face smiled affectionately at him from low on the ground, and she looked directly into his masked face and said, "How do you feel about a spring wedding?"

A loud sound like a jackhammer off to his right caught his attention just then, and he turned . . .

Daniel opened his eyes in confusion, consciousness returning to him. It was a strange sensation, this lack of the passage of time. He could sleep and even dream, but neither brought him any sense of sleep's normal, restorative effects, and he awoke as strangely tired as he'd been before.

The jackhammer sound he'd heard in his crazy dream continued on, and he realized this was what had awakened him. He sat up from his cot and looked around in the darkness for the source of the sound. The cot was situated next to the building's outer wall, to his left; the shattered light fixture was still scattered on the ground to his right. Lisa's cell was beyond the foot of his bed, straight ahead. She didn't seem to have roused yet, despite the loud battering.

"Lisa!" he shouted, and she stirred.

The sound was coming from the outer brick wall, and he jumped away from the bed as it came closer. *"Lisa!"* he shouted again. The two of them had long ago stopped worrying about alerting guards; more troubling was the *lack* of guards.

A pin-sized hole broke loudly through the wall about a foot above his cot. Lisa startled from sleep and rushed to his side, clutching him through the bars that separated them, as if prepared to protect him from this outside intruder. They could do nothing but watch as the hole grew in size, first to the dimensions of a fist, and eventually bigger and bigger until it was half the mass of a man.

A young boy, who must've been no more than sixteen, climbed halfway through the hole and gazed bright-eyed around the cell until his eyes found Daniel and Lisa. Daniel didn't recognize him. He faced the other side of the hole and yelled, "Hullo, what's this? I think we got 'em, mate!"

Lisa clutched Daniel harder, taking entire handfuls of his shirt into her hands and pressing his body painfully against the bars.

The boy disappeared and was quickly replaced by a sweaty, adult male face that was much more familiar. Daniel had only met the man once and didn't know if he could be trusted, but he was incredibly relieved to see him all the same.

"Come at a bad time?" asked Ethan Cooke.

"What are you— *How* are you . . . ?" Daniel asked as Lisa loosened her death grip.

"Don't worry," Ethan replied. "Jail's deserted; there's no one to stop us. I don't think anybody really cares what *anyone* does anymore. All government facilities and businesses are closed up. Parliament's the same—they say even the royal family's gone into hiding."

Daniel stepped forward and looked through the hole; outside was a narrow back street in the heart of downtown London. The young boy he'd just seen was now crawling into the passenger's side of a British police car and fiddling with the radio inside. He landed on a news station and turned the volume up. Daniel thought he heard the words "military buildup" crackle over the airwaves before he recovered and looked back at Ethan.

"What's going on?" he gasped.

"All that doomsday prophesy stuff about the Bringer?" Ethan replied, speaking fast. "It's happening. And there's no one left to fight it. Come on, I need your help. We're on our own."

Alex prayed that she would die.

She prayed that the blood oozing from her abdominal wounds would seep all of the life from her limbs and let her pass blissfully into the next life. It was hard to believe it was just a little while ago that she had been daydreaming about a future with Grant. In her vision, his feelings for her were as strong as hers were for him, and they decided to live out their days together as retired superheroes, away from the cares of the world.

She was reclined on a simple bunk inside the Turkish military base's barracks, arms at her sides and unable to look anywhere but up. Grant had seized the entire base, and after miles and miles of walking, it had taken a suggestion from

Devlin to grant them a break to eat and sleep. Via an unconscious signal, Grant gave the Ringwearers a choice: dine or rest? Either way, he would control their every action, from lying on their backs on a bed to opening and shoveling field rations into their mouths.

Most of them opted to sleep after being forced to walk for so long without stopping. Some of the more unfit Ringwearers were suffering from seized muscles and severe dehydration. Hector's skills would normally have been put to use in easing their misery, but even he was out of commission. And from what she'd overheard members of the Secretum saying to each other, this opportunity to rest would be very brief before Grant forced them to set out eastward once again.

But everyone else's suffering was nothing next to Alex's. Her excruciating burns still felt as if on fire, burning her now on the inside as well as out. If the clocks had still been working, she estimated it had to have been at least three days. Three days of living with pain beyond intensity, unable to even place a hand upon her waist for comfort, Grant's control forcing her legs to walk endlessly . . . She felt grateful she managed to remain unconscious for the majority of it.

So now, finally given the chance to recline and rest in a real bed, she found it a bitter irony that she couldn't get to sleep. The pain had taken hold again, worse than ever, and she pondered to what lengths she would go to make it stop, if she could. Even in her youth, in the life she'd known before she was called Alex, she had never, ever known pain that was anything like this. How long could she withstand it before her body simply . . . gave up?

Wondering who the soldier had been who just hours ago might have slept in the bunk she was resting in, she prayed that death would come for her soon.

14

"Well," Director Stevens said through heavy static on the other end of Ethan's phone, "I hear from you more frequently now than when you were under my command."

"I take it my intel proved useful?" Ethan said. He stood at the top of the stairs leading to the attic space, where he'd met Trevor earlier. His three friends had already gone inside.

"There's no denying the United States owes you a debt of gratitude for your information," she said with obvious reluctance in her voice. "Without your tip, it's unlikely we would have been able to obtain satellite images of the region before the satellite in question lost its orbit. But I need more, Mr. Cooke. I know you're holding back."

"The only way this works," Ethan retorted, "is if the flow of information isn't one way only. You've obviously seen pictures of what's happening in Turkey right now. Without me, you'd have nothing. I want to know what you're planning."

There was a static-filled silence on the other end, and Ethan could swear he heard her teeth grinding. "Fine. A short time ago, infrared satellite imagery clearly showed a small military base some thirty miles to the east of Antalya, home to about two hundred souls, completely laid waste in mere minutes. The life signs we picked up on the infrared inside the base flashed out all at once—at the same time we read an enormous power surge that erupted like a bomb blast at the base's front gate. When it was over, a single warm body stood in the center of the blast area. Imagery taken later showed that he was not alone. And, I might add, this particular individual's body temperature registered significantly higher on the infrared than any we've ever recorded."

"Oh no," Ethan whispered.

"Your turn," Stevens said. "I want to know who this person is. And I want to know why you're so certain that it's not your friend Guardian. Because this display of power falls right in line with what we've seen from—"

"Guardian's dead," Ethan interrupted, and then found he had nothing more to add.

"Then God help us all," Stevens said quietly. "Those black clouds and the ashen earth beneath them have already spread beyond Turkey's borders. The U.N. is holding an emergency meeting as we speak, and the president has been on the phone with foreign world leaders for hours. If you know anything more about this man and the threat he poses, now is not the time to play games with me."

Ethan took a deep breath and let it out quickly. "His name is Oblivion. And as I told you before, we've never built a weapon capable of taking him down. He'll swat anything you can hurl his way; we're little more than flies to him."

"But *what is he*? Where did he come from?"

Ethan sighed. They were reaching the limits of his knowledge. "As I understand it, and I don't fully . . . think of Oblivion as a primordial force of nature that has been set loose on our world. He's ancient—in the extreme—even predating the existence of mankind. Nothing can stop him. Anything that gets in his way will die quick and bloody. He's going to do whatever he's here to do, and no amount of human manpower or military armaments has a snowball's chance of slowing him down. I'm exploring other solutions as we speak, but I must strongly repeat my urging that you *not* attempt to engage him."

A pause. "I was hoping for more."

"You wanted to know everything I know about Oblivion. Now you do."

"Fine. If you manage to find out anything *useful,* do try and keep in mind the fact that the security of your native soil—not to mention the world—could very well rest on how much you choose to share with us. I have to go; my flight is about to take off—"

"Wait, where are you going?"

"Where do you think? The Turks have asked for help. We're going to war."

Click.

"No, wait!" Ethan shouted. It was no use; she was gone.

Had she not heard the part about not trying to engage Oblivion? Was the U.S. government insane? Wheels spun in Ethan's mind, his knowledge of the inner workings of Washington's halls of power coming to the forefront. He knew exactly what kinds of battle plans were being drawn up at this very moment, he knew what tactics they would use to try to take Oblivion down, and he had a good idea of how many soldiers they would send to the Middle East, probably pulled from nearby bases and places as far as Germany and Italy . . .

Oblivion and his makeshift army would be outnumbered by three hundred thousand to one.

And Oblivion would slaughter every last soul.

"I know you must be holding on to the hope that Grant can be restored."

Payton awoke to the sound of the voice he hated more than any other in this world. His eyes opened and swiveled to the sound of Devlin's latest accent—a thick Mediterranean sound appropriate to their location. The thing wearing Grant's skin was allowing him control over his eyes, to better facilitate his need for sleep. But he couldn't move anything else.

Devlin knelt over Alex's prostrate form, less than five feet away. He was applying bandages and ointment to her stomach; a military grade first-aid kit was open at his feet.

"Hello, Payton," Devlin said without facing him. "I can feel it when you watch me, you know. There's no supernatural connection between us. Just the unspoken silence that passes between mentor and protégé."

Payton's eyes turned as far as they could, trying to get a glimpse of Alex's face. He couldn't tell if she was trying to see him as well, or not.

"He didn't tell you, did he?" Devlin said, still looking at Alex and dressing her wounds. "Yes, it's true. Payton became a master swordsman under *my* tutelage. He and I have quite the history."

Payton tried with all his might to force his mouth to spit on the old man, but his body refused to obey.

A silence passed for several moments, and though Payton could tell that Devlin was continuing to fuss over Alex, he could make out no details. A strange sensation spread over Payton's body, a sensation he wasn't used to feeling. Not for a long time.

It was fear. He was feeling fear. How odd.

A moment passed before he realized that it wasn't his fear, but Alex's, that he was feeling. It had happened before—times when her emotions became so strong that her power forced them onto everyone around her. But for her feelings of fear to be intense enough to push them through Grant's control . . .

What was Devlin doing to her?

"Yes, yes . . ." the older man whispered, trancelike. "Terribly painful, isn't it . . .?"

Payton imagined a scenario where Devlin had gotten caught up in what he was doing, dressing Alex's injuries, and couldn't stop himself from . . . *playing* with her open wounds. To have her so completely at his mercy . . .

It was not only possible, it was probable. Payton knew this man all too well.

Devlin started, looking down at Alex with something like shock on his face. "Do forgive me, do forgive me," he said, in his most polite of tones. "If not for the tears gushing from your eyes, I might not have realized . . . I do apologize, truly. I suppose my curiosity got the best of me with you unable to resist . . . Well, you know what they say about power corrupting . . ."

Payton wanted to fling himself onto Devlin and gut his chest from top to bottom.

"You must think me quite the madman," Devlin went on calmly, now wiping his hands on a nearby towel. "Cold, cruel, heartless, caring little for the pain of others. And you would be exceedingly wrong. It is *because* of the imminent wrongness of pain, cruelty, and suffering that the Secretum has done all that it has done. I grieve for those who have died, just as I grieve for those still in pain. I grieve for you as well, my dear . . ." Payton couldn't see him, but Devlin's voice had become very far away, something akin to lament. "I grieve for us all . . .

"These burns are quite severe," Devlin said, snapping back to the moment with fatherly concern. "At least second degree, probably third. I'm afraid there's only so much I can do with these meager supplies, but this should keep you from infection or blood poisoning, at least for a time. Your friend Hector could patch you up, I'm sure, but Oblivion doesn't quite seem to grasp human concepts of pain and suffering. But I promise, I will point out to Oblivion that your effectiveness in the field may be compromised if your wounds go untreated indefinitely."

Oblivion? What was that?

Alex must've been showing Devlin the same question with her eyes.

"Well of course, you wouldn't know, would you?" Devlin said as he wrapped a roll of white gauze around her arm.

"That's what we call him. If he has a name of his own, no one alive knows it. But as I was saying before, I'm afraid your friend Grant is quite dead. Just as was prophesied seven thousand years ago, Grant's form has become the vessel of a being we call Oblivion, who now has access to all of Grant's immense powers, in addition to the terrible power Oblivion calls its own. The Secretum performed the Ritual of *Atrum Universitas,* allowing Oblivion to be born into human flesh."

Devlin glanced over at Payton, looking on him fully for the first time. Payton tried to struggle against the invisible bonds that held him immobile, but he couldn't even get his muscles to clench or stretch. Devlin, in reply, offered the slightest hint of a knowing smirk; he understood better than probably anyone alive the full extent of the murderous thoughts flooding Payton's mind.

"I promise you," Devlin continued, turning back to Alex, "there is no way to undo what has been done. Grant is dead, as is his sister. Yes, I'm afraid Julie Saunders' life was taken as part of the ritual as well. I'm sorry for your loss, but it was the only way. The Ritual of *Atrum Universitas* is one of the oldest and deepest secrets known to the Secretum of Six. And it can only be performed with the deaths of two individuals: the vessel, and a sacrifice. The sister's blood was drained from her body to give to the Hollow, to feed the birthing process. Only the Bringer could have been the vessel, of course, because he wore the Seal of Dominion. But the sacrifice could have been anyone who doesn't wear a Ring. It became Grant's sister purely out of convenience."

He stood, satisfied with his work on Alex's damaged skin. "You should both do your very best to rest. We have a long journey ahead of us, and I believe Oblivion is intent upon walking the entire way. He seems to relish the effect his touch has upon the ground. Exciting days are ahead, very exciting days. And you will both play crucial roles in what's to come. You are, after all, the deadliest weapons in Oblivion's army."

15

As Ethan told them his tale, Daniel sat and listened, Lisa at his side on the sofa holding his hand in hers. The young man named Trevor lingered alone immersed in the television, constantly flicking through the channels.

Before losing himself in the terrible images, Trevor offered his own history, explaining that for most of his life he'd been forced to work for the Secretum. The unique power his Ring gave him—to suppress the mental abilities of other Ringwearers—was of particular use to them. He explained how the Secretum had now all but disappeared from London, leaving him on his own for the first time he could ever remember. And he told how he'd tried to help Grant when he was in London, and how he pointed Grant in the direction of the Middle East in his quest to find his sister Julie.

Ethan took over the story from there, giving them a twenty-minute explanation of his new status. Lisa looked at Ethan, listening to him talk. Daniel stared absently out of the attic window to the streets below, which flickered in the distance with firelight from the rioting mobs.

As Daniel took all this in, Ethan explained how he'd been freed from a British police station several days before time stopped, and inducted into a secret security task force whose existence was known to only a handful of people around the world. It was this task force that explained Oblivion to him, and that the Secretum's endgame was to birth this creature into human flesh.

"Who are they?" Daniel interrupted.

"What?" Ethan paused.

"This 'secret task force' you mentioned. Who are they and what's their interest in all this?"

"Plus, how do you know they're the good guys?" Lisa added.

Ethan peered out the window, and Daniel had the impression that the blond man was searching for words. "That last part, you're just going to have to take my word for. I have my reasons for taking them at their word, not the least of which is that I'm a good judge of character. Always have been. Remember, I believed in Grant when no one else in the FBI did. I was the one to quit so I could stand at his side."

Even Lisa had to acknowledge this point; she sat back in her seat but continued listening and watching him. Daniel didn't move, nor had he, since this conversation began. He sat perfectly straight in his seat, one hand on his cane, which stood beside him, and the other holding Lisa's hand.

"Regarding who they are," Ethan continued, "they call themselves the Appointed. They haven't been around as long as the Secretum—only about five hundred years or so. But it is—or it *was*—their mission to stop the prophesies on the Dominion Stone from coming true. They apparently thought I could be of some help to them, though I don't know why they picked me."

"Well, these Appointed—this 'anti-Secretum' group—couldn't have been trying very hard, could they?" Lisa blurted out. "*We've* been trying to stop the prophesies from coming true for months, and where were *they* in all that time? Why haven't we ever seen them?"

Daniel knew it was a rhetorical question, but he watched Ethan's expressions carefully, and for a moment he almost thought Ethan was going to answer her. But the moment passed.

Ethan had already explained the mission the Appointed had sent him on, to infiltrate the Secretum's underground city in the hopes of stopping Grant Borrows from entering there should he ever attempt to. It was to Ethan's great shock and horror that Grant and his friends had already beaten him to the place by the time he got there. He then told them of Grant's fate.

The part about the underground city, Lisa had the most difficulty swallowing. Daniel, meanwhile, rarely said anything, unless it was to clarify something Ethan had told them. But he never released Lisa's hand.

"And Grant's dead? You're sure about that?" Lisa continued. "And some . . . *thing* . . . called 'Oblivion' has taken up residence in his body? And his being here is somehow causing the world to undergo this drastic physical change? And it's caused time to disappear too?"

"That's more or less the size of it," Ethan replied.

"So what do you expect us to do?" Lisa asked. "And why can't these Appointed do something to stop Oblivion?"

Ethan let out an impatient breath. "My understanding is that their entire focus was on keeping Oblivion from coming into being, at any cost. I didn't get the impression that they had a contingency plan for what to do if it ever actually happened."

"This is all just so *big*," Lisa sighed. "What are we supposed to do?"

"We do what we always do," Ethan said, sounding almost offended that she had to ask. "We help Grant. We finish what he started."

"How?" asked Lisa, incredulous.

"The Dominion Stone," Trevor spoke up, surprising everyone with these words. Daniel turned to face him, and the others did the same. But Trevor's attention never wavered from the television set in front of him. "I heard them talk about it loads; they were always intent on keeping it as far away from Oblivion as possible. As much as the Secretum reveres it—I think they're afraid of it too."

"I think we could work that," Daniel said softly. His mind was spinning, and he didn't miss the expression on Ethan's face either. This was clearly news to him as well.

"We have to get to Los Angeles, *now*," Ethan said. Daniel nodded in agreement.

"You're both crazy!" Lisa cried, nearly jumping up from her seat and pointing to the TV. "Have you seen the news reports? It's the end of the world, and you two think you're suddenly action heroes! According to your own words, Oblivion is all-powerful. He'll squash us or suck out our brains through our noses or—"

"If Grant really is dead," Daniel interjected and Lisa fell silent, "and his entire team is out of the picture, then it falls to us to take action. There's no one else."

"But it's hopeless!" she nearly shouted. Daniel was beginning to realize that she had changed since their experiences in jail. Where she once would brave the unknown, something about their shared time together, the things that had been said, and nearly losing him again had caused her to become much more apprehensive in the face of danger.

Lisa collected herself and then spoke with more calm. "Daniel, you've been through a second terrible ordeal in less than a year's time. I'm not sure you're thinking clearly . . ."

"No, I *am* thinking clearly, finally," he said, turning loose of her grasp and wobbling precariously to his feet. It was meant to be a gesture of bravado, but his broken body couldn't quite pull it off. "We have to do this because it's what Grant would do. It's something he tried to teach us through his actions."

"What did he try to teach us?" Lisa asked, and he had Ethan's full attention now too.

"On principle alone, evil must be fought," Daniel concluded. "The line between right and wrong has to be held. Good has to stand up to evil and not back down. Even if there's no chance of success, and there may not be for us—that fight, the struggle against darkness . . . it *matters*. It matters beyond the here and now."

In the silence that followed, Trevor turned up the television volume a bit, and the room's attention turned toward the latest report.

" . . . and though government officials are staying mum on the subject, it seems that there can now be no doubt that an international coalition of military forces is gathering in southeastern Turkey. We have no information as of yet regarding what the military buildup intends to do there, though there have been rumors that the devastating changes to the environment have their origins somewhere in Turkey. But as one eyewitness to the mass troop mobilization put it, 'They have enough weapons to take on God himself.' "

"They're doing it," Ethan whispered, and it didn't escape Daniel's notice. Daniel looked at the blond man and noticed that his entire body language was changing. He was sitting forward in his seat now, more alert. His eyes were focused on something far away, and his expression was grim and determined.

He suddenly stood from his seat. "I have to go."

"Go where?" Daniel asked.

"They're going to try and take on Oblivion with military might. I told them not to, but . . . they won't listen . . . So I have to go. I have to go where they're going to be—to the battle."

"But what can you do?" Daniel asked, logic racing to the front of his mind. "You already said they won't listen to you. You're just one man, Ethan."

"One man *without* superpowers," Lisa chimed in.

"I'm a trained, highly skilled federal agent, and I'm not going to run the other way while American soldiers are about to engage in a fight they have no chance of winning."

"But how do you know that?" Lisa asked. "If the TV report is right about how many troops are being sent, what makes you think they don't have a chance against Oblivion and his army of—what, twenty Ringwearers? At most?"

"You don't understand!" Ethan said, rounding on her with a fiery expression. "Everything I've been told by the Appointed has come true, and the one thing they told me repeatedly was that *nothing can stand in Oblivion's path*. If this coalition army gets in his way, he will mow them down without even slowing down."

He knows more than he's saying, Daniel thought, wondering just what these Appointed had told him of Oblivion's capabilities to make him so adamant about this.

"You haven't answered my question," Daniel said, and now he stepped around to block Ethan's path. "If Oblivion and his army are as powerful as you say they are, what can one mortal human hope to accomplish in opposing him? If you're determined to do this, I think at the very least, Lisa and I should come with you."

Lisa blanched at this suggestion; Ethan shook his head violently.

"Not a chance. No offense, Doctor, but neither of you have any training for armed conflict."

"I know how to fire a gun," Daniel said, intentionally not letting his gaze wander to Lisa, who alone among them would understand the significance of this. "I'm a good shot too."

Ethan examined Daniel carefully. "Are you good enough of a shot to kill your teammates—your friends? Because that may be what we're talking about here. I promised Alex I would save her and the others, and killing them may be the only way to do that. Could you draw a gun on *Alex* and put a bullet through her heart?"

Daniel frowned and finally shook his head.

"Look," Trevor said quietly, and for the first time he wasn't staring at the television. He was staring out the attic window behind them.

In the distant horizon, the faint but unmistakable edge of dark boiling clouds were visible. The clouds seemed to be holding back an inferno of flames that wanted to dance upon the planet's surface. And they were coming this way.

Ethan grabbed his small pack of belongings, then took Daniel's hand in a shake. He uncharacteristically placed his other hand on top of the two already clasped and squeezed tightly. "You two find that Stone. It may be humanity's only chance. If I make it through the fight, I'll find a way to meet back up with you in Los Angeles. Good luck."

Daniel turned loose of the handshake. "And to you."

With nothing left to say, Ethan stepped past them and made for the kitchen door.

"Hey," Lisa called, her voice curious.

Ethan turned back, pausing.

"These Appointed people . . . did they tell you what Oblivion is here to *do*, exactly?" she asked.

"Not in specific terms."

"I'll settle for nonspecific."

Ethan's expression was firm and rigid. "If he can't be stopped, Oblivion will systematically exterminate every living thing from this planet, until *nothing*—not a single bacteria—is left alive. He has the power and he has the will, and he won't stop until it's done. The Bringer brings Oblivion . . . and Oblivion brings all-encompassing death."

He grasped the door handle and turned away from their faces, which were filled with shock and fear as they looked after him, and he summed it up for them. "He's here to kill us all."

INTERREGNUM

"THINGS ARE FALLING APART, aren't they?" Grant asked.

"Why do you say that?" the other man replied.

"I'm not sure. I just . . . Things are unraveling somehow. I can feel that they are. War is brewing . . ."

"Things are unfolding according to plan, yes. But why do you care about what's happening to the world, Grant Borrows? You've left it behind. Your earthly troubles are over."

"I care about my friends. Are they all right?"

Mirror Grant shrugged. "They've had better days."

"Then I need to get out of here. I need to help them," Grant said slowly, adding weight to each word.

His doppelganger shrugged again. "You know as well as I do that they are not my—that is, *our*—concern. They never really were. What can I say? We're *that* selfish."

Grant took a step backward, examining his double. "Then what *is* our concern?"

"Now we're getting somewhere. Why don't you tell *me* what our concern is."

Grant wasn't breathing, so he couldn't sigh. He frowned instead. "I'm not sure I can. Right now, my main concern is helping my friends."

Mirror Grant watched him closely as if reading his thoughts. "No, that isn't true. And I'll prove it. Take a look, here's something you'll probably find interesting . . ."

Mirror Grant made no gesture at all as he stepped to Grant's left, and in the dark space there formed a scene inside a three-dimensional box. It was like watching a live play, only in miniature, and Grant could walk around it and look at the stage from all sides.

Inside, a lovely woman was in a great deal of pain on a hospital bed. Her legs were in stirrups and she was crying as she bore down and tried to push. A man stood next to her, gently telling her to push harder, holding her hand and drying her brow with a towel.

"Come on, sweetheart, you can do it!" the man said with conviction. His expression was a mixture of emotions . . . He was watching over her with great tenderness, but also trying hard to be strong and reassuring. There were traces of pain on his face as well, but he was doing his best to hide it. It seemed that watching his wife endure so much was deeply agonizing for him to watch.

She collapsed backward on the bed, spent. She was covered in sweat and tears, her face red from the exertion. "I can't!" she cried.

Grant looked closer at the room they were in. It was sparse but tidy, and he realized this was very likely a military hospital room.

"Yes, you can!" the man replied, squeezing her hand harder. "You're strong."

She opened her eyes and a flash of love and gratitude crossed her features before the pain of childbirth consumed her again, and she squeezed her eyes shut and bore down hard.

"Come on, just think about the baby . . . Our little girl's brother or sister is counting on you!" the man coached his wife.

She pushed harder, and with two more pushes, an older man wearing a surgical mask and sitting at the far end of the gurney announced, "It's a boy!"

The woman fell back onto the bed again and released her clenched muscles. She even began to laugh as the sounds of a baby's cry suddenly filled the room.

"Here we go," said the doctor kindly, handing the baby off to a nurse. The nurse carried the screaming infant to the next room over, where he would be wiped off and swaddled before returning him to his mother.

"Go," the mother said softly to her husband, who was looking longingly in the direction of the other room yet still clutching his wife's hand. "It's okay. He needs you."

The man smiled and gently kissed his wife on her forehead. "I'll be right back," he said.

She smiled in reply and squeezed his hand once more before he left.

The doctor, who had lingered in the background, watched this scene unfold, and then once the husband was gone he removed his surgical mask.

In the darkness where he watched, Grant's jaw tensed and he moved around the large box to get a look at the man from a different angle. He recognized the man at once, though he'd never known this person had ever been a doctor. His hair was already salt-and-pepper, but his face was full of charm and warmth. A stark contrast to the person Grant remembered.

Without a word, the doctor casually walked around to the side of the woman's bed, withdrew a silenced sidearm from somewhere deep within the folds of his garments, and shot her through the head. It was so calculated, so casual, so unremarkable . . . Grant hadn't had time to turn away from the image and had seen the whole thing.

He slowly closed his eyes, and ripples of fear and awe shuddered through his system.

She had died just like his sister. Just like *her* daughter.

A single bullet to the head.

When he opened them again, the scene had vanished and only the darkness and his mirrored companion remained.

"Well," the other man said, "that was a defining moment, wasn't it? One that would shape the fates of everyone in the world, as a matter of fact."

Grant was in shock, struggling to put words together. "That . . . that man—the doctor who delivered me—that was . . . my grandfather?"

"Of course," mirror Grant replied. "Maximilian Borrows murdered his daughter-in-law, right after delivering her son—his grandson. *You.*"

Grant could only shake his head. He was still quivering all over, fighting the urge to launch himself at his double for making him watch that. "I didn't—I had *no* . . . I never knew," he finally got out.

"That your grandfather conducted your delivery?" his doppelganger replied. "Surprising that you never deduced it. You knew he killed her immediately after your birth. How else could he have gained such easy access to her at that time?"

Grant continued shaking his head. "Why did you show me this?"

"You needed to see it," the other man replied. "You've always wanted to. One choice by your grandfather set into motion every single thing that's happened to you throughout your entire life. It made you into the man you are. A selfish, self-pitying whiner who grew up hating everyone, because his mommy died before he knew her."

Grant was clenching his fists at his side. Through gritted teeth, he replied, "That's not true. I don't hate people. Not anymore."

Mirror Grant cocked his head sideways, watching him closely. "You hate me. And our time together has barely begun."

16

Death.

It was everywhere Payton looked. It was Oblivion, living inside of Grant. It was Alex, whose every movement was an exercise in torture. It was visible on every surface their feet trod on this senseless forced march.

It was in the faces of those he'd just been forced to kill in Oblivion's name.

Death to Oblivion. Death to Devlin. Death to every last member of the Secretum of Six. How he dreamed of it. Fantasized about dealing out death to everyone who deserved it. And how he longed for it, for himself. But not before he'd killed Oblivion and the Secretum.

As the walking caravan continued on its eastern progression across the desert mountains of Turkey, his sword, sheathed within the scabbard on his hip, dripped with the blood of about two dozen innocents he'd been forced to slay. Two miles behind them lay a small, rural village that was now little more than a mausoleum for nine hundred and fifty-six corpses they'd left behind. The majority had been wiped out by Oblivion himself, with his terrible energy blast wave. Payton and a few of the others were sent to mop up the leftovers. Women. Children. They'd spared none. Oblivion wouldn't let them.

They were slaves. Machines with superpowers. Lifeless rag dolls to be put to use, played with, or cast aside at Oblivion's whim.

The silent march continued through the darkened desert. Black earth, dark skies with fire licking the edges of the violent clouds, and incredible heat given off by Oblivion's presence; this was the nature of the new reality created by Oblivion. Robotically, Payton's feet shuffled beneath him, the soles of his boots already wearing thin and beginning to shred. He could only imagine what this was doing to Alex's bare feet.

The Secretum members, including Devlin—curse him—had acquired a trio of Jeeps from the military base and were driving them slowly off to the side of Oblivion and his army. It seemed that their taste for following Oblivion on his relentless quest extended only as far as their own comfort could tolerate.

How Payton hated them. It was a sensation so strong, so much more than emotional or physical, he often wondered if they could feel it pouring off of him. He hoped so.

Hate was the only thing keeping him alive now. Hate was what made him refuse to block out any of the blood he was forced to spill in Oblivion's name. He knew this was far from over, but he would sear the faces of his victims into his brain and never let one of them be forgotten. And he would make sure that, in the end, Oblivion and every person belonging to the Secretum understood the error of their ways in all that they had done to him.

How much better it would have been had he died in that cave-in so many years ago in France. And how fitting that it was another cave-in that birthed him into this wretched new existence. The warrior he had become from that experience, the lies he had been told by the Secretum in tricking him to hunt down Grant Borrows—all in an attempt to . . . what? To unleash Grant's powers? To further him on this path to becoming Oblivion?

Is that why they made him into this deadly assassin, revered all over the world as "the Thresher"? Was it merely a part of their machinations for Grant's destiny? Was his destiny to always be a fist to be used by others—first by the Secretum, and now Oblivion?

His feet burning and aching and bleeding upon the hot black ash, he vowed upon the blood of all those he had been forced to kill and his own immortal soul that his hatred would become their end.

"What we know," read the newscaster into the camera, "is that a military coalition forged between Turkey and many of her allies descended upon the central Turkish desert to muster an attack that will attempt to repel what officials are calling an 'invading army.' Very little is known about this group. No one has yet managed to get close enough to the intruders to identify any members of the group." The newscaster was a handsome black man, with a full voice that resonated with authority. His was a face that the British trusted.

Trevor had returned to watching television the moment Ethan had left, and now as the others gathered their possessions, he watched with rapt obsession. Live helicopter footage videoed high above the Turkish desert was replayed for the third time since he'd stopped on this station. Filmed hours earlier, the handheld video footage depicted a long line of individuals walking through the charred black landscape far below. At the head of the line was a man Trevor knew to resemble Grant Borrows, though the footage was too far away to make him out properly. On the upper edges of the screen could be seen the boiling black clouds rimmed with fire that bathed the entire nation in darkness.

Oblivion suddenly turned his head skyward and looked directly upon the helicopter. The chopper's blades stopped spinning, the camera crew aboard cursed and screamed, and the vehicle fell from the sky like a rock.

The footage turned to static, and then the TV news station switched to a different set of file footage, this taken with a long-range scope lens that showed blurry images of the walking group from ground level. This footage showed the group entering an unidentified village in Turkey and destroying everything in their path. As he'd heard the newscaster put it earlier, it was as if the town refused to get out of this walking troupe's way, so they simply annihilated it. He could just make out various members of Grant's team using their abilities to lay waste to the town, leveling buildings, draining the life from its citizens, and leaving nothing but rubble and death in their wake. They never stopped marching the entire time.

Trevor's thoughts began to wander as he realized he would probably be forced to join their ranks at some point, and something occurred to him that he hadn't realized until this moment.

The newscaster's booming voice rocketed him back to the present. "This military coalition includes, aside from almost the entire Turkish Armed Forces, military representatives from Israel, Greece, Serbia, Croatia, Bulgaria, Syria, Azerbaijan, and the United States. The Americans are strongly urging all members of NATO and the U.N. to get behind this attack, as the bizarre meteorological and ecological threat emanating from Turkey has already breached its borders and is currently spreading throughout Europe, Asia, and the Middle East. Great Britain has pledged its forces to the fight, though the coalition is expected to act with great haste, and sources within Parliament have expressed doubt that Her Majesty's Armed Forces will reach the battlefield in time for the initial strike . . ."

Trevor looked up as Daniel walked in front of the television set, blocking his view. "I called your name five times," he said. He'd changed into a fresh set of clothes and was clutching his walking cane in one hand. A backpack was slung over his shoulder and a small luggage bag was in his other hand. "We need to get going, and you haven't packed anything yet."

Trevor hesitated. "I'm not coming with you."

Lisa quickly appeared, and Daniel reached behind to turn off the television set. "What?"

"I can't come with you," Trevor said quietly, looking away.

Daniel looked to Lisa, but she had no help to offer. "Look, son," he said, absentmindedly scratching at the back of his hand, "I know how you feel; this isn't easy for Lisa or me either. But we have to at least *try* to find the Stone—"

"I'm not afraid!" Trevor said, suddenly defiant and looking up into their eyes. He held up his Ring for them to get a good look at. "Don't you understand? This rotten thing is going to make me just like the rest of them—a zombie, enslaved to Oblivion's will—and if I'm near you when that happens . . ."

Daniel and Lisa exchanged looks once more, understanding now. He was staying behind, separating himself from them to save their lives.

Daniel leaned over and placed a hand on the boy's shoulder. "It's very noble of you. But we don't even know if it will take you like it did the others. Maybe it only happened to them because they were there, in the underground city, in close proximity to Grant, when Oblivion was born."

Trevor shook his head. "I just worked it out. It's the black storm—the changes to the earth are accompanying it. The world is dying, and it's because of his influence, his touch. When the storm reaches here, so will Oblivion's ability to control me."

They seemed to hear the wisdom in his words. In its own way, it was logical.

"The storm isn't far off," he said, remaining rooted to his seat. "You had better go."

Daniel looked down, set his shoulders, and then looked back up. "We'll come back for you if we can." He began making his way toward the tiny apartment's front door. Lisa followed closely.

Trevor smiled without happiness. "Don't, please. As I understand it, the Forging was an all-or-nothing deal, irreversible. Any attempt to rescue me—or any of the Ringwearers, for that matter—is suicide. And you know it."

Daniel opened the door, and Lisa filed out, but he turned back to face his young friend. "You said yourself the planet's dying. If we're all doomed anyway, no one should have to face the end alone."

17

Turkey

Ferocious black clouds barely concealed the angry fire above it, casting a dark gray tone on the desert below. Neither night nor day, the empty countryside was shrouded in eternal twilight.

From a mountain peak not far above the distant battlefield, Ethan surveyed what was sure to be the place of engagement for the coming fight. He'd returned by Conveyor to a changed landscape, a world of ash and swirling black dust in which every green plant was dying. And would continue dying unless this spreading rot could be checked. Hot-wiring a battered Jeep from a tiny town below the mountains, he'd followed Oblivion's all-too-obvious path of destruction leading east.

Facing almost exactly north from his current position, the dried-up Mediterranean Sea was at his back. The blue waters now all but gone, in its place lay muddy, drying black mushy ash. Seaweed, sponge, and other underwater wildlife were exposed and withering; all manner of fish, crabs, stars, and even a few larger creatures like whales and sharks—all a pitiful sight, either dead on their sides or taking their last gasps. Beached fishing boats and millionaires' yachts mirrored the fish, exposing their curved undercarriages as they rested on the muddy ash on one side or the other.

Ethan's journey here had followed the shoreline with endless views of the devastation to his right, and it left him numb. The impact this event would have upon the planet's ecology couldn't be overstated. After emerging from the underground Entry Node, he'd taken his stolen Jeep into Antalya to stock up on supplies. At a roadside food mart, he overheard two men speaking in heavily accented English about a massive cruise ship that had gotten stuck ten miles off the coast of Spain when the ocean began to evaporate there. It would take weeks if not months for the world's oceans to dissipate completely, but ships so close to shorelines were unable to outrun it. Hundreds of passengers had to be evacuated by helicopter.

Ethan turned to his left, watching through his binoculars. It was from this point that he knew Oblivion and the others would approach, though there was no sign of them yet. It wouldn't be long, though. Oblivion was still steadily walking, never pausing or slowing down.

To his far right, a deployment of military power the likes of which he'd never seen was taking up positions, forming a line that they would die to prevent Oblivion from crossing.

Die *being the key word,* Ethan thought.

The fact that the coalition had been able to put so many troops in place so quickly was nothing less than astounding. Unprecedented, even. He saw hundreds of tanks and light infantry vehicles, thousands of makeshift sandbag walls that had already been erected and reinforced, and hundreds of thousands of men and women, all of whom were no bigger from this vantage point than moving dark green specks of dust. Thousands of lights had been raised alongside portable generators. Hundreds of helicopters buzzed the battlefield at shallow heights. Thousands of tanks sat ready and waiting near the front of the line. Squadron after squadron of fighter planes and bombers flew by overhead every few minutes. Ethan knew that more than one of those aircraft would be carrying nuclear ordnance.

Still, the battlefield itself was largely empty. A wall of humans and machines and equipment on the right, and an unseen single-file procession of thirty or forty superhumans (or however many had been summoned to Oblivion's ranks so far) on the left.

On a collision course.

Ethan scanned the military encampments for something resembling a command center. Stevens had specifically told him that she was coming here, and she would be wherever the generals and senior military advisors would be planning and coordinating their attack. It was odd, to be sure—a director at the Federal Bureau of Investigation venturing to a foreign battlefield—but then, these were odd times. He suspected that her sudden insider knowledge about the mysterious individual behind this threat had something to do with it.

Somebody in a top position wanted her here as an advisor, because of what she knew. Ethan was willing to bet on it.

Which was all the better. Because what Ethan needed right now more than anything in the world was someone who could get him in, past the legions of soldiers and vehicles and weapons.

Oblivion hated life in all its forms. It was his nature.

And yet he was grateful to the humans. Peculiar, that. It was humans who finally allowed him to begin completing the function for which he was meant.

Eons he had waited. He registered few emotions, and impatience was not one of them, so the waiting had not bothered him. His irritation came from another source. For only a handful of times in all of human history had he been allowed to act freely, and even then his freedom came with heavy restrictions.

Now, at last, Oblivion could compose his masterpiece of death without impediments of any kind. Given autonomy to choose how he would operate, to dictate the strictures of his efforts, he would un-create everything that lived, in ways that no other being in the universe was capable of.

How ironic it was that here, in this human form, he would decimate the human race. The darkness he was spreading upon the earth, the absence of time, the fires, the blistered sky, the acrid smell, the raining blood, the heat . . . All of this was merely the canvas upon which his work would be done. Byproducts more than anything else.

The red mark on the back of his hand caught his attention momentarily, and he briefly wondered if its curved arc had grown longer. He dismissed the thought.

The tools of his beautiful death, his *army*, marched silently behind him. Those who had granted him his freedom, the Secretum of Six, rode nearby in machines built by human hands. The vehicles were slanted upward now as Oblivion and his army climbed a moderate ridge, a mountain beyond which they could not see.

The first of these vehicles drew near to him, and the one called Devlin began shouting words in his direction. Other passengers in the vehicle were eating field rations as they rode; most seemed bored.

Devlin was holding in one hand a small communications device that he and several of his fellows seemed to favor. Often throughout the journey, Oblivion had seen one or more of them speaking into these diminutive folding machines.

"Great one, a vast army has assembled ahead to oppose you," Devlin called out as Oblivion continued his relentless pace, one foot in front of the other. "Their number exceeds what we are able to count."

Humans opposing him. How expected. How inevitable.

How very pointless.

But then . . . So many humans had gathered all in one place, directly ahead. Terribly convenient of them. He would feast on their souls.

"They are immaterial," Oblivion replied, his voice cutting through the fabric of reality and echoing across dimensional walls. As ever, his voice was monotone, yet simmering with malice, as if barely able to contain the tremendous power housed within this human body.

Devlin faltered for a moment, then collected himself. "I do not doubt you in any way, great one," he shouted over the noise of his vehicle. "But I believe you should face them with the knowledge that their technologies and their weapons of war have advanced and multiplied significantly since you last faced human opposition. While I know they could never harm you, they have devised weapons strong enough to wipe out your entire army with a single blow."

Oblivion continued walking until he reached the top of the rise. On the other side came into view distant artificial lights, dark machine forms, and hundreds of thousands of human beings.

Unimpressive.

"They will die at my hands, all of them," Oblivion said. "The only difference between them and the rest of your kind is that they have chosen the location where their human existence will end."

He never slowed in his walk. He began sending silent orders to a select few members of his army. Their unique talents would be put to fine use.

18

"He's out there and he's coming. I need more, Director Stevens," said General Bradford Davies. He stood at the center of the high-tech coalition command center, surrounded by peers from other coalition nation armies. Stevens stood nearby, over the shoulder of a young man working on a computer station that simulated the battlefield and the coalition's deployments. "We all do."

"I'm working on it, General," Stevens replied nervously, standing up fully. "My contact is endeavoring to uncover additional information as we speak."

"We can't wait!" Davies nearly shouted. "Our projections show that this 'Oblivion' will be within range of our most powerful weapons in mere moments. I need to know how to take him down."

"I'm afraid you can't," announced a new voice at the outer edge of the room.

Four rifles from guards were trained on Ethan, and he froze where he stood, arms raised.

"Who is this?" Davies barked.

"He's with me," Stevens announced, and waved him through the guards. "General Davies, meet my inside source, *former* special agent Ethan Cooke."

Ethan was half-led and half-pushed by two men, with their hands on either of his shoulders, to the center of the room where the military leaders stood.

General Davies wasted no time in sizing him up. "What were you just saying about this Oblivion character, son?"

"Your opponent in this ill-conceived battle," Ethan defiantly declared, "is *the undefeatable enemy*. I'm forced to wonder if Director Stevens passed on *all* of my intel, because if she had, you might not be here at all, planning a war against an opponent you cannot overcome."

"And how," Stevens retorted, "do you *know* he can't be defeated?"

Ethan's eyes flared as he spun on one heel to face Stevens. He knew she hated him, but how many times had he told her this already? And now she was selling him out?

"It's a long story you don't have time for," Ethan replied, looking once more at the general. "The long and short of it is, I was told so by a group of people who know a lot more about what's happening here than any of us. And I believe them."

"Young man," Davies began, stepping forward imposingly, "this battle is about to start, regardless of your opinion of our military capabilities. You clearly have some kind of firsthand knowledge of this Oblivion, and you've no doubt traveled a long way to help us. So if you know anything that can save innocent lives—any hint of a weakness we could exploit—then I'm grateful to hear it. But if you withhold said information or if you're simply wasting time that we don't have . . . I've half a mind to personally stick you in front of a firing squad."

"Oblivion has no weakness to exploit, General," Ethan replied with urgency. "I can't say it any plainer than that. I am *trying* to save innocent lives, and that *is* the reason I came. And the only way to do that is to pack up your men and go home, as quickly as humanly possible. You're trying to stop a force of nature here, and I'm telling you—it *can't* be done!"

The military guards standing nearby tensed at Ethan's outburst.

Davies examined him carefully, while Stevens's head darted back and forth between them nervously.

"I believe that you believe what you're saying, former special agent Cooke," Davies said with calculated measure. "But you know a great deal more about this enemy than you're sharing, and that I will not tolerate in a time of war." Davies motioned to the guards. "Lock him up, but I want you to put him someplace where he has an unobstructed view of the battle."

Ethan's hands were cuffed behind his back, and the guards began leading him away. He looked imploringly at Stevens, but her gaze slid smoothly away from him.

"Every man or woman who dies in this battle . . ." Davies called out as Ethan was being led away. "You just sit there and watch it happen! I hope their faces fuel your nightmares from this moment on. They're on your head."

Ethan struggled against the cuffs in frustration and futility. "No, sir," he shouted. "They're on yours."

In the absence of an on-site prison, Ethan was taken to a small A-shaped tent two miles from the command center, a tent held up by two metal poles jammed into the ground. At the front pole, one of Ethan's handcuffs was released, wrapped around the pole, then locked again.

The view inside the tent was uninteresting; it seemed to be nothing more than a storage space for medical supplies, probably attached to the ground infantry unit that was deploying in the immediate vicinity around him. It looked like one of the smaller divisions working within the coalition; the four dozen or so men he could see were setting up stationary ground turrets, sandbag trenches, and one very large missile launcher.

The coalition forces would not advance on Oblivion. They had drawn a line that they intended to hold against him.

Oblivion would come to them. And as near as Ethan could tell, he was positioned near the heart of the battlefield.

To Ethan's immediate right was a narrow river running through the desert, about ten feet across. It had once been a river, anyway. Along with the other geological transformations caused by Oblivion, the river's water had dried up and been replaced by something hot, thick, and glowing red.

Lava.

Ethan was staring at a river of lava flowing through a Middle Eastern desert. The glow given off by the river gave his entire field of vision an orange hue, which contrasted with the dark background of the black earth and the dark, fiery sky. It created a striking, stark effect upon the landscape.

The wildfires scattered here and there, the ground made of volcanic rock, the boiling skies above, the river of lava, the intense heat, the smell of sulfur . . . Suddenly it all fit.

He was trapped in the center of Hell. And there was nothing he could do but watch.

19

A black man with an average build, a crisp-brimmed hat, and a voice that projected for miles bellowed orders to the infantry division into which Ethan had been plunked. The sergeant pointed and shouted without end, a line of sweat circling the area where his hat touched his head.

With nothing else to do, Ethan sized up this field officer. He wore no wedding ring, but he was older than Ethan by at least five years, Ethan estimated. He wore a stern and dour expression, but creases around the corners of his mouth betrayed lips that knew how to smile. His eyelids drooped almost halfway down over his eyes, but not in a listless way. He rather struck Ethan as world-weary, as if he'd seen it all and done it all before. Ethan couldn't help wondering how many conflicts this man had fought in.

Ethan also wondered if this commanding officer or his troops had any idea that they were about to die a very swift and efficient death.

As his men hustled to and fro with equipment and armaments, the shouting man paused long enough to approach Ethan's tent and introduce himself as Sergeant Paul Tucker.

"Ethan Cooke," Ethan replied automatically.

"I don't care who you are or why the brass sent you here for us to baby-sit in the middle of a war," Tucker bulldozed on as if Ethan had said nothing, "but you are going to do exactly one thing, and that is stay still and be quiet."

Ethan considered pointing out that that was, technically, *two* things. But this wasn't the time to argue.

"If you do *not* stay still and be quiet, I will draw my weapon and fire in your direction. The bullet may miss you. It may hit you in the leg, the foot, or maybe the arm. Or it could hit you someplace a lot more vital. In the heat of battle, I don't plan on spending a lot of time on shooting at anybody behind our lines. So unless you like the odds on my bullet missing a body part that you hold dear, I hope that we now have an understanding between us."

"We do," Ethan replied. With that, he compliantly seated himself on the ground, sliding his cuffed hands down the pole and wrapping his legs around the pole as well. It was one of the hardest things he'd ever had to do. But he wasn't an unreasonable man. There was no point in arguing; whether he died from the sergeant's gun or from Oblivion's superpowers, the result would be the same.

It was going to be a massacre.

Tucker frowned while grunting in approval and then marched off to continue barking orders to his men. One of them ran up to him with a radio in hand. Tucker took it, and then returned it to the soldier.

"Front lines report visual range on targets!" Tucker shouted at his men. "DEFENSIVE POSITIONS! *MOVE IT!!*"

He'd barely gotten the words out when Ethan instinctively pulled back. There was a great *whoosh* of air, like wind rushing into a vacuum. The rear pole holding up the tent tore free and took the tarp with it, but the pole he was chained to clung stubbornly to its roots in the ground.

Recovering his bearings, Ethan stood and looked around. The giant missile launcher was gone; tire grooves in the tiny black rocks the only evidence it had ever been there. Ethan followed the gazes of the infantry soldiers up into the sky to where the green missile launcher was soaring higher and higher into the atmosphere as if gravity had lost its claim. And it wasn't alone. Hundreds of tanks, Jeeps, troop transports, and every other kind of heavy machinery the coalition owned dotted the sky, ascending until they disappeared into the boiling clouds, one by one, tiny explosions the only trace they'd been there. Ethan guessed that the fire behind those clouds had ignited their weaponry or gas tanks and consumed them.

As he continued to stare upward, he caught sight of a few tiny black dots falling from impossibly high. His jaw fell open and he felt sick, his blood turning to ice.

The dots were soldiers who'd jumped from the vehicles and were now plunging back into the open arms of death.

And so the battle was joined.

Any other time Payton would be honored to charge first into the fray. He would never have it any other way. But here at the front of the Ringwearers, he knew he was little more than a weapon. A puppet whose strings were being pulled by those too cowardly to fight.

Payton cursed Oblivion, Grant, Devlin, and anyone else he could think of, again and again in his mind as he was forced to slice his blade through another soldier, and another. Like him, these men were warriors. They deserved enough respect to go down fighting, at least, but Oblivion refused them even this dignity.

Sweat saturated the sulfuric air like acid rain, pouring off of his super fast movements; whether the sweat came from the extra heat that had followed Oblivion into this world or from Payton's exertions, he couldn't say.

He silently vowed yet again, upon the blood of every man and woman he took down, that they would be avenged, that he would be the one to end Oblivion's bloody rampage. He promised that not a single one of these brave souls would be forgotten, that their sacrifices would not be in vain, that every last one of them counted for something, even if it was nothing more than fueling his rage.

Alex was so tired, yet adrenaline surged through her system now for the first time since this nightmare began, so her mind had returned to coherency. She knew immediately what Oblivion was up to, sending Payton in first and then her, Nora, and Mrs. Edeson close behind. She understood it because it was a tactic much like Grant would have used in a similar situation.

The line this massive army had quite literally drawn in the sand was huge—easily more than ten miles in length. They obviously wanted to be certain that Oblivion would not simply outflank them.

So Oblivion intended to punch a hole through the line at a strategic point and make his way to whatever central command outpost this army was using.

Cut off the head.

It was simple, timeless, effective.

As Payton sliced his way through the first of a series of battalions, Alex slipped in behind him. Tears straining to flow from her eyes, she sent feelings of blissful relaxation into as many members of the next battalion as she could, allowing her to get farther in and make things easier on Payton. Nora came next, erasing the soldiers' memories of their combat training, so that they wound up fumbling with their weapons, not remembering how to use them.

Hector appeared and did something that shocked Alex: A touch from him, which was usually a source of healing, became a source of pain and suffering. Apparently his powers could bring both healing *and* hurt. None of the Loci had ever known this, and she wondered to herself if Hector himself was aware of it. Her large, round Hispanic friend was already mute before Oblivion's imposed silence, so of course he had never spoken of it. And his unwaveringly kind, servant-like personality didn't seem prone to anything but offering help. The idea that he was being used to bring pain into this world horrified her, and she could only imagine the anguish that it brought to her gentle friend.

But she knew this wasn't Grant's doing. None of it. It was this fact that she took solace in as she wept internally. That, and not doing any killing herself. Payton was killing, but wasn't he used to it? She, Nora, and Hector, at least, could lay claim to the fact that for all the terrible things Oblivion was forcing them to do . . . taking a life was not among them. Even if they were making it easier for *him* to kill, he wasn't making them do it themselves.

Not yet anyway.

Mrs. Edeson pulled up the rear of this core group, using her control over willpower to force soldiers to shoot at one another. This proved most effective when forcing soldiers from one nation to shoot at soldiers from another, so that small pockets of confused friendly fire broke out.

The pattern was repeated again and again, and sounds of explosions and crunching metal from not far behind told Alex that Oblivion was closing in on her. She imagined that no gun blast would be able to penetrate his rock-hard skin, while any soldiers that managed to get close enough to attempt hand-to-hand combat with him would die at his slightest touch.

As she had so many times before, when her body was doing such unspeakable, terrible things outside of her control, she found refuge in thinking about Grant. She missed him and longed to be with him, wherever he was.

No matter what Devlin says, she thought while running toward the next hole in the line that Payton had created, *as long as Grant lives in my memory and in my heart . . . he's not really dead.*

20

Ethan heard the battle explode into action and knew instantly how poorly things were going from the terror of those around him. He knew he only had so long left to be afraid. Something was coming. The men had just taken up positions in their trenches and bunkers and were leveling their aim on something approaching from the east.

It was too dark to make out the attacker. Ethan knew it had to be one of his friends; he only hoped for the soldiers' sakes that it wasn't Oblivion himself. He tried to shield himself behind the narrow pole, which was no help at all. He was trying to force down his own fear when he heard Tucker shout at the top of his lungs.

"OPEN FIRE!!"

At the same moment, Ethan felt a wave of intense peace wash over him. He almost forgot what he'd been afraid of a minute ago, he was so relaxed. He felt like nothing in the world could harm him, that there was nothing to fear from this strange place, that everything was perfectly fine. He looked around and saw that he wasn't the only one; the soldiers and even Sergeant Tucker had stalled just as they were about to discharge their weapons on the approaching attacker.

As the individual in question came into visual range, Ethan got his first look. And the sight came close to rocketing him back to his feelings of panic.

It was Alex. Only he could hardly believe it was really her. She was filthy, covered in grime and sweat and cake-dried blood. Her long brown hair was matted to her scalp and hung limp, in dirty clumps. Her stomach and one arm were crusted with disgusting scabs, and her bare feet were blistered, burned, and bloody. She looked like a zombie who'd clawed her way out of a grave and never bothered to bathe. The red flickering light from the lava river nearby only enhanced her otherworldly appearance.

A tiny feeling was birthed in the pit of Ethan's stomach at the sight of her, and it grew to give a good fight to the peaceful sensations that Alex was flooding him with. He felt revulsion, pity. Mostly, he felt sorrow. If only he could help her somehow, but what could he do, tied to a pole?

He couldn't believe this was really happening. Had it truly come to this?

Alex surveyed the men briefly, caught a glimpse of Ethan but gave no sign that she recognized him, and then proceeded off to the next battalion, some five hundred feet behind them.

The feelings of peace and contentment were just beginning to wear off when Hector bounded into their midst and began touching the soldiers, one by one. With his slightest touch, each one of them fell to the ground, clutching their heads with both hands and yelling in torturous pain.

No no no NO NO!!

Enough was enough; Ethan wasn't about to let this continue. He stood and slammed his body into the pole. It showed only the slightest of dents around its midsection—not nearly enough to allow him to get his hands over the top.

The soldiers were backing up now, their weapons already dropped on the ground from Alex's influence. Hector was moving faster than Ethan would have guessed he was capable of, touching one after another after another before they had time to react. Hector was working his way through the entire line of men, moving in Ethan's direction.

Ethan pulled back as far as he could from the pole, trying to bend it with his muscles. It bowed slightly, but was jammed into the hard ground far too deep.

He jumped at the sound of distant explosions. He turned to look, as did many of the infantrymen. The sound came from the west, in the distance where Oblivion was. A three-mile-long stretch of the empty black ground had exploded in a perfectly straight line, as if a very long row of ground mines had been tripped simultaneously. The air was littered with black rock debris, weapons, and even soldiers, some of whom were no longer in one piece.

A few seconds passed, and then another explosion rocked the ground. This explosion was identical to the last, only it had moved about twenty feet to the east—in the direction of the coalition forces.

Oblivion.

He was going to wipe them out by blasting the ground beneath their feet.

We're dead. It's over.

Another explosion, louder and closer. Ethan estimated he had less than a minute before the blasts reached the infantrymen here.

Hector drew closer, and as Ethan flung himself at the pole once more, he saw Sergeant Tucker fall under the excruciating pain that Hector was inflicting. Tucker had managed to retrieve his own gun from the ground, but when he stood again and leveled it, Hector was already on top of him.

Another insanely loud blast from the earth. It was getting closer. Hector drew near, only two or three men standing between him and Ethan.

Ethan kicked and kicked at the pole, making more tiny dents but nothing else.

"Come on!" he roared at the pole, another explosion drowning out the sound.

Hector stepped forward and reached out to touch him, but Ethan ducked the movement and knelt to the ground. When Hector moved to grab him, Ethan kicked the large man hard in both knees.

Hector reached out instinctively for support, but no pain filled his eyes, no howl of agony escaped from his lips. Fortunately for Ethan, the object Hector chose to support himself on was the pole, which bent completely over until it snapped and Hector fell to his knees.

Ethan slid his cuffs off of the pole and grabbed the end of the pole out of Hector's hands as another explosion left a loud ringing in his ears. He had no time to turn around and look, but he knew the powerful blasts must have been right on top of them.

To his surprise, Hector rose to his feet, no longer favoring his knees.

Guess that healing power of his works on himself too.

Ethan stood, grasped the pole in both hands like a bat, and swiped Hector as hard as he could across the head. A nasty gash had opened up across Hector's face and he went down again, but Ethan knew it wouldn't last.

Ethan dropped the pole, ducked, and rolled sideways toward Tucker. On the back half of his roll, he grabbed Tucker's sidearm, a pistol from the ground near Tucker's feet, and already had it trained on Hector by the time he was standing again.

An explosion from just behind sent a shower of rock and debris pelting against his back and the top of his head.

Go go go!

Hector stood once more and advanced as Tucker moaned in pain at Ethan's feet.

Ethan made a split-second decision. His hands still cuffed together, he extended the gun with both hands and fired it into Hector's right shoulder. Hector tumbled backward onto the ground.

Ethan pocketed the gun, grabbed Tucker's feet and began dragging him, running as best he could away from the coming blast. Only instead of toward the coalition armies, he ran in the direction of Oblivion.

The blast came sooner than expected, and Ethan and Tucker were sent flying ten or twelve feet into the air until they were slammed back onto the ground. They were lucky, Ethan guessed; they'd barely made it to the outer edge of the blast, and now Ethan's ears were no longer ringing, but had simply gone altogether silent. All he could hear was the frenetic beating of his own heart.

Knowing he had a moment's pause available to him, he awkwardly lifted Tucker's agony-riddled body with his cuffed hands and slung the man over one shoulder.

He turned south, away from both sides of the battle, and ran.

21

"Oblivion, look to the sky!"

Oblivion was only mildly curious about what had caused this outburst from Devlin. He advanced—he never stopped—plowing through a rumbling cascade of explosions directly in front of him, moving toward the farthest reaches of this battlefield. But he averted his gaze momentarily from his destruction of the human military to roll his eyes up and crane his neck back.

He saw it instantly: a rocket or missile fired from far away. Possibly from one of the flying machines. Its fiery contrail was easily visible against the darkened sky. It wasn't the first missile the humans had launched upon him in this battle, but this one was different. Most noticeably, it was significantly bigger.

But he failed to understand Devlin's concern. No matter how powerful it was, it was just another impotent human projectile, another pointless attempt by these insects to sting him. He returned to his task, focusing again on the ground ahead of him, which was now a wasteland of destroyed human technology and shattered human beings.

Devlin stepped out of the Jeep in which he flanked Oblivion and ran toward his master. Stopping well short of touching Oblivion, he bowed deeply, then stood again, casting an anxious look at the rocket turning down toward them from high above.

"Great one, if I may . . . This missile houses a weapon capable of harnessing the power of the atom! If it detonates on the ground, *you* may go untouched, but your army—not to mention your servants among the Secretum of Six—will be killed instantly. Even your power cannot prevent our deaths if this bomb touches the earth."

Oblivion looked slowly upward again, and his eyes found the missile that was growing steadily larger as it thundered down toward the ground like a bullet fired from outer space. He considered Devlin's words. The Secretum . . . truthfully, he had no real need of either the Ringwearers or the Secretum. He could accomplish his work entirely alone. And even if he let them live, they would all die in the end, anyway. What would be the difference?

The answer came to him at once. The difference is that he would not have the satisfaction of killing them himself. Letting them die was not the same as ending their lives. And beyond the personal gratification, he had to admit that all of them had certainly earned the honor of dying by his hands. Despite his hatred for all life, it was because of the living that he had been birthed into this world. He despised the thought, but the completion of his work was made possible entirely because of their efforts.

Devlin sweated visibly. He seemed to be slowly trying to shrink into the ground beneath him, as if it would help.

Pathetic.

The bomb had dropped to five hundred feet and was falling fast when Oblivion stretched a hand skyward. At once, the missile jerked backward as if caught on a fishing line, and began flying into the sky in reverse. Oblivion cast it backward, sending it far beyond the dark clouds in seconds.

Almost as quickly as he'd focused his power upon it, the bomb exploded somewhere in the upper atmosphere, setting off a grand, potent shock wave that flared against the clouds beneath it, but could not disperse them.

Done, Oblivion rotated his head to face Devlin and flashed a menacing glower at the man, his fire-filled eye sockets flaring bright until the man shriveled from his presence.

It would be a long while before the human asked anything of him again.

Oblivion was turning his attention back to what remained of the battlefield when something within his perception changed. Hundreds of miles from the battle, the DarkWorld had spread to London, England. There, Oblivion's mind touched the consciousness of a young Ringwearer named Trevor, hearing an echo of Trevor's final thoughts before he was overtaken by Oblivion's will.

Oblivion always found the moment of connection disorienting. It was potent enough to transmit the emotions and thoughts of the mind he touched—but only the Ringwearer's feelings and thoughts from that exact moment. There was something in Trevor's mind at the moment of connection . . . A complication, an irritant.

The battle winding down, his enemies all but obliterated, Oblivion called back from the front lines two of his most useful soldiers. He had orders to issue, and these he would give personally, with his mouth and not his mind.

He looked up into the sky at his dark clouds, which stormed and swirled with ever greater agitation. At his urging, they grew even more unstable, stirring with a turbulent velocity.

Faster, he willed the clouds. *You must spread faster now . . .*

INTERREGNUM

"I FEEL . . . DEATH," SAID Grant Borrows, his voice far away. "A lot of people are dying—so very many."

"And how does that make you feel?" his doppelganger asked. "Guilty?"

"Are you saying these deaths are somehow my fault?"

"There are those who might think so."

"But why?" Grant asked. "A crime of absence? Is it because something's happened and I'm not there to save them?"

"Perhaps. But do you honestly believe that preventing their deaths saves them from anything?"

"It saves them from dying."

"But I've already told you," mirror Grant replied. "Death is not the end."

Grant looked away, confused and frustrated. What was he doing here? What did this strange entity want with him?

"How poetic," mirror Grant mused. "I'm boring you with the most important question in the universe."

Grant didn't know what to make of that. None of this made any real sense to him.

"All right then, back to work," the other man said.

Once again, Grant had no choice but to watch as a series of moving, three-dimensional scenes unfolded before his eyes.

Three years old, his sister was hugging him after just telling him that their dad was killed in a car accident and he wouldn't be coming home. Julie, her light brown hair pulled into the pigtails she sported as a grade-schooler, glasses much too big for her face, was sobbing. Grant, a toddler, stood emotionless, his face scrunched up in confusion as his young mind tried to process what his sister had just told him.

A few days later, a man he recognized as a much younger General Harlan Evers paced through an office—a space much more regal and lavish than the one Grant had met him in, several months ago—dictating orders to a young male officer who must've been his attaché. "Specific instructions, very specific instructions. That's what Frank left me in a locked box, and asked that I carry out his wishes in the case anything should ever happen to him," Evers was saying, pacing up and down his office. "I don't pretend to understand his instructions, but they are very, very explicit in regards to what is to be done with his children. He wants them placed into foster care immediately as wards of the state. And he wants their names changed, to protect them from—" he stopped abruptly, gazing thoughtfully at the young man seated across from his desk, taking notes—"well . . . for their protection. None of it makes any sense to me, but Frank always has—er, *had*—good reasons for everything he did. And I owe him my life, many times over. So I don't care how many strings we have to pull. If his last wish is for his children to be placed in an orphanage under fabricated identities, then that's exactly what we're going to do . . ."

Five years old now, and Julie was hugging him again, this time after delivering the news that she had been adopted by a couple who desperately wanted a child but couldn't afford to adopt him too. In the darkness, grown-up Grant's cheeks flushed as, unlike everything else he'd seen so far, he remembered this moment vividly. He clenched his fists again, recalling how that would be the last day he allowed himself to cry until he was an adult.

"So," mirror Grant said as the moving scenes vanished into nothingness, "let's see. That's three immediate family members who left you, one after another. First your mother, then your father, and finally your sister. Tell the truth, Grant: It never really mattered to you that none of them left you of their own accord. Did it?"

Ashamed, Grant shook his head, then looked away.

His double's eyes danced. "All that mattered was that everyone who loved you . . . *left you.* They left you all by yourself. Poor little Granty-wanty, all alone and missing his mommy-wommy . . ."

Grant looked up, fierce anger overshadowing his face. "Why are you showing me this?"

"To prove my point," mirror Grant replied, suddenly calm. "You're hopelessly self-absorbed. And really, it's not entirely your fault. It's who you were programmed to be, by all those who abandoned you early in life. At least that's what you told yourself. Isn't it?"

Grant didn't answer. He didn't have to. Somehow he knew, deep within his soul, that he couldn't lie to this strange mirrored being, whoever or whatever he was. There was no need to deny what was known to be true. He felt his jaw clench, his temperature rising . . .

"How much more *This Is Your Wicked Life* am I going to have to look at?" he spat.

"How easily provoked you are," the duplicate Grant said. "But then, this is hardly the first time that temper of yours has gotten you into trouble, is it? Don't lose yourself quite yet, Grant. We haven't even gotten to the part about your 'violent episodes' yet. Look, here's a good one . . ."

A new scene materialized in a floating cube before Grant's eyes, this one depicting his nine-year-old self rolling around in the dirt, fighting with Finch Bailey, the orphanage bully. Finch was a head taller than Grant and a few years older. Grant and Finch antagonized one another frequently, but for whatever reason, this day Grant had snapped and started tearing and clawing at every inch of his nemesis. The scene soon shifted to display the two of them standing in front of the orphanage administrator, sporting an assortment of busted lips, black eyes, and bloodied knuckles. Little Grant tried to maintain his best aloof sneer, though the Grant watching in the black space knew what that sneer concealed.

The images dissolved and reformed, and Grant saw himself as a young adult, starting out at his job as a computer technician. This was the man he was before the Shift, when he still thought his name was Collin Boyd; the bald spot had not appeared yet, and he wasn't as overweight as he would become in later years. But his surly disposition was well in place and quickly gave way to a red-faced shouting match with a difficult customer who was shouting back. The fight escalated until Collin picked up the laptop belonging to the customer and threw it out of a third-story window.

"Wait, wait, this is my favorite part . . ." said his doppelganger from the darkness, leaning in to speak softly into Grant's right ear.

The same scene continued to play out, but now Collin was standing before his employer, being publicly berated in front of the whole office. Before his boss had the chance to fire him, Collin's temper flared again and he quit on the spot, cursing his employer and a few of his ancestors. He ended by storming out with a door slam hard enough to break one of the hinges. It was dark by the time he got home to his tiny apartment, where he sat in his recliner, in the quiet dark, never bothering to turn on any of the apartment's lights.

The scene they watched had become so still and quiet that it might have been paused in freeze-frame, but Grant remembered all too well that he had sat there in the darkness for quite some time that night. And it was hardly the only time it had happened.

"Poignant, don't you think?" the duplicate Grant asked, walking slowly around the box-like frame of the 3-D scene. "There's something about this image that's just so perfectly symbolic of your life, your frame of mind, your outlook on the world. 'Nobody likes me, everybody hates me . . .' " his double sang.

"But everything you've showed me is from my old life," Grant pointed out. "I'm not like this anymore. I've changed. I'm not the person I used to be, and not just on the outside."

"Be careful, Grant. If I were you, I'd pay serious thought right about now to lying. Here in this place, lying can have . . . *disastrous* consequences."

"Ha!" Grant exclaimed. " '*If* you were me . . .' You admitted you're not me at all! Why don't you just tell me who you really are?"

"That time will come," the double replied. "But not until we find out who *you* really are."

22

Los Angeles

"Can I ask what makes you think we're going to be able to reach this place?"

"You mean," Daniel said, shooting her a bemused smile, "can you ask *again*?"

"Wasn't it destroyed?" Lisa pressed on, her words coming faster. "Deep-sixed? Buried under tons of earth and forevermore inaccessible by any living soul?"

There was something in Lisa's voice . . . Looking closer, he noticed that she was pale and clammy.

Daniel took her hand to steady it. They were seated side by side in a lonely Conveyor Pod hurtling toward their destination. Ethan had brought them to the London entrance and explained how to get to L.A. They were astonished at the scope and power of this transportation system of tunnels buried deep underground. The Conveyor created a hum that was on the high end of the auditory spectrum, but not ear-piercingly so. Daniel contemplated the heightened senses the entire human race was experiencing, thanks to the absence of time, and wondered if the Conveyor's hum was normally this loud, or if this was a byproduct of his newfound enhanced hearing.

"We know they had a Substation in Los Angeles, beneath the Wagner Building," he reminded her, "but the last time we were there, none of us knew that these tunnels existed. It's logical to assume there would be a tunnel stop near the Lambda Alpha Substation, providing access to the site."

"But 'the site' isn't there anymore. We were there, Daniel—we saw it fall. We barely escaped it. As we so often do."

"True," Daniel replied. "Grant leveled the place. But as I recall, the facility itself was a tall, pristine building standing in the middle of a large cavern. The cavern could conceivably still be standing even if the building is not. And if that's the case . . ."

" . . . then maybe we could sift through the rubble," Lisa finished, frowning with understanding. "Wonderful. I hate it."

Daniel offered her his best brave smile and threw an arm around her shoulder. It was such an easy gesture, so natural feeling, he couldn't imagine why he'd fought it for so long. "Someone has to do it. Who else is there?"

She didn't respond, just settled into his arm, covering his hand on her shoulder with her own. After a few silent minutes, she gazed up at the Pod's curved metal ceiling. "I wonder what's happening out there," she said, her voice barely a whisper.

The Pod began to slow, and the display screen at the front of the Pod indicated they were coming up on their stop. As he helped her to her feet, he decided not to tell her that her question was the same one that had consumed his thoughts for the duration of the ride.

The Pod opened to a subterranean platform halfway up the side of the enormous round tunnel. They stepped out onto a silver metallic grate. A small archway in the side of the tunnel waited, and seeing no other options, Daniel took her hand and led her through it.

The opening brought them to a small, round tunnel. It was a gloomy place with illumination coming only from either end of the tunnel. It was longer than Daniel felt comfortable entering, but the light at the other end kept them moving forward.

The tunnel angled upward a good twenty degrees, meaning the Conveyor system was deeper underground than whatever they were moving toward.

"This is so weird," Lisa commented, shaking her head.

"Which part?"

"*All* the parts," she replied, getting wound up again. "The whole world is slowly turning into some kind of nightmare, people just won't stop trying to kill us, three of our friends are dead, the rest are under the thrall of the thing living inside the skin of one of our dead friends, Ethan's gone off to get himself killed in the mother of all apocalyptic battles, and I don't even know what the two of us are doing down here . . ."

Daniel squeezed her hand. "We're here looking for the broken fragments of the—"

"*I know that!* But what makes us think this is going to help our lives become any less crazy? We're down here on the whim of some post-pubescent who *thinks* he *may* have heard something or other about the Secretum *possibly* being frightened of the Dominion Stone! It could be the biggest rabbit trail in the history of rabbit trails."

"Or it could be the key to stopping an unstoppable man . . ." Daniel reminded her as they neared the end of the tunnel, "or *whatever* Oblivion is."

The tunnel emptied into the mouth of the large cavern, but it was nothing like Daniel remembered it from his last visit. Twisted and destroyed, the once-immaculate research facility was nothing but ruined wreckage now, having crashed completely to the ground and spread its rubble throughout the space. Much of the cavern's high ceiling overhead had come crashing down as well, depositing tons of boulders and rocks on top of the decimated building. As a result, what remained above them was a craggy mess of cracked stones and sod that looked as though any piece of it could break free with the slightest provocation. It wasn't as big as the cavern containing the underground city, from the way Ethan described it. But it was breathtaking nonetheless.

"Oh, well okay, then," Lisa quipped. "We got this. Piece of cake."

Daniel wanted to admonish her, but what would be the point? The landscape before them was bleak, offering virtually no hope of success. It was also eerily silent.

On the far side of the cavern, Daniel could see the elevator access he remembered using when following Grant and Alex down here months ago, along with the Loci. They were standing directly opposite from it, entering the underground space from an entrance that was blocked to their vision the last time they were here.

"Well, we may as well give the sifting a try," Daniel said hopefully, scratching an itch on the back of his hand.

Lisa rolled her eyes in an exaggerated kind of way, but she followed him loyally as he moved into the cavern proper. They waded carefully over some of the smallest bits of rubble on the outskirts of the destroyed building. Daniel's eyes scoured the ground beneath his feet for any sign of the telltale brown stone, while Lisa couldn't stop staring timidly upward, as if waiting for one of the loose rocks or clumps of earth high above to smash her into a lump on the ground.

"I don't know how you do it," she said softly.

"What's that?" he asked absentmindedly.

"Keep going," she said, and he glanced at her before returning to his ground search. "Everything that life keeps throwing at you—you never stop. You keep searching for your scientific proof, your answers to whatever puzzle you're facing right now. I've never known anyone so focused, capable of being so single-minded . . . come what may. Of course, none of this is counting that two-month period where you hid in your office out of guilt and refused to talk to anybody."

He glanced at her again, not quite smirking. "I guess I just don't know how to do anything else," he replied. "I always keep going, I always have. Didn't I tell you about how I was always getting into dangerous situations as a kid?"

Lisa had stopped searching and was now held in rapt attention. She loved it whenever he divulged secrets from his past, because he so rarely did it. "All that stuff about how you used to stick your fingers into electrical sockets as a toddler and stuff?"

He nodded, smiling sheepishly with the memory. "My mom used to say that she believed there was a reason I was pulled from death's clutches so many times. She actually told me one time that I must have some kind of important role to play when I grew up, and that's why God continually spared my life. If you can believe that."

Lisa didn't hesitate. "Of course I believe it. She was totally right! Look what you did for Grant and all his friends. Look at what you've done for me . . ."

Daniel chuckled. "What, get you into more trouble than you ever wanted or needed?"

"No, silly man," she said, sidling over to him, and before he knew what was happening, she had clutched his hand in hers, soft but confident. He turned at her touch and she was right there, her face just inches from his.

Her eyes were searching his, hungry. Funny how he had never noticed before just how red and full her lips were. So, so tempting . . . How could he have missed something that prominent in her features? In all the time he had known her, how had he not noticed her perfectly spaced and proportioned brown eyes, her pink cheeks with just a hint of down-home freckles, her flattering bone structure—

Daniel's line of thought was interrupted when her lips pressed into his, and if time hadn't already stopped, he would have sworn that it had been bottled just now, just for the two of them, wrapped inside this perfect moment . . .

He was startled out of the kiss and pulled away from her suddenly. "Did you hear that?" he whispered.

She was grinning from ear to ear, giddy. "All I heard was my pulse racing past my ears."

"It sounded like hammering, or maybe some kind of crash—"

He heard it again, and this time Lisa's eyes grew at the sound too. It sounded as if someone had picked up a bunch of debris off the ground and tossed it out of their way. They both searched for the direction the sound had come from.

"What was that?" Lisa whispered.

"Someone beat us here."

23

Ethan couldn't believe it. His eyes were showing him a vision that couldn't be real. It was impossible.

But the world was now a place where the inconceivable had become reality.

Flat on his stomach at the top of a hill over three miles to the south of the battlefield, Ethan surveyed what was left of the site. Oblivion and his army had marched through the region and leveled everything in their path, in what Ethan felt had been only a moment.

Weak from running so far and carrying a grown man over his shoulder, Ethan could not keep going. Lying down on the ground seemed like a perfectly rational option. Adrenaline would take him no further. He had actually managed to doze off for a few minutes after collapsing on the ground, but the unconsciousness brought no real restoration, and soon he was awake again.

After unlocking his cuffs, he'd rolled over onto his stomach to take a look at the destruction Oblivion had wrought. From what he could tell from this distance, there seemed to be little if anything left of the coalition forces. Every tank, every weapon, every human being—it was all gone, swept clean by Oblivion's upturning of the ground as he marched. Even the fighter jets and bombers had crashed to the ground, mostly plucked from the sky by Oblivion's immense power.

Sorrow flooded into him at the reality and magnitude of the loss of life. This was no longer a battleground; Oblivion had transformed it into a mass graveyard. Hundreds of thousands of soldiers—possibly up to a million brave men and women—all dead. He'd tried to warn them. He knew he'd done everything he could.

He could only feel pity for Director Stevens and General Davies and their ilk. They'd brought this on themselves and all of the men and women under their command. True, Oblivion would have tracked them all down and killed them off eventually anyway, just like the rest of the human race, but they'd basically offered up a not small percentage of humanity to him, allowing him to kill so very many all at once. The fools.

This train of thought was stalled when he heard faint grunting sounds to his immediate right. Sergeant Paul Tucker was stirring awake at last, having passed out not long after Ethan slung him over his shoulder.

"What?" he slurred, opening his eyes. Back to the ground, Tucker startled himself awake, jerking back to reality. "Where . . . ?"

"Relax," Ethan said, pushing himself up onto one elbow, "the battle's long over, Sergeant." Ethan gestured with his head in the direction of the battlefield.

Tucker pushed himself up slowly, painfully until he was on his knees. Ethan was pleased to see the residual effects of Hector's pain attack seemed to have been only temporary. The effects of what his eyes were absorbing right now would last a lifetime.

Tucker tried to mouth a question, starting with the word *how,* but no sound came out. He merely stared, eyes wide open, unable to speak.

"I'm sorry," Ethan said. "They're gone."

"My men . . ." Tucker whispered, his demeanor unchanged. Tucker took a deep breath, his features still in shock from the devastation spread out in front of him, the loss of life.

"I'm sorry," Ethan said again.

The sergeant began getting to his feet. "Survivors . . ."

With great effort, Ethan stood to block the other man's path. "Oblivion wouldn't have left any."

Ethan's jaw cracked when Tucker sucker-punched him, and Ethan staggered backward until he partially fell to the ground, bracing himself with one arm. Tucker moved forward, blood in his eyes. "You dragged me away from the battle—from my men! And now they're dead! They are good men, loyal soldiers, hardworking . . . They deserved better than . . . And I wasn't even *with* them . . . !"

Ethan wiped the blood from his lips. "There's nothing you could have done. And I mean *nothing*."

"I should have been with them . . ." Tucker muttered, looking far off to the plains, a stricken look on his face. "Command . . . I have to report in, the Army has to know!"

Again, Ethan took up position in front of Tucker, but this time he was ready to duck. He'd let the soldier have his moment, but the longer they stayed here, the more people Oblivion would kill.

"Sergeant," Ethan said slowly, bracingly. "You really think there *is* an Army anymore?"

Tucker's arms fell to his sides, his shoulders and head going limp. He closed his eyes.

After a long moment of silence, with his eyes still closed, he asked, "What's happening? What *is* Oblivion? What's all this about?"

"The human race is being eradicated," Ethan explained, massaging his jaw again. "Utterly and without mercy. You want to help stop it, then help *me*. Now."

Tucker opened his eyes and raised his head, flashing Ethan an angry look. "I never asked you to drag me away from the battle! I'm a deserter!"

Ethan struggled to maintain his patience, trying to see the situation from the other man's shoes, but able to think only of Oblivion's rampage. "First—you didn't desert anything. Second—I didn't drag you, I *carried* you. Unconscious, over my shoulder. And third, there may be a way to end all of this, but I have to get back to my friends and help them. You want to stay here and mourn the dead, be my guest. I'm going to try and help the living ensure that *this* doesn't happen again."

"Who *are* you?" Tucker asked.

"I'm one of the good guys," Ethan replied. "So are you. We're fighting the same enemy. But guns aren't the way to do it. There's still a chance to save everyone who's still alive on this planet, but we could use all the help we can get."

Tucker seemed to consider this. "Why should I believe you?" he asked. "You were in handcuffs the last time I saw you."

Ethan sighed, his mind racing, trying to think of a way to break through the walls between them. "You have any family back home, Sergeant?"

Tucker's eyebrows knotted together as he looked Ethan up and down. "I have a son. He's with his grandparents right now, but he lives with me on the base. Fort Bragg."

"All right then," Ethan replied. "Do you want to go back to your son and watch him become the next dead body in Oblivion's wake? Or do you want to give your son, and the rest of the world, a fighting chance?"

Tucker looked down. His head rose to survey the dead battlefield once more, his eyes moving slowly across the miles of mountainous plains set out beneath them. Ethan found it nearly impossible to read the weathered soldier's expressions.

Finally, he turned to face Ethan again.

"What would I have to do?"

"Bring your gun," Ethan replied. "And consider yourself drafted by a higher power."

24

The source of the sound seemed to rise from the very heart of the ruined complex.

Without a word, Daniel began working his way in that direction, ducking around debris and climbing over where possible. His damaged foot, which had never been fully restored after the severe beating he took shortly before meeting Grant Borrows the first time, barely let him get on and he leaned on Lisa for extra support. She didn't protest for once, even though he knew she must be thinking this was foolhardy.

He didn't care. He was on a mission. He felt alive—truly alive—for the first time in a long time, and it felt good.

They had only gone about fifty feet before, to their far right, they discovered a pre-made pathway that appeared to lead directly into the heart of the destroyed building. It was as if the wreckage and remains and all of the boulders from overhead that had fallen in this area had made room for a narrow path that led far inward.

There was just enough room along the path for one person to maneuver through, so they had to walk single file. Daniel took the lead. Slowly, they worked their way deeper inside, until the rubble reached higher than their heads and the path became more like a canyon, very dark and towering well above them. There was a dim light source somewhere far ahead.

The sound still seemed to wait ahead of them, but it was definitely closer now. They heard it every few seconds, echoing throughout the tiny corridor and growing louder the farther they went.

"With our luck," Lisa whispered from behind, "it'll be Grant's grandfather back from the dead."

Daniel's mind focused only on what lay ahead. The ground beneath his feet didn't escape his notice either, his eyes periodically glancing down in the dimness to search in case they should stumble across fragments of the Dominion Stone.

They made it to within fifty feet of the light source when Lisa grabbed his arm from behind.

"Wait," she whispered, barely audible. A slight urgency and panic was in what he could hear of her voice. "What if it's, you know . . . somebody *bad*?"

Without looking back, he let the backpack fall off of his shoulder into one hand and pulled a black pistol from inside. He held it up just high enough over his shoulder for her to see.

She gasped. "Where did you get that?" she whispered, a little louder than he was comfortable with.

He stopped and turned to face her. "Ethan had five of them. And a whole bunch of ammo."

Her eyes grew in shock and disapproval, but Daniel didn't linger to watch her reaction turn to scolding, as he knew it would. He resumed his approach toward the end of the tunnel, now creeping slowly, his bad foot throbbing with the effort.

Twenty feet away, he made out another sound that accompanied the banging, a guttural grunt. It was the kind of sound a gorilla might make upon exerting itself especially hard. Daniel cast a quizzical gaze back at Lisa before continuing. He released the safety from his pistol and extended the weapon straight ahead, edging slowly forward until he reached the end of the tunnel.

There, he mashed himself back against the tunnel wall, and held out his right arm, pressing Lisa against the wall too.

Daniel held a finger to his lips and then peeked his head out from the tunnel into the larger open space beyond, where the sounds sporadically continued. But his view from this vantage point didn't encompass the whole room, and the banging and huffing were coming from a spot around the corner that he couldn't see without being seen.

This central chamber was the same large inner room where Grant and his grandfather had faced off against each other, not so long ago. Only it was mostly turned to garbage now.

Daniel held out a hand toward Lisa to signal her to stay put. He closed his eyes briefly and let out a calming breath. He tried to imagine what Ethan or Payton would look like, and swung himself fully out of the tunnel and into the room, gun extended with both hands in front of him.

He blinked.

An old man with a bald spot and gray hair was hefting wreckage in the center of the room and slinging it onto a large pile. He stood fifteen feet from Daniel, facing sideways relative to Daniel's perspective. He didn't look up when Daniel approached.

The man appeared more or less harmless; he was easily in his mid-sixties, with a slightly hunched back, leathery skin, and . . .

And he was missing a hand. His *left* hand to be exact, which instead bore a functioning, but quite obviously prosthetic replacement.

Something about this felt familiar, but Daniel couldn't quite sort it.

Slowly, Daniel lowered the gun until it was at his side. He put it back into his jacket pocket and waved Lisa to come out of her hiding place.

An expression of confusion and hesitation on her face, she stepped out and followed Daniel's gaze until her eyes landed on the old man. In barely a second, she registered the same shock and recognition that Daniel had.

"That's not Grant's grandfather," she whispered. Turning to look around them, she added, "And he's been here for a while."

Daniel saw that a camping tent had been erected off to one side in this wide open space, and a large backpack containing food and other supplies lay open on the ground next to it.

He looked at Lisa, eyebrows raised high. She shrugged, then took a step forward.

"Uh, hi there," she called out conversationally, as if talking to a child.

The old man looked up at last. He appeared a bit surprised that they had snuck up on him and appeared so close. He seemed to size them up for a moment, and then the moment passed. He grunted roughly and motioned for them to come closer before returning to his task.

"What's your name?" Lisa tried.

The old man merely grunted again without looking up.

Lisa said, "I don't know if he can speak."

Daniel nodded, his mind still searching for an echo of something he couldn't quite grasp.

"Oh," Lisa gasped. "Oh, wait! Didn't Grant say something during the L.A. riots about meeting a man with only one hand who couldn't talk?"

That was it! Of course! "Yeah, yeah . . ." Daniel muttered. "He somehow told Grant about the Three Unholy Acts—"

"—which were counting down to something," Lisa finished. "Guess now we know the big countdown was T-minus Oblivion."

Daniel nodded at the memory.

"So, uh," Lisa continued, but turning now to the older man, "you know Grant Borrows, don't you? Are you the man who met him at a nursing home during the L.A. riots?"

The old man grunted again and gave a barely perceptible nod.

"Was that a yes?" Lisa whispered.

"Grant said the man he met that day had damage to the speech center of his brain," Daniel whispered back. "If this is the same guy, then that's probably the best *yes* he's capable of. But why is he here?"

Lisa shrugged again and walked closer to the man. Daniel followed.

"We're friends of Grant's," Daniel said, deciding that this was not the time to mention that Grant was dead. "I'm Daniel and this is Lisa."

As they cautiously approached, the man waved them forward again, more urgently this time.

They rounded the pile of rubble and saw stacked neatly at the man's feet a collection of more than two dozen brown stone fragments.

"Those are fragments of the Dominion Stone!" Lisa cried, unable to stop herself. Her outburst echoed throughout the room and into the cave beyond.

25

The old man stopped his work at once and looked straight up at the barely attached boulders and stones hundreds of feet above. He watched closely until the echoing sound of Lisa's voice faded, then let out a shuddering breath. He threw her a nasty look of warning and returned to his work.

"Might want to pull back on the loud noises," Daniel whispered at Lisa. "I just wish he could tell us who he is."

The old man ignored this while continuing to sift through the rubble at their feet.

Lisa gasped again.

Daniel jumped at the sound. "Stop doing that!"

She pointed at something over his shoulder.

Daniel turned. Fifty feet behind him, sprawled upon the ground, was the body of a man with perfectly groomed salt-and-pepper hair, wearing a crisp suit and an expensive gold watch.

Daniel was certain he knew who this was, but he couldn't resist checking it up close. He had to be positive. Together, the two of them walked closer to the dead body.

The dead man lay face up, and the two of them were nonplussed to see that the man's wrinkled eyes were frozen open, staring directly ahead in shock. He had one arm on his heart, clutching it hard. He looked for all the world as though he'd suffered a heart attack and collapsed in shock. And stayed in that position at the moment of his death.

His body had already entered decomposition. It wasn't so much that he was unrecognizable, but it was more than enough to give off the distinctly sickening odor of rotting flesh.

"That's who I think it is, right?" Lisa asked.

Daniel inspected the body closely. "It's Grant's grandfather. But it looks like he's passed something on to the next Keeper."

He pointed and Lisa followed his direction. The silver Ring from his right middle finger was gone.

"So this is how Devlin retrieved it," Lisa observed. "Interesting that he came all this way to get the Ring but left the Dominion Stone fragments behind, don't you think?"

"Lends credibility to Trevor's suspicions about the Secretum fearing the Stone," Daniel replied.

They left Maximilian Borrows where he lay and walked back toward the handless man.

"Huh," Lisa remarked, shaking her head in wonder as the old man came into view again.

"What?" Daniel whispered.

"What are the odds," she whispered back, "that we venture down here to this destroyed Secretum base looking for the Dominion Stone, only to find some weird old man with one arm already digging it out, like he's waiting for us to arrive?"

"Add it to the List of Crazy," Daniel replied.

Daniel stepped up alongside the old man, who grunted at him again. This time the man precariously lifted a stack of Dominion Stone fragments off of the ground with his one good hand and tried to hand them to Daniel.

"Oh!" Daniel exclaimed. "Um, okay . . ." He fumbled, opening the pack on his back and allowing the old man to drop the fragments inside. Another couple of handfuls and Daniel had every piece the man had recovered.

"Have you found all of it?" Daniel tentatively asked, scratching his hand again.

The old man grunted and gave a halfhearted shrug, which Daniel took to mean, *I don't know, but what I found is probably enough.*

Without a word, the old man turned from them and began exiting the way they'd come in, through the narrow tunnel in the rubble.

"So . . ." Lisa stammered, "are we supposed to follow him?"

Daniel almost laughed at the absurdity of this. "I have absolutely no idea."

"Well, he seems to know where he's going, and that works for me," she replied, weary and ready to get out of this wretched place.

It took some time, but they followed the old man through the rubble and back toward the opening in the cave wall. Down the dark, sloped tunnel, and back out onto the platform where their Conveyor Pod waited.

Instead of boarding the Pod, the old man made a sharp left and moved to a three-by-three metal grate in the platform. Kneeling, he unlatched something and the square grate gave way to reveal a ladder leading to the bottom of the Conveyor tunnel below. Without preamble, he began to descend, something he managed with surprising ease considering he had the prosthesis.

Daniel and Lisa exchanged a significant look, and then followed him. At the bottom of the tunnel, the old man led them to a tiny side passageway, at the end of which was a very old door made of solid oak. Inscribed into the door was the six-pointed symbol of the Secretum, surrounded by extraordinarily ornate scrollwork that seemed to serve no purpose but look impressive. The number 102 was inscribed in the center of the symbol.

The old man opened the door to reveal a tiny, cylindrical room. On the other side of the room was a ladder that led up into the darkness, well out of their field of vision. The man grabbed the ladder with his single hand and began to climb as handily as he had descended the last ladder.

Daniel started to follow him, but Lisa tugged at his shirt-sleeve from behind. "Guy has an awfully intimate knowledge of this place, don't you think?"

He nodded in reply; truthfully, he'd been thinking along the same lines. Who was this old man, and how did he know so much about this place? Was he a member of the Secretum? Had he worked at this underground facility at some point in the past?

They climbed for what seemed like hours, and no one said a single word. Sweating hard at the effort, Daniel thought of what a bizarre trio they were. The old man with his one hand, Daniel with his ruined foot, and Lisa pulling up the rear, consumed with worry and fear.

This trip had confirmed his earlier suspicions: She really had changed after their experiences in London. She was more wary now, and much more apprehensive about engaging in anything dangerous. He thought back to her gung-ho exit from the plane in Jerusalem, only a week or so ago. While he had displayed much more cowardice about wanting to enter the destroyed city and help with the cleanup, she had basically grabbed a shovel and wouldn't let anyone stand in her way.

He supposed he had changed significantly from recent experiences too. His confession of guilt to Lisa had lightened the weight that had been consuming him internally. He was far from absolved for his offenses, but everything that had been holding him back seemed so irrelevant, so pointless now. He had a renewed vitality that he felt no desire to explain away with logic or science.

At the top, they found a small sliding door that opened into an elevator shaft. To the right was an elevator door opening to the bottom floor of whatever building they were in, and Daniel and the old man set to work forcing it open.

Climbing out, they found themselves in a downtown Los Angeles bank. The building was closed, and the floor-to-ceiling glass windows on the ground level displayed a dank, oppressive atmosphere outside.

A few rays of sunlight broke through the clouds, but twilight was spreading fast, thanks to the darkened skies and burning earth that were approaching. Empty drink containers and old newspapers tumbled through the deserted street outside. A lonely SUV flew by at a speed well above the speed limit, but otherwise no vehicles were in motion. Downtown was largely a ghost town, though a scattered few pedestrians were visible ducking quickly between buildings, eyes darting fearfully in all directions, as if they were hoping not to be noticed.

The bank they stood in was locked down, and Daniel was astonished they hadn't already set off an alarm. Maybe the power was out. Not much was out of place, with more than a dozen teller stations along the far wall, partitioned desks and offices to their right, and the front doors to their left.

"Everything's locked," Lisa said, moving to the front door and trying to open it. "How do we get out?"

Daniel retrieved his pistol, and Lisa screamed when he fired a number of shots into one of the tall windows, far off to her right, until it shattered, every shard of glass falling to the ground.

Alarms began to wail, but their new friend took no notice. Without waiting for the other two, the old man marched right through the broken window frame and out onto the empty city street.

Daniel and Lisa followed his lead once more, exiting the building and marching to a street corner to their south. The skies overhead were darkening fast, and Daniel was alarmed at how quickly the world was changing, and how fast Los Angeles—which was so far away from the events happening in the Middle East—had already reacted. An eerie quality had settled over the heart of this famous city, blanketing the concrete canyons in foreboding silence. Whatever few pedestrians they saw were speaking to each other in hushed voices, as if afraid to break the deafening quiet. Traffic lights were dark, lacking electricity; not even a single aircraft flew through the skies.

Daniel recognized the street they were on in the business district, and again he was amazed at how deserted the city appeared. Looters had strewn a destructive path, leaving behind broken storefronts and damaged goods and trash littering the streets and sidewalks. Abandoned cars clogged their path as well. Daniel imagined traffic being so bad to get out of downtown that frantic residents had left their cars behind in the street, opting to flee however they could.

They passed a homeless man sitting on the edge of the sidewalk, hugging himself with both arms and squeezing his eyes closed as tight as they could possibly be. He muttered under his breath, again and again, "It's not real. It's not real. It's not real . . ."

What was happening here? He'd expected mass hysteria or fistfights or broken water mains and gas leaks. Instead, it was like everyone had just run off to hide in the wilderness someplace. More likely they had packed up their families and hidden in basements or gone to stay with out-of-town relatives. It was as if hope itself had abandoned the globe and there was nothing left but to hide and wait for the end to come.

"Look!" Lisa cried, breaking the impenetrable silence.

Daniel followed her gesture to see that on the horizon, the firestorm was approaching. Violently ripping through the skies, it was a terrifying wonder that was as hard to look at as it was to take one's eyes off of.

The old man jerked him by the arm at the same moment that Lisa screamed.

He pointed across the street, where Alex and Payton stood, watching them with blank, dead faces.

26

Daniel's first instinct was to run and embrace his friends.

Well, Alex, anyway.

But his scientist's brain took in Alex's shattered, ghastly form and applied the terrible logic he knew to be true to the situation. Alex and Payton weren't in control of themselves. Ethan warned him of as much. Both wore bloodied clothes. Both were caked in mud, ash, blood, and sweat.

Of course—Oblivion would see no need for them to bathe.

With a single ominous step, Payton moved in their direction. He would vanish in a blur of movement any second.

"Run!" Daniel shouted, grabbing Lisa by the arm and slinging his backpack over his shoulder.

They were half a block away when Daniel felt himself overcome with terror. The sensation had hit him fast, like a panic attack, and in no time he was nearly shivering with cold sweats, his heart thumping like mad. But he swallowed the feeling and forced himself to continue running. His imagination went wild, conjuring up an endless variety of horrific shadows closing in around the two of them. He had known much fear in his life, but never had it consumed him so completely as this.

He knew this was Alex's doing, that she was forcing these emotions into his system, and he wouldn't be able to stop it. Still, he tried to logically compartmentalize the sensations, to push them aside and run mathematical equations through his head; it was a habit for focus and concentration he'd picked up in college. But the feelings Alex fed into him were much too powerful, and soon he lost control of his bladder, a warm liquid running down his pant leg.

He was too busy running to be embarrassed. But he stopped short when an imposing figure blocked his path at the next street corner just ahead. The figure's head was bowed with hands clasped in front.

Payton.

We're dead.

Daniel was about to turn around, Lisa still clutching his hand for dear life, when a dented Camaro screeched to a halt right between them and Payton. The passenger-side door flew open and a strange sound like a yell emanated from the driver's lips. It was the old man. In his panic, Daniel hadn't even noticed the man disappear from their midst.

Daniel flung Lisa into the front seat and fumbled with the back door before diving in himself. Payton was already striding atop the car, sword in hand, slashing downward. The blade sliced through the roof and barely caught with Daniel's left arm. He shouted in pain but was able to roll away.

Lisa crouched in her seat and he did the same, sliding down as far into the back as he could. The old man gunned the gas, and they were off, but Payton clung stubbornly to his sword, which was still embedded in the roof of the car.

The old man swung the car wildly from side to side in a crazed frenzy, slinging them madly between the cars parked in the middle of the street, yet maintaining deft control over their movements. The man was surprisingly calm, his eyes darting around to take in every detail of their surroundings in short, focused movements.

Above Daniel, Payton's sword sawed back and forth, slicing through metallic bits of the car's rooftop. The old man increased their speed, and the sword started to shift backward, slicing toward the rear of the car as the inertia finally caught up with Payton, who still knelt atop the car, holding his sword to maintain a grip on the vehicle.

The old man let out a ferocious yell, and Daniel raised his head just long enough to peek through the windshield; an eighteen-wheeler was blocking their path directly ahead, situated perpendicular to their approach. The old man aimed for the rear of the truck, in the empty space beneath the load, between the massive forward and rear tires. Daniel quickly tried to do the math in his head, calculating if the Camaro would pass unharmed beneath the truck bed, but it was coming too fast and he was still shaking off the aftereffects of Alex's panic attack.

At the last second, the old man slid down sideways in the car to lie next to Lisa, and the sword in the roof vanished. Payton had jumped free before impact.

The car bucked, followed by the awful shriek of metal against metal, but then they were clear. The roof had scraped against the underside of the truck bed, but the parts of it Payton hadn't sliced into held firmly to its moorings.

"They're really not messing around!" Lisa shouted, rising again in her seat to look behind for any trace of Payton.

Daniel dared to raise his head too, scanning the world on all sides of the car. "Oblivion knows we came for the Stone. I wonder if *he* knows what to use the blasted thing for."

A garbage truck roared into view just behind them as they rounded a corner. Alex was at the wheel, but Payton was crawling his way from above the roof of the truck—he must have leapt onto it after jumping from their car, Daniel figured—down into the driver's seat and pushing her aside. The truck slowed slightly as they reconfigured positions, but soon Payton had hold of the wheel and Alex sat beside him.

Payton poured on the speed, drawing close enough to their car to look Daniel in the eyes. Daniel barely knew what was happening as the windshield of the truck exploded and something shot through the back of his seat, stopping less than an inch above his prone body. It was Payton's sword; he'd thrown it at the Camaro in the blink of an eye.

"Faster!" Daniel yelled at the old man, eying the dangerous sword, which was still wiggling back and forth where it was jammed into the seat, and debating whether or not he should touch it. The old man replied to Payton's advance in kind, pushing the car's engine harder.

"Where are we going?" Lisa cried over the thundering engine, looking into her side mirror at the garbage truck that was barreling toward them like an unstoppable tank.

The old man gave a whelp and pointed straight ahead.

"I'll take any place that's far away from these two," Daniel agreed.

Daniel took a deep breath and retrieved something from his backpack, but it wasn't a piece of the Dominion Stone. It was the black Glock he'd swiped from Ethan.

He debated his options as the truck inched closer. He could try shooting the engine, but if he somehow hit the gas tank, the whole thing would blow. And Ethan had been right about him; he had no desire to kill his friends, even if they were possessed by an all-powerful evil.

An idea formed in his mind. Daniel reached into the front seat and put a hand on the old man's shoulder. "Let them get within twenty feet."

The old man made no gesture to indicate his understanding, but Daniel looked back and saw that the truck was closing in on them fast.

Kneeling precariously in the backseat, Daniel raised the weapon just over the seat to aim at the truck. He tried not to look at Alex, thinking of what she could do to his aim with another well-placed panic attack. And he didn't dare look at Payton, knowing what the assassin was capable of, lest he lose his resolve.

Instead, he angled his view downward and aimed at the truck's right tire. If he could blow one of the tires flat, Payton would have no choice but to stop. It might not slow them down much—they'd probably just commandeer another vehicle—but their chances were already slim and he'd take any advantage he could get.

Daniel zeroed in on what he could see of the tire beneath the huge grill, and fired. Lisa screamed at how loud the shot was, but he ignored her and fired again. Repeatedly he squeezed the trigger until he'd used up the entire magazine, but to no avail. He only had one mag left, and didn't see the point in wasting it on another attempt at such a difficult shot. He let the spent mag fall, replaced it with a full one, and jammed the gun back into his backpack on the seat next to him.

There was a blur from the front of the truck, and then the truck began to slow. He did a double take—Payton was no longer in the driver's seat! He'd vanished.

He turned; Payton knelt inside the car right beside him in the backseat. Daniel had been afraid of this; getting closer to the truck so he could take a shot had allowed Payton to get close enough to dive full-bodied into the car. In a smudge of motion, Payton had already freed his sword from the backseat and brought it down to bear upon Lisa's neck up front.

27

Daniel freed the gun from his backpack. He whipped his arm forward in Lisa's direction, just fast and strong enough to catch the sword's long hilt with his pistol at the last second. The tip of the sword blade touched Lisa's neck in the front seat, and she didn't dare move.

Daniel glanced sideways; Payton's flat, dispassionate eyes were locked on his.

Their surroundings outside the vehicle were little more than indistinct shapes, bulleting past at dangerous speeds. They passed beneath a dark cloud of the firestorm, and everything in the car dimmed. The old man wrenched the steering wheel wildly to the right, and the sword left Lisa's neck as both men in the backseat shifted left. Off-balance, Daniel fell right on top of Payton, and not knowing what else to do, he dropped the gun and grabbed the overlong hilt of Payton's sword, trying to wrestle it away from him.

Payton snarled as he elbowed Daniel viciously in the face, not once but twice, and Daniel shook the stars out of his vision while refusing to let go of his desperate grip on the sword. But it was only seconds before Payton regained his bearings and had vanished from beneath him. The sword disappeared from Daniel's grasp as well, and he was suddenly lying on the floorboard, grasping nothing but air.

"Where is he?" he shouted, struggling to rise from his awkward position. "Where'd he go?"

He looked up and saw Payton standing on the hood of the car, his sword already raised and preparing to strike.

The old man slammed on the brakes, and Payton leapt from his spot on the hood. At almost the same moment, something struck them from behind, crunching against the bumper. Daniel's seat was pushed up more than a foot toward the front seat.

Daniel turned. Alex had resumed driving the garbage truck and caught up with them during his struggle with Payton. Payton's leap from the car's hood had taken him to the top of the garbage truck, where he had regained his footing and now glared at the tiny Camaro, his sword still poised and ready to slice.

The garbage truck slammed into them again, and Lisa screamed as Daniel's seat jutted farther toward the front of the car, wedging him painfully between. He could only imagine what the back of the car must look like now. Lisa reached through and took his hand in hers, squeezing hard.

The old man took a hard right into a parking lot, jumped a curb, and blasted through a greenhouse. They burst through the glass with ease and didn't slow down, the garbage truck still hot on their heels. But the truck couldn't turn as easily as the car could, and the old man used this to their advantage, turning wildly again on the other side.

Daniel looked through the car's windshield, ignoring the tight squeeze around his abdomen. He watched as the old man turned left at the next intersection and then turned right quickly after that. Another right and a left they swung wildly, and it became obvious: He was creating a random pattern that would be difficult for the cumbersome garbage truck to reproduce. But the constant turning was reducing their speed, even though the car was screeching at a highly unsafe velocity against the ground beneath it, which was turning to black volcanic rock as the chase went on.

A crash came from behind and Daniel twisted as best he could to see that Alex had countered their zigzagging maneuvers by barreling through any obstacles that stood in her way. She had just crashed through a small drive-through burger place and her speed was increasing.

"Faster!" Lisa shouted.

The old man replied with an unintelligible roar; Daniel looked down in the front seat to see that his foot was already mashed against the floorboard as far as it could be.

The garbage truck edged closer, growling and snarling. Daniel watched, his heart racing fast enough to explode at any moment as the two large metal arms used to pick up dumpsters were deployed from their vertical positions at the vehicle's sides. The arms faced forward, low to the ground, like forked teeth ready to bite.

The old man made a daring wide turn to the right, trying to shake the truck, but Alex floored the gas just as they took the turn. The truck slammed into the right side of the car, and the entire Camaro rose up off the ground as the metal arms retracted.

The truck carried them sideways fast enough to take on a freight train.

Lisa screamed. Daniel turned to see a high bridge about half a mile ahead, and now they were angling to ram straight into one of the massive cement beams that held the bridge in place.

"Daniel . . . !" Lisa cried, squeezing his hand so hard he couldn't feel it anymore.

"Get out! Jump!" Daniel shouted.

"I'm not leaving you!" Lisa refused.

"GO!!"

"Forget it!"

Daniel looked up; the enormous bulkhead support holding up the freeway overpass was closing in . . .

He was aware of many things at once. The growing heat and darkness . . . The strong sulfuric odor permeating the air . . . The scattered wildfires that even now were springing up out of absolutely nothing . . . Fleeting thoughts flashed through his mind—of his mother, his career, his feelings for Lisa . . .

The old man turned in his seat and grabbed Daniel's face with his one hand and shook him back to reality. When Daniel snapped to, the old man pointed at Daniel's gun, still on the floorboard where he'd dropped it while facing off with Payton.

The roar of the truck's engine was overpowering as it rolled on, only two feet or so from where Daniel was trapped. He strained in his squeezed position between the compressed front and back seats to reach the weapon. He didn't dare look up, afraid that their proximity to the freeway support pillar might make him give up the struggle.

His fingers grazed the handle of the weapon, and straining for an extra inch or two, he finally got it between forefinger and thumb and tugged it free. Daniel was about to take aim at the truck when the old man hollered again. Daniel turned; the old man's hand was right beside him, open and waiting. Daniel placed the gun into his hand.

The cement pillar loomed ahead and they were closing fast.

The old man motioned for Lisa to hold the steering wheel steady, and then with surprising agility he opened the door, swung his head and shoulders up and over the roof of the car, and brought the gun up to bear on the truck's cabin.

Daniel turned back to face Alex, afraid the crazy old coot would shoot her dead. Instead, when the gun was fired, there was a horrendous lurch, and Daniel saw that the top of the truck's gigantic gearshift, which was visible thanks to a big black ball at its tip, was gone.

Gears somewhere inside the truck screeched and grinded powerfully against one another. The sound was so awful, Daniel had to cover his ears. The old man was already back in his seat putting his seat belt on as there was another strong lurch, and the Camaro fell free from the truck's grasp. The man floored the gas and they shot out of the truck's path with inches to spare.

Daniel looked back and saw the truck had suddenly roared into reverse and was stirring up tremendous amounts of the black soot-like ground into an angry maelstrom of dark dust as it struggled to end its forward momentum and move backward instead.

Lisa's eyes were ready to pop out of her head. "Did he just shoot their *gearshift*? Into reverse?" she shouted.

The old man thumbed on the gun's safety and then tossed it back into Daniel's hands, his eyes glued on the road ahead and nothing else.

"He saved our lives," Daniel replied, placing a hand on the old man's shoulder. "Thank you."

Lisa was too stunned to conjure any gratitude. She was still trying to catch her breath, and was looking from Daniel to the stalled truck in the distance behind them, to the old man and back again. "But . . . the gearshift . . ." she stammered.

The gearshift stick had been shot clean off the truck's dash. They wouldn't be able to get it back into Drive again, and would have to stop. By which time the three of them would be very far from here, with any luck. Daniel was astonished at the simplicity of it and how easily the old man had pulled it off.

Lisa, meanwhile, had stopped looking between Daniel and the old man and was now focused only on the gentleman beside her in the driver's seat. Her mouth still hung open wide, and she was breathing faster than ever.

"Who *are* you?" she shouted, her tone somewhere between astonishment and outrage.

The man never acknowledged the question or even looked in Lisa's direction. He merely drove, grinding the car into the eternal twilight.

28

"How long do you suppose we have?" Lisa asked.

"No idea," Daniel replied, glancing at his watch for the hundredth time, only to be reminded that time was not in motion. "They'll catch up sooner or later, and we'd better have some kind of a plan by the time they do."

They had stopped at a large gas station in the middle of Santa Monica. It was as far as the car would take them without needing more gas. Like downtown L.A., the hip oceanside suburb was almost completely abandoned. Fortunately, even though the power was out and no one was working there, the old man seemed to know how to get the gas pumps flowing again. While he busied himself fueling the car and prying apart the backseat enough for Daniel to sit there without hurting himself, Daniel and Lisa sat cross-legged on the ground just beside the car. This ground had once been oil-streaked pavement, but just like everything else, it had been transformed into black rock and dirt.

The skies above raged and churned, casting the gray of dusk and oncoming night onto the world below. Daniel and Lisa used the car's interior illumination for light but didn't dare anything brighter. Their tracks would do a good enough job of leading Alex and Payton straight to them as it was.

The one advantage this place offered was a clear view of the main road for a mile or more in both directions. Normally this would have been unheard of in Santa Monica, but they were close to the beach. Or at least what used to be the beach. Now the ocean was eroding, boiling to intense temperatures until it evaporated. The warm mist being generated by all this evaporation blew in across the coastline and made them moist and clammy.

Daniel poured the fragments of the Dominion Stone from his backpack out onto the ground, and the two of them set to work assembling them like a jigsaw puzzle. Ten minutes passed and they'd put together what they had, which Daniel estimated was ninety percent of the whole. The old man had done a remarkable job uncovering it.

"Okay, so we know that the Secretum is afraid of this thing," Lisa began, to refresh both of their memories, "which can only mean good things for us."

Daniel nodded in agreement.

"The question is," she summed up, "what exactly are we supposed to do with it that could hurt them?"

"These symbols here"—Daniel said, pointing and studying the Stone intently—"I'm pretty sure they're the ones for 'Dominion Stone.' But this symbol next to it . . . I don't know that one. The next one I'm sure I've seen before. And look, there it is again. Echh, this would be so much easier if Morgan were here . . ."

Lisa wrapped an arm around his. She was feeling Morgan's loss too.

"Do we still have her cipher notes?" Lisa asked.

"Think they're somewhere in my bag," he said absently.

She yanked open the bag. Setting a few things aside, she dug deep within to find the thin spiral-bound notebook upon which Morgan had once scrawled out her notes about the symbols on the Stone. Morgan had done more than anyone outside the Secretum of Six to translate the Stone's markings and uncover its secrets, spending more than a decade of her life attempting to decipher it. They were very lucky to still have her notes on the Stone's symbols and language.

Lisa was putting the displaced items back into the backpack when something fell out of her grasp and rolled across the ground. It was a CD.

"What's that?" Daniel asked, noting the CD even though he was still concentrating on the Stone fragment before him.

"I don't know," she replied. She stood and followed it until it came to a stop against a gas pump and toppled flat onto the ground. "Oh!" she gasped.

"Huh?" said Daniel.

Lisa stuck her finger into the hole in the middle of the disc and brought it back to show him. "This is Morgan's handwriting. Look."

She handed him the disc. It read, *In Case of Emergency*. He brought it closer to his eyes and looked at it intently through his glasses.

"You're sure it's Morgan's writing?" he asked.

"Positive."

"I don't think this is an *audio* disc," he said. "Where was it?"

Lisa sat again, combing through the stacked notebooks and other items inside Daniel's bag. "Here, it fell out of this, I think," she said, picking up a book. It was a novel: *The Remains of the Day* by Kazuo Ishiguro. She turned to the back flap, where she found a square envelope just big enough to hold a CD disc. It had been taped to the back cover, beneath the dust jacket. "I saw Morgan give this book to Julie to read. It was the first day of the riots in L.A. The two of them had gotten into the habit of trading books . . ." Her voice trailed off.

Daniel's thoughts of Morgan now included Julie as well. They were dead, the both of them. It was a hard thing to digest since he hadn't witnessed either. In his mind, they were as alive as he was.

He looked again at the disc in his hand. " 'In case of emergency,' " he read aloud, thoughts drifting to a time and place far away from here. Morgan had been doing a great deal of research about the Secretum of Six around the same time as the L.A. riots.

And didn't she tell us she'd figured out what it all meant—everything from the Secretum to the Bringer?

He looked around. It was unlikely this gas station had any technical equipment that would be useful in this situation . . . "We've got to find something to play this on. A DVD player or a computer maybe."

Daniel placed the disc carefully back into its paper sleeve taped to the novel and returned his attention to the Stone spread out on the ground. He thumbed open Morgan's notebook and began looking for the third symbol—the one he recognized. The pages were already becoming spongy in the heat and moisture.

He scratched the itch on the back of his right hand, which had grown into a red, angry bump.

"Here it is," he said, and Lisa drew up just beside him and rested her head on his shoulder as he read from the book. " ' . . . difficult translation . . . unable to determine if noun or verb . . . Seems to indicate some sort of uncontrollable movement, like an aimless wandering. Also used to describe something that was strictly confined but is set free to move without a prescribed course.' "

"Hmm," he said. "I wonder if she has anything on the other . . ."

His voice trailed off at the sound of a powerful, wordless yell that fluctuated in its inflections. The old man was screaming. They looked up and saw a silver Mustang tearing down what used to be a road, racing in their direction, less than a mile out.

"They found us," Lisa whispered.

29

Daniel and Lisa snatched up everything that was on the ground and tossed it onto the backseat of the car as fast as they could. Pieces of the Dominion Stone fumbled out of Daniel's grasp, flying into the front seat as well. They jumped in the car, which the old man already had started and was waiting to gun.

With them safely in, he took off before Daniel had even closed his side door.

Crouched down low, Daniel chanced a glance up over the back of his seat and caught a glimpse of the silver sports car approaching them from behind at blistering speeds. It was like being chased by a sleek, muscular shark in wide open waters. There was nowhere to go now, no place they could take the Camaro that the smaller Mustang couldn't follow.

It began to rain as they sped along the open road, but it wasn't water that was washing over the car. It was blood.

They'd lost the front windshield in their last encounter, so the man at the wheel and Lisa were both soon wet with the hot, sticky blood.

The Camaro may have been older than the other car, but it could certainly accelerate with the best of them, Daniel thought. In no time at all, they had matched paces with their pursuers and were doing their best to put any distance at all between them, despite the suddenly wet weather.

The old man veered to the right, slinging Daniel and Lisa around in the car like rag dolls and skidding across the blood-wet ground. Daniel looked up to see that an entrance to the 10 freeway was about one mile straight ahead, and they were making a run for it.

Even if they reached it, they were far from safe, so Daniel grabbed Morgan's notebook off the rear floorboard and began skimming through it quickly for the mysterious symbol that he didn't recognize.

"Look out!" Lisa screamed, and their vehicle was violently smashed into from behind.

Daniel had been hurtled onto the floorboard, then wrenched himself back up on the seat. But he stayed low, continuing to thumb madly through Morgan's pages.

Come on, come on, where is it? Is it in here . . . ?

They hit the on-ramp and Daniel looked up as they approached the top. The westbound lane had plenty of cars in it all right, but they were abandoned, just like the cars in town had been.

How strange, the thought occurred to him. *During the riots, everyone was consumed with escaping from town, but now it's like everyone has gone home and holed themselves up in basements or whatever. Guess they know there's really nowhere to run. Nowhere to go that the raining blood won't soak you . . .*

There was a tap from behind, but this time they managed to avoid a major collision, even though Payton and Alex never slowed down. They were darting in and around the stationary cars, barely missing most of them.

Payton was behind the wheel this time, a vicious, predatory expression painting his features.

So this is what it feels like to be hunted by the Thresher . . . Daniel mused and felt a momentary pride that they weren't dead yet. Few made it this long.

He snapped back to the moment. *Focus, Daniel! Focus!*

The notebook fell out of his hands and onto the floorboard again, but this time Daniel froze before picking it up. The page it had fallen open to bore the symbol he was looking for.

"I got it!"

"What's it say?" Lisa shouted without raising her head over the top of her seat.

" '. . . body, breath, or life,' " he replied. "So . . . we have 'unconfined movement' . . . and now 'life.' "

He saw Lisa peek over her seat at him, her dark hair now soaked with blood and matted down to her scalp, her eyes big and unable to look away from the car right behind them. "What do you think it means?" she asked urgently.

"Not sure," he replied in the voice she often referred to as *maddeningly detached* when he was going into scientist mode. "What's another word for 'unconfined movement'?"

"Freedom, maybe?" she offered.

"No, I think in this context maybe it's more like leaking, or spilling . . ." he replied, feeling another jolt from behind as the old man tossed them back and forth. He surmised that they had to be doing speeds well above a hundred miles an hour. "What happens when something gets spilled or leaks out?"

Lisa nervously pulled at her wet, stringy hair, still watching the Mustang. "I don't know, it runs over?"

Daniel stopped in mid-thought. "It *flows*," he said. His thoughts turned back to the passage on the Stone and the order the symbols were in. "Dominion Stone . . . life . . . flow . . ." He looked outside, at the otherworldly storm that was making visibility on the freeway increasingly hard . . .

And he had it.

Knowing exactly what to do, he peeked over the top of the seat at the passengers in the Mustang. It wasn't easy to make them out through the gushing drops of red falling from the sky, but he was pretty sure that neither of them were wearing seat belts.

He ducked back down and whispered silently so that only he could hear, "If either of you survive this . . . please forgive me."

Daniel reached through the gap between the two seats up front and grabbed the old man by the arm. "Slam on the brakes! Now!" he shouted, squeezing the man's arm firmly.

"What? Are you crazy?" Lisa replied.

The old man grunted a similar-sounding question.

"I know what I'm doing!" Daniel snapped back. "Just DO IT! Do it NOW!!"

The old man frowned but jammed his foot down on the brake pedal as Lisa and Daniel both braced themselves.

It worked. Almost too well. Payton obviously hadn't been prepared for it, and the Mustang slammed even harder into the Camaro, with Daniel getting wedged once again in his seat. This time he was so far down he couldn't get out.

But soon the car came to a screeching, grinding halt, and he opened the side door and squeezed out into the pouring red rain.

Please, God, let them be alive . . .

Alex was on the ground some thirty feet in front of the Camaro. Payton seemed to have used his unique agility to gain some kind of foothold and jump onto the roof of the Camaro, but then fallen onto his back. Neither of them were moving.

Daniel reached inside the car and grabbed a fragment of the Dominion Stone from the floorboard and then ran toward Alex.

Whether it was her blood on the paved freeway or the kind falling from the fiery clouds above, he couldn't tell, but she was most definitely unconscious. Yet when he was ten paces out, she stumbled to her feet, her eyes were still blissfully shut. Daniel stopped in his tracks, unnerved by the sight of her moving like a marionette, and knowing that Oblivion was holding her strings. Her right arm came up slowly, grasping for him, but Daniel was moving too fast.

He ducked under her arm and slammed the Dominion Stone fragment into the black crusty scars covering her abdomen. He scrubbed at the scabs until a spot of raw, pinkish flesh appeared, along with a fresh oozing of blood, and he thrust the Stone fragment into it fully.

The Ring on Alex's right middle finger glowed, casting a diffuse white glow in a four-foot circle around where she stood. The rain stained it red.

Alex blinked awake. A scream burst forth from her mouth, the kind of agonizing, howling scream that could only pass beyond lips that had been forcibly held closed for days, perhaps weeks. She collapsed in a heap on the ground, shriveling practically into nothingness and trying to drift off into death's cold arms.

Lisa screamed in the distance.

Alex jolted awake and, like Daniel, looked up just in time to see Payton standing atop the Camaro, his sword twirling in his hand and preparing to strike at Lisa, who stood outside her side door just below him.

Alex stuck a hand out in his direction. "No," she whispered.

Payton nearly dropped his sword from whatever emotion she'd shot at him, then staggered backward onto one knee, seemingly unable to get his bearings.

Daniel seized their one opportunity. "Lisa, touch his blood with one of the Stones!" he shouted. "The symbols say *blood flow*! Touch his blood with a fragment of the Dominion Stone, and Oblivion will lose his hold!"

Lisa's eyes searched the car and spotted a three-inch shard of glass resting on the dash; it was all that remained of the windshield. She grabbed it and jumped up onto the hood, where she reached down and slashed a deep cut right into Payton's left cheek.

The old man had already retrieved a piece of the Dominion Stone, and he tossed it to her. She dropped the glass with one hand, caught the Stone fragment in the other, and mashed the Stone into his wound as hard as she could.

Payton started at the pain in his face, then blinked several times as if waking up from a long sleep.

Alex fainted into Daniel's arms. He scooped her up as best he could and realized how hot her skin was. Under the battered frame, she boiled with fever. The scabs covering her stomach and right upper arm were black and crusty. The soles of her feet were covered in red sores and blisters, most of which were open and oozing pus. Her leg muscles twitched now and again, a sign of exhaustion and overuse.

Daniel carried her slowly back to the car, doing his best not to let his weary legs slip out from under him in the blood pooling on the freeway in the rain.

When he got back to the car, no one spoke. Payton was still lying on the roof of the car, grasping his sword with one hand like it was a safety blanket, his only root to reality. He appeared coherent, watching the actions of everyone else, but the pained, bitter look in his eyes was thousands of miles away.

With the Camaro wrecked beyond use, the old man had found an old station wagon with the keys still in it and a mostly filled tank of gas. Daniel placed Alex carefully in the backseat of the car, where the old man got to work dressing her wounds with some supplies from Daniel's backpack. She stirred awake at his ministrations and clutched her stomach in agony. She stifled powerful emotions that forced tears streaming down her cheeks, crying out in great heaving sobs of anguish.

Daniel planted himself in the driver's seat and leaned back. Out of breath and drenched in blood and his own sweat, he was pretty sure he never wanted to get up again.

INTERREGNUM

"YOU REALLY THINK YOU changed, after you were given a new body?" asked Grant's duplicate.

"Yes," Grant replied without hesitation. "I care about people! I care about everybody. I risked my life to save them."

"Certainly true," his reflection admitted. "But in the end, you could not prevent them from suffering the terrible fate that is now upon them. Many have already been lost. Do you even know *why* you saved their lives again and again?"

Grant paused, not sure what his companion was expecting to hear. "It was the right thing to do."

"And why does doing the right thing concern you?"

Grant had no answer. He remained silent for so long that the mirror man finally spoke again.

"Let me put it another way. Your sister, Julie Saunders, is dead."

"My fault . . . She tried to warn me . . . I led her to her death."

"Yes," the double said. "Perhaps that responsibility does lie at your feet. Or perhaps it's because of the actions of others. Either way, can you accept that there is nothing you could have done to save her, in the end?"

"Never!" Grant cried with conviction. "With all the power I had, I could've . . . I *should* have—I could've stopped the bullet or pushed her out of the way, or—"

"No, no, no," the other man interrupted. "You misunderstand my question. Even if you had saved Julie's life from Devlin's bullet, you could not have stopped the disease that was ravaging her muscular system from ultimately degenerating her quality of life until she was dead. Understand this, it is crucial: In the end, her fate would have been exactly the same. So I ask again: Can you accept that even you could not have prevented her from dying? Whether it occurred on the same day that you died or twenty years after?"

"No," Grant admitted. "What was any of it for, if not to help people avoid pain and suffering?"

"An admirable goal, if ultimately futile . . . Still, I'd like to believe that you changed, but the evidence is simply too damning. See for yourself . . ."

A new scene materialized in the blackness before Grant's eyes, and this one he knew all too well. He relived it in his thoughts and nightmares often.

A broken window in a high-rise penthouse. Grant, kneeling on the ground by the window, Alex nearby. Cradled in his arms was Hannah, the life draining out of her from a bullet wound to the neck.

"Don't let them take . . ." Hannah said groggily, fading fast, "your soul . . ."

He cried out her name at the same moment that she stopped breathing. He held her in his arms, unwilling to let her go, even at Alex's attempts to snap him back to manifest . . .

In the blackness, the Grant of the here and now watched his own visage change in the 3-D image, becoming dark, vengeful, full of rage. The whole room began to shake as if an earthquake were happening, but it was no earthquake. It was his wrath made reality.

The scene faded. "No need to relive the whole thing," Grant's doppelganger said. "You know what came next. The skies turned dark, fire threatened to fall from the sky, and the lives of everyone in Los Angeles were nearly extinguished. All because of your inability to control your rage."

Grant said nothing. A series of scenes flickered to life in the darkness, coming faster and faster now, some so quick that he only caught glimpses of them.

He saw himself standing in Substation Lambda Alpha, beneath Los Angeles, facing down his grandfather with an explosive eruption of anger . . .

He ran into a street in the heart of the Old City of Jerusalem, his breathing fast, looking like he was ready to detonate, when the walls surrounding the Old City flew up into the sky and burst into powder . . .

He was storming into the attic hideout of the Upholders of the Crown in London. He marched inside, dictated demands to the four Brits, and threatened them to within an inch of their lives if they didn't obey . . .

He was inside the same attic sometime later, sitting on the couch, all focus on his teammate Nora. Her body left the ground and was pinned up against the far wall as she struggled to loosen an invisible hand around her throat . . .

Devlin was leading him into the heart of the round cavern known as the Hollow, toward the gaping, howling hole at its center, and Grant was following him blindly, ignoring the pleas of his sister to stop, to turn back . . . Moments later, her blood splattered on his face, his eyes turned red, and he was shoved in the back by Devlin into the hole . . .

The images dissipated, and Grant's double walked slowly around and stepped in front of him. "Tell me again about how you've changed."

30

The old man did his best on Alex, and she'd fallen into a feverish sleep. The others, near collapse from exhaustion, had sat in stunned silence until Lisa finally suggested that perhaps they should move someplace that wasn't so exposed. Who knew what Oblivion would do now that Payton and Alex had been freed? Payton mumbled something about knowing a place, and so he hot-wired a broken-down sedan that was abandoned nearby, and Daniel joined him, taking the driver's seat. The old man followed in the station wagon, carrying Alex, who was unconscious, and Lisa, who tended to her.

They drove east on the 10 in silence for hours, or possibly days. There was no way to be sure. The state line came and disappeared, and Arizona directed them to a northbound turn onto I-17 at Phoenix. Thirty miles north of Phoenix, not far from the Interstate, Payton motioned for Daniel to get off the highway. Payton directed him through a series of black, mountainous desert roads until they came to a stop at some kind of cliff-side factory.

Purely utilitarian, the place must've been twenty thousand square feet, if not more, with dingy cinder-block walls and a flat aluminum roof. It was a relic, like something airlifted out of East Germany or the old Soviet bloc. A single metal staircase on one side led up from the ground to a small grated landing in front of a normal-sized door. Near the back of the building, beyond the stairs, was a cluster of electric generators that prevented the building from depending on local power.

The rain had stopped long ago, leaving a clotting glaze over the vehicles and the blackened ash-like roads, and a musky, metallic odor drifting through the damp air. Alex never awoke as Daniel and the old man carried her up the stairs, following Payton and Lisa. Payton mumbled a sequence of numbers, which Lisa typed into a keypad to the right of the door. They heard a tiny clack as the door unlocked.

Inside, they were greeted with a completely open space, much of which held a massive gymnasium outfitted with state-of-the-art equipment.

"What is this?" Daniel asked, the first time he'd spoken since before they'd left California.

Payton leaned against a wall for support, refusing help from any of them. He peeled off his blood-soaked black shirt and tossed it in a trash bin near the door.

"My home," Payton replied, his voice barely audible but echoing throughout the giant chamber.

Everyone took their turn at resting and showering and changing into fresh clothes. Alex required help just moving, so Lisa aided her in a quick bath and change of clothes before she was allowed to sleep. More bomb shelter than home, the place was stocked with enough food to last through a nuclear winter, so everyone enjoyed being properly fed for the first time in a long time.

A lofted second floor extended over the open area to the right of the entrance. It was open and visible to the main area below, but sectioned off by the long stairway that led up to it. Typically, Payton slept here, but now he insisted it be used by Alex for her recovery.

Daniel and Lisa worked with the old man for hours assessing the damage: Payton was more or less his usually fit self, though profoundly dehydrated and in desperate need of sleep.

Alex, on the other hand, they could barely believe was alive. She suffered from second- and third-degree burns on her stomach and right arm, which had created dark scabs. Each had gone far too long without being properly treated, and the resulting infections now boiled in her bloodstream. She also had a severe concussion and a few broken ribs due to her ejection from the Mustang.

Payton's home came complete with every medical supply one might ever need, including painkillers and strong antibiotics to fight Alex's infection, and these were administered not long after their arrival. But combined with the concussion, she was largely confused and incoherent when awake, vomited occasionally, and had a dangerously high fever she could not seem to break.

All five of them—even Payton, who rarely spoke and spent much of his time among his training equipment—feared each time Alex fell asleep that she might never reawaken.

With every moment feeling like *now*, it became difficult to fall into the routine of day and night, but they all did their best while waiting for Alex and Payton to recover. Makeshift beds were created from whatever could be found. Meals were shared. And they waited for a sense of what to do next. They tried to engage the one-handed man and discover his secrets, yet he refused to share even his name, seemingly content in his silence.

It was sometime during the *awake* period after their third sleeping cycle that Daniel and Lisa seated themselves in front of a gigantic flat-screen television and turned it on for the first time. Payton's high-tech equipment allowed them to pick up on signals still being transmitted by some of the major news networks, but most were intermittent and unreliable, since the satellites that normally broadcast their transmissions were slowly dying, one by one.

They were in a small seating nook near the facility's kitchen, located directly beneath the second floor, where Alex rested. It wasn't long before they were joined by the old man—who'd taken to staying at Alex's side whenever he wasn't sleeping—and Payton, who showed up covered in sweat, his sword held tightly in one hand.

The news was not uplifting. The darkness and the blackened earth had spread completely, covering the entire planet. It was done; transformation complete. Video reports from all over the world showed much of what they had already seen—the volcanic rock and scattered wildfires that covered the earth, the oceans that were still evaporating, the occasional raining blood, and the rivers that had turned into hot lava.

Natural springs and wells had become dark pits of deadly flame—flames so hot, no one could safely approach them. The global suicide rate had peaked to an all-time high, and there were countless reports of people losing their sanity. Going completely mad, these individuals were breaking into homes where others were huddled in fear, and killing them all—or worse. Bizarre new religions popped up all over the globe, most of them taking their cues from the bloodred rain, utilizing ritual sacrifices of animals or even human beings in attempts to appease whatever gods had been angered into unleashing these horrific conditions upon the planet.

The slow loss of the world's oceans was having a dramatic effect on sea life. It was unprecedented: Both the fish and underwater plants were dying and drying up, starting with those nearest to shorelines. Every kind of ship—from tankers and ocean liners to battleships and submarines—made for the nearest port they could reach. Many of them made it. Several thousand did not, some hitting land on the dried-up ocean floor, others opting to sail for the central areas of open sea still existing, hoping to ride out the phenomenon for as long as possible.

Similarly, the fiery storm clouds enveloping the entire planet had caused authorities to ground all aircraft. Astronauts manning the International Space Station managed to send a few grainy images of the earth down to the surface; the pictures showed the opposite of what those on the planet's surface saw. Instead of black clouds with fire peeking through, these new images revealed what at first seemed to be a small sun.

The world was on fire.

Three sleep cycles later, with everyone else asleep, Payton sat up, unable to achieve unconsciousness.

He watched the news footage, alone in the kitchen nook, the volume low. The sounds were of little interest to him. His attention was focused on the blurry video of Oblivion. It seemed no one was able to get close enough to him to get his picture, but whether that was Oblivion's own doing or that of the young British girl Charlotte, who was still held under Oblivion's thrall and could control electrical transmissions, was open to debate. The best the news had been able to achieve was this one fuzzy image, shot with a super-high magnification from miles away.

Payton didn't need to see every detail to know exactly what he was looking at. He remembered Oblivion's cold, lifeless face, his eyes of fire, and his stone-gray skin all too well.

Oblivion had led his army and the Secretum eastward toward Syria until finally turning sharply south. He was already approaching the northern Syrian border, and speculation was rife among the newscasters as to where his final destination might be.

Most of them agreed that in all likelihood . . . he was headed for Israel. Though there was no evidence anyone could come up with to support this theory, somehow it just seemed to fit.

What Oblivion had done to Payton, what he'd done to Alex, what he was doing even now to the rest of the Loci, not to mention his march of destruction upon the world . . .

It was unforgivable. There was no punishment too harsh, no anger too severe, no death he could give to Oblivion that would be slow or painful enough. Oblivion would pay for this, and so would the Secretum. Every last one of them.

In conjuring Oblivion into human flesh, the Secretum had betrayed the entire human race.

And as far as Payton was concerned, betrayal was the worst sin in the book.

31

Twenty-Four Years Ago

"Girls," he chided the three young ladies sitting at the back of the classroom. "Pass that note to the front of the class, please. It will be read aloud before this period is over."

There were groans and sighs at the back of the room, while snickering presided over the front. It was a small room at the private Catholic school, allowing for no more than twelve students at a time, and even now it wasn't full.

But this was many a student's favorite class, a fact that Father Bernard prided himself in. Who would have ever guessed that Theology could become *any* teenager's favorite subject? It reinforced the instinct he followed when, fresh out of seminary, he'd chosen to spend the first few years of his career teaching, influencing the lives of the younger generation, before moving on to his own parish.

"Now, we were discussing the passage in Joshua where God struck down the city of Jericho and every living thing in it, for Israel's sake, so that the Israelites could move into this land. As you should recall, God had promised this land to the Israelites many generations before, so this action was taken to restore to them what was rightfully theirs."

A hand shot up. "Father?"

"Yes, Simon," he replied to one of his favorite students, a brilliant young man with tremendous potential. Father Bernard had high hopes for this one.

Simon had a quizzical look upon his oval face. "The passage says that God wiped out the entire population of the town—that's tens of thousands of lives. And under the rule of King David, the Israelite army decimated countless peoples in God's name, butchering and slaughtering their enemies. Yet back in Exodus, the Ten Commandments command us never to take a life. And later in the New Testament, Jesus raises the dead and heals the sick and commands His followers never to kill."

Father Bernard smiled. "Yes. Quite the paradox, is it not? You have stumbled upon one of the great mysteries that theologians and scholars have wrestled with for centuries. But I believe the answer lies in the book of Romans—chapter six, verse twenty-three." He waited, watching the boy, knowing his keen mind could very likely call up the passage from memory.

Simon's shoulders settled. He had an *aha!* look on his face. " 'The wages of sin is death,' " he quoted.

Father Bernard nodded. "Whether or not any of these peoples died at the very hands of God himself, the important thing to remember is that they were all wicked, deceitful, *depraved* people. Do you understand?"

"So they deserved to die? And their wickedness made it *okay* for God's people to murder them?"

Father Bernard tilted his head to one side in thought, and then shrugged. "Far worse than their mortal death was the eternal punishment they received *after* death. And that fate would have awaited them regardless of how and when they met it, because they were unrepentant. It doesn't matter if we agree with their deaths at the hands of the great patriarchs of our faith; it was a different age, subjected to a different way of life. What matters is that they were deemed unrighteous in God's sight."

The lesson ended; Father Bernard went home for the day and thought no more of the conversation he'd had with Simon. Late that night, he received a telephone call from the school's administrator, who informed him that one of the girls sitting in the back of his classroom that day had accused him of inappropriately touching her.

An investigation was launched, and Father Bernard was placed on administrative leave. He was sure he would be cleared of the charges, but the girl who'd accused him had prepared her story too perfectly, and it was eagerly verified by several of her friends. Even his best students looked at him differently when he came in to speak to the administrator. No one volunteered to speak up in his defense.

He was never convicted of any crime, but the damage was done. Despite his innocence, he swiftly lost his job, and his rights and title as a priest were revoked.

Nineteen Years Ago

In a small city in northern England, over two hours away from his previous home, Bernard resettled and tried to find some peace in his life. His kindhearted brother, Frederick, had been good enough to offer him a job, believing that the charges against him had been fabricated.

Bernard served as the manager of the meager office supply company owned by his brother. The hours were long and the work was far from thrilling, but he liked the people he was working with, and he smiled and laughed with them often. And no one here knew anything of his past or the false charges that had ruined his career.

One spring morning he was recounting a funny story to his employees when two police officers arrived at the office.

"Yes, can I help you?" he asked the approaching officers.

"Please turn around and place your hands behind your back, sir," one of them ordered. "You're under arrest for defrauding your tax filings for the last five years. We have evidence linking your office to the laundering of more than fifty million pounds."

Bernard pleaded with them, certain it was a mistake. He had always kept spotless records and was strict about ensuring that his employees did the same.

A few days later, word reached Bernard's ears inside jail that his brother had unexpectedly left the country in a rush, leaving no forwarding information or reason to believe he would ever return.

Bernard fell physically ill upon hearing this news. He remained silent and inconsolable at the trial, where he was sentenced to an eighteen-year prison term with a possibility of parole after eleven years.

Seven months would pass before he would receive the news that Frederick had been found in the United States; his brother was found dead, and with him the only soul who knew of Bernard's innocence.

Twelve Years Ago

Bernard tossed and turned in his cot, unwilling to wake up.

What was the point? There was nothing to look forward to, here behind these bars. And the prospect of leaving prison in a few years left him just as cold and empty inside as staying here for so long had.

Knowing the warden would be by any minute to rouse him for the morning meal if he wasn't up and ready in time—and knowing the warden wasn't famous for his gentility and charm—he opened his eyes. And gasped.

Bernard wasn't in his prison cell. He was in a stylish bachelor's bedroom, all twisted up beneath fine bed linens. What was going on here? It had to be a dream.

Quickly disentangling himself from the sheets, he got up and ran to a bright window next to the bed to look outside. He was on the second story of a quaint apartment building; old-fashioned shops lined the street below. It was a part of town he couldn't recognize.

What was happening?

He felt a lurch in his stomach, like he might vomit, and ran out of the bedroom to find a bathroom. It was right across the hall, but instead of throwing up, he froze when his body filled the frame of a large oval mirror over the sink.

His appearance had changed. His *whole body* had changed. He'd slept in pajamas his entire life, but the man staring back at him wore only a pair of shorts. The physique of this man was stunning: Toned, chiseled muscles covered his entire body. Shrewd eyes were set deep within a bald head. An expensive-looking gold ring sat upon his right middle finger.

And in a blink, though he had no idea how it had happened, Bernard embraced this new life that had been miraculously given to him, as if his years as a priest and in prison had all been a bad dream and his life had truly begun at last.

He was free; he had a different identity, a new name, and nothing to tie him to his past. He could never be sent back to jail, and there were no records to connect him to the unjust events at the high school, so long ago. It was a miracle.

A second start. Everything was a new discovery, and he found endless reasons to appreciate each arriving day. What had happened to him was enough to make him believe that maybe there was someone still up there watching out for him after all, and maybe, just maybe, there were still some good people left in this world.

Nine Years Ago

In a hospital bed in France, Payton awoke. His body was in considerable pain, but his first thought rested on one thing only: *Where's Morgan?* He tried to sit up, his heart filling with fear . . .

"Calm down, friend," said the older gentleman standing with his hands clasped at the foot of the bed. "You were in an accident. A cave-in. Your heart even stopped for a few minutes, but they revived you."

"Morgan!" Payton's dry, raspy voice tried to shout. "What happened to Morgan?"

"You were found alone," the man replied.

Payton sank back onto the bed, not believing these words. She wouldn't have left him. She wouldn't.

She loved him. Just as much as he loved her.

She did, she had to.

"No, you don't understand," he said to the man, sitting upright again, ignoring the pain. "We must go back and find her; she must've been trapped in the cave-in—"

"A thorough search of the cave has been conducted, and there was no one else found. You were alone," he repeated.

Impossible. She was the only thing he'd ever really loved. She was his reason for living . . .

The thought turned his blood cold.

32

Payton was not asleep when the alarm sounded. He was unmoving, yet wide awake, in a small foldout cot, his mind racing from thought to thought—from Morgan to Oblivion and everything in between. Mostly his thoughts lingered on Oblivion, about the exact number of pieces he would cut him into . . .

Hearing the alarm, he vanished from his cot and unsheathed his sword to hold it underhanded, sprinting at superspeed for a small alcove of video screens near the front door. There were no windows in the building looking out, but he had a top-of-the-line security system that showed views pointed in all directions from the outside of the building.

Payton had been concerned about this since his and Alex's escape from Oblivion's thrall. Oblivion might not be able to control them anymore, but could he still sense them, could he *see* their location? Grant had always been able to. If so, then Payton had expected Oblivion to send someone after them, or even come after them himself—and he'd expected it to happen long before now. It wasn't like Big Evil to delay gratification. This was the one trait Payton respected about Oblivion, because they shared it in common.

Daniel and Lisa appeared, running toward the security alcove. Soon they stood next to Payton, both of them out of breath.

"What is it?" Lisa asked.

"*Who* is it?" Daniel asked.

The old man rounded a corner from a room behind the kitchen: the armory. He carried a Beretta 92 in his hand, and he popped the clip in by slapping the gun's handle against his hip. He strode toward them, cold and focused, eyes on the front door. He chambered the pistol's first round by grasping the slide with his teeth and pushing the gun sideways across his mouth. Ready, he took up position on the other side of the door, pointing his weapon at the door and glancing at Payton.

Payton leaned in to examine one of the monitors closely, and frowned. There were two people standing on the other side of the door at the top of the small exterior stairway. The weather outside had turned on them again, and it was raining blood once more, which was messing with the monitors' system. The images were grainy and distorted, and the rain had quickly become a downpour, making it nearly impossible to make out the visitors' faces.

"Huh," Lisa commented, tilting her head to one side and squinting. "It kinda looks like they're trying to ring the doorbell."

"There is no doorbell," Payton replied.

Lisa glared at him. "I know . . . I'm just saying . . ."

"Do we run?" Daniel considered, looking behind them and up to where Alex lay, still sleeping.

"Run where?" Payton replied, and in a flash he was standing beside the front door, opposite the old man, sword still held reversed in only one hand.

Daniel and Lisa ducked down behind the row of monitors and watched as Payton placed his hand on the door's metal handle. With practiced lethality, he flung open the door, grabbed the first man and threw him on the floor inside. Continuing his momentum from his initial movement, he whacked the second man in the face with the blunt end of the sword, and then grabbed the man's shirt lapels and shoved him up against the wall just beside the door. He swung around with one foot and kicked the man on the floor in the side of the head while pressing the edge of the sword against the standing man's throat.

The old man stepped out and covered the guy on the ground with his pistol.

"Wait, wait!" shouted the man on the floor, throwing up a hand. "It's me!"

"You know this man who's about to get shot?" the man pinned against the wall said, his throat vibrating against the blade. Payton looked down and saw that a glistening black pistol was being held just shy of touching his chest.

Not bad, Payton had to admit. He hadn't seen this man draw his weapon.

"You're sure these are the good guys?" the gunman asked.

"Last time I saw them they were," Ethan replied, rubbing the side of his head, a lump already rising where Payton had punched him.

Payton turned loose of the man up against the wall but didn't offer to help Ethan up. "What are you doing here?" he asked darkly.

"How in the world did you find us?" Daniel echoed, emerging from behind the security alcove, Lisa in tow.

Ethan looked down and saw that Daniel was scratching the red welt on the back of his hand. "Sorry about the rash on your hand," he said. "That's my doing. When we parted ways in London, do you remember when we shook hands? I tagged the back of your hand with a subdermal tracking device. Don't worry—it's advanced tech, untraceable to anyone who doesn't know the frequency." At this, he held up a small device like a palmtop computer, which showed a rudimentary map; a blinking blue dot indicated the source of the signal. "Knew I'd never find you again without help."

Payton was unimpressed. Daniel seemed to be taking a moment to process this.

"Who's the new guy?" Lisa asked, sizing up Ethan's new companion.

"Sergeant Paul Tucker, ma'am," said the man against the wall, who was rubbing his throat now that Payton had released him. He holstered his weapon.

"Who's *your* new friend?" Ethan asked, noting the old man, who had lowered his gun as well.

But Payton focused solely on Ethan, closing the outside door and sheathing his sword. "What happened to you in London? You disappeared."

It took Ethan a minute to catch up with Payton's question; he was thinking of his last experiences in London, with Daniel and Lisa and Trevor. Payton was talking about a time several days earlier, before Grant had died, before any of the most recent events—including the extraordinary changes in Ethan's life—had occurred.

"I got a new employer," Ethan replied. "It's kind of a long story."

Payton crossed his arms. "Dying to hear it."

"Me too," called out a weak voice.

They all turned. A very pale Alex was standing at the edge of the upstairs sleeping quarters, an IV on wheels attached to her arm. She was clutching the metal railing on the second floor and looking down at Ethan with a mixture of curiosity and deliriousness.

She swayed dangerously, and as one, all six individuals on the ground floor made for the stairs.

33

It was a tight space in the upstairs sleeping quarters, but the seven of them found places to sit, even if it was on the floor.

Payton was the first to reach Alex, catching her before she collapsed completely. He promptly escorted her back to bed before she was reprimanded by just about everyone for getting up in the first place. But their chiding was softened by their amazement in seeing her moving at all. It was the most coherent and awake she'd been since arriving here.

The condition upon which she agreed to go back to bed was that Ethan would tell his tale where she could hear it. So they all remained upstairs with her, much to her satisfaction.

Her fevered nightmares had been twisted re-creations of her time under Oblivion's thrall, reliving the physical pain and emotional anguish and the terrible loneliness of it all . . . To exist in the midst of so many people, yet be completely helpless.

Thankfully awake now, she decided that she didn't want to be alone ever again.

"That was a very emotional night for us all," Ethan began his story. "Grant and Alex had just escaped from the secret room beneath the London Library, and the rest of you were hit with the news that Morgan had died. We gathered in the attic loft of your British counterparts. Tensions were running high as I recall . . . Grant and Nora exchanged some heated words—"

"I'll cut your insides out," Payton's gravelly voice intoned, "if you don't get on with it."

Ethan cleared his throat nervously. Alex looked closer at Payton from where she reclined on her bed. He looked much as she remembered him, pre-Oblivion. He was nearly back to perfect physical condition and his personality—or lack thereof—was stronger than ever. But she perceived something new in his face. He concealed it well, but she saw flashes of it at times when his patience was put to the test.

His practiced composure was cracking. The caged animal they knew waited below the surface seemed closer than ever and was doing all it could to get out.

"Well," Ethan continued, "I left the attic and walked into the arms of the British authorities. They'd been tracking me for a while, but thankfully I was far enough away from the loft when they found me that they didn't trace me all the way back there. The FBI had issued a warrant for my arrest."

"Why?" Payton asked.

"Mostly for ticking off my supervisor. She was . . . well, she was kind of . . . *charm-free*." He glanced up at Payton, whose hard expression did not change one tic.

"Anyway," Ethan went on, "to make a long story not so long, I was taken into custody, and that's where they found me."

"Where who found you?" Alex asked.

" 'The Appointed.' That's what they call themselves. They're sort of a rogue security agency, answerable to no government, operating outside of the law. They believe they're doing nothing less than the work of God himself. I don't know everything about them, but they told me they've been around for centuries, and their primary mandate was to undermine the work of the Secretum of Six in bringing about the coming of Oblivion."

"Umm . . ." Lisa raised her hand cautiously.

Everyone faced her.

"I don't buy it."

"Buy what?" Ethan asked.

"These Appointed people. That they've been around for hundreds of years, fighting against the Secretum. I mean, if it's true . . . then they've done a bang-up job!"

Ethan smirked.

"No, seriously. They have one task and they failed miserably. And they certainly haven't tried to help the rest of us. Just exactly *where* have they been?" Lisa was shouting now. "Where were they when Daniel and I were stuck in a British jail and nearly killed? Where were they when the Loci were strung up like puppets for Oblivion to control? Where were they when Grant died, or when Morgan died, or Julie? Where were they when the Loci were Shifted and given Rings? I'm sorry, but I don't know how you can believe any of this."

Alex looked back at Ethan, who was taking in the expectant gazes of the entire group. She almost felt sorry for him, having to rationalize the difficult choices he'd obviously had to make.

"As it was explained to me," he said slowly, "the Appointed have intentionally limited their numbers and resources over the centuries so as not to alert the Secretum to their existence. There are only about a hundred of them in the whole world. And they move very cautiously, with great deliberation, because the fact that the Secretum doesn't know they exist is their one advantage."

"Why you?" Payton asked, his dangerous voice somehow making every statement feel like a threat.

"Excuse me?"

Payton leaned in a bit closer. "Why did they recruit *you*?"

Ethan hesitated. "While I'd like to think it was my FBI training, or perhaps my boyish good looks and boundless enthusiasm . . . honestly, I have no idea," he sighed. "But I'd barely met a handful of them at some sort of local meeting place in London when they sent me to Antalya on an observation assignment. I was to infiltrate the Secretum's underground city—which they knew how to find and breach, though I don't know how—on the off chance that Grant might turn up there."

"Why did they send you away so quickly after indoctrinating you?" Daniel asked.

"Because I mentioned that Grant was on a mission to find the Secretum. The Appointed knew of Grant and his status as the Bringer, but they knew that as long as he stayed away from the Hollow, there was no reason to engage him. The underground city was the key. However the Secretum pulled it off—killing Grant while allowing Oblivion to inhabit his body and take control of his powers—apparently it couldn't happen anywhere else in the world. So I was to keep Grant from entering that city at any cost. The Appointed thought this would be easy for me since I'd already earned his trust."

There was silence around the room as everyone digested this.

"Where are they now? The Appointed?" Lisa asked.

"I'm not sure," Ethan replied. "I was told that they never use conventional methods of communication, so there was little point in my trying to contact them after my assignment was done. Or hey, maybe they thought my assignment would never *be* done, or that I would never return from it. In any case, I did try to contact them after time stopped and Oblivion unleashed Hell, but it got me nowhere. I couldn't reach them, and now with all the satellites falling out of the sky, I doubt I ever will."

Something Ethan had said triggered a memory Alex had forgotten. Lost in thought, she mumbled the word, "DarkWorld."

Everyone turned.

"What?" Daniel asked.

Tired, she took a few breaths before answering. "Devlin and some of the Secretum people said it a lot: 'DarkWorld.' I think they were using it to describe what Oblivion was doing to the earth."

"This *is* the DarkWorld," Payton explained. Apparently Alex was not the only one to have heard this term in use. "We're living on it."

No one had a reply to this. It was an evil, wicked thought. It was terrifying.

"There's something else you should know," Daniel began. "Morgan left behind . . . well, I think it's some kind of recording. We found it in Julie's things. I've been waiting to take a look at it until everyone could see."

Alex's eyes drifted once again to Payton, who had stiffened noticeably at the mention of Morgan's name.

"We should let Alex get some rest and continue this later," Lisa said, standing to her feet. The others seemed to agree and began rising as well. "It's—"

Lisa let out a chuckle and Sergeant Tucker noticed. "What?" he said softly.

"I almost said 'it's getting dark out,' " Lisa replied. "I forgot for half a second that it's *always* dark now."

Payton was already at the top of the stairs, preparing to go down, but he turned halfway back. "I hadn't noticed the difference."

"What do you mean?" asked Lisa, and everyone froze in place, waiting for his response.

"Death consumes everything. It's a universal constant, and it is all-powerful. The world has always been dark. And spiteful. And full of misery," he replied as he began descending the stairs. "It's just a bit more obvious now."

34

Alex wasn't sure how long she'd slept when she awoke to the sound of arguing downstairs. She felt stronger today, so despite the old man's wordless protestations, she insisted on going downstairs for the first time since she'd arrived here at Payton's sterile, function-before-form home.

She took the stairs slowly with the old man's help, her feet aching with each step and her stomach still anguished. But her frequent pauses let her listen and watch the argument unfold, just to the right and bottom of the staircase. No one seemed to notice her. Most of them were sitting around what looked like a small breakfast nook; Payton stood off to one side, arms crossed, body leaning against one of the six metal I-beams that were holding up the interior of the three-story-high building.

"But he's unstoppable! Facing him is suicide."

"How do we know that for sure?"

"Agreed," Daniel was saying. "Let's not forget that we have a weapon now—a *real* way of fighting back. We can release Ringwearers from his control. And I think it's safe to assume that once we've touched their bloodstream with the Dominion Stone, Ringwearers disappear from his internal radar—from the Forging—too. Oblivion can't see Payton and Alex anymore, or their location, or else we would have been found by now. So why shouldn't we free more of them?"

"Because what good would that do us?" Lisa replied. Alex was surprised to see these two falling on opposing sides of an argument. She'd noticed the glances and furtive hand-holding between them at the last group meeting. "Freeing Payton and Alex nearly cost us our lives. And even *if* we somehow freed every last one of the Ringwearers, do *any* of them realistically have a chance at stopping Oblivion?"

"I will stop him."

The conversation halted. Everyone turned to look at Payton.

"How?" Alex called out, descending to the bottom stair.

There was a bit of commotion as some of the others protested her appearance out of bed, but she refused to return. She wanted to see Morgan's message. So the others slid around the curving seats at the table and gave her a place to sit. Her one-handed caretaker sat next to her, watching over her IV line. She'd become accustomed to his presence and even found it oddly comforting.

"I said," Alex repeated, once everyone was situated, "how do you plan on stopping Oblivion? And if your answer involves anything other than finding a way to draw Grant out from inside Oblivion . . . then you can just bury that plan right here and now."

She'd spoken with such icy resolve that no one dared question her, at least not at first. She and Payton stared each other down with such intensity that a few of the others held their breaths as they watched.

"B-b-but . . ." Lisa stuttered nervously, not taking her eyes off of the standoff between Alex and Payton, "but I thought . . . that guy Devlin said Grant was dead. Didn't he?"

"I don't care what he said," Alex replied, looking at Lisa with hardened eyes. "I don't care what anyone says. Oblivion may not be Grant, but that doesn't mean Grant's not still in there. And if he's in there, he's fighting to get out, to regain control, to stop Oblivion from massacring any more people. So we're going to help him. All other options are off the table, as of this moment. Are we clear on this?"

She slowly looked at each of them in turn, ready to quell any arguments that might arise. She ended with eyes locked on Payton, the only other person in the room who knew how she was feeling, having just survived their shared ordeal at Oblivion's hands. Yet she knew that his idea of a solution to stop Oblivion would not be what she had in mind.

"Very well, love," he said softly. "You try it your way. But if no such way of reaching Grant can be found, then I will test my fate against his."

An uncomfortable silence followed. Daniel cleared his throat.

"For sake of argument," he said in his best professorial tone, "let's say Payton *did* try to take Oblivion on, mano-a-mano. From what the two of you have told us, his skin has turned to something hard, like cement or granite. How would you even—"

In a flash, Payton whipped out his sword and slashed a perfectly horizontal swipe at the load-bearing post he had been leaning against.

Everyone jumped at the sudden movement, and then gasps were heard as each of them realized there was now a perfectly straight line running through the entire beam, separating it into two pieces, one resting on top of the other.

Payton had sliced through it like it was a wet noodle.

"How did he do that?" Lisa whispered to Daniel under her breath. And then louder, at Payton, "How did you do that?"

He held the weapon out and examined it with great care and admiration. "This sword was forged centuries ago by those who knew exactly what the Bringer would become, and what it would take to kill him."

"The Appointed," Ethan said, nodding. "I suspected they might be responsible for such a weapon. I wonder how the

Secretum got their hands on it, if they don't even know the Appointed exist?"

"The sword has had a prominent, if little-known, role in mankind's story. It was passed down for generations, through the hands of many key historical figures—"

"If I might interject," Sergeant Tucker spoke up, his hand halfheartedly raised a few inches off the table. "Could we get back to the part where we free more of your super-friends from Oblivion? No offense to Mr. Sword Guy here, but I'm thinking we need all the help we can get."

"Second," Lisa added, raising her hand.

"Seems to me, we're now faced with two problems," sighed Ethan. "How to find the other Ringwearers, and how to decide which ones to free. We can't realistically get to them all. For one thing, Oblivion would notice, just as he's no doubt noticed you two gone from his *radar* or whatever," he said, nodding at Alex and Payton.

"Finding them won't be a problem," Payton said, sheathing his sword and leaning back against the pillar again. "They will be wherever Oblivion is. They will be drawn to him by his will. All of them."

"That complicates things," Daniel said with a frown. "But Ethan's right—we can't hope to go after them all. So who do we pick? We can all think of Loci we would love to have on our side because they would be useful, or because they're our friends and we don't want them to suffer under Oblivion's thumb anymore. But we have to be objective about this; we're talking about the good of mankind here. The more Ringwearers we try to free, not to mention the longer we risk getting close to Oblivion, the more we risk losing everything. So who do we absolutely *need*?"

"Hector," Payton said quietly, not looking at anyone else.

"I'm not sure I see how—"

"For Alex," Payton interrupted.

Alex was touched at Payton's concern, despite their earlier tension. But then it wasn't the first time he'd surprised the rest of them.

Daniel swallowed and nodded, apparently unable to argue. Hector could very likely heal Alex completely, with a single touch. Though Alex wondered if the scars she bore on her stomach and arm would ever truly heal.

"All right then. Hector. Who else?" Daniel asked.

"Shouldn't we go for the most powerful?" Ethan asked. "They would be most useful in a fight."

"I wouldn't count out tacticians like Fletcher—*yes*, Fletcher," Lisa said, adding the last part when she saw skeptical looks around the room. "Like him or not, he's brilliant, and could probably see solutions the rest of us might never pick up on."

"I'd like to get Nora. She could help us cover our tracks," Ethan offered. "And that stuffy British woman, Mrs. Edeson. She controls willpower, right?"

Alex nodded.

"What about that electricity guy I saw you all with in Jerusalem . . . William?" Ethan asked.

"Wilhelm," Alex corrected.

"I don't know . . ." Lisa admitted, timidly. "I still feel like we're unprepared for this. Should we maybe take some time and rethink—"

"No one deserves being enslaved to Oblivion's will," Payton said with quiet resolve. "The notion of doing *nothing* is more offensive to me than any physical violation could ever be."

Payton's tone of voice had left little room for argument. Alex understood. He spoke from bitter personal experience, and if this was what he wanted to do . . .

"Alex?" Daniel asked. "What do you think? Is planning a mission like this foolhardy? What do *you* want to do?"

"Want?" Alex nearly laughed humorlessly. The word was alien and almost nonsensical to her. "You know, I'm not sure anyone has ever asked me that question before. Oblivion never asked what I wanted. *Life* has never been too concerned with my wants either."

When Daniel made a funny face in reaction to this dismal proclamation, Alex became incensed.

"Did you know," she said, painfully sitting up a little straighter, "that before I was Alex, I was a girl named Becky, born with a degenerative spinal condition that never allowed me to walk on my own? And that I am the only person alive to *willingly* undergo the Shift, knowing full well what would happen to me? Did you know that in fourteen years, I have not once laid eyes on my real family? And that I think about them every day and wonder what's become of them?"

The old man placed a calming hand on her shoulder, but she ignored the gesture.

"What do I want? I want to find my little brother Mark and sit him on my lap, like I used to, and listen to him giggle. I want to ask Morgan about the meaning of life, and listen to her soothing voice as she assembles all of the pieces for me. I want to walk hand-in-hand with Grant through an idyllic fairy-tale meadow, and then have a picnic under a cloudless sky . . .

"No one has *ever* cared about what I want, so why start now? Why are we sitting around talking about stupid things like what people want? For crying out loud, somebody get that disc of Morgan's and let's see what's on it already!"

35

Little was said in the wake of Alex's outburst. Finally, feeling awkward and self-conscious, Daniel excused himself from the table to retrieve the disc in question. Passing by Payton, he mumbled quietly, "You got a laptop or something?"

He then went to find his bag and fished the disc out of it. Returning to the table, Payton had already set up a small computer for him.

Daniel reseated himself and opened the drive, slipped in the disc, and closed the drive. The computer whirred to life, the only sound to be heard, and soon a video application launched. Frozen in the very first frame of the video was Morgan's face, very much alive and offering the slightest creases at the edges of her lips in a tiny smile.

Daniel's heart sank at the sight. He hadn't realized until now just how much her absence had been suffered. He felt very much like they were all children whose mother had passed away, and now they were trying to find their way on their own, without her infinite wisdom and care to guide them.

He glanced around the table and saw that similar emotions were written on Lisa's and Alex's faces. Payton's expression was impossible to read, while Ethan, Tucker, and the old man—none of whom had ever met Morgan—stretched around to see the video without realizing the true significance of what they were taking part in.

Daniel placed his hand over the keyboard and paused there, reverentially, before finally clicking the cursor's button to select Play.

Morgan's image snapped to life. Daniel's free hand was soon covered by Lisa's, under the table. She squeezed tight.

"To whoever is watching this video," Morgan said in her gentle British clip, "and I hope that it is Julie, or perhaps Alex—the fact that you are watching this means that two things have probably occurred. First of all, I am most likely dead. If that is the case, I would ask that you do not grieve for me, please. I am sure it happened as it did for a reason, as I believe everything does. Though I do hope I went in the night while sleeping. Or better yet, *reading.*

"The second thing that has probably occurred is that something drastic and terrible has happened to my friend Grant Borrows. I would be very surprised if he is with you, listening to me now. You see, I have suspected for quite some time now that the Secretum's designs for Grant involved *altering* him in some fundamental way—remaking him once again, this time to serve their purposes.

"I pray that I am incorrect about this, and only *my* death has prompted the viewing of this video. In that case, then my greatest fears have been unfounded, and perhaps the events I fear the most will never play out. Grant, if you are there, watching this now, then I owe you an apology for keeping what I know to myself.

"Please allow me a moment to explain myself, and in time you may come to understand why I did not believe that anyone else was ready to know what I know. You see, it is my belief that whatever has happened to Grant—it was unavoidable. I believe that the Secretum's designs for Grant would eventually lead him down a very dark road—one that he could not turn away from, even with the very great power that he commands."

She cleared her throat and sat up straighter in her seat. Around the table as they were watching these last words from their friend, no one dared utter a sound. Lisa leaned into Daniel a little farther, her expression taut. He squeezed her hand back.

"If Grant is indeed dead," Morgan said, "then I suspect he has been replaced by someone or some*thing* of terrible, ferocious power. And I fully expect that this has been the work of the Secretum, playing itself out. Again, please allow me to emphasize that no matter how much willpower Grant possesses—and we all know he possesses a great deal of willpower—there was no way for him to avoid this fate. Invisible forces have been at work, bending him toward this purpose, since long before any of us were born.

"The day I first met Grant, I visited an old woman living in my facility named Marta. Marta had the peculiar ability to see eventualities, making her the closest thing to a prophet the world has seen in centuries. That day, she told me that Grant was, to use her words, 'part of something greater than all of us. Vast and powerful, it reaches back through the fabric of history to the very beginning of time. Those like him have been with us since it all began, in one form or another.'

"Some time later came the day of the firestorm over Los Angeles. It was that fateful day, when Grant squared off against his grandfather, that I believe we first got a glimpse of the true power of the Bringer. We all watched what happened as Grant lost himself to his grief over Hannah's death: The skies boiled and fire threatened to rain down upon us. While all of this was happening, Grant's grandfather kept goading him, pushing him to 'unleash the whirlwind,' as it were. It was on that day that I realized the Secretum wanted more than just Grant—much more. I came to believe, over time, that what we saw that day was merely the first stage of something much larger. If Grant is dead and he's been replaced, as I suspect, then you have probably seen that firestorm blossom into something much worse, something big and terrible enough to consume the whole world.

"I took my suspicions about the events of that day with me as I began a journey of learning all I could about the Secretum of Six, most especially its prophecies and plans. Since that time, I have become consumed and obsessed with discovering the secrets of the Secretum in the hopes of seeing if there is any way of undoing what would one day be done to Grant. I confess I cannot provide an answer to this question with any degree of certainty. But I have a theory that may be of help to you now.

"In my research and investigations, I found it very difficult to turn up any information about the Secretum of Six in historical records. I eventually realized that any references to their existence, their activities, their prophecies—all would be shrouded behind references to other peoples throughout history, other groups and organizations. It was a kind of code used by those few historians who knew that an organization like the Secretum existed, but had no name for them or proof of their existence.

"Looked at in this light, my research began to come together at last. Blessed as I am with perfect memory, all I had to do was cross-reference various records in my mind, and I came up with some answers, which I shall now share with you.

"I have discovered that there are precisely 299 Rings of Dominion, not counting the Seal of Dominion, the most powerful of the Rings that's currently worn by Grant Borrows. It's my belief that if used in concert, by 299 Ringwearers, the combined might of all of the Rings of Dominion *could* be enough to overcome Grant—or rather, whatever Grant has become.

"So as I'm sure you're coming to realize, the question facing you now is: How many of the Rings of Dominion are currently in use? I believe that all of them are. Well . . . *almost* all of them. My belief is that Grant was the last person to be given a Ring, so the other 299 were given out first. I know this conflicts with the sudden appearance of the Ringwearers in London who are calling themselves the Upholders of the Crown. They seemed to emerge after Grant was given the Seal of Dominion, and I have no explanation for this. But to the best of my knowledge, there are no missing or unused Rings. Or as I said before . . . *almost* none.

"You see, I may not be there with you, able to help you in what must now be done, but I do not leave you empty-handed. Hidden in the spine of the same book in which you found this disc, you will find a key to a safe-deposit box at the First National Bank branch in downtown Los Angeles—the one not far from Chinatown. Retrieve that box. Inside it you'll find nineteen unworn Rings of Dominion. If you think about it, you will remember when and how these Rings came to be in my possession.

"Before you face whatever it is that Grant has become—and I believe you *must* face him, for whatever the Secretum has brought forth this being to do, I am certain it is meant to undermine life as we know it—you must unite all 299. All outstanding Ringwearers must be found, and nineteen civilian souls must be willing to wear the remaining Rings. I leave this in your care—as my final gift to you."

Daniel sat back in his seat, the reality of Morgan's words sinking in. He was overwhelmed at the task that was now set before them.

"It is not my wish to leave you in despair or overwhelmed at the task that now faces you. And again I pray that my words are unnecessary, that Grant is listening to this recording now, and my fears are unfounded. I apologize for not revealing this information to you sooner, but I have my reasons for believing that none of you were yet ready to know all that I know. It's my intention, at the time of this recording, to reveal this information to Grant myself, over time. But I have decided to leave this recording in case anything should happen to me before then. It would be irresponsible of me to die on you without some record of this knowledge outlasting me.

"If Grant is gone, and you now face this enormous task without him, please take heart, my friends. There is light at the end of this road. If you were there, you may recall that I came to Grant around the same time I was undertaking this research into the Secretum, and I conveyed to him my belief that I'd 'figured everything out.' I was not exaggerating when I uttered these words.

"Whatever has happened to you, whatever has happened to the world—it is not the grand orchestrated masterpiece that the Secretum wants you to believe it is. Please hear me, my friends. I have read and studied nearly every word written by the hand of man, and I am absolutely convinced that there is meaning to this existence, that we are not here by chance. This conspiracy is but one volley in a war that has been waged for countless ages. The events unfolding around you are no work of prophetic genius, no matter what they tell you. It is a cheap imitation of truth. A pathetic fake.

"Stay true to one another, remember my words, and you will discover this for yourselves. The purpose for our lives is all around you, waiting for you to see it. We all have a part to play in the outcome of this struggle, and I trust every one of you will discover the part you are meant to play."

Daniel blinked when the video went black. That was an odd note to go out on. She didn't wish them luck, or even say good-bye.

Another thought occurred to him. "Morgan was a Ring-wearer too," he said to no one in particular. "We'll have to find her Ring, and someone to wear it."

"That makes twenty," Alex said, and there was a quaver to her voice. "Twenty Rings in need of wearers."

Daniel looked up and saw that both Alex's and Lisa's cheeks were wet. Lisa squeezed out of the round booth and walked away, a single hand covering her mouth.

36

Neither Alex nor Lisa could be coaxed into talking right away. So the choice was made to take one more pause before deciding what to do next. Each took the opportunity to get some additional rest, and then the group gathered one last time around the circular bench to finally begin formulating their plan.

The first thing decided—or rather, dictated—was that Alex would be joining the mission. And she would entertain no arguments against this. Her mind was made up, she was coming, and that was all there was to it. Anyone who wanted to try to stop her would find out what it feels like to cry uncontrollably for hours on end.

"So where *did* Morgan get those remaining unworn Rings?" Ethan asked, changing the subject.

Alex and Payton exchanged a look.

"The fire," he said.

Alex nodded in response, then turned to Ethan. "Morgan used to own some private property where Ringwearers could go to stay in safety. This was long before most of us knew much about the Rings or the Bringer, before Grant was Shifted and given his Ring. An enemy of the Loci set fire to the place. Most of the Ringwearers got out, but nineteen of them died in the blaze. Morgan gathered the Rings from their bodies, for safekeeping."

"So we'll find those at the bank," Daniel said. "We have two further tasks to overcome. Find wearers for the Rings and then intercept Oblivion's group to free as many Ringwearers as we possibly can. Obviously our end goal is to take Oblivion down before he can enact his endgame, but I think we're all agreed that these two tasks have to come first."

Everyone around the table nodded.

"So the question is," Daniel continued, "do we leave now for the Middle East and try to reach Oblivion's group before they reach their destination? Or do we head for Los Angeles first to get the extra Rings? Which is more important?"

"Oblivion."

"The Rings."

Payton and Alex had spoken simultaneously.

"The more Ringwearers we have going into this, the better our chances," Alex argued.

"If we don't get to Oblivion before he arrives at wherever he's going, then all of this is for naught," Payton countered.

"And just exactly what are *two* superpowered people supposed to do against the all-powerful Oblivion and his army of supers?" Alex shot back.

Payton withdrew his sword and threw it across the wide open training area behind him. It pierced the head of a fighting dummy, pinning it against the far wall.

"Use your imagination, love," Payton replied.

Alex's mouth was already open with a ready retort when Ethan jumped to his feet. "Let's make this simple!" he announced. "Billions of people's lives are on the line; we don't have the luxury of arguing. Personally, I agree with Alex, because . . . well, what if we get over there and realize there's no time to come all the way back for the Rings before we have to take Oblivion on? So . . . raise your hand if you think we should go get the Rings first?"

Everyone around the table raised their hands, except for Payton and Tucker.

"And if you think we should go after Oblivion *now*?"

No one raised their hands. Payton didn't have to; everyone knew where he stood. When Ethan looked curiously at Tucker, he said something under his breath about being unsure if his opinion counted.

"Los Angeles first, then," Daniel stated. "But who's going to wear the extra twenty Rings?"

There was silence at the table for a moment, then Ethan said, "I'll wear one."

The old man still had his right hand—his left was the missing one—but no one attempted to suggest that he should wear a Ring. He'd been through enough.

When no one else spoke, Daniel said that they would need to find some volunteers, as Morgan suggested, though none of them knew where said volunteers might be found. He ended the meeting with, "We should probably get going."

With that, everyone at the table began to rise.

"Wait," Tucker said. "What about weapons? We need to be armed."

"We do?" asked Lisa, uncertain.

Tucker stood to his feet. "Well *I* do," he replied.

"I don't like the idea of shooting at our friends," Alex said, as dubious as Lisa.

"Don't kid yourselves," Payton spoke with his gravelly, dead intonations. "We're talking about the fate of the entire world. It may well come down to *us* or *them*." As if that was the only argument required, he turned to Tucker and said, "There's a weapons room in the back—help yourself."

Tucker nodded. The old man motioned for Tucker to follow him; he would show the sergeant to the guns.

"Flesh wounds only," Ethan quietly reassured Alex.

"Get as much sleep as you can, all of you," Payton announced. "We leave as soon as everyone's had a chance to rest."

Tucker and the old man, who had frozen on their way to the armory, turned and resumed walking. When no one was looking, Lisa snuck away and followed them.

"So. What's your story?"

"Sorry?" Tucker replied, as he opened the double-door cabinets that revealed a surprising variety of weaponry, from blades and staffs to crossbows, pistols, and shotguns.

"You're a cut-and-dried military officer," Lisa explained.

"Enlisted," he corrected her.

"Whatever. Point is, what's your part in all this?"

"Ethan," he replied. "He saved my life."

"Oh," Lisa said, nodding. "So it's like one of those 'life debt' things, between you and him?"

Tucker looked confused. "Not really."

"Then why are you here?"

"I'm here to fight the bad guys, ma'am," he replied. "I have a son, Jake. He's twelve. And the world isn't safe for him to grow up in. Ethan promised me a chance to change that. Way he tells it, we're 'operating outside of time.' What kind of father would I be if I didn't do everything I could to ensure that my son gets to have a future?"

"Only in this case, that's not actually a metaphor," Lisa mused.

Tucker shrugged. "Ask *you* a question?"

Lisa shrugged. "Knock yourself out."

"You really think you all can do this? Free the rest of your friends and take on this Oblivion character? Because I've seen firsthand what he can do, and I don't know of a power anywhere in this world that can stop him."

"We've made a habit of defying the odds."

"I hope so," Tucker said, his face grim. "I'm career military, ma'am, joined right out of high school. Been doing this a long time. One thing I know about going to battle against vastly superior numbers—it's that casualties are a given. It's the first thing they teach you: Whoever has the most soldiers with the biggest guns, wins. And I haven't seen anything in your arsenal capable of even stubbing this enemy's toe."

"We'll surprise you," Lisa said.

"Unless you do . . . none of us has a chance of surviving this."

INTERREGNUM

"So I have a temper!" Grant tried to shout, though the sound of his voice still refused to echo through the emptiness. "So do lots of people! And there were good reasons whenever I lost it! What difference does it make now?"

His doppelganger eyed him intently. "It makes a difference when you give in to it and allow it to influence your decisions and actions. Every choice carries weight and consequence, Grant."

Grant paused, his thoughts racing. He looked around in the darkness, but he wasn't trying to focus on anything in particular. He was thinking back over the events of his life.

"I don't disagree," he said tentatively.

"Good," replied his duplicate. "Because now we're coming to what I *really* brought you here to discuss. Your choices are not the only ones that influence the fate of the world. Every choice made by every person alive has the potential to have positive effects or negative effects on the human race. Would you agree?"

Grant thought a moment. "I suppose."

"Then would you say that the positive choices outweigh the negative, or vice versa?"

"I . . . I don't know."

His twin smiled, amused. "It was not a rhetorical question, Grant. Give me your honest opinion."

Grant frowned and gave in to the loaded question, though he couldn't figure out where this was going. "Then I suppose there have been more negative effects upon humanity based on people's choices throughout history."

Mirror Grant began to walk slowly, circling him like a college professor offering a particularly insightful lecture. "Then here is the question to end all questions, Grant Borrows. This is the reason you are here, with me.

"I want you to think about the damage that has been done to mankind because of the choices of men and women. Think of the suffering, the anguish, the loss. All of it, throughout human history. Wars waged throughout the ages, using ever-escalating weaponry that is crafted to bring about newer and more efficient ways of killing the enemy. The horrors and atrocities of Hitler's concentration camps. Barbarism. Pornography and the sex trade. Slavery. Organized crime. Genocide. The list goes on.

"Think about these things, and ask yourself . . . Wouldn't the world be better off if humanity lacked free will? If people did not have the ability to choose their actions for themselves, but were *forced* to behave as they should?"

Grant didn't answer immediately. He retreated inside himself, digging deep for an answer to his twin's question that would be honest and real, but wouldn't be pessimistic. He found that he couldn't come up with one.

"I don't know how to answer that," he replied.

"Of course you do," his double said at once. "You just don't *want* to. Let me simplify it for you.

"Make it personal. Think back on your own life. All of the people who claimed to love you, but then abandoned you. Being dealt one hand after another that you neither chose for yourself nor wanted. Facing responsibilities that no one else on earth could possibly understand, as the most powerful man in the world. Losing the people you love the most. It's not right. It's not fair. You didn't ask for any of it, but it's what happened.

"Think about all that's happened to you, and all that's been done to you intentionally . . . And tell me why you fight. Why do you try so hard to help others who are in need? Why do you fight for the rest of the world, when the world has done nothing but bring you pain?"

Grant hated this. He wanted to grab this twisted duplicate of himself—whoever he was—and throttle him for making him think about this.

Truth was, this was not a new question for Grant. It plagued his thoughts often, even as he was fighting to save the world. Did they really *deserve* to be saved? Was the world even worth fighting for?

He had to admit, even if it was only to himself, that sometimes he wondered if playing the hero was worth it. Because that was all he was doing—pretending. Posing as the figure they needed to believe could save them from themselves. When the truth was that he was just as flawed and lost and fragile as they were.

Had he actually made that much of a difference as the public's hero, Guardian?

"I guess," Grant replied at last, "I fight for them because I don't think anyone should have to suffer. And if I can alleviate anyone's pain, then I want to."

Mirror Grant stopped circling him and stopped right in front of him. He placed a hand in the center of Grant's chest, and Grant felt a prickling sensation that quickly turned to intense, painful heat, which he could not pull away from.

Holding his hand in place there upon Grant's chest, the double leaned in close to Grant's ear, and whispered one word.

"Liar."

37

Los Angeles

Chinatown sat poised on the brink of implosion.

No longer day yet never fully night, fierce billowing clouds had settled dusk permanently over the dingy streets of downtown Los Angeles. Oriental lanterns dipped low over North Broadway where it ran straight through Chinatown. On one side of the street stood an unblinking line of Chinese nationals, perfectly still. On the other waited a gang of terrifying-looking men and women, with wild eyes and flesh smeared with blood.

Between them stood Alex, Payton, Daniel, Lisa, Ethan, Tucker, and their handless friend. They hadn't asked to be here, and they would gladly leave now if not for the fact that the First National Bank and the precious contents held in its vault were blocked by this violence. Ethan had no idea what had transpired to bring about this confrontation, but he realized they'd stumbled into something dangerous.

At least one skirmish had already broken out, because both sides of the conflict were battered, few without some sort of bruise, scrape, or ripped clothing. Many of them were still breathing hard. All held weapons of one kind or another.

No words were spoken or movements made by the Chinese, their faces both old and young, a mixture of dour and dispassionate. A variety of guns, knives, and bats were held in their hands. Their silent message was louder than any words could transmit.

Get. Out.

The gang on the other side of the street looked like deranged figures of all races from some post-apocalyptic zombie movie. Faces, arms, and hands were smeared with dried blood. The red fluid had been used to draw vulgar symbols and crude line drawings everywhere their skin was visible. The clothes they wore were shredded around the cuffs. But nothing about their appearance was as disturbing as the objects carried in their hands.

Instead of knives or guns, they carried bones. Human arms, legs, jaws, even skulls—anything sharp or big enough to do damage to a living body. The bones they carried were as bloody as they were, some of them stripped clean of muscle and tissue, others still dripping with ligaments, nerves, and meat. Their eyes were set deep within their flesh; their mouths recalled those of rabid wolves.

"English?" Ethan called out, facing the Chinatown residents.

A moment passed in silence as the Chinese men and women stared at him with disdain, unmoving and unspeaking. But the line parted, and a woman stepped out into the street to approach Ethan.

"I speak English. Yen Xue is my name."

"I'm Ethan. It's nice to meet you, Xue."

Tired creases formed around the corners of her lips as she eyed Ethan thoughtfully. He understood; she likely hadn't met many Westerners who knew that Chinese names placed the family name ahead of the given name.

An older man with a self-important presence and authority in his every inflection said something to the female in Cantonese, rapid-fire. His meaning was clear, even to the outsiders.

The woman named Xue was in her late thirties and dressed head to toe in brightly colored traditional Chinese attire. Her dark hair was tied in a large, tight bun. Sandals peeked out from beneath her dress, sheltering her feet.

She didn't face the elder gentleman as she replied to him with something equally severe that Ethan could not understand. A hint of distaste tainted her lovely features when she replied to him. And when she spoke to Ethan again, she became more cordial, her voice carrying virtually no accent. "You are friends of Guardian. I saw you on the news with him," she said, shooting a knowing look at Alex. "But where is he now?"

Alex couldn't hold Xue's piercing gaze. Ethan spoke instead. "I'm afraid he's dead."

She turned downcast. "Then I fear the madness that has come to our streets will destroy more than Chinatown."

"Why are those people here?" Ethan gestured at the gang on the other side of the street.

"They sacrifice the innocent," Xue explained in an undertone, "believing they may appease the gods who have brought the darkness and fire and destroyed the soil. They ingest their victims so the blood of the innocent may cleanse them, inside and out. I do not know what specific purpose has brought these dangerous men here, but they appear to be . . . hungry."

The older man behind her said something else, which Xue ignored.

"*He's* not glad to see us," Payton interjected.

Xue took a step back and gestured dutifully to the older man. "This is Yen Wei, my uncle. He is a venture capitalist by trade, though he owns much more in this city than buildings, if you follow my meaning." A slight frown played at her lips, yet the grace and dignity with which she carried herself remained intact. "He is a powerful man; cross him at your peril. He has strong opinions about what is happening to the world. He knows who you are, and he believes that you are servants of the evil one."

This instigated a rallying cry by the cultists, who let out unholy yells and screams that sounded like a pack of wild animals preparing to attack.

"You have not come to help us," Xue inferred. There was no question in her voice, nor was there judgment or disappointment. "So what *has* brought you here?"

Ethan's mind spun fast. "Guardian died trying to prevent all this from happening to the world. We're trying to finish what he started. But to do that, we need to reach a safe-deposit box in the bank up ahead."

"I know this building," Xue replied. "My uncle owns it. I could get you inside."

"We'll get inside, love," said Payton, "one way or another."

"But we can't leave you to this," Ethan finished.

"My uncle will never accept your help," she said. Nonetheless, she spoke to her uncle in Cantonese. He replied to her and an argument ensued, with each successive statement growing in volume.

Xue turned to face Ethan once more.

"What did he say?" Ethan asked, noting with anxiety that two dozen men near her uncle had just taken an imposing step forward.

"He is a fool. He said that death smiles on you."

And as a cry arose that seemed to erupt from everywhere at once, North Broadway exploded.

38

When he roused, Daniel heard only ringing. He was in the middle of the street, Lisa facedown on top of him. He tried to sit up to check her, but found his equilibrium too unstable to move.

"LISA!!" he screamed.

He was sure his mouth had formed the word, certain his throat had vocalized it. But he'd heard nothing. Nothing but the ringing.

Daniel raised a hand, wiped the sweat from his brow. Blood dripped from his hand, thanks to a gash above his wrist.

He looked around. Chinatown burned, ablaze in billowing fire. The blast seemed to originate from the cultists' side of the street, so there were only a few dozen of them still alive. The Chinese had fared better; the elder man named Yen Wei still stood exactly where Daniel had last seen him. His niece was on the ground next to Ethan.

Lisa moved. Her head lifted until she saw the position she was lying in, directly on top of him. Their eyes made contact, and she almost smiled.

She started speaking, her mouth moving slowly, but Daniel still couldn't hear.

His arms had wrapped themselves around her. He wasn't sure how that had happened, but even amid this chaos, he had little inclination to disentangle himself from her.

She leaned forward and kissed him. It was an action of desperation, of panic. Daniel welcomed it, lifting his head off the ground and mashing his lips into her with passion and intensity. She pressed back even harder, throwing her arms around him and closing her eyes. Like him, she was losing herself to the moment . . .

A tingle in the back of Daniel's neck made him open his eyes. Payton stood over the two of them, an impatient grimace all he had to offer.

He offered a hand and pulled the two of them to their feet. Lisa cradled her left arm in a way that told Daniel she'd hurt her wrist. Sprained if lucky, broken if not.

Two hundred feet away, a residual blast went off, the result of the blaze reaching something highly flammable. It could have been any number of things in a densely populated area like this—the gas line to a stove, a kerosene heater in somebody's apartment. Daniel recoiled slightly from it, and was comforted only by the realization that he'd *heard* the explosion.

Payton vanished and Daniel caught sight of him a few hundred feet away, helping to pull an old woman from a burning building. Ethan was getting up from the ground and helping Xue to do the same. Poor Alex at first looked unconscious again, but he saw her fingers twitch and her head roll to the side. The old man without a hand was next to her, patting her gently to awaken her. Sergeant Tucker was mixed into the Chinese crowd, trying to save lives.

"I told you to kill them!" a commanding voice shouted. "Kill them all!"

Daniel turned. It was Yen Wei, shouting to his men, some of whom were still on the ground.

Yen Xue was on her feet. "Uncle? Did *you* do this?" She gestured at the fires burning Chinatown all around them.

"You are too young to understand!"

"This is because of China, isn't it?" she said slowly. "Because of the quarantine?"

She was referring, of course, to the Zhuan Virus. It was one of the first natural disasters to break out a few months ago, killing well over a million of the nation's population, and because of it America and the rest of the world had closed their doors to China. Cut them off. Protests erupted across the world, but the policy never changed.

The fact that the virus had mutated and not killed anyone in more than two months had changed few people's minds that the world had turned its back on China and left her people to die alone.

Enough of this madness, Daniel thought, uncharacteristic adrenaline surging through him. Seeing an opportunity, he stepped away from Lisa, reached inside his jacket pocket, and melted into the pandemonium surrounding them.

"The world has gone mad," Wei replied to his niece. "We need to get their attention. Remind them that we are still here. We exist and we will not be forgotten!"

"Even if it means killing ourselves!?" Xue screamed in his face.

He turned away from her, back to his men. "I said kill the intruders! NOW!!"

His men moved fast, at least two each taking positions around Alex, Payton, Lisa, Tucker, Ethan, and the old man. Payton was already in striking position, and Alex settled her shoulders, eying her first emotional target.

Daniel appeared behind the old patriarch and buried the muzzle of a pistol in the old man's ear. "We haven't formally met," he said, loud enough for the whole area to hear.

The surrounding men turned on Daniel, each tensing like a cobra.

"My friends and I are trying to save the world, and we need to get into that bank to do it. Now, I'm sorry about the quarantine in China, but you can't hold us responsible for that. So you're going to call your men off, or I'm going to blow your brains all over this pavement."

The old man's eyes shifted sideways, and he smiled. "I am one of the most powerful men in this city. I own a third of downtown Los Angeles. I have no interest in helping you without something in return. But currency has lost its value in this brave new world. What can you offer me?"

"How about the continued use of your mind?" Daniel replied. He pointed his free hand at Alex, who was watching them both, expression grim. "*She* can fill it with nightmares so potent you'd commit suicide to be free of them. Or maybe you'd like to keep your entourage?" He pointed at Payton. "That man is the *scariest human being alive*. He could kill every one of your men in under a minute with nothing but a very thin sword."

"Your friends and their powers do not frighten me."

Daniel rounded on Yen Wei and mashed the muzzle of the gun into his left eye socket. "Then how would you feel about losing your own life? Because the man holding a gun to your head right now is more dangerous than anyone else here. I have no superpowers . . . but I am a murderer."

He thumbed the hammer back and pressed the gun even harder into the old man's closed eye.

A beat.

Yen Wei spat on him. "You search for hope in a hopeless world. Waging a war that has already been lost. You are fools, all of—"

His words were cut off by the end of a sword protruding from the front of his chest. He gulped, the sword was pulled free, and he fell to the ground.

Daniel's gun hand fell. "You didn't have to kill him!"

"I punctured no major organs," Payton replied, emotionless. "He'll live. But we won't if we don't get to the bank. Now."

Daniel turned, as did everyone else, at the sound of an approaching mob. There was another group of blood-smeared cultists now between them and the bank. Coming this way.

“These people . . .” said Alex, clutching her stomach, “if we leave them now—what’s left of them—they’ll be killed by that mob.”

“*Everyone* will be killed if we don’t stop Oblivion!” Payton shouted, raising his voice for the first time in a long time. “This is not an argument, Alex, so don’t bother! Get it through your head: *He has to be stopped!*”

The silent tension within the group was augmented only by the sound of crackling fire and the distant thumping of approaching feet.

“Can you really do it? Are you capable of stopping the evil one?” Xue broke the silence, ignoring her uncle on the ground and his moans of pain.

Ethan faced her. “We’re going to try.”

She hesitated, but only a moment. “Come with me. I know another way.”

The mob of cultists was building, over a hundred of them now, and they held death in their hands and in their hearts.

“You heard the lady!” Ethan called out to his friends, ending the discussion, brandishing his gun and pulling its slide. “Load ’em if you got ’em.”

39

The group's roundabout trip to the bank, lit by the blazing fires set to Chinatown, took them to an employee entrance through an adjacent building that patrons would have never known about.

The luck they'd had in making it to the bank didn't hold. Once inside, Xue led them to a set of stairs that would lead them to the sub-basement that held the vault. The cultists outside took immediate notice of their activities and used the bones they wielded as weapons to break through the building's glass front doors.

"Go," Payton said, stopping at the top of the stairs. "I'll hold them here."

Wordlessly, the old man, who was hefting a large duffle bag on his back, dropped the sack on the ground near the entrance to the stairs and retrieved a shotgun from inside. The bag's zipper now open, it was easy to see its full contents, comprised of a huge stockpile of guns from Payton's secret arsenal.

He nodded at Payton, grim, as he hoisted it one-handed against his shoulder. No one bothered to argue with his obvious decision.

Sergeant Tucker stepped out as well, digging into the duffle bag for an automatic rifle. "Rambo Senior and I will guard the door."

"I should stay—" Ethan began.

Tucker shook his head. "No, you go with them. In case we fail . . ." He didn't need to finish the thought. Should anyone get through their makeshift blockade, Ethan would be the only trained soldier there to help them.

Xue led Alex, Ethan, Daniel, and Lisa down into the dark basement.

"I'm sorry about your uncle," Ethan said quietly.

"I'm sorry he's my uncle," Xue replied. "I have interned at many of his companies over the last five years. My parents insisted. It was a daily lesson on the dangers of power."

"It corrupts."

"Yes," she said. "It corrupts."

They found the vault door already open, ripped canvas bags containing money strewn about the floor. It probably seemed like a good idea at the time to whatever employee or thief had broken in. Only now it had become largely worthless since the global economy had collapsed in Oblivion's wake.

Inside the enormous vault, the five of them split up to hunt for Morgan's safe-deposit box. They could only hope that whoever had robbed the vault hadn't been able to access any of the boxes.

The vault was poorly lit without power, with only battery-powered emergency floodlights casting angled spotlights in sporadic locations.

A deep clang reverberated throughout the vault.

"What was that?" Lisa's voice called out from the dimness.

"It sounded like the vault door," Xue replied.

"We're not alone in here!" Daniel shouted, and Ethan heard the sound of him chambering a round in his pistol.

He was right, Ethan decided. The five of them had been locked inside the vault, and probably *with* some of the cultists, who had somehow gotten past the others upstairs. He had no time to think about that last part.

"Payton will get us out," Alex said. "Just find that box."

"What number are you looking for again?" Xue called out.

"2342," Daniel replied with a raised voice.

Ethan looked down. He saw it.

Before be could announce the good news, all sound was drowned out by a great shout right behind him. It was an unearthly cry, a roar of death.

"They're here!" he shouted. He whipped out his pistol and fired a few shots in the dark before he was on the ground and all light had been blocked out by the bodies crashing into him.

Alex's heart thumped harder, sensing the bloodlust that had suddenly broken out in the vault. There was so much of it, she couldn't get a bead on how many of them there were.

"Ethan!" she screamed. He had the key to the box; without that key, they had no chance.

She ran, trying to zero in on Ethan's emotions. A typical adrenaline junkie, he gave off an unusual emotional fingerprint during a fight—something like giddy excitement.

But not now.

Her empathy failing her, she decided to just follow the noise. She maintained a safe distance, concentrating on filling the minds of the cultists with peace and contentment. But it was difficult to block out the intense savagery these men and women gave off.

That was her last thought before one of them bashed her in the back of the head with a heavy bone.

Ethan was being battered by sharp-edged bones and grappling for control of his gun as he heard more footsteps approaching. He angled his head and saw Xue's sandaled feet run into view.

"Take this!" He caught sight of her briefly and tossed her the key to the safe-deposit box.

He put a hand up to protect his face while managing to strike another man who was pinning him to the ground. One of them bit into his forearm and tore off a mouthful of flesh. He screamed involuntarily.

Someone stomped on his hand, and he turned loose of the gun reflexively. It fell away from his reach, clanking against the tile floor.

From somewhere nearby, he heard a jangling sound, followed by the loud clap of something heavy hitting the ground. Ethan turned his head to the side while more blows fell, and his eyes met an upturned safe-deposit box that had fallen to the floor. A handful of tiny golden items were freed from the box and rolled in all directions.

"What is this?" cried Xue's frantic, confused voice.

Ethan made a split-second decision. It was a terrible risk, but he was low on options.

He strained hard against his attackers and spun on his back until his left hand was able to land on one of the objects rolling across the floor.

Alex had filled her attacker's mind with regret and gotten to her feet when there was a bright crackle of light. She turned to the mound of bloodied people on the ground, beneath which she knew was Ethan, and saw the piercing light break through the spaces between them, shining out in all directions in blinding beams.

The light faded and then another glow, an underwater-like shimmer, caught her attention. It came from her Ring, and it was gone as fast as it had appeared.

She looked back up just in time to see Ethan's attackers fly backward in a wave surrounding him. He stood, his body bruised and ragged, his arm awash in blood. Though he looked no different, Alex knew exactly what had just happened.

Ethan Cooke was a Ringwearer.

40

Ethan guessed he looked like a grisly mess, but he couldn't help himself. He grinned, poised triumphant over a dozen cultists.

He looked down at his arms, which hadn't changed, yet he regarded them as if new. "I could really get used to this."

Alex looked at him curiously. He expected her to reprimand him for throwing caution to the wind and taking on one of the Rings of Dominion. Instead, she asked, "What, did you get superstrength?"

Ethan was almost speechless with glee. "I uh . . . I think so, yeah."

She scowled. "I hate you."

Daniel appeared, Lisa at his side, and marched up to Ethan. He placed something against the open bite wound on his arm. He recoiled in pain, saw what it was: a fragment from the Dominion Stone. "Just to be safe," Daniel said.

Another cult member lunged at them just then with an especially thick femur polished like a police baton. Ethan put up a hand to block the bone and his hand smashed into it and it broke into pieces. He almost laughed as he clutched the attacker by the shirt and threw him into a wall of safe-deposit boxes as if the man were a wet noodle.

Alex gathered up the fallen Rings with Xue's help while Ethan made fast work of the remaining enemies. That done, he marched to the thick, oval vault door, pressed finger grooves into the shiny metal, and used them as grips to rip the door free from its foundation.

"So how is superstrength a mental power?" Lisa asked, exasperated. "And why am I always the one who asks that?"

Daniel shrugged. "The mind regulates every function of the body. I'd guess that Ethan's body chemistry was altered by his brain, magnifying the density of his muscles, bones, et cetera."

Lisa's irritation disappeared. It was replaced by a cute smile and eyes that stared dreamily into his. "Is there anything you can't explain?"

He returned the gesture, a longing expression gazing into her hungry eyes.

"Seriously, you two," Alex said, rolling her eyes. She turned to Ethan. "Let's go, Thor. You lead the way."

What was that?

Who was that?

Oblivion stopped walking. He'd felt it. But then, just as fast, it was gone.

Still, in that moment he'd taken all he'd needed. A new Ringwearer. One of the humans had put on a Ring of Dominion. Ethan Cooke, former FBI agent, born in Atlanta, Georgia, thirty-one human years ago.

But how could this plain man have encountered one of the Rings, and then known what would happen when he put it on? That should be impossible. Almost all of the Rings were accounted for, anyway.

Unless he'd found one of the Rings belonging to Alex or Payton, after they died. What kind of brainless man would dare . . . ?

But no, that was not possible either. Because one of the thoughts in Ethan Cooke's mind he'd overheard before losing contact was a fleeting glimpse at Alex, who stood nearby, alive and well.

Oblivion had *felt* her die. Or thought he had when his connection to her severed. But what if she hadn't died? What if they'd found a way to escape his control?

If Alex was still alive, then Payton could still be alive as well, and if that was the case . . .

Then the humans had found a way to unbind him from his army.

And the freed Ringwearers would be coming. Some kind of misguided attempt to intervene in his work.

A thought back to his brief connection to Ethan Cooke confirmed his suspicion with a sliver of thought, anticipation, excitement . . .

Let them come. Hope would only make their deaths sweeter.

The final leg of Oblivion's journey was at hand; he and his army would enter Israel soon. He remembered previous occasions when he had been to the tiny nation. One notable instance had brought him to the slaughter of seventy thousand humans at one time. It was the closest thing Oblivion had to a fond memory.

The rebel fools believed they could stop him.

He had butchered countless of their kind, and no one could do a thing to hinder him.

He was unstoppable.

The others had held their own against the attacking cultists, and with Ethan and Alex coming in as backup, that fight soon ended without further injury for any of their team, Assessing their situation, all agreed Los Angeles was too unstable to stay in much longer and voted on a quick Conveyor ride back to Payton's home in Arizona where they decided it best to spend the "night," catching some sleep before heading for the Middle East, and Oblivion.

They returned with one more member than they'd arrived. Her home destroyed and her one living relative a monster, Yen Xue opted to leave with them. By way of explanation, she merely stated that actions speak louder than words in her culture, and that was that.

Exhaustion finally caught up with everyone, and before long they were sleeping. But Alex soon awoke to the sounds of violence.

Quickly reading the emotions of everyone in the building, she knew that their hiding place hadn't been compromised. There was no sense of danger within these walls.

She rose from the upstairs bed and descended the metal stairs quietly so as not to rouse anyone. The source of the commotion was the clanging of metal on metal, fists thumping against vinyl padding, and feet shuffling across thatched, dojo-style training mats. Much of the sound came in the form of grunting and hard breathing.

Payton was momentarily visible in his special training area, then disappeared again. Alex approached guardedly, watching as Payton slashed, sliced, and thrust with precisely measured moves that reduced the room's contents to bits and shards. Payton's body and clothes were drenched in sweat that dripped to the ground like a rainstorm.

Alex settled in a seat well outside of the training area. Impressed with the meticulous nature of Payton's thrusts and parries, she realized he never did anything without a very specific reason. He didn't eat, walk, speak, or sleep unless it served whatever purpose he was currently pursuing. And here, shortly before they would be leaving to face the greatest threat the world had ever known, he was honing his skills with a ferocity she'd not seen from him before.

At long last, his bursts of speed ended, and Payton laid the flat side of his silver samurai sword against the back of his opposite hand. He stood perfectly still, breathing hard and soaking wet, his eyes searching every inch of the blade for . . . Well, Alex didn't know what he was looking for, exactly. Stains? Rust? Imperfections? He protected that weapon like his life depended on it, and she knew that in his line of work, it almost always did.

Silence fell as his exertions came to an end, and it struck Alex that he was the one thing in the entire room still standing.

"Hope you've got another one of these training rooms somewhere," she said softly.

Payton looked up as if noticing her for the first time, but Alex knew this was just a formality. He always seemed to know a person's actions before they did themselves.

"You should be sleeping," he said, returning his gaze to the sword.

"It's overrated," she replied. "Besides, I just have nightmares about Oblivion, about what it was like under his control. You ever have nightmares?"

Payton shot her a fleeting glance that was all the confirmation she needed.

Alex wanted to ask if he missed Morgan, but she knew better than to go down that road. He was still examining his sword like it was an appendage, a piece of himself he couldn't live without. "So . . . is war really our only option?" she asked.

He offered no reply. Instead, he moved across the room and retrieved a towel with which he polished the sword. It was a ritual; he'd done this many times before, Alex noted.

She sighed, her thoughts wandering. "Payton . . . Do you ever find yourself reflecting back on the person you were before the Shift?"

"As a rule," he said quietly, wiping his face with the towel, "I try not to."

"Why not?"

"Because I have nothing worth looking back upon."

"I was disabled," Alex said, not knowing why she was saying it out loud. "A paraplegic, and a burden on my family that they didn't deserve."

"Then you have nothing worth reflecting on either."

"But that's just it. It was painful and it was hard and I was so ashamed of myself for bringing so much grief to everyone who loved me . . . but sometimes I miss that life so much that I *ache*."

Alex stopped speaking, waiting for him to comment. When he didn't, she said, "Come on, there has to be something about your old life that was good, something you miss."

He shook his head, still refusing to look at her. "There's nothing."

"Then I pity you for a life without joy, or love," Alex said defiantly.

"I pity *you* for a life blinded by love," he shot back. "Love is an illusion. A chemical process. Ultimately it's futile."

"A chemical process, huh? If that's how you define love, what's your take on killing?"

"Dealing death is necessary to the survival of the collective population. Not everyone has the stomach or the capacity for it. But some people are too dangerous to be allowed to live, and if they are not removed from society, then the world will spiral into anarchy. As it is in danger of doing now."

"I won't let this be done to him," Alex said, suddenly all business. "Not Grant. They can't just rape his identity like this. He deserves better."

"Yes, he does," Payton replied. "But it's done. And he's gone."

"No," was all Alex could say.

Payton looked up at the ceiling as if trying to figure out how to explain a complex concept to a little child. "He's gone, Alex. Grant is gone. Forever. The thing that killed him is wearing his face. And I'm going to destroy it."

Alex let out a long, slow breath. "I know what you're saying is true, but what I feel won't go away. I can't turn it on and off like a switch. I look at the abomination that is Oblivion, and some part of me still sees Grant."

Payton sheathed his sword and cast his eyes toward the wreckage he'd created.

"I don't want to hurt you, Alex," he said. "Don't force me to."

Alex didn't hesitate. "I meant what I said before. You try to hurt him, and I swear I'll stop you."

"And I'll cut down *anything* that gets in my way."

For the first time, their eyes locked on each other, just for a moment.

"I'm gonna save him," Alex said.

"I'm going to kill him," Payton said.

INTERREGNUM

GRANT SCREAMED.

The heat pouring into his chest was searing, burning his very soul. He had never felt anything more visceral, more *real.* His eyes were closed tight and he was screaming, but his arms and legs had gone limp, and there was nothing he could do to stop the flow of white-hot pain.

Still his twin spoke to him, and he heard and understood every word, over his own screaming and writhing.

"Face the truth, Grant. You're not altruistic. You were never a hero. Not really. 'Guardian' helped people for his own self-serving motives . . . just like you did everything else."

"That's not true!" Grant yelled over the pain. "I wanted to help people! I wanted to do what was right!"

Mirror Grant smirked. "At best, you were a selfish loner who went around 'doing good' because he craved the love no one else ever gave him. So you sought it out from the public at large—it's their *gratitude* you coveted more than anything. Because even though it's fleeting and even though it's not sincere love in the way that you long for . . . their adoration *feels* to you like a close enough approximation of a parent's unconditional love."

The pain increased tenfold, to an intensity Grant didn't think he could withstand. He shrieked and flailed, but it was worthless.

Long past the point where he felt he could stand no more, the other man's hand left his chest and the pain subsided at last. The duplicate turned his back and walked away.

Grant had no need to breathe here in this dark place, wherever it was. But he was bent over double, clutching at the residual pain in his chest, and he felt hatred boil up inside him until he could hold it back no longer.

He lunged.

Wrapping his arms around the other man's waist, he tackled him, pulling him to the ground, and he began punching, kicking, pulling, tearing, clawing at his double with everything within him.

"I HATE YOU!!" he screamed. *"I hate you I hate you I hate you!"*

"Sticks and stones, Grant!" the other man shouted back. "You're not the first to ever tell me that!"

The two men became intertwined, fighting hard against each other and rolling about on the utter absence of ground.

"Just admit it, Grant!" the mirror man shouted. "I want to hear you say it! Mankind's multitude of poor choices has made the world a hopeless cause, and in the end there's no real reason to fight for it! SAY IT!"

"NO!!" Grant roared, trying to poke the other man's eyes out, then resorted to beating against his head, shoulders, and chest with both hands.

"You wouldn't lift a finger to help anyone if there wasn't something in it for you, and you know it!" the other man shouted at him. "Such a shame too, since they need you now more than ever . . ."

Grant hit him and kicked him and scratched at this hated creature like he was nine years old again, still scrapping in the dirt with Finch Bailey.

"And what about . . . *her?*" the duplicate man asked knowingly. "We both know your only interest in the opposite sex extends no further than what's in it for you! You could never love a woman like Alex unselfishly!"

Grant launched himself at this enemy anew, pulling at his hair and trying to rip the skin off of him. "That's not true! It's *not* true! *It's not* . . ."

41

Central Israel

"Stand down, or be killed," said the heavily accented voice.

Ethan hated being on the wrong end of a gun. Especially the business end of an assault rifle five feet away with a nervous Israeli soldier holding a noticeably quivering finger on the trigger. The young fighter blinked hard to see through the sweat rushing down his forehead; the motion added more of a tic to the finger that was already twitching, struggling not to pull the rifle's trigger.

A wildfire raged ten feet to Ethan's right. Aside from the heavy breathing coming from the small Israeli barricade and the occasional soft clanking of their weaponry, the hissing of the fire was the only sound in this lifeless desert under the dark sky.

"Move out of our way," Ethan replied in kind, "and we won't have to cripple you."

The soldier looked sideways at his fellows, trying not to betray a nervous weariness. Ethan wondered if this skeleton crew manning a makeshift outpost so close to Jerusalem had somehow lost its commanding officer. He almost felt sorry for the young soldiers; they were only doing their duty as best they could.

But there wasn't time for this.

"You will stand down!" the young soldier suddenly shouted with halfhearted conviction.

At this, Ethan took a big step forward until the rifle's muzzle was inches from his chest. Quickly, he grasped the rifle midway down its barrel with a single hand.

The soldier was stunned momentarily, but then tightened his two-handed grip on the weapon as if preparing to wrestle for control of it. His finger touched the trigger . . .

Ethan smiled lopsidedly at the boy. Then he squeezed.

The black metal crumpled in his hand like putty. When he let go, the front end of the barrel looked as though it had melted, bent in a smooth arc toward the ground.

Safeties were clicked off from the other soldiers' weapons, and every gun was trained on Ethan.

Yen Xue stepped forward from the group, which was situated more than fifty feet behind Ethan. She approached quickly yet walking with grace and dignity.

As Ethan continued to stare down the Israeli soldiers, Xue extended her right hand in their direction, the nearby wildfire glinting off something on one of her fingers.

The soldier on the far right end of the barricade gasped. His rifle had flown free from his grip, whirling through the air until Xue caught it lengthwise in her right hand as if it were a baseball flying into a mitt. A moment later, twenty-three more rifles wrenched themselves from their wielders' grasps and flew at the rifle Xue still held in the air as if a powerful magnet.

A few of the dazed soldiers recovered quickly and tried pulling out long bowie knives, but it was a futile gesture. Soon these too were soaring through the air until they clung stubbornly to Xue's rifle, held aloft in her hand as if it were nothing more than a feather.

"My friend has a way with metal," Ethan remarked. He turned and pointed behind him at Sergeant Tucker, who stood at the edge of the crowd. "*He* has a way with . . . well, you're happier not knowing. Time to give it up, fellas."

The officer up front, the one who'd first targeted Ethan, motioned to his men. As one, they stood at ease.

Ethan glanced back at the group and they soon joined him. As the others were walking past these depowered military men, Ethan looked once more at the young man in charge.

"Also . . . We're taking your truck. We need it to save the world. You understand."

Fifteen miles southeast of Tel Aviv, not far from the West Bank border, the group split into two teams.

Payton, Alex, and the old man waited atop a small dune, fairly close to—of all things—a nice, not entirely unmodern housing development that did not match anyone's expectations of what might be found in a Middle Eastern country. Alex and Payton both knelt low, staring through binoculars in a northwesterly direction. Alex traded hers frequently back and forth with the old man.

A mile to the south, the others huddled by their commandeered truck parked between a row of tall, dying trees near a main northbound road. The trees seemed out of place amid the arid landscape, but there was a small village behind them; apparently the trees had been transplanted here as part of some sort of planned community. Ethan and Tucker hid behind tree trunks, scanning the northwestern horizon, also with binoculars. Xue stood nearby, listening and watching.

But even with Ethan, Xue, and Tucker now wearing Rings, they were still dangerously outnumbered. Aside from the Secretum of Six members still at his side, Oblivion would have by now drawn all the remaining Ringwearers under his thrall to him as well—all 277 of them.

Still following the news reports wherever possible, they'd discovered that Oblivion had led his people south through Syria and Beirut, and he was still going. Oblivion's march continued along the Mediterranean shoreline, so the group deduced together that after Tel Aviv, they knew where he was headed.

A journey by Conveyor guaranteed they'd arrive before him, and hopefully they could stop his army before he ever reached his target. But their plan was a perilous gamble. Placing themselves here, between Oblivion and his final destination, made them prime targets, since Oblivion had displayed a penchant for annihilating anything and everything in his path. Or they could be wrong, and Oblivion might continue south and make for another destination, such as Cairo or something even farther away like Marrakech.

"I got 'em," Payton announced into the walkie-talkie at Ethan's side. "Approaching precisely due northeast, as expected. Oblivion is still in the lead."

He tacked on that last part after a moment's pause, and Ethan thought he detected a hint of hunger in Payton's voice.

42

Payton had always been a remarkably single-minded individual. Capable of intense focus where others' attention spans drifted, he could sit and maintain a thought vigil on the same topic for hours.

It was a useful trait for an assassin. He found it particularly useful today, watching the slow but steady approach of Oblivion, followed by two Jeeps carrying the Secretum members, and the enslaved Loci behind that, nearly three hundred in number. Impressive, considering there were less than two dozen of them who'd left the underground city with Oblivion back at the beginning. It was exactly as he'd predicted: The Loci, all around the world, were drawn to Oblivion. They couldn't stop themselves from venturing to wherever he was. Soon, all of them would help him destroy what was left of the world.

Unless Payton acted. Now.

"I can see Nora," Ethan whispered through his walkie-talkie. "Mrs. Edeson is near the front of the line, not far from Oblivion. Haven't spotted Hector yet . . . the line is so long . . . Yeah, that's definitely Nora, pulling up the rear, kind of on her own."

"Perfect," Alex replied into the walkie that the old man held close to her mouth. "You grab Nora. We'll get closer to Mrs. Edeson, see if we can get her."

"Copy that," Ethan replied.

Alex switched off the walkie and carefully rose to a crouch. She watched the tiny figures just coming into view on the horizon, knowing the thing living in Grant's body was right there at the front.

Her thoughts lingered on him for a moment, trying for the hundredth time to think of something—anything—she could do to try to bring Grant back. She wouldn't believe he was really beyond hope. She *would not*. Grant touched the supernatural daily with his awesome powers, so why should he be irretrievable from the mortal grave?

"You ready?" Payton asked, standing.

"Absolutely," she replied.

"Good. Wait here."

She turned—

And Payton was gone in a blur.

No!

She knew exactly what he was going to attempt, just like she knew there was no way to stop him. She'd been afraid of this.

He'd played her—played all of them—all this time, back at his home. Agreeing to their plans, putting up just enough of a fuss that they wouldn't question it when he finally agreed to do things her way . . .

She cursed his lone-wolf tendencies. He was going to get himself killed, and he was going to do it now, when they needed him most.

But Payton was here for one reason, and one reason only.

Ethan and Sergeant Tucker were crawling as low to the ground as they could, approaching the back of the line. Xue stood watch at the tree line behind them, ready to come to their aid if needed.

"Don't let Nora see you, no matter what," Ethan advised.

"Why?" Tucker replied.

"She could wipe clean every memory engram in your brain."

"You're joking."

"We've got to do this from behind. Cut her shoulder or something and press the Stone into the wound."

"And all this without her seeing us, or alerting anyone else," Tucker said. It was nearly a question.

"Yeah," replied Ethan, pulling out his gun. "My strength isn't going to help either. Stealth is the key here. And it has to be done *fast,* or . . ."

The two men cautiously ran up behind the long, single-file line of men and women walking upon the black soil, holding their guns low and hoping to never have to use them. The DarkWorld's properties were working in their favor, masking their approach. They wore black jumpsuits like the ones Payton preferred, and they'd painted their faces with dark grease, so they blended in easily with the ground and the sky above.

"So, uh . . . what will she do, exactly, if she sees us?" Tucker asked in a hushed tone as they neared her position by less than fifty feet.

"About five seconds after she sees us, we'll forget who we are, why we're here, how to speak, chew food, and lose all motor coordination we were trained with as infants. Then Oblivion will come and separate our bodies' molecules."

"All you had to say was 'we'd be dead,' man," Tucker replied. "That's all I needed to know."

Daniel watched Lisa from the tree he hid behind. She was crouching behind another tree herself, her head peeking out from one side. Ethan and Tucker had left their binoculars behind, and she'd picked them up to look through. Xue's keen eyes traced them from her position behind a tree twenty feet away.

With a deep gulp, Daniel carefully, cautiously left his hiding place and slid over next to Lisa. She didn't notice his approach, her peripheral vision cut off by the binoculars pressed against her face. Daniel bit his lip as he awkwardly extended his right arm and placed it around her shoulders.

Lisa reacted only slightly, the binoculars pulling away from her face by an inch. She realized it was Daniel without looking directly at him, smiled to herself, and then replaced the lenses at her eyes.

Daniel knew her well enough to know that a wild assortment of happy thoughts were thundering through her overactive brain right about now, but he had to hand it to her for playing it remarkably cool. He hadn't expected that. Maybe this wouldn't be so uncomfortable after all.

"What do you see?" he whispered, strengthening his hold on her slightly.

"They're almost there."

"What about Payton and Alex?"

She turned. "Let's see . . . There's Mrs. Edeson, still marching in the procession. But if the two of them are anywhere near her, I can't see 'em . . . no, wait, I see Payton, he's . . . what is he *doing*?"

43

With a sharp nod at Sergeant Tucker, Ethan sprinted for Nora.

But Tucker was the faster man and got to her a second before Ethan could reach her, tackling her limp, weary body onto the ground.

Oblivion stopped.

He turned.

He'd felt it. One of his Ringwearers had been shoved to the ground.

With a fleeting thought, he awakened twelve other Ringwearers in her vicinity.

Tucker was sitting on top of Nora, where she'd fallen facedown onto the black ground. He held her arms behind her back. She was writhing about with surprising strength.

But no, that's not her strength, Ethan reminded himself. *That's Oblivion.*

"I think we woke the neighbors," Tucker whispered, looking around warily.

Ethan dropped to his knees and slid the last foot or so until he was able to touch Nora. He holstered his gun. The Stone fragment was in his left hand; he reached into a pants pocket with his right, only to find it empty.

"I didn't think to bring a knife!"

"Well *I* don't have one, man!" Tucker replied as Nora nearly bucked him off her back.

Looking around for anything sharp, he had to find something he could use to pierce her skin just enough to get the Stone to touch her bloodstream . . . He glanced up just long enough to see about a dozen Loci walking toward them robotically from all directions, like zombies that would arrive much faster than it seemed they could . . .

The rocks on the ground were craggy yet too small to cut human flesh. Maybe he could just slash at her with the Stone fragment itself? But this piece was flat and dull, not nearly as sharp as some of the others . . .

Ringwearers were coming; he had to do something!

He was still thinking hard and searching the ground around him frantically when a gunshot went off. The blast was so close, his ears started ringing.

Nora's hand had a disgusting, bloody, burned hole going straight through the center of her palm. Tucker held his sidearm tight with one hand, its muzzle still smoking.

"Do it!" he shouted, nodding at Nora's hand.

Ethan pressed the Stone into the hole, and Nora went limp almost immediately.

Tucker climbed off, Ethan hefted Nora easily with both arms, and the two men ran. No good going back to the trees now; that would give the others away.

Ethan surveyed their surroundings. They weren't far from the small housing community he'd seen earlier, and it looked like it had lots of places where they might hide.

"This way!" he shouted.

"Daniel," Lisa whispered. "Look."

Daniel stole his view away from what Payton was doing to see that Hector was walking alone, less than thirty feet away. Daniel glanced about and saw that other Ringwearers were scattered across the plain in every direction; it appeared that Oblivion had split them up, sending his army out to search for others who might be here with Ethan and Tucker. It was a stroke of luck that Hector had ventured so close to them.

"What do you think?" Lisa whispered, clutching a Stone fragment tightly in her right hand.

She clearly wanted to go for it, and he was leaning toward agreeing with her. He whirled around to get Xue's attention, but she was looking the wrong way, still following Ethan's and Tucker's movements.

"Come on, he's *right there*—we'll never get a better chance!" Lisa whispered again.

Without waiting for him, she jumped out from behind her tree and entered a dead sprint toward Hector, who was facing away from her.

Daniel took off behind her, but she had a ten-foot head start on him, and he couldn't run with his permanently damaged ankle. The best he could manage was a fast limp, leaning on his aluminum cane for leverage.

As she was nearing Hector, the gigantic man turned at the sound of her running footsteps. He stuck out a hand and grabbed her by the neck just as she came into view. His enormous arm lifted her off the ground easily, and Daniel struggled to reach them as Lisa's features contorted into anguish. She couldn't breathe, but that wasn't the worst of it.

Daniel understood what was happening from what Ethan had told him: Hector's touch was draining Lisa's body of health, causing her intense physiological grief.

She was unable to stifle a bloodcurdling scream, and the sound echoed throughout the barren plain.

Alex dared to step out into the open.

She couldn't help herself. Grant was only a hundred or so feet away. She didn't care that the last time she saw him, he'd flung her into a wildfire. Didn't care that his skin was gray and hard, or that his eyes were on fire.

He was still Grant.

He had to be.

She was about to move when the old man appeared in front of her, his expression different than she'd ever seen it. It had softened, but carried heavy creases around those sharp, bright eyes.

His lips formed a grim smile, a pained expression of love. He slowly reached out with his one hand and placed it flat over her beating heart. He nodded slowly at her as if wordlessly speaking an unspoken message, and she read the myriad emotions running through him in that instant as warm and caring, yet regretful and determined.

Reluctantly, he withdrew his hand. And then he turned on his heel and ran. Away from Oblivion, away from where Payton had disappeared, away from the truck where the others were hiding.

Alex stood in stunned silence, watching as his elderly frame grew smaller on the flat open ground, until he rounded a distant mound of black ash and was gone.

He'd left her. Left them. Abandoned them all.

Confused, her thoughts drifting, Alex subconsciously directed her feet to begin carrying her forward.

And suddenly all of her thoughts snapped back to attention as her eyes landed on Oblivion. If only she could get closer to him, maybe she could flood him with feelings of love, of compassion and joy and hope—maybe it would be just enough to give Grant a chance to return to the surface . . .

Her line of thought ended when a scream pierced the silence from somewhere in the distance, far off to her right. Oblivion turned toward the sound as well, looking—

A hand snapped over Alex's mouth from behind, an arm around her shoulders.

She tried to shout, but only a muffled sound came out.

"Alex!" Payton whispered into her ear. He turned loose and grabbed her by the hand, dragging her off.

It was only after they rounded a small hill and Oblivion was no longer in sight that she noticed there was an unconscious man slung over Payton's left shoulder. Which didn't seem to be slowing Payton down in the slightest.

She recognized the sleeping man.

"What are you *doing*?" she asked, a little louder than she'd meant to. "This isn't what we came for!"

Payton held her tightly by the hand and continued to drag her half running in a direction opposite of Oblivion and his army. "Pencil me in for a good row over that once we're far away from here."

44

Daniel whacked at Hector's head with his cane, but it only resulted in putting a dent in the metal walking stick. Hector backhanded Daniel, and he landed with a harsh thud against the black ground.

Xue appeared, using her powers of magnetism to draw Daniel's cane to her. Once the cane was in hand, she tried to sweep Hector's feet out from under him, from behind. But he was too big a target to be felled so easily, and soon she too was on her back on the ground.

Hector dropped Lisa and looked around, looked down at his own two hands, looked at the two people lying at his feet. He was utterly mystified, bewildered, as if he'd lost his—

Nora.

Daniel's head spun and he saw the black woman being carried in Sergeant Tucker's arms. Her dazed, barely conscious gaze was focused on the three of them, a bleeding hand outstretched and trained on Hector.

Tucker ran until he stood face-to-face with the big man. "Sorry, man," he whispered. He brandished his gun and shot Hector in the shoulder, creating a tremendously loud sound that would draw the attention of everyone in the area.

Daniel didn't bother to watch what happened next; he crawled over to Lisa, who had turned red in the face. Now she was clutching her head with both hands, as if her brain were about to explode and she wanted to contain the blast. He sat cross-legged and pulled her close, until he could hold her in his arms. She cried out in pain as he rocked her back and forth.

A hand extended down from above and touched her on the shoulder. Lisa's hands fell away from her head and she looked up. Daniel followed her gaze.

Hector, unharmed and smiling, beamed down at them both.

"Good to have you back, big guy," Lisa mumbled wearily.

Hector placed a hand on Daniel's shoulder and he instantly felt a lift, a boost in energy, and the calm centeredness that always came from the man's healing touch.

The two of them got to their feet and saw that Nora was standing as well, with just a little help from Ethan for balance. Her hand was mended, no longer bleeding. She still appeared wobbly, but she was definitely in control of herself again.

Daniel was about to ask what they should do now when Alex and Payton appeared, running toward them. Payton carried a man over one shoulder, unconscious.

It was Devlin.

"Follow me," Payton said, and he turned and ran toward the housing development in the distance.

There was no choice. They'd gotten two of their best fighters back, but they were still outnumbered and thoroughly exposed. The Ringwearers possessed by Oblivion's will were closing in.

They had to hide.

The housing development stood all but abandoned. Daniel quietly speculated that the residents were in hiding elsewhere. Or, Lisa added, maybe they'd fled when it was apparent that Oblivion was coming their way.

Payton prepared to slice through a doorway to grant them access to a random house deep within the neighborhood, when Tucker stopped him. The Army man pointed out that any enemy on the hunt would notice something as obvious as a door that had been hacked open. It didn't escape Daniel's notice that such an oversight was out of character for the assassin.

Ethan knelt next to the door and picked the primitive lock in impressive time.

The door opened into a dingy living room bearing the distinct smell of, as Lisa put it, "old people." Off from the main room there was a separate bedroom, bath, and tiny kitchen. They couldn't afford to turn on any lights, leaving them to feel their way through the room past vague, blocky shadows.

Contact with anything in the room gave off a musty odor. Nora found her way to a linen-draped sofa and lay down; Hector sat on the floor at her feet. His touch had repaired the wear and tear done to her skin, muscles, bones, and ligaments, but she had gone on miniscule food and water for far too long, leaving her body nearly desiccated.

Payton slung Devlin's unconscious form on the floor without grace or pity. Devlin grunted softly and began to stir awake; Payton swiftly kicked him in the head, and Devlin slumped, asleep again.

"You abducted him?" Daniel asked.

Payton gave one curt nod.

"But why?"

"*You* wanted to fight Oblivion smart," Payton replied. "This man is our one chance at doing that. Wouldn't you like to know if Oblivion has any weaknesses?"

"Where's Julie?" Nora asked weakly, barely able to stay awake.

Hector was about to administer his healing touch on Alex when he froze, hand outstretched. Instead of looking at Nora, his eyes met Alex's; he knew she would have the answer.

"She's not here," Alex replied. Her words didn't express the truth, but the tone of her voice had.

Hector seemed to withdraw into himself. His usual dogged smile, his most prominent feature, faded. His eyes searched the ground as they grew bigger.

Alex put a hand on his round shoulder. He didn't react.

"You loved her . . ." Alex whispered. "Oh, sweetie . . . I had no idea."

Lisa blinked to life, squeezing Daniel's hand harder. "Hey, where's the old guy?"

"Wait, the one Payton was talking about, or somebody else?" Nora asked, still dazed.

"He left," Alex replied.

"The man without a hand," Lisa explained to Nora.

Nora's mouth opened, but she said nothing. Flummoxed, she grappled for words. "The guy Grant met back in L.A. during the riots? *That* old kook was with you? But . . ."

"Yeah, tell me about it," Lisa said under her breath.

"Quiet!" Payton hissed, his sword drawn and ready. He was looking outside through a small gap in the curtains behind a smallish front window.

Everyone fell silent.

"What is it?" Alex whispered.

"The Easter Bunny," Payton whispered, without turning from his post.

"Attitude, now? Really?" she shot back.

"I said *quiet*!" he seethed.

Ethan joined him at the front window, looking out to the distant right. There was a bit more light in the dusk outside than the tiny, darkness-filled room. His sharp eyes focused on something in the distance.

"Is that—?" Ethan asked.

"It's Cornelius," Payton replied, referring to the elder British statesman of the Upholders of the Crown. "He's not aware of us yet, but the search pattern he's using will lead him straight to us."

Daniel thought back. Cornelius could force others to think about whatever he wanted them to think about. It would be a simple matter for him to subdue them; he would simply distract them all with thoughts of flowers or chipmunks or something, until Oblivion arrived.

"We have to move," Payton whispered. "Now."

"Where?" Daniel asked.

"Whole town's crawling with them," Ethan added, nodding in the other direction.

Daniel joined them at the window. He followed Ethan's gaze and saw another shadow sweeping through the street, this one much farther away, but also moving in their direction.

45

The journey to a safer location deeper in the maze of houses nearly ended in disaster. With Payton leading them through the darkness, they almost crossed paths with three different Ringwearers. Each time Payton broke away from the group to create subtle diversions elsewhere that would draw away the danger, so the rest of the group could continue moving.

When they finally reached a more secure hideout, Payton was nowhere to be seen, but before the last of them could step inside he appeared at the rear of the line and followed them in.

"Mrs. Edeson isn't far, but she's moving in a different direction," he replied. "Stay put and stay quiet. I'm going to grab her."

Ethan stepped forward. "Can I lend a hand?" he asked eagerly.

"No."

Ethan recoiled slightly. "But I could—"

Payton was already gone, in as long as it had taken Ethan to blink.

Alex felt significantly better, now that Hector had had a chance to help her. His hand had lingered on her flesh longer than his usual brief touch, his eyes closed tight in concentration, but once done, her pain vanished and her strength had fully returned. The skin over her stomach and right arm were permanently scarred; there was nothing he could do about that.

She retrieved cloths from the small bathroom, ran them under cold water, and brought one out into the living room for everyone. Most everyone placed the cool cloths on their foreheads or the backs of their necks to cool off. Ethan and Tucker wiped the greasepaint from their faces.

Alex found a broken menorah in the closet bathroom. She saw no stand for the yard-long candelabra, but she thought it might be useful nonetheless. Along with the menorah, she found a bottle of oil and a matchbook, so she lit the tiny cups of oil at the end of each branch. She found the floor stand out in the living room.

The glow it created gave them enough light to move about safely, while still dim enough not to attract any outside attention.

In what seemed like no time at all, Payton reappeared. Alex stopped what she was doing, as did everyone else.

Rather than carrying Mrs. Edeson, he was guiding her with his arm around her shoulder, though she was quite capable of walking under her own power. While clearly freed from Oblivion's influence, she had a wild look in her eye and repeatedly tried to yank herself from his grip. Her refined, tailored attire had seams that were falling apart, bits and pieces of it hanging in slivers from her slight frame. Her makeup had long since worn off, and like everyone else in Oblivion's service, she desperately needed food, water, and a shower.

But none of this explained the crazed way she was wrestling to pull away from Payton.

"Get your hands *off* of me!" she shouted in a blind rage.

"Shhhh!" Alex, Daniel, and Lisa all said at once. Even Hector motioned at her with a finger over his lips.

"It's all right," Payton replied. "They're leaving, resuming course toward Jerusalem."

"And every minute we waste, the farther away they get, don't they!" Mrs. Edeson cried with a savage furor.

"What's going on?" Alex said, asking the question that was on everyone's minds. Even Nora rose from her incline on the couch to sit up and listen closely.

"We have to go back for him! NOW!!" she screamed.

"Who?" Alex responded.

"Ryan, of course!"

"Who's Ryan?"

Mrs. Edeson froze, recognition dawning in her eyes. "I never identified him by name to you, did I? Ryan is the young man from our group—the Upholders."

"But," Daniel interjected, "what's the rush? Let's formulate a plan for taking on Oblivion first, then we can track him down inside Jerusalem . . ."

"No!" Mrs. Edeson cried. "I will not leave him to suffer under Oblivion's thumb, all alone. He won't understand what's happening. He may never recover as it is . . ."

"No, Daniel's right," Alex said. "Let's figure out our next move, then we'll look for your friend first thing when we get to Jerusalem—"

"You people are not hearing me!" Mrs. Edeson shouted, frantic. "*I will not help you* unless we save Ryan! Right now!"

Silence filled the room.

"Why? What's so special about this boy?" Daniel asked.

"He's my SON!!" she bellowed, tears pouring from her eyes. "Ryan is an autistic savant—he can't have understood what's been happening to him all this time in Oblivion's enslavement, and I fear the damage already done could be irreversible! Please . . . He's my son . . ."

Alex was stunned, and by the looks of everyone else, the others felt the same way.

Potential Ringwearers had always been selected at random by the Secretum. Grant's grandfather told him that the Ringwearers were chosen because they were the outcasts or forgotten members of society. They were the ones no one would miss.

They never knew one another prior to becoming Ringwearers. As such, there were no two members of the same family among them. Until now.

Payton spoke up. "Ryan's Ring allows him to combine the powers of other Ringwearers."

"So we would want him on our side before we face Oblivion," Ethan summed up.

"All right," Alex heard her confused voice say. "If we're going to rescue your son, then we have to go right now, before they get any farther away."

"That's what I've been trying to tell you!" Mrs. Edeson cried in exhaustion.

Hector got to his feet and gently placed a hand on her shoulder, healing her cuts and bruises and the exhaustion hiding beneath her adrenaline-fueled frenzy to save her son.

"Three groups. We'll need two distractions this time," Payton said, clipped and precise. "We used one last time; Oblivion won't be fooled the same way twice. So they'll ignore our first group and pursue the second, while the third group sweeps in and grabs the boy. And someone will need to stay here and watch . . . *that*." He nodded in the direction of Devlin, who was facedown and still unconscious on the floor.

"We'll stay," volunteered Lisa. "Daniel and I. We don't have powers; we wouldn't be much help to you anyway."

Daniel appeared slightly surprised by this, but made no argument.

Alex stood and the others followed her lead. "We'll be back soon."

Everyone else, including Nora and Mrs. Edeson, made for the front door. Payton took up the rear, but as he was leaving he called out, "You'll want to bind Devlin. And for your own sakes, don't talk to him until I return."

46

Daniel and Lisa talked quietly in the bedroom as they tore lengthwise strips of the bed linens to create makeshift ropes for tethering Devlin.

He wanted to ask her about her comment from before, about the two of them not having powers. Was there more behind this comment? Now that the remaining Rings had been found, they *could* have powers. Did she think they should?

"Tell you what, now?" Daniel asked as he continued to tear the sheets. He decided to ease into the conversation, let her take the lead.

They were at the rear of the house, seated on the edge of the bed, looking out a back window at the desolate surrounding geography. Like everywhere else, it had turned into a charred shadow of its former self. Despite this, Lisa was obviously enjoying this chance for a brief private moment between them.

"A *joke*," Lisa repeated. She sat at his immediate left, tearing a bed sheet of her own by hand. "I know you live off in Danielville, always thinking about all your science-y stuff, but surely you're familiar with the concept of a punch line?" she teased.

He threw her a smile. "I may have heard a joke or two over the course of my life."

"Then tell me! And I promise to laugh no matter how bad you butcher it."

"Oh well, thanks . . ."

"Come on, please?" she begged, somehow managing to mock and entice him at the same time.

"Okay, okay," he said, finding it harder than ever to resist her. "Let me think . . . Okay, I may not tell it quite right . . . A group of dark-haired NASA scientists were joking one day about how dumb the blond members of their department were. A blond scientist overheard what they were saying and reprimanded them. After her scolding, one of them said, 'You know, we sent twelve men to walk on the moon, and not one of them was blond.' She replied, 'Big deal. We'll be the first ones to walk on the sun.' The other man responded, 'Don't you think you'll get a little burned?' She talked down to him as she said, completely serious: 'We'll go at night.' "

Lisa laughed—a little too hard, Daniel thought. It was a polite laugh. A pity laugh. But he couldn't bring himself to stop her. She had a brilliant smile.

Thinking hard as her laughter subsided, he came up with another one. "Do you know what the rear end of a *trilobite* is called?"

She replied, "If you're about to say a 'trilobutt,' I *will* hurt you."

He laughed, and she did the same. It was a great feeling.

"You know," Lisa said, her face still smiling but her tone more serious, "I couldn't help noticing that you haven't volunteered to wear one of the unworn Rings."

"Well, Ms. Hazelton," he said jovially, "it didn't escape my notice that neither did you."

"I thought about it," she replied, noncommittal.

"I really thought you might," Daniel said. "A few months ago, you wouldn't have hesitated. What happened? What changed?"

She opened her mouth. Closed it. Studied him with a knotted brow.

"I almost lost you," she said, her voice fragile. *"Again."*

He nodded slowly, his suspicions confirmed. "London."

"London. You almost died on me, for the second time in one year. It was frightening, but it's not really fear that's holding me back."

"Then what?"

It was the first time Daniel had ever seen her at a loss for words, grasping. But he wouldn't allow himself to rush her.

She sighed, her eyes darting back and forth. "When I was in college, after my dad passed away, before we met, I just . . . I, uh . . . I never found anyone I wanted to let into my life. When I met you, it wasn't that I let you in my world—I wanted into *your* world. Heart, body, and soul. I let myself start to care about you. And then you got hurt. Those guys beat you and left you for dead, and it felt like it had been done to me. It changed things. The thought of losing you became painful. Unbearable. I knew that whatever happened to you, wherever you went or whatever you did . . . I had to be there with you. No matter what.

"If you want to wear a Ring and get yourself some superpowers, then I'll be proud to stand beside you and get some of my own. What matters to me isn't the powers. I just want to stand beside you. I want to be wherever you are."

Daniel was smiling. He wasn't sure it was appropriate for such a tender moment, but he couldn't help it. He grabbed her hand and squeezed it.

"Tell the truth," he said. "You want to see me be a superhero, don't you?"

She smiled, sheepish. "I think I do. But then I think that if anything ever happened . . . if I really did lose you . . . I don't think I could keep breathing."

Her last words came out as a whisper. The two of them paused for air at the same moment, and their faces came closer together. Daniel felt himself flush, but didn't take his eyes off of hers. They inched even closer. The hunger was upon him once more, how he longed to taste her . . .

Daniel's vision went bright white. Something hard had hit him on the back of the head. He clutched at his skull and felt blood oozing from the blunt force trauma.

Lisa screamed, and Daniel's vision cleared just as the same object came down ready to hit her, but she ducked sideways, barely avoiding it.

Daniel tried to get his bearings, but his reaction time had been reduced to a crawl, like slow motion. Finally he saw Devlin standing on the other side of the narrow bed, the menorah in his hand, ripped free from its base. The oil wicks had all gone out, and a few of the branching candleholders appeared to have broken off as they'd hit the side of Daniel's head.

Lisa screamed again as Devlin dove at her.

47

Daniel regained his wits enough to lunge at Devlin, whose age belied unbelievable speed and strength. Daniel managed to shove Devlin to one side, but Devlin kicked back with his feet and vaulted Daniel completely over top of him, sending him flying upside down into the nearby wall. Lisa roared and pummeled Devlin's head with her fists, but he backhanded her viciously and she slumped against the same wall as Daniel, out cold.

Devlin reached down with both hands and grabbed Daniel by the legs. He spun in place, slinging Daniel like a rag doll, and flung him against the bed. Daniel's head crashed into the headboard with a crack, and he could only hope it was the bed that had made the sound.

Devlin advanced on him, the menorah raised above his head, ready to strike. A rage in Daniel kindled. He needed to fight back. Lisa's prostrate form lay unmoving in his peripheral vision and he saw in his mind again how hard Devlin had hit her.

Jaw gritted with savage intensity, Daniel let out a furious growl, sprung from the bed, and tackled Devlin, forcing the older man all the way to the floor. Before Devlin could get his bearings, Daniel landed two solid punches to the older man's face and felt satisfaction rising in his chest.

Devlin grabbed him by the throat with both hands and squeezed as hard as he could. His air cut off, Daniel stopped hitting and began flailing at Devlin's arms, trying to get him to loosen his death grip.

Think! What would Payton do? What would Ethan do?

The answer came to him at once, and he brought both of his arms up between Devlin's and fanned them out. Devlin's hold was broken, but he kicked Daniel in the groin, and Daniel fell to his knees, the stars he'd seen only moments ago returning and bringing some friends along.

Devlin stood and looked about for his candlestick as Daniel clutched helplessly at the pain in his groin.

"Daniel!" Lisa screamed, coming to. She looked at Devlin, saw that he was holding something in his hands, and leapt to shield Daniel on the floor. She landed facing him on her knees, love and fear written in her eyes—

—when the bottom end of the candlestick burst through her stomach.

Lisa froze; Daniel flinched hard, every muscle in his body going rigid. Blood squeezed from the puncture, a trickle at first, and both Daniel and Lisa looked in disbelief at the ragged stem of the candlestick jutting from her abdomen. Then the blood began to flow quickly, and Lisa whispered Daniel's name as she fell forward into his arms. As she slumped, the weapon was pulled out of her.

Daniel looked up just in time to see Devlin swinging the rod like a bat. He released his hold on Lisa and put up a hand to catch the candlestick right before it could hit him in the head. He grasped it hard and yanked it from Devlin's hands. He launched himself from the floor wordlessly, landing on top of the other man. With the bloodstained menorah held wide in both hands, he pressed it down hard against Devlin's larynx.

Devlin struggled, grunting. He punched Daniel in the face, but even as his head snapped around, Daniel was filled with rage and he never faltered, never allowed himself to be deterred from his task, pressing the golden stick down until the life was drained out of this vile excuse for a human being who deserved any and every pain that Daniel could visit upon him . . .

"Daniel?" Lisa's weak voice called out.

Devlin had just closed his eyes, passing out, when Daniel heard her voice. He let go of the menorah at once and returned to her.

She was lying on her stomach, and he gently rolled her toward him, cradling her in his arms, on her back. Already he felt her blood soaking through his pants.

"Hector!" he bellowed as loud as he could, knowing there was virtually no chance that any of his friends would hear him now.

His heart was beating fast, he was wet and sticky and sweating, and Lisa's life was draining away . . .

"Daniel . . ." Lisa whispered.

"Why did you do that?" he shouted at her. "Lisa!"

He was at a total loss. He was so stunned, he couldn't even cry. *"Why . . . ?"*

She opened her tired eyes and focused on him, smiling even in her pain. "Silly scientist . . . I told you already," she said. "The choice was mine to make. And I made it."

Daniel looked around, helpless, desperate to do something, anything, to stop this from happening.

"I'd do it again," Lisa whispered, her voice growing more and more faint with every word. "I would have never left your side. No matter what. I promised you when you were in the hospital I'd take good care of you. And I did, didn't I? Daniel?"

"You did. You took care of me." His eyes and face were so wet, he could barely see her. "You always—"

"I love you," she said, her voice fading. "I love you so much, Daniel."

Daniel opened his mouth, but there were no words for what he felt. This wasn't happening, it couldn't be.

"Do you love me?" Lisa asked, her voice down to almost nothing.

"I—" Before he could finish the sentence, her chest slumped and her eyes fell closed.

She was gone.

"I do!" Daniel cried, as if hearing the words might bring her back. "I love you! Lisa, I LOVE YOU! *I LOVE YOU!!*" he screamed. He kissed her, only the third time he had ever done so, trying to will her back to life with the act.

He was a fool, and he deserved to die for it. He should have kissed her a hundred times. A *million*. He should have wrapped her body in his and held her, safe and whole. He should have told her every time he opened his mouth how he knew he would never have made it this far without her, how empty he felt when she wasn't around, how she made his life fuller and richer, how happy he was to know her and to love her.

How life wasn't worth living without her.

When the others returned, they found Devlin first, unconscious, bound, and crumpled in the corner of the living room. Then they saw the blood. Alex and Ethan rushed into the bedroom first and discovered Daniel sitting on the bed, rocking Lisa's bloodied body gently back and forth, leaning over her.

Daniel barely took notice, but he heard their voices and Ethan's quick shout for help. He felt the jolt of panic from Alex's surprise. Hector came—too late of course—and touched Lisa's forehead. But she didn't stir.

Daniel ignored the others and pushed Hector's hand away absently. His eyes were locked onto Lisa's cold face, his lips moving just barely, mumbling things under his breath—all the things that he should have said to her. And the more he said, the more came to him that he wanted to say, that he *should* have said . . .

He stayed there, immovable by anyone, for an eternity. With time gone, it might as well have been.

48

Alex sat in a rocking chair in the tiny, dark living room, her gaze far away from this place. Tears rolled down her cheeks, one by one, even though she repeatedly tried to blink them back.

How many had they lost now? It was more than twenty, she knew that much, but found it hard to take a complete count.

The first soldiers to go down were the victims of the fire at the asylum in L.A. None of them had asked to be there, none of them realized they were to become cannon fodder in a war of ideologies, a war of heroes and villains. A war that was ultimately about power—who had it and who could get more of it.

Then came Hannah. The arson victims had left Grant hollow inside, but losing Hannah had nearly cost him his soul. But he persevered. Then there was Morgan, who was more of a mentor to all of them than anyone had ever been. She died alone, in the hands of the Secretum, far away from her friends. Julie, the soul and conscience of the entire group, but most especially to Grant. Grant himself, fallen at Devlin's hands. And now Lisa.

Wait, why did she include Grant? She didn't believe he was really dead.

She didn't.

No. Even now, after seeing death once again in such vivid real-life detail, up close . . . she didn't accept that what happened to Grant was anything like what happened to Lisa. Alex's heart refused to entertain the notion, rebuffed any thoughts that led her down that path. The others could think what they wanted; Grant was alive. It was true in her heart, and that was all that mattered.

In her periphery she saw Ethan pacing relentlessly back and forth in the tiny room. It was driving Alex insane. He dropped the magazine out of his pistol's grip, caught it with his other hand, and slammed it back in place. This he did again and again as he trod over his own footsteps, again and again.

"What do we do now?" he asked, his words coming out rapidly. "Do we head for Jerusalem, try to free the rest of the Loci? They'll be almost there by now, right? But we still need Morgan's Ring, so what good would it do to take on Oblivion without finding that first?"

Nora, like many of the others, was despondent. "Shut *up*, man."

Ethan rounded on her, on all of them. "Look, I'm sorry about Lisa. Really, I am. But Oblivion has sent the world to Hell and he's getting ready to finish the job. We can't afford to just sit around and grieve—that's exactly what Devlin expects us to do."

The words had no sooner left his lips than Daniel entered the room, and everyone stopped to look. His face was empty, his expression muddled, his arms hung limp at his sides as though he was drugged. Nora and Xue rose from their seats to offer them to him, but he shook his head without meeting anyone's eyes and turned away, situating himself on the floor in a corner at the far end of the room. He sat very intentionally opposite Devlin, who was awake, lying sideways and watching everything in calm silence behind his gag. His skin was pale, his circulation probably being dangerously cut off, but no one bothered to loosen his excessive bonds.

Daniel stared at the ground just beyond his own feet, and made not a sound.

"Devlin should be interrogated," Payton broke the silence. "It's the reason I brought him here."

Alex thought of the pain Devlin had caused her when she was lying in that military barracks in Turkey, still under Oblivion's thrall and only reluctantly being allowed to rest. He'd actually reveled in adding to her anguish, lost to the power he held over her. But then, he'd also taken the time to dress her wounds, personally.

He didn't have to do that.

It didn't matter. Devlin was evil incarnate. Look at what he'd done to Grant.

Her thoughts returned to the moment, and she faced Payton.

"*You* brought him here," she said to Payton, before she could stop herself. "And look how well that turned out."

"Don't you dare blame me for what happened to the girl," Payton seethed. "I couldn't have known—"

"Because you never bother to, Payton!" Alex said, jumping to her feet, a newfound fire blazing in her chest. She needed to lash out at someone right now, and it might as well be Payton with his lone-gun lunacy. "If you weren't always going off on your own and doing things without telling the rest of us—"

"At least I'm not sitting around waiting to be told what to do by a dead man."

Grant.

Alex stood toe-to-toe with Payton, and she was ready to knock his bald head off, when a quiet voice broke the tension.

"I want to talk to Devlin," said Daniel. His voice was numb and raspy, protruding from a throat that was raw.

Everyone stared in silence as Daniel crossed the short distance between himself and the silver-haired Keeper of the Secretum.

"This can't be a good idea," said Alex, crossing her arms over her chest, her argument with Payton all but forgotten.

"We should just lock him in a basement somewhere and throw away the key."

She empathically felt her way around the room, hoping for support from anyone who might agree that Daniel was about to embark down a very dark path he might never return from. Hector remained perfectly still. He hadn't yet made a move to ease the minor injuries Daniel had incurred during his fight with Devlin. He seemed to know Daniel wanted the pain. Nora, sitting on the couch across from her, didn't meet Alex's eyes. Instead, the woman locked her gaze on Devlin, hatred and rage boiling from her.

Sergeant Tucker stood guard at the front window, gun in hand and ready to spring into action as the need arose. He didn't seem to be paying attention to the events unfolding inside the house. Xue was seated in an armchair on the outer edge of the room, deferentially holding her tongue about affairs she wasn't intimately familiar with. Mrs. Edeson sat beside Nora on the couch, an arm around her son Ryan. She watched the discourse in the room with tremendous interest, though she said nothing to the others. Instead, she continued to dote over Ryan, whispering soothing words to him in tones only the two of them could discern. Ryan, healed after his ordeal with Oblivion, looked about the small room, absorbing every detail, but Alex read his emotional state as blissfully ignorant.

Ethan was Alex's last hope at an ally. He'd holstered his gun and stood at Alex's right, his arms folded. But aside from mild twinges of grief over Lisa, he was giving off his usual exhilaration and impatience, which she chalked up to thoughts of using his superpowered muscles to beat the living daylights out of Devlin. He would be of no help to her either.

"I don't know, Alex," Daniel argued, turning to face her with hardened features. "This man and the group he represents have manipulated and affected the outcome of the lives of every person in this room, either directly or indirectly. I think we're long overdue for finding out why, don't you?"

Payton helped Daniel get Devlin to his feet, and then guide him, hopping, to a small, armless chair. The two men applied extra bindings to hold him to the chair and keep him from wiggling to his feet. Devlin's calculating eyes surveyed the room, moving from one person to the next.

"This is ludicrous," Alex said, walking behind the two of them, watching. "Anything he tells us will be a lie."

Payton tore the cloth around Devlin's mouth in half and yanked it free. Spitting out the few threads that were lodged in his mouth, Devlin looked at Alex and spoke in an American accent. "That's not true, my dear. If Grant were still here, he could vouch for the fact that I never once lied to him."

"Fine," Daniel began. "Then tell us everything. The Secretum, Oblivion, all of it."

"Ah, I'm sorry, you misunderstand," Devlin replied. "I won't lie to you, but I do, however, refuse to cooperate with your inquiries."

"Oh yes you will!" Nora fought her way to her feet with Hector's help. Her knees wobbled, her stance precarious. "You're gonna tell us everything, or I'll rip through your brain and take it from you, one synapse at a time."

"I have nothing to lose, my dear," Devlin replied, unmoved. "The dark and terrible storm has come, and there's nothing anyone can do to stop it now."

"Then by your own logic," Payton observed, "there is nothing to be lost from answering our questions. You once told me, long ago, that only a fool says one thing and does another."

Devlin almost smiled. "It is a terrible thing to hear your own words repeated back to you by your former protégé." He seemed to mentally shrug and said, "Very well, then."

"I still don't trust anything he says," Alex said.

"There is no rationale for pretense or subterfuge on my part," Devlin explained. "Payton is quite correct. There really is no reason not to tell you everything now. You might as well know the truth, before the end. Ask me your questions; if you even *suspect* me of lying, Payton here can run me through."

"I think it's a given he'll be doing that either way," Nora said with satisfaction.

"It no longer matters," Devlin replied, smiling grimly at the entire group. He faced them from the far side of the room where he had been perched. His smug expression and polite demeanor was enough to generate hatred from all of them, even the few who knew next to nothing about him.

Ethan began pacing again. Alex remained standing, while Daniel returned to his seat, the black, murderous glint in his eyes refusing to fade. Payton hovered over his old mentor, looking down on him with dark satisfaction. Everyone else—Hector, Nora, Tucker, Xue, Mrs. Edeson, and her son Ryan—watched with rapt attention.

"What happened to Grant?" Alex asked. "And what is Oblivion?"

"As I have told you again and again since this began, Grant is dead. He has been replaced by Oblivion—death's avatar on the physical plane."

" 'Death's avatar'?" Nora repeated. "You mean Grant's turned into the Grim Reaper?"

Devlin chuckled at this.

"Is he possessed by Lucifer?" asked Payton, glaring.

Alex wasn't entirely surprised that this question had been spoken aloud; it was a possibility that had occurred to her long ago as well. But she *was* surprised to hear it asked by Payton.

"No." Devlin shook his head, smiling again in amusement.

"Then what?" Daniel screamed, his face scarlet. "Stop playing games and just *tell us*! WHAT IS OBLIVION!?"

Devlin let out a slow breath. "He is the Angel of Death given human form and flesh."

49

"The Angel of Death," Daniel repeated, disbelieving. "As in the Angel of Death who killed the firstborn sons of Egypt—the last of the ten plagues prophesied by Moses? If you believe in that sort of thing."

"One and the same," Devlin replied. "And I do believe in that sort of thing."

Silence hung thick in the room as everyone processed Devlin's admission. Only Ryan was blissfully oblivious to what had just been revealed.

"Why?" Payton asked.

"Why what?"

"Why summon the Angel of Death and give it a human form?"

"To answer that question, I must explain to you who we really are—the Secretum of Six." Devlin watched the others, thoughtful for a moment. "How much do you know about the dawn of time?"

"You mean, like, the Big Bang?" Ethan replied.

Devlin rolled his eyes. "Have you never read the book of Genesis?"

"Sure," Alex said. "My mom used to read Bible stories to me as a kid."

"But you can't take that 'on the first day, on the second day' stuff literally," Ethan added.

Devlin tsk-ed. "You really are laughably naïve, all of you. To have seen and done all that you have, and still not know the truth? Honestly . . . Have you never studied the ancient texts contained within Genesis? Examined them, scientifically, for the historical records held within?"

When no one answered, he continued.

"The Creation account in the book of Genesis tells us that when Adam and Eve brought two sons into the world, one of them murdered the other in a fit of jealousy. I am of course referring to Cain, the first murderer. As we all know, it was a downward spiral for mankind from that point forward: theft, rape, defilement, debauchery . . . Any depraved notion human beings could think of, they *did*. It became so horrendous that the Maker decided to wipe clean the slate with a Flood so terrible it would cover all the earth."

"Noah's Ark," Ethan interrupted. "You're telling us this is somehow connected to Noah's Ark?"

"Indeed. The Flood was a brutal, violent act of mass murder by the Creator, expunging mankind from all that He had made. That is, all but a handful of chosen survivors, who were descended from Adam's third son, Seth. Following this line of reasoning, every person alive today traces his or her origin to the line of Seth."

Devlin paused so long that Alex finally said, "So what?"

"So . . . what if I told you that the children of Seth were not the only people to have survived the Flood? Abel, the second son of Adam, was killed by Cain before he could bear any children. But Cain . . . Genesis chapter four states that Cain found a wife; where she came from is a mystery that did not survive historical accounts, but Cain and his unnamed wife bore a son, called Enoch. Enoch bore a son named Irad, Irad bore Mehujael, Mehujael bore Methushael, and Methushael bore Lamech. Curiously, the text provides the names of these first descendants, but does not provide any details about who they were, how long they lived, or the lives they led. Instead, it skips on to the next man in Cain's line and provides more detailed information about him. Why? Could it be because the writer of Genesis—commonly held to be Moses—was unaware of what became of Cain and his first descendants?

"What the Bible does not record is that somewhere along the line, these men—Cain and his five firstborn descendants—discovered a cavern deep underground. You know the cavern I speak of; many of you have been there. They built a city there, far below the original site of the Garden of Eden, the birthplace of mankind. The cavern was impossibly huge in size, yet completely sealed off from the earth above, and flowing with water and geothermal heat . . . It was as if it had been set aside just for Cain and his children to inhabit. At the bottommost point of this multilevel cavern, they found a unique chamber they called the Hollow, which was inscribed with a colossal six-pointed symbol. The Secretum would later adopt this powerful symbol as its insignia; they named it 'Cain's Lament.' "

Devlin paused to allow this to sink in.

"You're saying," Daniel said slowly, "that you and your people—the Secretum—are the descendants of Cain?"

Devlin nodded, then continued his story. "Genesis chapter four, verse seven, tells of a profoundly significant moment in the life of our father Cain. Just after his brother has been honored and he has been shamed, God tells Cain that sin waits like a hungry lion to devour him, but he must overcome it. Master it. *He* . . . must *master* . . . *sin*." Devlin repeated with great emphasis.

"After Cain murdered his brother and was sent away as an outcast, he reflected on these words, and came to regard them as a personal charge, a singular purpose that could only have been assigned to him. At last understanding the magnitude of what he'd done in taking his brother's life, Cain couldn't reconcile himself with the fact that God has spared *his*. Not only was his life spared, but God promised vengeance 'seven times over' upon anyone who killed Cain. Why such drastic measures to ensure Cain's survival? Cain made the connection between these two divine statements quickly: He'd been spared for a very special task. He alone would find a way to master sin. It was his destiny.

"The Bible records that in those times, people lived a great deal longer than we live now, aging up to one thousand years old, even older. Yet the Good Book does not reveal how long Cain lived before his death. *We,* his children, know that he lived a very long time, long enough to still be alive when many of the very same descendants I listed a moment ago were born, and grew to be men, and had children and descendants of their own. Together with this group of his five most direct firstborn sons, Cain forged his own society. A secret culture that would live hidden beneath the world in the place that had been prepared, to preserve them against the coming Flood, so that they could carry out the great task the Maker had set before Cain: to master sin."

"You really believe all this?" Daniel said, leaning forward in his chair. "That Cain's descendants have been alive all this time, hidden away where no one knew about you . . . so that you could attempt a preordained task to 'master sin'?"

Devlin eyed him knowingly. "Who better than the first murderer to find a way to undo the wickedness inherent in man's heart?"

"So how does that get you here, to all of this pain and devastation?" Daniel's expression turned dark again, and he settled back into his chair.

"There were six of them, including Cain himself," Devlin continued, "and the Secretum of Six is named in their honor. We are more than an organization, more than a religion, more than a nation. We are a complete, self-sufficient society that has grown and flourished and evolved independent of the rest of the world.

"The Flood ravaged the earth and exterminated the human race, but the Flood did not reach the Secretum's home, so perfectly sealed off it was, and so we continued to multiply and survive in our underground home. But over time, Cain's people became aware of the Flood, and we believed it to be confirmation of what we were called to do.

"You see, from its inception, the human experiment was flawed. The Creator imbued His creations with free will. He set out to see if a self-aware, sentient species that had the ability to choose its own path would willingly choose the path of light. The Secretum watched from a distance as the depravity in Noah's time led the Maker to resolve that He would wipe away humanity with a great disaster. It was the answer to the experiment—cold, hard evidence that man is incapable of choosing the path of light for himself.

"But God loved Noah, so much so that, after the Flood, he promised Noah that He would never again wipe out earth's populace with a disaster. God, being perfect and existing outside of time, knew from the very beginning of His creation that He would make this promise to Noah, just as He knew that binding himself by this promise would make himself incapable of violating it.

"Which is why He provided the children of Cain with a prophecy, to guide our actions. You know the prophecy; seven thousand years ago it was inscribed on the object known as the Dominion Stone, which is a piece of the Hollow itself."

"But where did this prophecy come from?" Daniel asked.

"Cain's wife. She was a seer possessing insights into the nature of the universe that made sane men tremble. Her most important prediction was recorded on the Dominion Stone and preserved there for millennia, and the Secretum began the difficult task of gathering the resources necessary to ensure that everything in the prophecy came true."

"That's why you've been interfering in human history for thousands of years," Alex observed.

"Of course," Devlin replied. "The prophecy states that the Secretum will guide the coming of the Bringer, and the Bringer will set free the Angel of Death, giving him free reign and dominion over the earth. This is precisely what we have done."

"But *why*?" Alex pressed. "If humanity's free will is the problem, how does bringing forth Oblivion fix it?"

"Oblivion will annihilate mankind. Without man, there will be no free will, and all of the pain and trouble it has wrought will finally, beautifully, be wiped away."

50

"So let me see if I understand this," Daniel began thoughtfully. "You took a being whose sole purpose is to end life . . . You took this creature and you shoehorned it into a Grant Borrows–shaped wrapper, giving it the powers of the Bringer. You essentially provided it with a lifetime supply of steroids and energy drinks. Oblivion is an all-powerful killing machine with the ability and the will to destroy the entire planet . . . and you made it infinitely easier for him to do that." He paused. "Are you people out of your minds?"

"By your standards, perhaps we are."

"By our standards," Payton spat, "you're not even *people*."

"You're an intelligent, civilized human being," Ethan said, bitterness etched into his voice. "How can you allow this? We're talking about *billions* of innocent lives!"

Devlin snorted.

"What's funny?" Alex asked.

" 'Innocent.' How casually your people use that word to describe yourselves. One could *choke* on the irony."

"You should be so lucky, you miserable git," Payton threatened, a hand on his sword's hilt.

"Death is a necessary part of our task," Devlin explained with horrifying calm. "It's unfortunate, we do not relish it, but it is required. The Creator's promise to Noah prevents Him from wiping out all life on earth again, or surely He would have already done so—look at how far mankind has come since Noah's day! Human sacrifices and slavery. Mass ritual suicides. Torture and violence celebrated in art! Child predators! Sexual degradation at your fingertips! We've fallen further into depravity than even those in Noah's time. Can you imagine how much lower mankind will go, given time?"

"You actually believe you're the good guy here, don't you?" Ethan asked, incredulous.

"The Secretum of Six worships Jehovah, the God of Cain. Our purpose is to carry out His greatest work—the work that He cannot and will not carry out himself."

"The Angel of Death," Payton replied, scoffing at the words. "Oblivion is the *Angel of Death*?"

"He has many names," Devlin replied calmly. "The Destroyer. The Destroying Angel. The Angel of the Lord. The Angel of Death. Now, for the first time ever, he lives within human flesh, and in that form he is known as Oblivion. But he has existed since the beginning of time. He entered the houses of the Egyptians and smote their firstborn sons. He struck down some two hundred thousand Assyrian soldiers when that conquering nation threatened Jerusalem during the reign of King Hezekiah of Judah. He delivered the plague that David chose as punishment for his sin of pride—a plague that killed seventy thousand in just three days. And he is the fourth horseman of the Apocalypse, who will ride a pale horse at the end of time."

"But time *has* ended, hasn't it?" Nora spoke up and asked. "Is this the Apocalypse—what's happening now?"

"I rather think that time has merely . . . taken a breather. Once Oblivion has finished his work, the Creator will create life on this planet anew, and time will resume."

"What do you mean, 'create life anew'?" Alex asked.

"Do you still not understand?" Devlin observed, mildly surprised. "Like the Bringer before him, Oblivion wears the Seal of Dominion. And the Seal unlocks the Gates."

"What gates?"

"The center of the earth. Another dimension. A dark spiritual realm. Whatever framework you think of it in, it's a real place that exists. And it's not the 'fire and brimstone' prison you were taught about in Sunday school. The simplest definition for it is that it is the place where evil *lives*. Thrives. Grows. And from which it spreads.

"Evil infests that place, and like all that is vile, it lusts after *more* of everything. It is confined there, but it eternally rages against its bonds like a caged animal. And it grows ever more restless. The Gates are all that keep that terrible place from pressing in on our reality. The Seal is the only known object in existence that can peel back the boundaries between dimensions and let Gehenna loose to consume our world. Which is precisely what Oblivion has done. Look around you. Does this place now not contain the physical properties of all that is bad, all that is wrong and cruel and impure?"

"So earth is being . . . *annexed* by Hell. Wonderful. But why would Oblivion unleash this if he's just going to kill us anyway?" Alex asked.

"He cannot do otherwise," Devlin replied. "Revelation 6:8—'I looked, and there before me was a pale horse! Its rider was named Death, and Hades was following close behind him.' Where Oblivion goes, Hell must follow."

"That's why the sky is burning and the land has turned to volcanic rock and why there are wildfires spread out all over the place," Daniel said, more to the others than to Devlin.

"Where you see Hellfire," Devlin corrected, "I see the very fires of creation."

"So why did time stop?" Alex asked.

"Time did not 'stop'; it has simply been . . . removed. Time is a scientific law imposed upon mortal reality. Its forward motion defines our existence. But we are no longer existing in a realm defined by the strictures of mortal science. When Oblivion was birthed into human flesh, the Gates were opened and that terrible place began to spread into our reality. This place is earth no more. It is the DarkWorld, possessing the same properties as that place of suffering and torment—a place that exists wholly outside of time and space."

"You haven't answered my question," Alex said. "What did you mean when you said Oblivion was making it so that the Creator can 'create life anew'?"

"Oblivion has come to earth," Devlin replied. "He is the Unmaker. Everything that is living, he will turn to death. And he will not stop here. Once he is finished with our world, he will spread his reach into the very cosmos and render all of the stars and other planets as nothing but ash. If any other life exists in the universe, he will destroy it as well.

"He will lay waste to existence itself, and once he has consumed the mortal plane and everything within it, once the earth has faded into primordial ash, it will be a void, formless once more. Just as it was in the beginning. And the Creator will have a blank canvas upon which to start again.

"He was bound by his own promise to never again exterminate the human race, so we have done it for Him. Now, He will be free to create a new race who will *always* do that which is right, and in whom He can delight without regret."

"You mean a race without free will," Daniel said.

"Precisely," Devlin replied.

51

"So that's it, then," Daniel said with finality. "That's what all of this has been about? The Bringer, the Dominion Stone, the Rings, the prophecy, every single way you've manipulated all of our lives . . . It was about you pressing some kind of cosmic reset button."

Devlin merely looked at him, but there was a hint of triumph upon his face.

Daniel was unmoved. "Alex isn't the only one who heard Bible stories as a kid. My mom even sent me to Sunday school once upon a time. And in all this time, for all your centuries of preparation, I can't believe you missed the point," Daniel said, shaking his head bitterly. "*I* understand it better than you do, and I don't even buy in to it. It couldn't be more obvious: The Creator *wanted* us to have the choice between right or wrong. Because in our choosing, we prove not only His goodness, but His very existence. He has no interest in mindless robots—He wants those who *choose* to do what's right."

"But we cannot!" Devlin cried. "If allowed to proceed unchecked, humanity will only dream up newer and more deplorable subversions of what the Creator intended!"

Daniel looked upon the older man with loathing. He stood and casually removed a pistol from the back of his pants—a gun no one knew he had—and pressed the muzzle against

Devlin's right temple. Everyone reacted in shock—some almost cried out—but no one made a move.

"I should kill you where you sit," Daniel said coolly, "but would that really end this debate? Would that action be right or good? It would *feel* good, after what you—" His voice broke, and he couldn't finish the thought. Tears burned behind his eyes.

"Daniel, I'm not sure you're thinking clearly," Alex said softly, alarmed and trying to feed calm into him. But his emotions were much too strong for her to overcome now.

"How do you know that, Alex? How do any of you know what the real me is like? Maybe the real me isn't a scientist at all, but a cold-blooded killer. I wasn't lying when I told Yen Wei I was a murderer. Did you know it was me who killed Matthew Drexel? I shot him in the forehead with a gun just like this one."

"Don't expect any tears over that death," Payton scoffed. "Drexel was a predator who deserved a far worse fate than a quick demise."

"But that was different," Alex argued.

"The only difference is that this time, *Lisa's dead*!" Daniel thundered, face red and eyes bulging. "We're all going to die anyway—what difference would it make if Devlin went a little early? Not a soul here could argue that he doesn't deserve it!" Daniel said, facing Devlin. "You might just deserve it more than any single individual in recorded history. If the full extent of your crimes were known, any jury in the world wouldn't just convict you, they would personally tear you limb from limb! And no one would feel bad about it after! Just like *I* won't."

He pressed the gun so hard into Devlin's temple, the weapon nearly broke the old man's skin. Devlin never flinched or even closed his eyes; he simply watched and waited.

Daniel's damaged body was taut, a coiled spring. He gripped the gun viciously, as if pouring all of his sorrow into its gleaming black form. He gazed into Devlin's unconcerned face with malice, anger, pain, and grief . . .

Slowly, as everyone watched with breath caught, Daniel pulled back the gun and released the magazine, allowing the bullets to fall out of it. There was a single bullet still in the chamber, and Daniel held stiffly to the weapon as if unable to separate his hand from it.

At last he released his grip on the gun, but flipped it in the air so that he was holding the barrel. With a move so fast it made even Payton blink, he reared back with the same hand that held the gun and swung it horizontally so that the butt of the handle collided with Devlin's head. He released the gun as he ended his follow-through. It clanked and rattled as it settled on the floor several feet away.

"That was for her," Daniel whispered.

A purple egg rose instantly on Devlin's forehead. His neck bowed and he struggled to maintain consciousness.

"Why . . . why didn't you kill me?" Devlin slurred.

"Because the choice was mine to make," Daniel replied. "And I made it. I don't expect you to understand."

As everyone watched, uncertain of what Daniel might do next but unwilling to stop him, he put a hand in his inner jacket pocket and withdrew a small baggie, inside of which waited sixteen Rings of Dominion. He retrieved one from the bag and tossed the rest to Ethan. Out of another pocket, he dug a piece of the Dominion Stone and pressed it into a gash on the neck he'd suffered at Devlin's hands.

It was eerily quiet inside the tiny house, all alone in this deserted neighborhood. There were no sounds of life, traffic, or nature outside. Inside, all that could be heard were the sounds of breathing.

As everyone watched, Daniel clung tightly to the Stone that touched his own blood while sliding the Ring onto the middle finger of his right hand.

Daniel stared at the Ring as it slid into place and said aloud his answer to the unspoken question on everyone's lips. "I think . . . she wanted me to."

Here in the infinite quiet, every detail stood out as he slipped the Ring on. The same blinding white light, shining from the Ring's burgundy gemstone. A light so complete that it enveloped Daniel until he himself was glowing. Faint and distant, there was a sound of tearing and rending, as if reality itself were confused and revolting against such an unnatural act.

When the glow subsided, Daniel touched the Ring to find that it had bonded to his skin and would not come off.

And then he vanished where he stood.

52

Daniel reappeared standing next to Alex, at almost the same moment he'd disappeared.

"Whoa . . ." he said, placing a hand to his head and shaking out the cobwebs.

"Did—did you just teleport?" Ethan asked.

Daniel didn't reply. He was leaning over, holding one knee for support.

A wave of nausea and discomfort washed over Alex. She glanced at Daniel, who was still doubled over. Whatever he was feeling, she was feeling it too.

But she wasn't using her powers on him . . .

"I think he's using my empathic powers, spreading his anxiety to me," Alex said.

"I feel it too," Nora added, moving to the far end of the couch as if to get out of range of the effect.

Hector raised his hand in agreement, then reached around to touch Daniel on the hand, alleviating his queasiness. Testing a theory, Alex placed her own hand on Daniel's shoulder after Hector had turned loose of him. The anxiety she felt vanished as well.

"How could he be using your powers?" Ethan asked.

"Before that, was that Payton's speed, when he disappeared and reappeared?" Alex asked.

"Yeah, maybe . . ." Ethan replied. "It looked just like Payton when he enters superspeed."

"Daniel," Alex said, "I think your power is to mimic what other Ringwearers can do."

Daniel nodded, seemingly having already arrived at the same conclusion. "Proximity seems to trigger it. Fascinating . . ."

"Indeed it is fascinating. And pointless. You act as if your deaths are not foregone conclusions," Devlin said. "You are fools. We are all going to die, just as it was meant to be. Oblivion is nearing the city limits of Jerusalem as we speak. He will walk to the Old City, and once he's there, he will put into action his endgame. And everything will end, once and for all."

"What will he do in Jerusalem, exactly?" Payton asked.

"You are familiar with the Bringer's ability to send out a blast wave of pure energy, yes?" Devlin replied. "According to the prophecy, Oblivion will use this final stopgap to let loose a blast of extraordinary energy, a wave so powerful it will envelope the earth and obliterate everything—and everyone—in its path. The skies will open and fire will pour out and cleanse the land, wiping away anything that remains."

No one knew what to say. What could anyone say or do in the face of such awesome primordial power?

"So what do we do?" Ethan asked.

"What would Grant do?" Alex asked, though it wasn't really a question.

"Grant is gone, my dear," Devlin said with sincerity. "There is nothing left of him. You should try to remember that."

"You're wrong," Alex replied, even though she felt no deceit in him.

"Alex . . ." Ethan began. "We're at the end of the world here. Maybe it's time to finally let Grant go."

Alex looked around, and everyone was watching her in a similar fashion to Ethan, as if she were a starry-eyed idealist clinging to some romantic notion.

"I don't believe that," Alex replied without hesitation. "Julie wouldn't believe it. And neither would Morgan."

"Oblivion has total control over his body," Ethan went on. "*If* Grant is somehow still in there—and that's a huge 'if'—none of us knows how to draw him out again."

Alex looked to Daniel, who merely nodded his head in agreement.

"Then we won't try," Payton said.

The others turned to him and waited.

"Oblivion is a threat. Our job is to eliminate that threat. If one must die so billions can live, then that one will die."

53

"No!" Alex cried, jumping to her feet as well. "Grant has saved your life a dozen times over, and this is how you'll repay him?"

The edge in Payton's voice grew harder and more savage by the moment. "Yes, it is. I have known from the first time we met that the Bringer and I would end this—*all* of this—in a confrontation between the two of us. And only us."

"Don't you even think about it," Alex nearly whispered.

"You were there!" Payton roared, a terrible sound that was louder than anyone thought the British man could speak. "You saw what I did to those people! You saw what Oblivion *made* me do!"

Alex's mind filled with images of a possessed Payton cutting, hacking, stabbing, and slicing his way through countless people while on Oblivion's march.

Counting the coalition soldiers he'd taken out . . . there were *hundreds* of them. Possibly thousands.

"You're an assassin!" she yelled. "You kill people for a *living*! How is what Oblivion made you do any different?"

"I DON'T KILL THE INNOCENT!!" he thundered. "I have *never* killed the innocent! I knock off serial murderers, rapists, career criminals . . . the ones who have no intention of changing. But *never* do I take a job that endangers an innocent!"

Silence filled the space as each person digested this in turn.

Payton spoke up again. "You don't want to hear it, but this final confrontation is the reason he and I are both mentioned on the Dominion Stone. We know now why the Bringer was created. And now I know why the Thresher was created. I am here to keep him in check. If anything should go wrong, I am the only person alive capable of taking him down. It was meant to happen this way. It's the *only* way."

Alex's eyes flared, and the menace she felt pulsing through her veins overflowed from her and filled everyone in the room. *"You will not touch him."*

"I *will*," Payton said, stepping toe-to-toe with her. "I swore in an oath of blood long ago that I would be the one to kill him. I have the weapon forged millennia ago of purest silver. I was meant to do this, it is my purpose, it is the reason I died in that cave ten years ago and was revived. In killing the Bringer, I am fulfilling the function for which I was born."

"Try it and I swear I'll stop you."

"Don't embarrass yourself, love."

"I've stopped you before. I could reduce you to a quivering blob of infantile hysterics right here and now! And maybe I will! Ask me, it's long overdue that someone took you down a peg, *Thresher*!"

"Why so much emotion over one man?" Payton said, shaking his head, incredulous. "Grant of all people would approve of my intentions. He would do everything in his *own* power to take down Oblivion, if he were here."

"Why am I trying to explain myself to some *machine*, like he's a normal person with normal feelings? What makes you think you could ever understand anything about real human emotions?" Alex rebutted.

Payton spat upon the ground where Alex stood, and she jumped back an inch. "Whereas your life experience is summed up entirely in selfishness and need. What do you know of pain and misery and loss? Have you ever lost someone you loved more than you love yourself?"

"YES!!" she screamed.

"WHO?" he shouted.

"Who do you *think*!" she said, and now she was crying with very real tears while shouting at the top of her lungs. "I love *him,* all right! I was—I *am*—I'm in love with Grant!"

Everyone but Devlin looked at one another nervously, and no one dared make a sound.

Alex caught her breath and then spoke again, deflated. "I love him. I can't let him go. I won't."

Even Payton was looking down now, examining his own feet. When he spoke, his voice was barely audible. "If what you say is true . . . then you, above all, *must* let him go."

"The way you let go of Morgan?"

From a distant corner of the room, someone gasped. The rest dared not make a sound. Every eye was on Payton, because Alex had just crossed the uncrossable line.

Payton was lethal, and Alex could feel it. It was taking everything within him not to strike Alex where she stood.

"Wait—Morgan's Ring!" Ethan exclaimed, breaking the moment. "We have to have all 299 Rings, according to what Morgan said in that video, and without hers, we're still one short. We need to find it before we can go to Jerusalem—"

"No need," Payton said, still staring down Alex. Without facing Devlin or moving from his position at all, he whipped out his sword and cut a sideways gash into the older man's shirt. Hanging there over his heart was the last Ring of Dominion, dangling from a thin gold chain. "Saw the bulge when I grabbed him."

"Of course," Daniel said, nodding. "He would already know everything Morgan told us. And that only proves that it's true—that all 299 of us stand some real chance of stopping Oblivion! He'd want to keep the last Ring close to himself, so he didn't run the risk of someone else finding it. If he had it on him, he knew *we* didn't have it. But we have to hurry . . ."

Daniel stepped forward and tugged hard on the gold chain so that it snapped. He tossed the Ring to Ethan, who put it in the bag with the others.

"Where in the Old City is he going?" Ethan asked Devlin.

"Where would *you* go, if you were Oblivion?" Devlin replied.

"The Temple Mount," Alex and Payton both said at the same time.

"Of course," Ethan remarked. "The Dome of the Rock, original site of Solomon's Temple. The most significant spiritual location in the world. Where better to defile—"

"Wait, I don't buy it," Alex chimed in, her brows knitted together in furious thought and her tone completely changed from just a moment before.

The others stared at her with curiosity, with the sole exception of Daniel, who caught on at once. His eyes lit up with a newfound energy, and he nodded at her.

"If Oblivion is so all-powerful," Alex went on, "then desecrating a sacred site is not a very compelling reason to wait this long to finish us off. He could've wiped every living creature from the face of the earth any time he wanted. What difference does it *really* make where he's located when he works his big whammy?"

No one responded.

"It's not Oblivion showing restraint or patience. It's Grant," she concluded.

"But Grant didn't survive the transformation," Daniel argued, even though his voice betrayed the fact that he wanted to believe it.

Devlin turned to face Alex. "Oblivion waited to enact his plan according to the specific series of events that the prophecy—"

"Forget the *prophecy*!" Alex shouted. "You said that even the Creator swore not to get involved in matters of human free will. So what else is there that's powerful enough to hold Oblivion back? It's got to be Grant! Wherever he is, *what*ever he is—he still has some influence over Oblivion's actions, and it's *him* that's kept Oblivion from ending this until now. Grant is still in this, and he's bought us some time. So we're not going to waste it—we're going to finish this thing."

"Alex, that's an awfully big leap to think that Grant could still be . . ." Ethan said, shaking his head.

"But," Nora spoke up, her voice clouded with doubt, "what if we can't get through to Grant? Oblivion is too powerful for any of us. What if we can't—"

"There are other sources of power in this world than death or telekinesis or magic Rings," Alex replied. "And if you didn't learn that in all the time you spent with Grant, then I don't know why you're still here. There's power in words. There's power in tears. And there's power in *blood*. I promise you, this is not over."

"There's also power in steel, and that's good enough for me," Payton proclaimed, placing a hand on the hilt of the weapon at his side. "The rest of you can do what you want. I'm done waiting. Sit here and wait for the blast wave to reach you, for all I care. I'm going to find out what happens when that prophecy about a final confrontation between the Bringer and the Thresher comes true."

INTERREGNUM

"WHAT IS THE POINT of this, Grant Borrows?" asked the man Grant fought with, still tearing at him with all he was worth. "Why do you fight a battle you know you cannot ultimately win?"

Even as he struggled against this creature in this place of dark, black nothingness, his thoughts raced back to something Payton had said to him as they trekked together into the bowels of the Secretum's underground city. And to what Payton's observation about the nature of the universe had made him think to himself . . .

"Because," he answered, "I believe our actions have consequences that reach beyond anything we can see. Because standing in the face of darkness and choosing not to succumb to it is the most powerful thing anyone can ever do."

Mirror Grant pulled away and stood up, extricating himself from the fight.

Grant stood too, ready to tackle him again, but he froze at the sight. His twin was covered in blood, bruised, battered, and beaten.

"Why?" the doppelganger asked.

"Because . . . maybe the fight . . . is more important than the outcome."

The duplicate man placed both hands behind his back. He didn't smile, he didn't frown, he didn't argue. He looked upon Grant as though meeting him for the first time.

"You see it at last," the other man said. "The answers have been in front of you all this time, but only now do you finally allow yourself to see the truth of who you are. Who you have always been . . ."

A bright light flashed against the emptiness, and Grant was staring at himself, running through the underground tunnel that led away from the Inveo Technologies plant. Hannah was far ahead, calling for him to hurry, but he was talking on his cell phone. "There are no coincidences," said Daniel's voice into his ear.

Another flash, and Morgan was sitting in one of the bedrooms at the old asylum, talking to an elderly Hispanic woman. "Your friend," said the old woman known as Marta, "is part of something that stretches back throughout history. Those like him have been with us since the very beginning."

Flash. Grant was sitting in his penthouse condo at the top of the Wagner Building, talking to Daniel face-to-face for the first time. "Where you see random occurrences," Daniel said, "I see design. I see meaning. I see *purpose*."

Flash. Grant was on an airplane, sitting next to Morgan. "You are more than I ever had any right to hope you would become, after all you've been through," she said. "You're kind, compassionate, strong. You place the welfare of others above your own."

The images faded away, replaced instantly by the horribly damaged face of the man who looked exactly like him. Grant was sickened by what he saw. He'd beaten this man, this being, to a pulp. He was no hero, he was a ten-year-old brat in a man's body who had frequent temper tantrums.

How could he be responsible for hurting someone this way?

"Others see more in you than you see in yourself," the double said. "This is always the way it is."

"I'm sorry . . ." Grant blurted out. "I'm sorry about everything."

The other man smiled through his broken teeth and bruised face. "You're not the first to wrestle with me, you know. People do it every day. And in the end, it doesn't really matter."

As Grant watched, the injuries across the other man's face and body faded and vanished, until he was whole once more.

"What matters are the choices I make," Grant said.

The other man nodded.

Grant felt himself smile. It was a most pleasant sensation that he had nearly forgotten.

"I think I know who you are now," Grant said. "It *is* you, isn't it?"

"It always has been."

"You're nothing like I expected you to be," Grant admitted.

The other man actually laughed, and it was a warm, gentle laugh that was soothing and refreshing to Grant's soul.

"So what happens now?" Grant asked.

"This is your story, Grant," the other man replied. "How do *you* want it to end?"

54

Alex watched the skies.

No birds sang in the air above Jerusalem. No leaves rustled, nor did the dying trees provide soothing shade.

The clouds above roiled and churned like never before, billowing to incredible size in mere seconds, and then vanishing in a blink. The fire behind the clouds burned with a new intensity as well, desperately seeking to break free from the clouds that held it back, and Alex could swear she felt greater heat than before radiating down on them from so high above.

Wild animals roamed across the black desert, savages searching for prey of any kind. Even non-carnivorous creatures had been driven wild and hungered for blood and meat instead of plants.

Jerusalem was dead or dying, breathing its last weary gasps before a restless death. Not even a breeze brushed against the ancient city to cool its wounds.

No longer resting on a hill, Jerusalem had collapsed into a valley shaped like a shallow bowl, just one week before the DarkWorld was born. Many of her ancient buildings had fallen during the event, reduced to smoking heaps of white Jerusalem Stone. The death toll was catastrophic. Now it was burning, destitute. Writhing in a pain all its own.

Jerusalem had succumbed to Hell.

The DarkWorld was an unnaturally quiet place, thanks to the way people fled from Oblivion's coming. But pandemonium ruled Jerusalem's streets as Alex led her people through the outskirts of the city. Hundreds of thousands of souls had fled in panic to the refuge Jerusalem provided, but now they were trying with all their might to get out.

Everyone knew that Oblivion had come to town.

Numerous languages were represented among the shouted exclamations from the people, but Alex made out a few snatches of "The Destroyer is here!" and "It's the end of the world!" or "The Evil One has come to Jerusalem!"

There was so much to take in, but Alex kept finding herself watching the skies.

From an Eastern vantage point at the far edge of the Jaffa Road, the New City was a stark contrast to the Old, with modern architecture and automobiles, posh hotels, government buildings, and pocket neighborhoods tucked here and there. Very little of it was untouched by the sunken earth.

The Old City lay in the distance ahead, to the southeast of their position, near the bottom-most part of the bowl-shaped valley. Her historic walls made of white Jerusalem Stone were all but gone, blasted away by Grant when he was here last, in a fit of uncontrollable frustration. He hadn't meant to do it, Alex knew. But after days and days of cleaning up dead bodies and destroyed historic sites, he could no longer keep his emotions—which had always had a strong link to his powers—in check. The display of raw, awesome force had terrified Jewish authorities, who then turned on him, no longer welcoming his help but threatening war should he refuse to leave the country's borders.

A horrific thought occurred to Alex. What if she was wrong about Grant slowing Oblivion's plans? What if Oblivion had selected this site from which to end the world because he was getting even in some way for this residual memory he still had? Or, as Devlin inferred, was this some inescapable bit of instinct or programming that he simply could not deter? He was an ancient creature; perhaps instinct drove him to this place.

No matter the outcome of the events about to unfold, she would probably never know why this location was chosen. She only knew she was not happy to be back here.

Alex asked Daniel, Tucker, and Xue to come with her. Nora, Hector, Mrs. Edeson, and her son Ryan she sent off in a branching direction that would run them parallel to their path. Hopefully it would mean at least some of them would make it through the unseen obstacles that she knew had to be blocking the way leading to the Old City.

Ringwearers, Alex guessed. Two hundred and fifty superpowered individuals who would blend in with those people who'd stayed behind, hunting them with their enhanced and diverse array of mental powers. It seemed impossible that they would make it into the Old City without being discovered. Sergeant Tucker had pointed this out earlier as they were leaving the house.

Payton, meanwhile, refused to travel with either team. He had broken off early, pushing Devlin ahead of him. Alex wasn't entirely sure why Payton had brought Devlin along, but she was happy not to have the Keeper anywhere around.

And Ethan also had taken on a special solo mission.

There are so many ways this could go wrong, she thought.

"How do you filter out all these strong emotions?" Daniel asked as they walked. She glanced back and saw that he had put his hands over his ears, as if trying to block the same sensation that she was now feeling: panic, fear, paranoia, and so much more, flooding through hundreds of thousands of individuals. Navigating the streets was challenging enough, what with so many frightened people rampaging through the city like caged animals that had been set free, without having to experience everything that they felt along the way.

"You don't," Alex replied.

"Then how do you deal with it? I mean, do you ever get used to it?"

Alex was about to reply when a sudden wave of nausea hit her, and she whispered, "Get down!"

Daniel, Tucker, and Xue each hit the ground just as she did, and the four of them crawled between the sea of feet and legs, behind the gates of a small dried-up garden adjacent to a tiny house.

Daniel lurched and vomited onto the ground next to him. Tucker fought to keep his down, while Xue had reservedly turned her head away from where Alex could see. Such an instantaneous reaction could only mean one thing.

"What's going on?" Daniel whispered, wiping his mouth with a sleeve.

"It's got to be Trevor; he's somewhere close by," Alex replied. Her head popped up over the edge of the fence just enough to get a look around.

"Who's Trevor?" Tucker asked.

"Trevor?" Daniel repeated. His expression changed.

The young British boy had the ability to nullify the powers of other Ringwearers, and an unfortunate side effect to this involuntary power was that they often felt sick in his presence. And now Trevor was under Oblivion's thrall, no doubt combing the area for intruders . . .

Daniel squared his shoulders, glanced at her.

"Don't even think about it, Doc," Alex said, knowing what he was probably planning.

"Do you trust me, Alex?" he asked.

She froze. "That depends on what you're about to do."

"We *are* here to free the Ringwearers, aren't we?"

"Yeah, but—"

"Go on without me," he said, and Alex was already starting to protest when Daniel put up both hands to stop her. "Please, just do it. I'll catch up. I made a promise and I have to keep it."

He stood to a stoop and hobbled on his weak foot, hunched over, until he was around the corner and out of sight.

Alex sighed, looking helplessly at Tucker and Xue, the two people on the team she knew the least.

I really wish Grant were here.

Payton forced Devlin to crouch as they approached the Old City, and crouched likewise himself. Devlin's hands were tied in front of him, but Payton relied on nothing else save his sword to keep his old mentor in check.

Unlike the others, who entered the city via main roads, Payton used back alleys and empty fields to make his approach, doing all he could to avoid the thousands of panicking people.

"Poor Thresher," Devlin whispered as they knelt just outside the remains of the Damascus Gate. "Always fighting the hopeless, bitter cause."

"It's hardly hopeless if I'm still fighting," Payton remarked, his alert, coiled body taking in their surroundings and making sure they hadn't been followed.

"I shall never understand you," Devlin said, ignoring their surroundings and the shoulder-to-shoulder crowd between them and their destination, and focusing entirely on Payton. "You hate this world as much as I do. Yet you keep fighting to save it, despite your disdain."

"And what does that tell you?" Payton asked idly, with very little interest in hearing the old man's answer. Tactically speaking, as long as Payton could keep his mentor talking, he wouldn't be trying to escape and warn Oblivion.

"It speaks volumes to your greatest weakness, my boy," Devlin replied. "After everything you've been through, all the times when those you loved and trusted turned on you . . . Even though you would *kill* another man for even suggesting it . . . Be honest with me now, at the end. You still believe that the human race is a thing worth saving. Don't you?"

How Payton loathed this man. Why had he brought him along? Truthfully, he wasn't entirely certain. Mostly he wanted to beat Devlin, to overturn all of his grand plans, and he wanted Devlin to be there to see it with his own eyes when it happened.

Yet he considered the words Devlin had spoken. None of his observations about humanity were incorrect.

Was it true? *Did* he believe that people were still worth fighting for? Payton was a legendary assassin, his skills honed to a razor's edge and unmatched by any fighter in the world. He knew that by definition, humans were selfish creatures, given to letting their survival instinct outweigh nobler concerns.

So what *was* he doing here?

Didn't the world deserve what it was about to get, courtesy of Oblivion? Hadn't it unapologetically merited this fate since mankind's earliest days?

Hadn't this world betrayed him countless times?

"I never kill the innocent," he'd told Alex. Yet by definition, there *were* no innocent to be found among humanity's numbers. Not one. All were guilty, all deserved death.

Payton stood, slowly and watchfully.

"You're not going to answer me, are you?" Devlin replied, his eyes still locked maddeningly on Payton. "You fear the answer, I know you do."

Payton considered gouging Devlin's eyes out, but then Devlin would just be that much harder to manage, and Payton needed to remain unencumbered.

"Bear witness to what I do next . . . and you shall have your answer."

55

Alex might not understand, but Daniel knew he was the only one who had a chance of getting close to Trevor.

If he could creep close enough to the boy to tap in to his powers and mimic them, Daniel believed he could reverse those powers back onto Trevor, canceling out his nullifying effect. It was a sound scientific principle, like two equally polarized fields aimed at each other, but he could only hope it would work in practice.

Daniel ducked quickly and quietly into the swarm of human beings, simultaneously trying to blend in and covertly look for Trevor. The boy had to be here somewhere among the crowd for them to have felt him so close before, but now the sensation had passed. Perhaps Trevor was doing some kind of sweep through the crowd.

Which way would he have been moving? The possibilities were too countless to consider, and Daniel had no experience with this sort of thing. Covert ops were Ethan's forte.

Daniel gave a feeble jump on his limp foot, trying to get his head high enough over the crowd to catch a glimpse of Trevor. Nothing. No sign of the kid.

The ground gave a tremble, the first quake Daniel had felt since that moment when time stopped.

He turned in place, looked off in the distance toward the Dome of the Rock.

Are you in there, Oblivion, waiting for us?

Are you in there, Grant?

Oblivion stood before the ornate double doors that led to the interior of the Dome of the Rock.

This was it. The place where he would end it.

The doors were bolted shut and sealed to prevent outsiders from intruding. Oblivion stepped toward them, as if he would turn incorporeal and phase through the solid doors. But at the last moment, the doors and the frames that held them in place blew inward, stirring up a cloud of dirt and dust and soot. Oblivion marched fearlessly through the smoke and into the revered building.

The building seemed to hum or tingle as if in anticipation of what he would do here. So much history. So much of mankind's beliefs and struggles and hopes and deaths sown into this ground. The earth itself felt welcoming to him, felt as though it were breathing a sigh of relief that all of the pains this ground had known were finally coming to an end.

Oblivion's reverie came to an end when he heard footsteps behind him. Two teenage boys had seen the open door and followed him inside.

They ran in, approaching Oblivion from behind. He remained facing forward, showing them his back.

"Hello?" one of them shouted in Hebrew. "Is it safe in here?"

Oblivion waited until they drew near. He turned, revealing to them his granite face and burning eyes. His face was implacable, his head tilted slightly to the right as he examined them.

The boys froze in place; one of them tried to scream but no sound emerged from his lips.

"Safe," Oblivion replied calmly, "is no longer a reality."

Oblivion jutted out both of his arms and grabbed their faces. A single gasp was heard before Oblivion made contact, and then the boys slumped to the ground, dead from his touch.

Oblivion looked down upon these boys, these mere children. He felt nothing for them. He did not consider himself cruel or uncaring or vicious. He was doing what he was created to do.

"Why don't you try that trick on me," said a voice he remembered hearing for a moment before it'd vanished.

Oblivion turned to find Ethan Cooke standing three feet behind him.

Ethan, fist wrapped to protect himself, slammed into him with a right hook that made hard contact with Oblivion's rocky hide. For the first time in his existence, Oblivion was surprised.

He slid backward across the floor, his dense shoulders, arms, and feet digging grooves into the ground. It shook violently beneath him.

Alex decided to honor Daniel's request. If Daniel was intent on finding that kid, she might as well let him. But she couldn't wait around forever.

"Hold it," Tucker whispered, holding out a hand, and the three of them ducked low behind the fence.

A moment later they peered over the fence as an animal crossed the driveway adjacent to the small house. At first Alex thought the creature might be a fox, but its fur was striped black and brown with scattered tufts of white and a white furry tail. Its head slinked lower than its body as its black eyes seemed to look through them, and it bared its sharp teeth, a white frothy liquid dribbling from its mouth. It passed in silence, either not noticing them or not stopping if it did. The sounds of chaos reached them from the main road, and Alex silently prayed that this thing wouldn't find the other team.

At the sound, the animal's head darted around to look, and then it was running at great speed into the dark.

"What was that?" Xue whispered as the three of them rose to their feet.

"Hyena, I think," Tucker replied.

"It was rabid," Xue observed.

"I think *all* the animals are rabid," said Tucker.

They stood carefully, watching the nearby crowds disperse as the hyena entered their midst. A few screams spread until they became many.

"Come on," said Alex, "let's find Daniel."

They returned to the Jaffa Road and worked their way through the crowd. The ground was unequivocally sloping downward now as they marched deeper into the heart of the great city, eyes scanning for Daniel. The Old City loomed a mile or so ahead, electrical lights scattered inside, illuminating the boiling sky.

Alex thought she caught a glimpse of someone who looked like Daniel and made to shout when a powerful electrical volt surged through her body and the bodies of her two companions. She seized violently, her whole body writhing as the energy poured through her system.

The electricity stopped for a moment, and all three of them fell to the ground, limp and weak.

Alex was on her back, and into her field of view stepped an unkempt, mousy Ringwearer she'd first met in Los Angeles the day of the riot. His name was Wilhelm, and he could exude electricity from his body at will. Grant had left him behind in Jerusalem to help with the cleanup and reconstruction when the team was forced out of the city.

He looked down at her, his dead, expressionless features all too familiar. Alex panicked, knowing exactly what this meant.

Game over. Oblivion knows we're here.

The ground quaked as electricity jumped from his fingertips again, rushing through them until smoke rose from their skin.

56

Daniel had wandered farther than he meant to, he realized, when he looked back and couldn't find the house with the garden where he'd left the others. The Old City loomed closer in his path ahead as well.

An outcry of screams made him spin in place, and he saw flashing sparks of light some two hundred feet away. His view was largely blocked by all the people, many of whom were trying to get away from the source of the lights.

Fighting the urge to panic and with Trevor still nowhere in sight, Daniel hastily made a platform out of a wrecked sedan and, standing at the top, bellowed, "TREVOR!!" as loud as he could.

Hundreds of faces turned in his direction. Daniel hopped down from his perch and waited. He felt Trevor before he saw him. But it was mere moments after calling out the kid's name that he felt the rising nausea in his gut.

Daniel closed his eyes and concentrated, forced himself to breathe slowly. He could very nearly sense the boy's powers emanating from somewhere nearby. He hadn't had to do anything to activate his mirroring ability with any of the others, so there was no reason to assume he would need to do anything to trigger the effect here. The one stumbling block was that the focal radius of Trevor's powers was known to be at least one hundred feet, possibly even wider. Daniel's powers required much closer proximity to work.

He swallowed down the food rising in his throat, forcing himself not to retch.

"Trevor . . . ?" Daniel called out, not as loud this time because he was dizzy and struggling to stay upright. He put out a hand to brace himself on a tree. Eyes darting in circles, he had to find Trevor, had to get a bead on the kid if he were to have any chance . . .

Come on, kid . . . Where are you?

The vertigo became overpowering and he toppled. Daniel's head was on the ground when he turned it to his left and saw a pair of torn blue jeans standing twenty feet away.

Trevor, dirty and exhausted, stood just out of Daniel's range, staring at him impassively.

Fading in and out of the unconsciousness brought on by Wilhelm's electrical attack, Alex caught fleeting images of things happening around her.

Light flashing on their surroundings as the electricity poured from Wilhelm . . .

Agonized screaming emerging from her own lips as well as her two friends . . .

No more flashes . . .

Wilhelm was on the ground, not far away . . .

He seemed to be rolling around, wrestling with someone . . .

Commotion all around as new legs and feet entered her field of view . . .

Someone was prying Wilhelm's attacker off of him . . .

Alex came to with Hector's hand upon her shoulder. She felt better instantly and stood up. A crowd had gathered around her—Tucker, Xue, Wilhelm, and the rest, all of whom appeared healthy and fine, no doubt thanks to Hector.

They stood over a dead animal on the ground—it was the hyena they'd seen only minutes earlier. Wilhelm appeared to be in control of his faculties again, with fresh red cuts all over his arms and chest. Hector touched his hand, and the cuts stopped bleeding and vanished.

Another earthquake asserted itself, this one enough to nearly knock most of them off their feet.

"Somebody please tell me what just happened," Alex said, rubbing her head to try to fight the onslaught of emotions from the people watching them and refusing to move on.

"I'm sorry" was all Wilhelm could muster. He looked even more diminutive and self-conscious than she remembered. And with good reason: He'd very nearly killed them.

"I summoned the animal, I think," said Sergeant Tucker, staring at the hyena lying in a sickeningly twisted position on the black earth. "I remember thinking about needing help when we were being electrocuted, and then the hyena appeared and attacked the short guy as if it were following my orders. And when we hid from it earlier, I felt something odd . . . I think I was *sensing* it. Its instincts, its intentions, its hunger."

Alex took this in. So that answered that. Tucker could sense and bend animals to his will.

She turned to Hector and his team. "How did you know we were in trouble?"

"How could we *not*?" Nora replied. "The light display was so bright it lit up the sky."

Alex took this in stride. "Wilhelm," she said, "you've been in this city for a while now, and I'm sure you know some of the people here. If Oblivion didn't know we were here before, he certainly knows now, which means the rest of the Ringwearers are no doubt converging on us as we speak. We need to get out of here, but we're going to have to recruit some local help if we're going to finish this."

Wilhelm hesitated as if too ashamed to contribute to the conversation.

"What you did wasn't your fault," Alex comforted him, placing a hand on his arm. "Believe me, I did much worse while I was under Oblivion's influence."

"I may know some people who can help," Wilhelm replied softly without looking at her. "But we must hurry."

Stay on the offensive, Ethan told himself, chanting it in his mind like a mantra. *Stay on the offensive!*

Dropping his guard long enough to let Oblivion get a blow in would mean his death. His only chance was to keep pummeling Oblivion, blow after blow, not giving the immortal being a chance to get his bearings.

His blood sped through his veins at dangerous speeds, and he loved every ounce of sensation. He wore thick gloves and a jumpsuit to protect himself from Oblivion's touch of death. A balaclava over his face, allowing only his eyes to peek through behind a pair of sunglasses, completed the effect.

Ethan hammered Oblivion again, sending him flying this time until he broke a hole in the outer wall of the ancient building and blew through it. The ground shook again, and Ethan ran over the moving earth, eager to catch up with his quarry before he recovered. He vaulted through the hole, rolled, and leapt to his feet running.

Oblivion was thirty feet away, getting to his feet already . . .

Ethan closed in on him, but Oblivion flung up a hand before Ethan could make contact. Ethan was sent soaring in reverse by Oblivion's psychokinesis back toward the Dome, but he turned quickly in the air so that he was moving feet first. His powerful legs absorbed the impact and he immediately kicked off of the brick wall. Oblivion had no time to react as Ethan barreled into him again, tackling with the force of a battering ram. The earth quaked once again in response.

Oblivion put his hands into the dead earth and dug in with four rocklike fingers on each hand. With deadened eyes that pierced Ethan's soul, the Angel of Death didn't move a muscle as he shot Ethan wildly into the air, aimed at the golden Dome.

57

"Are you all right?" asked a frail voice.

Daniel looked up; an elderly woman stood over him, leaning on a cane not unlike the one Daniel himself used to rely on.

He used one hand to brace himself against the ground and extended the other to the woman above him. With great effort, he was able to get to his feet, but he couldn't lean on her; she was too feeble. The nausea intensified, and he nearly doubled over from the abdominal pain.

This brought him at eye level with the old woman's cane.

"Borrow this?" he asked, grasping the cane with his free hand.

He threw it and it spun circles in the air. It clunked against Trevor's legs, and the boy went down.

Swallowing a fresh taste of bile, Daniel half-ran, half-crawled. Lurching toward Trevor, he made it just before Trevor got to his feet again. Daniel's powers finally kicked in and the queasiness immediately vanished.

Daniel pulled a sharp piece of the Dominion Stone out of his pocket and slashed Trevor across the palm of his hand with it. The Stone made contact with the boy's blood.

Trevor gasped, blinked, shook his head violently as if he were waking from a bad dream.

"You all right, son?" Daniel asked, catching his breath.

Trevor picked the cane up from the ground and returned it to the old woman. He was battered and weak, but he stood tall and looked Daniel in the eye. "Never better," he said.

Daniel appreciated the boy's attempt at bravery through his pain, but knew that finding Hector needed to be their first order of business.

"Come on," Daniel said, leading the way.

"Stay back!" a voice ordered over a bullhorn as Wilhelm led Alex and the others to a reconstruction encampment. "We do not wish to shoot you, but we will if you force us!"

A small city of tents had been erected where the cultural center of town had once been, but now was little more than black dirt with remnants of buildings piled on top. Parked between the tents was a row of military trucks and Jeeps that had seen a lot of hard use since the city's collapse. Spotlights running on portable generators shone on collapsed buildings where workers had recently been sorting through wreckage, cleaning up and trying to find bodies. Tens of thousands were still unaccounted for.

Alex guessed that the searching had stopped when Oblivion came to town.

She looked up; Daniel came hobbling onto the scene with Trevor in tow. He took in what was happening and wisely chose to stay back, out of the way.

One of the bright lights had turned at their approach and now Alex and the others were staring directly into the beam, making it hard to see much of anything else.

"Amiel! It's all right!" Wilhelm shouted back. "My friends have come; they're here to help us!" He stepped out from the crowd and walked forward, directly into the light.

The ground shuddered again, much harder this time, opening cracks and fissures in the earth and sending Alex and many of the others down to their knees. Alex could only wonder what was happening to Oblivion right now to cause him to lose control like this.

She looked to the skies, saw tiny holes opening in the boiling clouds and the raging fire beyond it, ready to pour down upon them.

"Wilhelm?" called out the voice on the other side. "Are you yourself again?"

"The others found a way to free me, to free all of us!" Wilhelm replied.

The light turned away, and when her eyes cleared, Alex saw a line of twenty men standing at the edge of the tent city, each of them holding a semiautomatic rifle. But they stood at ease, weapons pointed at the ground.

A short man Alex remembered from the last time she had visited Jerusalem stepped forward, welcoming them into the camp. His name was Amiel Yishai, and he'd quickly become friends with Grant after the city's collapse when Grant and the Loci had arrived to help with the cleanup.

"It's Alex, yes?" Amiel asked, a smile on his face.

She tried to smile back, but couldn't conjure up any semblance of happiness or warmth. "It's good to see you again, but I'm afraid we don't have much time. We're going to need your help . . ."

Her voice trailed off when she caught sight of Wilhelm carefully approaching a frightened-looking child, who sat nearby. Slowly, cautiously, he knelt and allowed the girl to approach him. Wilhelm knew this kid, Alex realized. But the girl was no doubt frightened by what had happened to Wilhelm when Oblivion overtook him, and was unsure of whether or not to trust him.

Wilhelm smiled and made a silly face, tugging on his ears and sticking out his tongue.

The girl's face broke into a timid grin, but she kept her distance. "Willuhm?" she said. Some sort of nickname, Alex supposed, or the girl's best attempt at pronouncing his name.

The fearful way the little girl looked on Wilhelm was having a profound effect on him; he was near tears. He looked helplessly at Amiel, who walked over and held the little girl's hand.

Amiel said something in Hebrew. It sounded comforting, reassuring.

Wilhelm faced his young friend with sorrow in his eyes, an unspoken request there. She said something soft in reply, looking down at the ground.

"She asked why you were so angry before," Amiel said.

"Oh . . ." Wilhelm moaned. "I wasn't angry, sweet girl. I wasn't angry. I . . ." He didn't know what to say. "I was . . . I was *sick*. My heart, it was . . . it was sick. Diseased. I didn't know what I was doing, I couldn't help myself. I'm sorry, little one, I'm so, so sorry."

She turned loose of Amiel and stepped forward into a hug by Wilhelm's welcoming arms. Wilhelm looked as if he'd just been brought back to life, and she squeezed tears from his body with her tiny embrace.

Alex moved a little closer, watching as the girl said something else.

Amiel translated. "The 'bad man,' " he said, "she wants to know if *he's* angry, or if his heart is sick like yours was?"

Wilhelm smiled through his tears, bittersweet at her innocent question.

"I . . . don't know, little one. He's just . . . he's not himself."

She replied, and Amiel translated again.

"Can you stop him, Willuhm? Will you make the bad man stop?"

Wilhelm hugged her harder, but cut his eyes across at Alex.

We'll stop him, Alex vowed. *One way or another, we'll stop him.*

58

The Tower of David, also known as the Jerusalem Citadel, rested inside an ancient fortress that touched the far western edge of the Old City.

Payton followed the main vehicular road through a gap in the ruins of the Old City walls. Inside, he moved southward, following the outline of where the walls had once stood, until he came upon the fortress. Largely medieval in design, with stone parapets and stairs, the structure was multileveled and tiered. Modern metal walkways and stairs had been added in various spots, providing tourists easy access to otherwise unreachable rooms and lookouts. The entire structure was crowned by a pinnacle tower that showcased Muslim architectural influences.

The Tower itself was a perfectly cylindrical minaret. Miraculously, it showed few signs of damage from the recent cataclysmic earthquake. Payton was amazed it hadn't collapsed, as it looked extremely old and fragile. But looks could be deceiving.

Payton's feet carefully navigated the uneven cobblestones atop the old structure as he directed Devlin toward the minaret. They stood on a grass-lined stone walkway, above ground level and so untouched by the DarkWorld's effects. To his right and above was a narrow white archway made of white stone—most of which was barely still standing.

Shortly after entering the Old City, he'd torn an entire sleeve off of his black jumpsuit and fashioned a gag for Devlin to prevent him from alerting anyone to their presence. He maneuvered them through the central courtyard until they faced the minaret.

Payton crouched low beneath a higher platform of stone and elbowed Devlin in the face. He lowered his old mentor to the ground, unconscious. But Payton did not rise to his feet once more.

Instead, he decided that it would be here, well out of sight, where he would watch and wait.

Ethan opened his eyes and found himself sprawled on his back near the top of the Dome of the Rock. The burning clouds seemed nearly on top of him, being up so high. But that view only held him for a second because the next thing he saw was an Israeli army truck rocketing through the air directly at him.

He jumped with all the enhanced might his legs would give him, barely making it out of the way as the truck slammed into the massive gold Dome. He heard a horrific crash behind him as the truck plunged through the roof and crashed onto the floor below.

His jump had taken him too far down the side of the Dome to get a handhold, the gold tile set too close together, and he tumbled on. Finally, at the bottom, a wide ledge separated the lower walls of the building from the Dome, and Ethan's feet found purchase there.

He glanced down at the ground. Oblivion was not where he'd last seen him; he couldn't spot those fiery eyes or that slate gray skin anywhere.

He turned to get another look at the gaping hole above, and saw Oblivion standing there, up the side of the Dome.

Ethan kicked off against the ledge, his superpowered legs sending him fifty feet high before gravity took over and he began to descend. He collided with Oblivion on his way down and gave him the best sucker punch he had.

The ground quaked immediately and a flash of sheet lightning lit up the city as Oblivion's frame blasted through the

Dome, creating another hole in its surface, and his immense dead weight silently plunged beyond it to the ground underneath. Ethan grabbed on to the lapels of Oblivion's brown leather jacket, riding this ancient creature all the way. The impact Oblivion caused created a small crater in the building's interior, and he was folded sickeningly within it.

Ethan got to his feet. He had one shot. Thankfully the many holes they'd smashed into the Dome let him orient himself to the rest of the city, and he grabbed Oblivion by the lower legs and began to spin in place.

Hope I gave this enough time, he thought. *Hard to tell without a watch that works. But I can't risk dragging this out any longer.*

He spun faster, twirling like a discus thrower, calling on every ounce of strength his superpowered muscles could muster.

Please let this work . . .

With everything he had, he finally let go and sent Oblivion soaring like a rocket, flying off into the dark, treacherous sky.

Oblivion met land again nearly half a mile to the west.

He made a spectacular crash into another ancient structure on the far edge of the Old City, digging another giant crater into its center. But he would not be deterred.

He wasted no time returning to his feet, taking in his surroundings.

He knew this place.

Oblivion climbed a cobblestone staircase to a secondary level and rounded a corner. He spotted a tall, narrow tower in the farthest corner of this castle and decided to walk toward it. Higher ground was always the best vantage point for his work.

But something wasn't right. He heard hushed footsteps, moving rapidly in his direction.

Oblivion had just turned a corner, moving toward an opposite entrance to the interior of the Citadel, when he stopped in place.

A lone figure blocked his path, forming a dark silhouette against the harsh surroundings. Oblivion saw the tip of a sword touching the ground. The sword was held perfectly vertical, and his flaming eyes slowly traced its long, gleaming silver edge upward until he found the hand that held it. A hand with a golden ring attached to it, a burgundy gemstone inset in its center.

Oblivion recognized this man, just as he recognized the weapon he wielded. Was he surprised to see this one alive? Not really.

This one had a particular knack for survival.

"Thresher," said his piercing, booming voice, an aberration of nature.

"Bringer."

Payton burst forward with his liquid speed, sword in both hands, before Oblivion could meet the oncoming attack with his burning eyes.

Payton fell upon him, slashing as hard and fast as he could with his powerful blade.

"The Bringer shall be slain at the hands of the Thresher," Payton said as he followed through, breaking away and slowly rounding catlike on Oblivion.

Oblivion had suffered a vicious, disfiguring diagonal gash across his face, but it didn't faze him. A tiny flicker of his head and Payton was zooming through the air. His body crashed against a stone wall behind Oblivion and was held in place there.

Delirious from the crash, Payton held stubbornly to his sword as tightly as his broken body would allow.

"That's what the prophecy says," gasped the Thresher before spitting on Oblivion's face. His words came in a fast exhalation as Oblivion sent crushing pain throughout his body. "Funny how the prophecy was so concerned with your arrival, but it said nothing at all about how long you would *stay*. I'm here to let you know: Time's up."

59

The sky flashed with terrible thunder and vicious lightning, and Oblivion flung Payton against another wall. Whether this went on for minutes or for hours, Payton could not tell, but on it went.

And yet. In the midst of the torture, he'd noticed something.

The curved scar on the back of Oblivion's hand had expanded into a circle. It was a circle that lay flat, wrapping around his wrist until one edge of the curve touched the other. It looked different somehow than the rest of the granite.

Payton swallowed bile and willed himself to stay awake. He was certain he had broken bones throughout his body, and imagined he had a good deal of internal bleeding. But he would not give in to death, not this death, not now. His part to play was not over yet. And he would refuse Oblivion this prize for as long as he could; every additional second Payton drew breath was a victory, and remaining alive was the only way he could fight back against Oblivion's merciless beating.

They were still outside in the courtyard, though Oblivion had dragged or thrown him from one end to the other and back again. He sneered at Payton repeatedly, an unusual display of emotion from this all-powerful being, and Payton was forced to wonder how much Oblivion knew of the prophecy about the Bringer and the Thresher.

The Bringer shall be slain at the hands of the Thresher, the prophecy stated. Perhaps Oblivion was enjoying proving it wrong.

"Poor, pathetic fool," called out a voice that did not belong to Oblivion.

Devlin strode into view, and Oblivion momentarily paused in the thrashing he was giving to Payton. So, the old man had gotten free.

"Did you really think you could kill Death incarnate?" Devlin asked, striding toward them with a smug expression, hands clasped behind his back.

Payton laughed out loud. It was a sound of rebellion, of not giving in. He savored the moment and the way his laughter made both Devlin and Oblivion recoil slightly.

"I didn't come here to kill him, you arrogant fool," Payton replied through broken jaws, still laughing. "I came here . . . to take back . . . what doesn't belong to him."

His left hand was balled into a fist, but neither Oblivion nor Devlin had yet noticed what he held within it. With every last ounce of strength left, he summoned his speed one last time and burst forward, digging the Dominion Stone fragment he'd been hiding into the giant slash he'd made across Oblivion's face, hoping against hope that the Stone would find some remnant of blood that still remained inside the body of Grant Borrows.

Alex, Daniel, and the others suddenly stopped. Their Rings vibrated and gave off a shimmering glow. "Did you feel that?" she asked.

"I did," Daniel replied.

"It was like . . . it was like a surge . . . like something passing *through* me," Alex explained. She looked around; the others nodded back. They'd all felt it, and though the sensation had passed, all of their Rings were still glowing.

Amiel Yishai was among them now, wearing one of the Rings of Dominion, along with many of his fellow cleanup workers. With the help of Amiel and Wilhelm, every unworn Ring had found a wearer among the good people of Jerusalem.

"This could be it, come on, we've got to hurry—" she said.

"Help me . . ." mumbled a new voice.

Alex spun. Stumbling toward them from behind a dying hedge was—

"Fletcher!" she shouted.

He collapsed on the ground, his eyes rolling back in his head, his Ring illuminating the area where he lay.

"Hector!" Alex called.

Their round friend bounded his way to the spot where Fletcher had collapsed, and touched him gently on the cheek. Hector closed his eyes and concentrated.

Fletcher's eyes fluttered, his cheeks filling with color again.

"Alex . . ." he said weakly, "I just—I got free. On my own."

"No," said Nora, "you had help."

Alex stood to her feet and spun in place, taking in the sight of hundreds of bright lights that were shining like tiny stars, dotting the city in every direction. In fact, there were almost *three hundred* of the impossibly bright, shimmering lights . . .

Understanding washed over her at the sight, and her heart began beating faster . . .

"Look!" she cried, smiling and pointing at the lights. It was the first time she'd smiled since Grant died. "I'm guessing there's no need for us to sneak around anymore."

The others took in the sight, and as they did, Alex turned to her team. "Time to split up! Find them—all of them! And hurry! Oblivion will throw everything he's got at us now!"

"I'll go with Hector," Daniel volunteered. "If I stay close, I can use his powers to heal, and two of us can work faster than one."

Alex nodded, turning her attention now to the Old City as the group split and ran off in all directions, and to the storm overhead, which had grown increasingly turbulent and powerful. A torrent of blood rained upon them, but this time Alex smiled.

He did it.

"Looks like somebody's not happy," she said to herself with a rush of satisfaction.

Oblivion screamed. He howled and protested in an outraged fury, knowing pain for the first time in his existence. Every muscle within the body of Grant Borrows was clenched as Oblivion bore down and flung his arms as wide as they would go.

Lightning struck at the moment he stood outstretched that way, and the walls of the Citadel tore themselves apart as the ground shook even harder than before.

His true voice broke through the frail vocal cords of Grant Borrows and screeched and clawed and scratched at the fabric of existence until it was heard by every ear across all four corners of the globe.

So potent was the sound that it pierced the veil of reality, and for one single moment the scales fell from every human eye and the true nature of the universe was laid bare. The unearthly glimpse seen in that terrifying moment revealed an unseen world full of beautiful, powerful beings bathed in light, and shadowy creatures that skulked and slithered, drawn to the dark. Like a painting by Bosch, details of surfaces and crevices and devices unknown to man were suddenly everywhere, and there was far more to take in than any human eye could conceive.

Nowhere was this more evident than in Jerusalem, where countless numbers of these beings, both dark and light, were seen locked in an unimaginable battle. Swarms of them filled the skies and tromped across the lands. And everywhere there was a man, woman, or child, a small radius surrounding them held creatures of light and dark clashing against one another.

The moment passed as soon as it had come. Oblivion's scream ended, the otherworldly vision faded, and once more all that could be seen was what was real and tangible in the mortal world.

Oblivion staggered, weakened by some conflict or reaction taking place within him. He forced himself upright and crushed the piece of Dominion Stone Payton had used on him into powder. But he broke it while Payton's hand was still clinging to it, so Payton's hand and all five fingers were crushed as well.

Oblivion flung Payton across the square one last time until the swordsman slammed into another wall, then fell limp onto the ground, face first. Their Rings both glowed, but Oblivion neither noticed nor stopped to investigate.

He had bigger concerns. Inside his head, all was suddenly, deafeningly quiet.

How was it possible?

This feeble human had severed his link with the army he'd called to himself. Those he'd wielded had vanished as if cloaked in the night. He could no longer hear their thoughts, see their movements, or command their actions. He had already dispatched the remaining members of the Secretum himself before entering Jerusalem; they were of no further use to him. They were gone, and now the Ringwearers were gone as well, and he was left utterly, thoroughly alone.

But then, he had always been alone. From the time before time began, he existed as no other could. No one could share this experience with him, no one but he in all the universe would know and appreciate what he was about to do with the intimacy and beauty and attention to detail that he would utilize.

They thought to cripple him with this maneuver. How poorly they understood him.

It was destiny that this happened. The Thresher had done

this because it was meant to be. It suited Oblivion to do it this way. He needed no one's help to fulfill his purpose, his design.

He would kill them all. Butcher them. Slaughter them. Annihilate them.

He alone.

INTERREGNUM

How do I want this to end? Grant echoed the words in his mind.

"Can I go back?"

"There is no going back, not in the sense that you think of it. Another being has taken your place—a creature that does not belong in your world. This creature has caused tremendous harm and suffering, but there is still a chance to end his reign of destruction. You are the one person in all creation capable of ending it. You alone can send him back to where he came from."

Grant swallowed this. It was a lot of information to take in, and yet . . . A part of him had known this was the case all along. Something tickled the back of his mind the moment he arrived here—wherever *here* was—and had remained there, tugging at his soul, telling him that the natural order of the world he'd left behind had been disrupted by something unimaginable. Something he had been inextricably linked to, in coming here.

"How do I set things right?"

"If I tell you this, Grant Borrows—if I explain to you how to rid your world of the creature that has been set loose upon it—then you will be committed to that path. And no matter what, you *must* see it completed. You cannot turn back once you know this one final truth.

"So I give you now a last chance to change your mind, to leave behind the suffering you have known all your life, to remain here, at last, and rest in eternal peace. The choice is yours, just as it has been always."

"But neither option leads to an easy road, does it?"

"No. If you leave this place to stop the creature, pain and death will follow you. If you remain here, pain and death will be suffered by all the world, including those you know and care about."

"You already know what choice I'm going to make, don't you?"

"My prior knowledge of the outcome does not alter the fact that the choice is yours to make."

"If I stay, will I be with my sister? And my mother?"

"You will."

"But if I go back . . . Can I be with *her*? Can I be with Alex?"

"I cannot answer without revealing that which will commit you to this path. But I can tell you this: Regardless of your outcome, you can save *her* from a fate worse than death."

Grant looked down, saddened by the thought that he might never be with Alex. But if he could save her . . .

The other man studied him thoughtfully. "Grant, a man named Harlan Evers once told you that when you first experience loss, it feels as though all of the magic goes out of the world. I understand these words better than you might imagine, but I think there might be a little magic left after all. The only question that matters is: Will you fight for it?"

"I don't want to fight. I don't like to fight. But this isn't about what I want, it's about—"

"It's about what you're willing to do."

Familiar words. Grant had heard them before. So very familiar.

"Then I've made my choice."

But wait . . .

"Wait! Before you tell me, before we do this . . . I have to know: Who am I, really? Am I Grant, or Collin? Am I the Bringer? Guardian?"

His companion smiled patiently. "Those terms are man's limited means of trying to understand. I see things . . . differently. Like all others, I gave you your real name before I made you. And I alone know it. It is *my* name for you, and thus it is your one true name."

Grant paused, gazing around again as if a fly were buzzing over his head. "Are you going to tell me my name?"

"Your name can only be given to you at the end of your mortal journey. But we both know you're not ready to hear it yet."

"But why did it have to be me? Why was I made the Bringer?" Grant said, the one question he had wanted to ask more than any other, passing through his lips at last.

"Because there is only one thing that you have ever wanted in your entire life, and it is not power, nor possessions, nor fame. All you have ever wanted, Grant Borrows, is to be loved. But understand—this desire does not make you unique. It does not set you apart, or make you 'worthy' or 'chosen.' What it makes you . . . is human.

"You are as ordinary as they come, and this fact alone makes you extraordinary. The Bringer was intended to be a man with a lust for power and a willingness to give in to his darkest temptations. These impulses would facilitate the task that was to be placed before him. You have your faults—a strong temper among them—but deep within, in spite of the many terrible circumstances life has heaped upon you, you are still a lost, lonely child who craves love above all else.

"So while the Secretum plotted for a cruel, vicious man to be born as the Bringer, I had other plans. And *my* plans will not be undone. Not even against seven thousand years of man's cleverest schemes.

"Take heart, my child. The moment of truth is about to call for you. And if you answer it, you may yet find that there is one thing in this universe more powerful than death."

60

"Great one!" Devlin called out. He had climbed to the top of the western edge of the Citadel, and was looking out upon western Jerusalem. "The enemy comes for you! You must end it, now!"

A collection of Jerusalem Stones tore themselves free from the Citadel and formed a slanted walkway from where Oblivion stood over to the western side of the Citadel. Oblivion stalked up the ramp slowly, appearing unconcerned by Devlin's warning.

But the sight before him gave Devlin great pause. Because what he saw there shouldn't have been possible.

Oblivion joined him, looking out over the ramparts, to see almost three hundred Rings glowing in the darkness. They were spread out in clumps on all sides of the Old City, converging on the Tower of David.

"Great one, you must unleash the whirlwind!" Devlin pleaded.

Oblivion's eyeless face, his eye sockets burning with flames that grew in intensity by the second, turned slowly to lock onto Devlin's. "Never presume to dictate actions to your better."

Oblivion reached out a hand in Devlin's direction, and Devlin was certain he was about to die, but the hand passed him by and stretched toward the minaret beyond him.

The tall cylindrical tower ripped itself free from the Citadel and, following the motions of Oblivion's arm, flung itself in the direction of the approaching lights.

"What is that?" Fletcher asked, pointing to the sky.

Alex looked up. "Look out!" she cried.

She dove for the ground and took Fletcher down with her, rolling over onto her back to see the towering white object soaring down out of the sky straight onto them.

Just at the moment she expected it to crash into them, it stalled, about three feet off of the ground. It was more or less vertical, but wobbling and leaning like the Tower of Pisa, as if supported by a crucible that wasn't stable.

Alex sat up. Ten feet to her right, Ethan stood, holding the base of the Tower with both hands underneath, like he was lifting a heavy box.

"You always have great timing," Alex said. "How do you do that?"

He grinned. "Takes practice. Don't try it at home," he grunted.

Ethan was straining hard, the bloodied rain pouring off of him in sheets, but he held his ground. With a mighty roar, he pushed against the ground with his legs and shoved the minaret back up into the sky. The motion carried him up at least twenty feet into the air himself, before he landed back down on the ground, kneeling with one leg and a single arm on the ground in front for support.

Alex watched as the minaret soared high up into the air and then back down toward the ground from the very spot it had come from. It impacted the Citadel in a terrific explosion of white powder and dust. They were close now, less than half a mile from the Tower of David.

Ethan stood to his feet and turned slowly to look at her, his eyes gigantic, a grin spreading across his face.

She didn't want to smile back at him, but his zeal was too infectious. "Yeah . . . Okay, that was pretty cool."

Lightning struck near the impact point of the minaret, and the ground quaked with newfound ferocity.

"GO!" she shouted. "MOVE!!"

As they drew closer, it became quickly apparent that something was very wrong. Around the base of the Citadel, what looked like more than one hundred thousand men, women, and children were bunched up in a giant clog of humanity. Many of them had pained looks on their faces, but their arms clung to their sides and their legs were rigid and unmoving. Oblivion held them. He'd gathered them together like stones or bricks, stacking them together as a living barrier.

Only this was one barrier Alex and her people couldn't blast their way through.

"What's the word, boss?" Nora asked. "What should we do?"

"He wants us to choose," Daniel said absently.

Alex turned to him. "What?"

"He's making us choose," Daniel replied, thoughtful. "Are we willing to kill all these people to get to him, or do we let them live and watch the whole world die?"

"That's insane," Alex replied.

Daniel pointed at the sea of human beings, the incredible sight of it being all the argument he needed to offer.

There's no time for this!

"We don't kill innocent people," Alex said.

"We can't stay here and do nothing!" Ethan shouted. "Oblivion is going to unleash his big mojo any minute now . . ."

"Alex, we gotta go!" Nora prodded her.

"No!" Alex stood her ground. "I want another option!"

"No need." Daniel's eyes slowly swiveled upward, a sickening look on his face. "Looks like Oblivion is forcing the issue."

Alex turned. Something was flying through the air toward them, something with flailing arms and legs . . .

She gasped.

One hundred or more of the people that made up the barrier had been flung toward them as if snapped from a slingshot. They soared through the sky wet with blood, aimed at Alex and her people.

"What do we do?" Nora asked.

Her heart skipped several beats.

"Alex?" several voices called.

She could only stare at the sky and watch the people falling out of it.

61

The blood that fell from above soaked Payton's clothes and skin, yet his broken form did not stir. Even when an explosion only twenty feet away rocked the Tower above him and sprayed him with tiny white rocks, he did not rouse.

He twitched involuntarily, the pain overloading his senses, but he did not move. Consciousness returned to him only in strobed glimpses. He knew Oblivion had flung the minaret at his friends, and he knew it had been returned to him. But he had no idea what Oblivion had done after that; he knew only that it had created a quiet stillness throughout the valley that chilled him to the bone.

Unable to fight the coming blackness, Payton descended into a dark sleep, losing himself in dreams of years long ago and the one woman he'd truly loved with his whole heart . . .

But he could not descend any deeper and eventually he opened his eyes to stare implacably into the chaotic sky. He felt hot, sticky wetness covering his body, but he couldn't tell if it was his own blood or that which was falling from the sky. Probably both, he decided.

The rain seemed to get its second wind, pouring so hard that it howled, soaking the blackened soil, the trees, the ruined buildings, and every person alive or dead in dark red blood.

"Gonna have to catch 'em!" Ethan cried. He locked eyes on a woman who was flying overhead. Picturing a football in her place, he went long.

Daniel stuck close to Ethan, trying to feed off of his powers enough to catch a young girl that was rocketing his way.

Xue found a dumpster full of trash and debris, and sent it speeding down the road in an attempt to soften the plunge for a teenage boy who was dropping out of the sky. Happy with the dumpster's position, she set off to save another . . .

Alex's mind was racing. How could they use some of the others' powers to save these people? Hector could heal the ones who managed to survive their plummet, but what of the others?

More falling bodies were coming terrifyingly close to the ground now. A few had already made impact . . .

Tucker's sway over animals would be of little help; there was no time to summon anything useful . . .

Wilhelm couldn't help by electrocuting them . . .

These poor people, each one of them was somebody's son or daughter or father or mother, and now they were dead . . .

Ethan was bounding off in another direction, having caught the woman he was aiming for and now attempting to seize a second . . .

Nora's memory control, Mrs. Edeson's power of persuasion, Alex's own empathy, these were powers with no real influence over the physical world. These men and women were shooting through the air at them and Alex could do nothing to stop it. They were all going to die.

But there were three hundred Ringwearers here, and a flurry of activity had been ignited among them. Some of them worked solo, others teamed in pairs of two or more.

Alex lost count of them all and their various efforts. Two dozen saved had to be . . . No, more than that. Maybe significantly more . . .

They couldn't save them all. Around a half-mile radius, one stomach-turning crunch after another pelted the ground, or crashed into rooftops or cars or trees. A car alarm went off somewhere.

Alex's hand was covering her mouth in shock, though she couldn't remember putting it there. How many people had died? Just like that. And tens of thousands more blocking their path, waiting to be used as cannon fodder against them.

Even with all of the supernatural power at their command, there was no way to keep all of these people alive. It would be a massacre on par with the multinational military standoff in eastern Turkey.

Oh, God, help us, please . . .

A hand touched her shoulder, and she jerked around in a frenzy. There she saw the last person she expected.

Payton's body, near death, drank in every sensory experience around him. The hard patter of the pouring rain and the warmth of the sticky substance as it touched his skin. The fire behind the clouds so high above, ready now to pour out on the ground and burn everything it touched. The oddly distant sound of his own shallow breathing.

"Great one, they are here!" Devlin cried, and Payton heard alarm in his old mentor's voice. "I don't understand how—a few of them got through, and they're coming right n—"

"Let them come," Oblivion said without inflection.

Payton believed the two of them were upon a parapet some thirty feet behind and above him. His body lay flat on the main cobblestone walkway inside the Citadel's inner garden, located near the very center of the structure.

He opened his mouth, prepared to call out to let the others know where he was. But his voice would not come, his collapsed lungs unwilling to give him the breath needed to call out.

Something white and hot flashed against the darkness and he strained his head to look up. It was Wilhelm, unleashing crackling sheets of electricity into Oblivion.

The earth rumbled and shook, and pieces of the old Citadel broke free and flew over Payton's head. He couldn't see what became of Wilhelm, but the electricity stopped.

It was quickly replaced by a shower of shovels, knives, guns, hubcaps, and dozens of other metallic objects, firing on Oblivion in concert. Payton caught a glimpse of Xue running sideways in the distance, directing her magnetic powers over the metal that was attacking Oblivion now.

"There!" Ethan's voice shouted. "I see him!"

Payton swiveled his head. Oblivion was descending the stone stairway, swatting at the flying metal, and moving straight toward him. Ethan's loud proclamation hadn't been lost on Oblivion; Payton wondered if even now the ancient creature was realizing his mistake in not finishing Payton off.

Oblivion was only footsteps away, and Payton glanced around, looking for Ethan, but his friend was nowhere to be seen.

Some part of Payton's brain wondered what had become of Devlin. The old villain had vanished as soon as things got dangerous—a skill he was particularly good at.

Oblivion soon stood over Payton's prostrate form, and his head tilted sideways to look directly into Payton's eyes. Payton braced himself for what was coming: Oblivion rending every organ in his body, crushing every bone. He hoped death would find him quickly.

Payton was sure the deathblow was on its way when someone called to Oblivion from quite nearby.

"Taste of your own medicine," said Daniel.

Mirroring the Bringer's powers of psychokinesis, Daniel rammed a hand straight forward and, without touching him, sent Oblivion catapulting at great speed toward the far end of the Citadel.

Another tremor quaked, this one enough to create cracks in the ground.

Daniel knelt over Payton, whispered, "Don't die, we've got you."

Payton tried to focus his weary eyes on the place where Oblivion had come to a stop, and saw Ethan there, pummeling Oblivion with one devastating blow after another.

Hector's buoyant frame came into view, and he placed one of his chubby hands on Payton's head just as the darkness took him.

"Is he okay?" said Alex's voice.

Payton opened his eyes. "I seem to be, yes," he said.

She pulled him to his feet. Daniel and Hector stood nearby. Behind Alex was the old man who was missing his hand, and he was not alone. Several dozen men and women wearing grim faces and carrying automatic weapons stood over his shoulder.

"I'm still fuzzy on the details," Alex explained, "but it appears that our friend here called in some major league favors. Not sure how that happened since he still can't communicate. There are several hundred of them on the main grounds below the Citadel, and we were able to break through Oblivion's defenses with their help."

Payton let out a breath, taking this in.

"Where is he?" he asked.

Before she could answer, Daniel shouted, "Look!"

He pointed straight up. An enormous hole had opened in the churning clouds directly over Jerusalem, and now fire was spilling over the edge of it, a great hot liquid magma rushing out of the hole and plunging toward them . . .

Alex looked at Payton. "Are you able . . . ?"

He gave a curt nod, squaring his shoulders. With a swift kick at the ground, his sword leapt up into the air and he snatched it with a firm grasp of the hilt.

Alex looked upward and Payton followed her line of sight. Dark figures stood atop the ramparts encircling the entire Citadel in the artificial night. Though he could not see their faces, he knew they all had to be there: Alex, Daniel, Hector, Xue, Mrs. Edeson, Cornelius, Ryan, Charlotte, Nora, Trevor, Ethan, Tucker, Henrike, Nigel, Lilly, Thomas, and countless others he'd never met. Hundreds of them, forming a unified circle around the stronghold, awaiting her signal.

"Tell him to do it!" Alex shouted. "He has to do it now!"

62

Oblivion stood within an archway in the heart of the fortress, his scarred face radiant with the glow of the brimstone spilling from the heavens. Ferocious heat and the acrid smell of sulfur poured off the fire—a savage column of heat and flame that would consume every man, woman, and child in Jerusalem. Except for himself, of course.

His Ringwearers, the living weapons that had been taken from him, lined the outer walls of the Citadel, desperate to stop him.

In moments, they would burn.

Even the Thresher could not move fast enough to outrun this doom.

After all, was he not the most powerful of all of the Creator's handiwork? Who could hope to withstand the Angel of Death? To think that anything alive could was folly.

His fire was at two thousand feet now and falling fast . . .

These human beings regarded him as a malevolent entity, but he knew himself to be nothing of the sort. He was present for the formation of this entire universe. His power forged in the fires of creation itself. That power was primordial and pure, the likes of which these humans could not even conceive.

Every creature had its purpose, and this was his. As sure as the ebb and flow of oceans' tides or the seasonal rotations of this planet, his purpose over all creation was to destroy it.

He was doing precisely what he was created to do.

As he stepped out of the doorway and into the open courtyard, the Thresher spoke right into his ear: "Did you *really* think our earlier fight was the main event?"

Oblivion's enraged eyes poured forth fire.

Payton grabbed both of his jacket lapels in one hand, lifted Oblivion high with inhuman strength, and then slammed him vertically into the ground, upside down. Oblivion's head was driven through the Jerusalem Stone boardwalk until he tasted dirt.

"Guess being around since the dawn of time doesn't teach you how to spot a bluff."

Oblivion's last view of the air was of his magnificent column of fire dissipating into wisps of gray smoke and then vanishing altogether.

Alex stood by, watching. From twenty paces away, inside an enclosed area of the Tower, she did the hardest thing she'd ever done in her life.

She watched as Payton attempted to kill the man she loved.

Her eyes shifted to the ramparts, to the spot on the east wall where she knew that Mrs. Edeson and her son Ryan were standing, side by side. At her behest, Ryan was focusing his ability to unite the powers of every Ringwearer—all 299 of them—and focus them on the man facing off against Oblivion now, the man with the sword.

Pour it on, she thought in their direction.

Her attention shifted back to Payton, who was simultaneously holding Oblivion frozen in place before him, electrocuting every inch of his rocklike skin, and punching him again and again at superspeed, with superstrength, over his entire body. Wearing thick gloves like Ethan's, he placed blow after blow on Oblivion's face, his stomach, his chest, and anywhere else he could land a devastating hit.

Don't kill him . . . Don't kill him . . .

The ground shook violently, and a portion of the ground beneath the inner garden gave way, disappearing into the dark soil. From the screams she could hear in the distance, she doubted that it was the only piece of the earth to do so.

Come on, Grant . . . Please . . .

Payton fought.

Punched. Kicked. Unleashed the full devastating array of powers now at his command.

At Alex's request, he kept his sword sheathed at his side for now.

How do you beat a man made of stone to within an inch of his life?

More important for Payton was, how do you avoid taking that last inch?

The storm increased in intensity, howling now in a ferocious hurricane-force wind that threatened to sweep them all away. The fire pouring down from above had returned to its place behind the swirling clouds, but terrific lightning and angry thunder echoed through the skies as the blood rain pelted into his skin with giant drops.

His attack on this creature was brutal yet efficient, and he proved himself more than a match for this supposed Angel of Death. Where were the awesome powers of the Bringer now? Payton kept him too off guard, too preoccupied, never letting up, unrelenting in his aggression. Oblivion would be given no chance to fight back.

Payton found that he rather enjoyed this feeling. Maybe Devlin had been right about power corrupting, but right now, Payton didn't care. He chipped off pieces of Oblivion's stony skin with every hit, and it felt good. If there were still bones inside that body, he would break every one of them as well. Oblivion would pay for the sins of the past.

Oblivion was the administrator at the Catholic school, dismissing him from his post and stripping him of his title and position.

Oblivion was Payton's brother, framing him for crimes he didn't commit, and never even bothering to explain why he hated his own flesh and blood so much.

Oblivion was the one person in Payton's whole life he'd given his heart to and who'd walked away when Payton needed her most. He was Morgan.

Payton froze. Sick.

Oblivion did not hesitate. Finding his feet again, he lifted his arms to end this, ready to unleash a powerful blast of psychokinesis.

Payton snapped out of it just in time, reared back, and threw a vicious uppercut at the same moment that Oblivion let loose his own attack. The two men flew backward from each other.

Both fell to the ground, unmoving.

Lifeless.

63

Through the terrible wind and the blood-filled rain and the frequent lightning strikes, through the shaking of the ground that threatened to send each of them crashing to the ground far below, she saw Oblivion fall.

He lay there, eyes closed. Dead? Asleep? If the skies above and the still-trembling earth were any indication, he was merely unconscious.

But how he looked like the man she loved, lying there so peacefully . . .

Come on, Grant! Fight back! Fight this monster! Do it now!

Please be in there, somewhere, sweetie . . . You have to be . . . Please be there, for me . . .

I love you.

She teetered between a mad desire to run to him and the fear that nothing had changed.

Alex glanced sideways at the old man, who still waited at her side. Their eyes locked, and she sensed wisdom and understanding behind them. He gave the gentlest of nods, glanced at the place where Oblivion lay, and returned his gaze to her. He flashed a very quick smile.

The prostrate man on the ground was less than thirty feet away.

Alex took a tentative step away from the old man and moved toward Oblivion.

"Alex! NO!!"

She whipped around. Payton's voice came from far off to her left, but now he was standing in front of her, blocking her way.

She looked around; most of the Ringwearers were watching them. It was as if all of the chaos of the last few minutes had paused, holding its breath.

"I know what you're thinking, Alex," Payton said. "But he's *not Grant.*"

She looked at him. She was tired. Tired of pretending to know how to lead the Ringwearers in Grant's place. Tired of arguing with everyone about Grant. Tired of living without him.

"I don't think I care," she said softly. "I just . . . I need to—one last time . . ."

"You touch him, you *die,* remember?"

Alex never took her eyes off of the pitiful creature prostrate on the ground before her. "I remember," she whispered.

She sidestepped Payton and walked slowly forward, searching Grant's gray, rock-hard face for the man she believed was still in there.

"Alex, he's right," said Daniel, who stood not far away near the old man and his small army. "What do you hope to accomplish? It's insanity."

"No, it isn't," she replied, kneeling on the ground next to Oblivion, close enough to touch him. She glanced back at Payton. "You said that death consumes everything." She faced Oblivion once more, swimming and lost in his face. "But I believe there's something more powerful than death. Just one thing."

Tenderly, but without caution, her hand reached out and cradled the side of Grant's face.

Eyes still closed, Grant's hand came up and grabbed hers. It did not push her away. It simply clasped her hand tightly. And Alex squeezed back, alive and flowing with joy.

Grant's eyes opened, and they were real eyes. They were bloodred, but they were no longer on fire. They fixed on her face, and then they blinked closed again, squeezing out tears that ran down the side of his rocklike face.

The entire world seemed suspended in this moment as the rain continued to howl and blow against them like a storm at sea and aftershocks shuddered. No one dared move; no one dared breathe. They watched.

Grant opened his eyes. A torrent of memories flooded his consciousness. It was overwhelming, all that this being had done within his skin. And somehow he knew it still lived within him. It was there, it was going to wake up, and it would reclaim him. There was no time for recrimination, yet he couldn't stop himself, the death toll was mind-boggling, the horror of what Oblivion had done . . . what *he* had done . . .

Everything was terribly confusing, and here inside this body that felt so alien now yet was utterly familiar, he was uncertain where he ended and where Oblivion began.

Both of his hands came up to his face as if to block out the world, to hide himself from what he'd done and all those he'd done it to.

Alex peeled away his hands and gently lifted his downcast chin. She smiled at him, the kind of gentle, loving smile reserved for the most profound bond that can exist between two people.

"What do your eyes see?" she whispered.

Grant heard the words that recalled the phrase that his sister had made all of them memorize. It was a lifetime ago that she'd done that. Wasn't it?

He looked around at the crowd of men and women watching, some from close by, others from the tops of the castle walls. Some of their faces were written in horror, aghast at the sight of the embodiment of death. That was what he'd become, wasn't it? But those he was closest to showed more concern.

And the one before him, the only one he noticed now. All he could do was focus on Alex's burns and scars and remember how this pain had come to her because of him . . .

Grant stared at his hands, which were outstretched before him. He saw no pale flesh or wrinkled skin.

He saw blood.

Tears spilled down his cheeks.

It was the blood of so many who had died because of those hands. Just like Morgan's blood had once stained them . . . Just like Hannah's . . . Just like his sister's.

What did it matter that he wasn't directly responsible for any of those deaths, or all of the horrors Oblivion had caused? They were the same hands, the same fate.

He pulled away from Alex, crawling backward as if trying to escape from himself. His mouth moved but nothing resembling words came out. Only guttural sounds of anguish and pain.

He was shaking, as if trying to will away the memories that filled his mind, the intimate knowledge of all that Oblivion had done. It was more than knowing what he'd done; Grant could remember how Oblivion had felt in carrying out each and every action. He felt vile, corrupted; he felt tainted. These hands, this body, they had been permanently stained and would never be okay again.

He trembled violently, fell flat on his back—

Another set of hands clutched his, steadying him.

Grant's eyes slowly, as if fighting his command to obey, followed the trail of these hands. His hazy, tear-filled eyes flowed carefully up one narrow, burn-damaged arm, across the shoulders, climbed the neck, past the mouth and the small button nose, to look into the other person's beautiful brown eyes.

But the eyes of hatred, accusation, and vitriol that he deserved were absent.

Instead, the eyes that delicately held his were full of light and hope.

"Alex . . ." He had coughed the name out through his terrified quivering. It was not the ear-shattering sound of Oblivion's voice that came out. It was his voice, the voice of Grant Borrows.

Alex's breath caught in her throat. Tears streamed from her eyes, but she made no attempt to stop them.

"Grant? Grant, is it you? Really?"

"Alex . . . ?" Grant whispered. "What's happening?"

"I'm here, I'm here, it's okay . . ."

"No no no, it's not okay . . . I remember it all. Everything I did, everyone I killed . . ." His eyes shifted down to the tender scars on her arm from where she was burned. He was horrified.

Alex hesitated only briefly, and then placed a hand over his heart and looked past his eyes and deep into his soul. She offered him the softest hint of a smile. "It wasn't you," she said. Her voice was gentle but firm, and full of conviction. "You didn't do this to me, and you didn't hurt anybody else. *It was not you.*"

Another set of memories raced into his mind, and it was like a charge that went off. He blinked, looked around, settled his earnest gaze onto Alex.

"I know how to end this," he said urgently. "I know how send it back! We can make everything right—"

"IMPOSSIBLE!!" called out a hate-filled voice. From somewhere off to Payton's right and not far above.

Devlin.

64

Grant, the normal flesh tones of his skin returning and his eyes blue once more, recoiled in horror at the sight of the Keeper of the Secretum as he emerged from the far end of the courtyard.

"You couldn't have planned this!" Devlin screamed. "I was with you! The whole time! You never had a single discussion about *any* of this!"

"Actually, that's just how you *remember* it," called out Nora's voice from somewhere on the southern ramparts.

"But—but . . ." Devlin mumbled, and Alex flashed Grant a tiny satisfied smile. The realization that was coming to Devlin right now, Grant understood instantly. Nora had tampered with his memories.

Devlin's expression darkened. "This world is dark and evil and it must be destroyed to balance the cosmic scales, to make way for the new world!" he shrieked. "Do you really think your deception—or this *touching* display of emotion—makes any difference?"

"It makes a difference to me," said the small, tired voice of Grant Borrows.

Devlin became even more enraged. "The Bringer will finish this, one way or another. So it is written, and so shall it be! DESTINY CANNOT BE DENIED!!"

He took another step forward, raising his hand toward Grant. The hand that bore the one and only silver and blue

Ring of the Keeper, the Ring with the power to see the souls of man, and Shift them . . .

Grant was processing it too slowly . . . It was already too late when he realized that Devlin meant to exchange bodies with him, and allow Oblivion to return and reign in him . . .

Into his peripheral vision, Payton was a blur running toward him, but he was going to be too late . . .

What power could prevent the Shifting of souls?

Grant put up both of his hands, as if he could prevent what was about to happen through surrendering. But there was nothing he could do except to watch the gruesome satisfaction apparent on Devlin's face as his Ring began to glow a bright blue light.

He closed his eyes tight, trying to block out what was happening, but he was powerless to resist. A warm rushing sensation went through his body, and then everything in the universe blinked and suddenly the sounds of shouting coming from the crowd were changed. They reached him from a different angle now and he knew it was done.

Devlin's hand—now Grant's—was still stretched out in front of him, its bright blue glow beginning to fade.

He ran across the courtyard, toward the place where his former body lay, now possessed by Devlin. Grant watched a wicked smile spread across the face that had been his only moments ago. Alex still held to Devlin's hand, but she quickly turned loose at the look on his face, and Devlin stretched Grant's arm straight out, unleashing the powers of the Bringer. The earthquake returned with vengefulness and brought everyone standing to their knees. The clouds overhead parted, the fire pouring out again . . .

Devlin cackled with a demented malice. "You cannot defeat Oblivion! No one can defeat Oblivion! The plans of the Secretum of Six will prevail, and the God of Cain will reward his servants in the afterlife—"

And then Devlin was screaming in pain, the hand bearing the Seal of Dominion gone from his arm. Grant looked to the right; Payton was following through on a throwing motion. His sword was gone from his side, and now Grant saw it to his left, stuck in the ground not far from where Alex sat, a severed hand leaking blood onto the cobblestones right next to it.

Grant's mind raced. It wasn't over. Devlin was still inside Grant's body, and so was Oblivion, and even without the powers of the Bringer, Oblivion would still be able to finish his work.

There was only one way to end this. One solution, the one given to him in a dark place outside of time and space.

Grant stretched out Devlin's wrinkled old arm and focused on his own body, across the courtyard.

"NO!!" Devlin screamed with Grant's mouth.

The familiar flushing sensation enveloped him and he closed his eyes.

When he opened them, a powerful pain was washing over him, originating with the place where his right hand had once been.

Devlin was still screaming "No!" but now the sound was coming from the old man's own mouth.

They were both back where they belonged.

Someone tapped Devlin on the shoulder from behind.

He turned. There stood the wrinkled, aged, balding face of a man he hadn't seen in almost thirty years. A man he'd thought to be long dead.

As he reacted in surprise at the sight, the other man balled up a fist with his one hand, reared back, and punched him in the face.

The storm in the skies above briefly subsided, the earthquake quelled. But the earth was still dark, the skies still enraged and threatening. Oblivion was not yet vanquished.

"Alex . . ." Grant called out, his voice weak and his strength waning.

She was there at once, a hand on his shoulder. Her eyes pouring love and warmth into him.

He smiled at her, took her hand with his remaining one, and squeezed it. "I'm so sorry. For everything. This is not what I wanted for you. For us."

"Grant . . ."

"Payton?" Grant said.

A moment later, Payton stood at his feet. His sword was still stuck into the grass several feet away.

"I need you to take your sword," Grant said softly, "and kill me."

65

"What?" Alex cried.

"It's the only way," Grant said. "They brought Oblivion into this world by binding him to a human being. The only way for him to pass out from this life again is for death to take the one he's tethered to. He'll go kicking and screaming, trying desperately to maintain his purchase on this reality. But he'll have no choice but to return to wherever he came from."

"No, Grant!" said Alex, tears spilling from her and touching his cheeks. "Please, no . . . You died on me once already. I don't know how to let you go again—"

"How do you know this will work?" Payton asked. He blurred and then reappeared, holding his sword.

"I just know," Grant replied. "For the world to live, I must die. And it has to be *now*, before Oblivion comes back. I can already feel him starting to awaken and stir inside me . . ."

Daniel joined the three of them, kneeling on Grant's other side, opposite Alex, resting his weight on his good foot.

"Hello, old friend," Grant said, throwing him half of a smile.

"It's good to see you," Daniel offered. "I overheard . . . Grant, you don't deserve this."

"We *all* deserve this," Grant corrected him.

"But why don't we just Shift you and Devlin again, and let Devlin die with Oblivion?" Daniel asked.

"Because Devlin will never surrender to death."

Alex wept loud and long, oblivious to what others thought or felt.

"I need you to be strong, Alex," Grant said. "For me. This power is too great, man was not meant to wield it. It has to be this way."

"But I never . . ." Alex whimpered. "We've never even kissed."

"Then do it, now, before the end," Grant said softly. "The Bringer, Guardian, Oblivion—just let it all end with me."

She leaned in and pressed her lips firm against his. He closed his eyes, squeezing out tears, and lifted his head off of the ground to press his own mouth into hers. He felt overpowering emotions leaking out of her, and in those feelings were love, joy, desire, anguish, rage, and desperation, among so many others. He felt everything she felt, and he wanted more than anything to pick her up in both arms and run away from all of this with her, to just *be* with her for the rest of his mortal life.

He couldn't keep one heartbroken, heaving sob from shaking his shoulders, but he swallowed the rest. He pulled back from her.

"Do it, Payton," Grant said, pushing down his internal conflict. "Do it now."

"It isn't fair!" Alex cried, and her body collapsed on top of his. "I don't want you to go!"

"I don't either . . . I don't want to go." His voice sounded like that of a child, yearning, longing for acceptance, approval. Love. "But . . . but you love me?"

Alex raised up and looked him in the eyes. "I have always loved you. I loved you before I knew you."

Payton raised his sword, ready to strike. But Alex threw out a hand, stopping him.

"Payton, kill me too," she said. "I don't want to live anymore if this is what life has become. I don't want to be here."

Grant stroked her chin and forced a smile.

"But you *are* here."

Alex pulled back, unsure if she wanted to watch this.

Payton was going to get his wish at last. He was going to kill the Bringer.

She hated him for it.

Daniel wasn't watching either; he was staring at something on the ground nearby. He turned back to face Grant, and suddenly he blinked.

"No, you can't—" he began.

Grant held up a hand to silence him. Then he motioned for the doctor to lean in close.

Daniel complied, and whispered words were exchanged. Alex couldn't understand what they were saying. Probably mutual apologies for the way things had turned out and how they'd treated each other in the past.

When it was over, Daniel pulled back and stood to his feet, an uncharacteristic display of emotion coloring his face. But he didn't turn away; he watched with an unreadable expression on his face as if debating whether or not to say something more.

"Do it," Grant asked one last time. " 'The Bringer shall be slain at the hands of the Thresher.' "

"I'm sorry," Payton said, his jaw set. He lifted his sword high above his head.

"I love you," Alex said, and then turned away.

The last she saw of Grant was a peaceful, resigned smile.

The deed was done. The act Payton had been waiting ten years for, accomplished at last. But now that it had come to it, Payton found no satisfaction in its execution.

There was a time he would have found that odd.

He paid his last respects, grasping Grant's left hand—receiving an odd scratch on the back of his hand from Grant's fingernails in the process—and then letting it go. He rose from the body and walked away, leaving Alex and Daniel to weep over their fallen friend.

The dark clouds in the sky above them began to roll back. The black volcanic-type rock that covered the ground was slowly withdrawing and the brown sand and dirt returning.

A few feet from Grant's dead body, Payton found Devlin on his back, unconscious.

Payton kicked him in the side, and Devlin stirred, looking up into the eyes of his protégé.

"You failed," Payton said, smoldering. "You. Failed. You worthless piece of rubbish. The Bringer is dead. Oblivion is gone."

"But . . . *what*?" Devlin stammered, backpedaling. "That's impossible, I don't believe you—"

He started to sit up, but Payton placed a foot on his mentor's shoulder and pushed him back down to the ground.

He held his gleaming silver sword pressed against Devlin's neck.

"You and your people have brought nothing but pain and suffering to the human race for thousands of years. You are personally responsible for the loss of more human lives than anyone in history."

"Payton, listen to me—"

"The wages of sin," Payton said softly, lightly, "is death."

He struck.

66

Everyone could feel it in the very air they breathed.

Time was passing once more.

An hour after Grant's death, the first ray of bright yellow sunlight streamed down and touched Alex. She sat on the edge of one of the Citadel's higher platforms, staring at nothing, trying to think of a reason to go on living. She had no more tears left in her, no more strength, no more life.

How could it have come to this? The whole thing felt wrong. She had been so sure that she would save him, that Grant would come back to her and everything would be all right again.

Grant was the "good guy" after all. Wasn't he supposed to "live happily ever after"?

. . . with *her*?

Little by little, the DarkWorld dissipated. The fiery clouds vanished first. At the same time the earthquakes had stopped and the rain as well. And then to the wonder of all, the scorched earth was receding, reverting to normal soil. She'd even heard one of the Loci mention something about hearing that the seas and oceans were filling with water again. The changes to the earth had been mystical, and once the cause of them was gone, the natural order was returning.

One thing that would never come back was the lives that had been lost. Whether they died at Oblivion's hand or from the various forms of madness that his appearance had caused, death was an unchanging constant.

Much like how she felt inside. Alex was vaguely aware of the initial swells of hope and contentment spreading throughout the city. People were just beginning to walk out into the sunlight, realization dawning that everything they knew was becoming whole and right again.

Nothing would ever be right again for her.

Not without him.

There was no normal. No happily ever after. No rosy sunset to ride off into with the man she loved.

Daniel had refused to leave her side at first, immediately after it happened. But the old handless man had come to them and dragged Daniel away after ten minutes or so. She hadn't seen him since.

Several of her friends came and went—Ethan, Nora, Hector, others—offering to do for her whatever they could. Alex mechanically gave them her thanks, never making eye contact. She repeated to each of them her desire to be left alone, if only for a little while.

"Alex?"

Daniel. She didn't look up.

"Alex, I need to talk to you," Daniel said softly.

"What's up, doc?" she asked humorlessly, still not facing him.

"I'm not a doctor," he said quietly.

Her brain didn't register this. She was too spent to really hear it.

"Alex?"

She sighed, looking up at last. "What, Daniel? What do you want that you can't leave me in my misery? What more do you think I can do for you, or for the others? I'm sorry the city is in such a fragile state, but you'll excuse me if I'm in no condition to spread calm just now—"

An inexplicable smile spread over Daniel's face as he reached out and placed a hand over her moving mouth. "Shut up, will you? I'm trying to tell you something."

Bordering on crushed and hurt, she stopped talking and looked on him, incredulous.

He removed his hand and let out a nervous breath. "I still don't know exactly why he did it. I was ready, I was prepared. I knew what I was giving up, and it pained me, but I'd made my peace with it. The world was at stake, and I—"

"One of us isn't making any sense, Daniel . . ." Alex said, "and I'm starting to worry it might be me."

Daniel smiled again, gently. "Devlin wasn't the only person here today who had the power to Shift human souls, was he?"

Huh?

She searched her weary mind. "Well, *you* would have been able to mimic Devlin's—"

She broke off. Lifted her head fully and gave him her undivided attention for the first time, looking him in the eyes. "What are you saying?"

"You remember the moment when he and I whispered to each other, just before the end?" Daniel asked. "That was right after he did it."

"*Daniel* . . . ?" Some tiny part of her heart fluttered, but she didn't dare believe . . . "Are you . . . ?"

"Just listen," he replied, taking her hand. "After it happened, he motioned for me to lean in so he could say something. I asked him what just happened, and he said that he wasn't sure it would even work with Devlin's Ring, since Devlin's silver Ring was of a different make, but apparently all such Rings draw from a similar power source.

"Of course I protested, but he said to leave it. 'She needs you,' he said. He said he was sorry for the wear and tear, but he joked that at least this would get me from A to B. And he asked me to let the others think it was me. That it would be easier, better for all of us this way."

Alex's hand jumped up to cover her mouth, and a few tears she thought were long gone suddenly fell out of her eyes. But she was afraid to speak, afraid to do anything to break the spell cast over the two of them in this moment.

"Just before I pulled away," he went on, his words coming out slower now, "he asked me if I loved you. And I said that for you, I would give up my life. He said, 'Promise me you won't let one day go without telling her that.' "

Daniel slid off of his perch and landed on one knee, still holding her hand in hers.

"So I came over here . . . to keep my promise."

Alex's shoulders shook as she threw her arms around this man. This diminutive scientist who was no scientist at all. Her head rested on his shoulder, and even though it was a foreign shoulder to her, it was the first time in a long time that she felt like she'd come home to exactly where she belonged.

The shoulder may have belonged to Daniel Cossick, but the man she held tight to was the one person in all the world whose life and happiness she valued more than her own.

Sobbing giant tears and soaking Daniel's shirt, she decided that the package didn't matter, that the bones and musculature and organs and everything else tangible she held in her arms was transitory and meaningless. And she decided that leaning on this shoulder was something she wanted to do for the rest of her life.

67

Some time later, after the cleanup had begun, the two of them finally made it out of the Old City and down to Amiel Yishai's tent city, which had become a crude headquarters in the wake of the DarkWorld's devastation.

The Loci labored on bringing relief and aid wherever they could. Though many of them were still grieving over the death of the greatest of them, the death of Guardian, it wasn't unusual to see pained hugs exchanged between individuals wearing Rings of Dominion. Wilhelm was spotted playing with the local children while providing power to a bank of ambulances and their equipment.

Alex spoke first as they wandered through the sparse tents together. "Why did you bring me down here?"

"We're here to meet someone."

"No more surprises, I hope," Alex remarked.

"Just one," he said.

"Hello, you two," said a voice somewhere behind them, a voice Alex didn't recognize.

They turned. The strange old man with only one hand was standing ten feet away, smiling.

Alex's jaw fell at seeing him talk, but then she got it. Of course. "Hector?"

The old man smiled wider. "Hector."

"So," Alex said conversationally, "you're finally going to tell us who you are?"

"Do you really need me to?" the man replied. "You haven't guessed?"

Alex grinned at the man next to her, the man who was most decidedly not Daniel Cossick. "I think I'd like to hear you say it."

"My name is Frank Borrows," he said, his gaze going back and forth between the two of them.

Alex nodded. It was huge, but not altogether surprising. "Grant's father. Aren't you supposed to be dead?"

Frank looked at her companion and couldn't suppress a knowing smile. "Like father, like son, I suppose."

Alex looked at the man beside her, and back at Frank Borrows. "So . . . you know?"

"I don't know anything," Frank replied. He said no more on the subject, but threw her a faint wink that no one but Alex could have possibly seen.

"I owe you an explanation, both of you," Frank picked up the conversation.

Alex sensed that he was about to tell his story, so she grasped the hand of the man next to her and settled in to hear it.

"After all these years, after so much struggle and pain and sacrifice . . . he really did it. I always knew he would. You have no idea what a relief it is knowing that it's finally done."

His audience of two said nothing, waiting patiently for him to continue.

"My son was destined from the moment of his birth to be the downfall of the Secretum of Six. He is the last in a line of sacred custodians, a line that stretches back for generations all the way to the time of Noah, and even further. The Secretum believed that no one in the 'External' world knew of them and their plans, and that was exactly what we wanted them to believe.

"When my son was born, I had already been made the latest in this line of protectors. My own father—the man you knew as the previous Keeper of the Secretum, Maximilian Borrows—was bypassed for the role, because the custodian before him knew that my father was an immoral man. My father spent years bitter over this dishonor, and jealous of me, his own son.

"While I was busy working for the Appointed, I attempted to infiltrate the Secretum and gain the confidence of one of their acolytes. Her name was Cynthia, and not only did I gain her confidence, I won her love, and she mine. She was born into the Secretum but disenfranchised with it and their secretive plans and manipulations. When I came along, she found the way out that she'd long sought. She brought me into the Secretum, I was given their brand, Cain's Lament, and I learned all that I could about the organization from the inside.

"But what I saw was big enough and frightening enough that I knew this 'secret society' had grown past the point where the resources of the Appointed could overcome them. We'd known of their existence and some of their manipulations of surface society, but the true scope of their aims was astonishing to me. So Cynthia and I came up with a plan; we would turn ourselves in to American authorities. In exchange for our cooperation and inside information on the Secretum, we would be assigned to a special military unit dedicated to taking the Secretum down. We were even given military ranks, though this was largely ceremonial.

"Unknown to me at the time, my father learned of our actions, and Cynthia's true heritage. When she became pregnant with Grant's sister, she asked to be relieved of her duties so she could raise our children. My superior, a man who came to be my best friend, Harlan Evers, happily agreed. When Cynthia became pregnant again, a few years later, my father learned of the Secretum's belief that the one male child in all the world who was born from the line of Cain *and* the line of

Seth *both*—a boy who resulted from the union of an External and a Secretum member—would grow up to become the Bringer.

"My grandfather used this information to gain entrance to the Secretum, and he used his considerable influence and charismatic personality as well as his profound familial connection to the Bringer to seize control of the Secretum as its newest Keeper. His appointment did not go uncontested. He was an outsider from the line of Seth. The first to ever join the ranks of the Ruling Council. Devlin was next in line for the job of Keeper before my father came along, and I understand that there was a bitter rivalry between them.

"But rather than following the dictates of the prophecy, my father secretly became obsessed with twisting the prophecy and using it for his own purposes. He wanted power, and he meant to use Grant to get it. He believed that, despite the prophecy's statement that Oblivion would be born in the Hollow, he could mold and shape Grant into taking control of Oblivion's powers *outside* of the Hollow, without bringing forth Oblivion himself.

"Learning of my father's beliefs about Grant, I came up with a plan of my own. With Cynthia dead, there was a way I could see to it that Grant stayed out of his grandfather's clutches until he became a man: I had to die as well. My father would not want his personal connections examined too closely—a requirement, should he ever try to gain custody of Grant in my absence. So I arranged my own death to save Grant's life.

"With that accomplished, I faded into obscurity while returning to my role as the custodian of the Appointed. I watched over my son from a distance, always keeping an eye on him and doing what I could to help him. This is a role that has now, at last, come to an end. It was almost fifteen years ago when the Secretum began putting its endgame into motion, by giving out the first Ring of Dominion to a British librarian, a remarkable woman I believe you knew."

"How did you lose your hand?" Alex asked, eyeing the prosthesis that was in its place.

Frank sighed. "The custodian, the warrior of the Appointed, is always identifiable by a mark. A perfect circle that wraps around the wrist and touches its other side. It was probably decayed beyond recognition by the time Grant saw it on my detached hand in London, so I doubt he even noticed it. But the mark is passed by a symbolic gesture. A dying touch, from one hand to another, from the last warrior to the next.

"Unfortunately, the speech center of my brain was damaged during the aforementioned faked death, and the secret of this dying touch was known only to the one person in all the world bearing the mark. Meaning I alone knew who and what I was, and that I meant for Grant to be the next in line as custodian of the Appointed. But I had no way of telling him, and he believed me dead anyway, which was better for him, for his protection.

"So after he was Shifted—something I wasn't prepared for—and molded by his grandfather into the Bringer, I took drastic measures. I cut my hand off and placed it in a hidden location while it still bore that dying touch meant only for Grant. And made absolutely sure that he found it."

"But how could you be sure?" Alex's companion asked. "That hand being where it was, falling out of the ceiling and scratching my—um, *his*—hand like that . . . It was totally random, wasn't it?"

Frank smiled. "That's how I meant it to appear. Before leaving the Secretum and turning ourselves in to the Americans, Cynthia and I undertook quite the daring adventure within the halls of the Secretum's underground city. When we made it out alive, we had four Rings of Dominion in our possession, which we held in secret. We never even told Harlan about them. Those Rings were still in my ownership at the time I cut off my hand, so I decided the time had come to put them to use."

"How?" Alex asked.

"He gave them to us," Mrs. Edeson spoke up, stepping forward. Neither of them had seen her standing in the background, waiting for her part in the story to become clear. "Ryan, Charlotte, Cornelius, and myself. We all became Ringwearers after Grant did, didn't we? None of us were Shifted like the rest of you. We simply received the Rings, along with a job offer from a member of the Appointed. We were to draw as much attention to ourselves as we could, in the heart of London, in an attempt to bring Grant Borrows to us. And we were given very specific instructions on where to leave that hand. If Grant hadn't found that building on his own, thanks to the clues planted by Mr. Borrows, we were going to have to steer him toward it somehow. My apologies for the deception and all the trouble we gave you, but we were under strict orders to ensure that Grant found his father's hand and thereby claimed his birthright."

"That's why you and your son are both Ringwearers," Alex said. "No two people related to one another have ever been chosen to be Ringwearers, but then everyone else was chosen by the Secretum. You were chosen by *him*." She pointed at Frank.

"Yes," Frank confirmed. "I told your friend Ethan Cooke that Grant wasn't what he appeared to be."

"You sent him the messages?" Daniel asked. "Gave him clues and pointed him in the right direction?"

Frank nodded. "I recruited him into our group. We've learned to be very careful when approaching potential new members. I had to be sure that he was an honorable man before I could extend the invitation."

Frank closed his eyes and reveled in the feeling of the warm, soothing sun. "I believed that I could destroy the Secretum from within by joining it, but it was my son who ultimately realized my goal.

"The Secretum believed that man's free will was a flaw in our design. So everything they did was an attempt to remove *choice* from the human equation. It's human nature to desire control. We want to control our lives, our surroundings, our paths, even our loved ones. Because we can make our own choices, we believe that this gives us *control* over our lives and everything that happens to us. But in our design, we were given *choice*; we were *not* given control. It's an important distinction—and one the Secretum never understood. Our free will is not a stumbling block. It's the defining characteristic of our subsistence—and the very universe itself.

"The Secretum's grand plot was doomed to fail from the beginning, because in their arrogance they chose their greatest enemy to be their Bringer. And now it's done. The Secretum is dead. And there shall be no more sacred custodians of the Appointed."

Alex thought idly of Payton and how the last time she'd seen him, he was absently scratching at a curved scar on the back of his hand.

She couldn't help smiling to herself.

EPILOGUE

The sun filtered down between white clouds as two people sat under a very familiar bus stop.

"So. Why are we here?" Alex asked.

Seated beside her, he squeezed her hand. How was he going to answer that question? There were almost more answers than he could possibly give.

"It was one year ago today that we first met, right here at this bus stop," he replied. "I had to—I needed to see . . ." he struggled for the words. He sighed. "I had to know for sure that it was all real. That it happened. I thought it would bring us both some closure, to come back here to the beginning."

"And does it?"

"Not really," he said. "I mean, nothing's the same, is it? I've changed, you've changed—*so much* has changed from that first moment we met right over there in front of that store. Most people are lucky if they get a second chance in life. I think I'm on something like my fifth. I may look and sound like Daniel Cossick, but we both know he's dead."

Alex tilted her head sideways, watching him carefully, determined not to rush him.

He looked down at the hand that was clutching hers. His right hand had only four fingers now. Remembering what the mercenary Konrad had once attempted to do to him, he'd come up with the idea of having his right middle finger removed.

Alex argued against it, of course, but he had no desire to wear Daniel's Ring, or any other Ring, ever again.

Payton had done the honors. Doctors at the hospital wanted to surgically reattach the severed finger, but they were baffled when he refused. He convinced them to simply sew up the wound, so that was what they did.

Alex, on the other hand, still wore her Ring. As did most of the other Loci, who were still out there in the world somewhere, doing good, helping people, and righting wrongs. They were reporting now to the organization known as the Appointed, which had changed and grown and had made itself and its existence known to the public at large.

Ethan, now head of the Appointed, personally saw to it that the Seal of Dominion and the silver and blue Ring of the Keeper had been thrown into the deepest part of the ocean, where they would never again be seen by human eyes. With Alex's blessing, Ethan took the Appointed public, along with Grant's story and that of the other Ringwearers. The people of earth were hungry to learn of the man who was unwillingly transformed into a hero, was twisted into something evil, but sacrificed himself to save the world. All 299 Ringwearers became famous as superheroes, but Grant's story was the most famous of all. And as far as anyone knew, his story ended in his death. Some refused to believe that he was really gone, and "Guardian Lives!" became a popular phrase appearing on everything from bathroom stalls and graffiti-painted walls to T-shirts and posters held high at sporting events.

Alex alone knew the truth.

"All of those people—Collin, Guardian, Oblivion, the Bringer . . . They're all gone," he admitted slowly. "I'm still not really sure what that leaves."

"It leaves you, sweetie. And that's enough for me. But you didn't bring me all the way down here to tell me that. So what are we really doing here?"

"Actually, I want you to meet someone," he replied cryptically. "He's arriving on the next bus."

Alex smiled mischievously at him, enjoying watching him have his little mystery.

"And does our mystery guest have a name?"

"His name is Mark," he replied.

"That was my little brother's name," Alex said, looking away, lost in thought.

"Yes, I know," he went on. "He was frequently in your thoughts when Oblivion had you."

Her head snapped back up. She nearly laughed out loud. "Don't tell me how you did it, I don't care!"

She threw her arms around him and kissed him long and hard. He returned the gesture.

"Are you sure it isn't weird?" he said when they broke apart. "To be kissing Daniel's lips instead of mine?"

Alex rolled her eyes. "I know who I'm kissing when I kiss you, sweetie."

He smiled, weakly. "I still can't shake that feeling that I owe the world . . . something. I mean, I know it wasn't me. I wasn't even here, I was *dead*. Or whatever. But I remember all of it, and in some weird way, even though it wasn't me, it *feels* like it was."

"We've been over this," Alex said. "You're responsible for no actions but your own."

"But even at that," he went on, "the world governments are still looking for a scapegoat for all of the terror and death and destruction that Oblivion wrought. Maybe if I offered myself to them, it might bring everyone some kind of closure. I mean, look at you. I don't care what you say, I know those scars still cause you pain. How could I ever make up for that; it could never possibly be enough—"

"Stop it," Alex said firmly. "It's not up to you to offer penance for the pain of the whole world. Now get this through that head of yours. And if you hear nothing else I ever say, I want you to hear this. Forgiveness is not something that can be bought or earned. It's a gift, free and clear. And I for one have already given it to you.

"Now that business is over and done with. And I don't want to hear another word about it."

With those words lingering in the air, hand-in-hand they sat and waited, and never spoke of it again.

THE END

ACKNOWLEDGMENTS

Thanks to . . .

Karen, my one true love, my soul mate. You're the most amazing person I know.

Evan, my precious son. I've waited so long to be a dad, and you made me one. I adore you and I always will.

My family and all my friends. Your love and support mean the world.

My agent Beth Jusino and everyone at Alive Communications. You rock.

My genius editor David Long. Your instincts and attention to detail are impeccable.

My Father above. I'm always amazed by all the little ways you show me how much you love me.

Last but not least, I would be remiss without offering endless appreciation to a man I revere but have never met: Philip Yancey. His writing is among the most important of our time. His book *Disappointment With God* helped me make sense of the nature of the universe and our existence, and I am eternally grateful for it.

More Page-Turning Action from Robin Parrish

The return of NASA's first manned mission to Mars was supposed to be momentous. But when the crew loses touch with ground control before entry, things look bleak. Safe after a treacherous landing, the crew emerges to discover the unthinkable—every man, woman, child, and animal has vanished without a trace. Alone now on their home planet, the crew sets out to discover where everyone has gone—and how to get them back—only to discover they may not be as alone as they thought.

Offworld by Robin Parrish